Don't Make Me Laugh

Julia Raeside

Bedford
Square
Publishers

First published in the UK in 2025 by Bedford Square Publishers Ltd,
London, UK

bedfordsquarepublishers.co.uk
@bedfordsq.publishers

ISBN
978-1-83501-185-0 (Hardback)
978-1-83501-186-7 (Trade Paperback)
978-1-83501-187-4 (eBook)

2 4 6 8 10 9 7 5 3 1

Printed in Great Britain by CPI Group (UK) Ltd, Croydon CR0 4YY

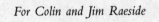

For Colin and Jim Raeside

Comedy is very controlling – you are making people laugh. It is there in the phrase 'making people laugh'.

It's Always Something
GILDA RADNER

One

His hair was wild, like he'd slept in a field. On TV he was clean-shaven, styled with gunk. But on the small stage in front of Ali, Ed Catchpole looked feral, unpredictable.

She couldn't look at him now from her seat on the front row. Too risky. But she could feel him looking at her. She froze, like a field mouse as a hawk flies overhead.

'What's your name?' Ed drew level with her, holding his mic out towards her mouth. Shit, she thought.

Her face muscles locked into a grimace and she heard, 'Alison' come out of her mouth, her voice squeaking. Why did she say that? Only her mother called her Alison.

Ed broke into song. 'Aaaaaaa-lison,' he crooned. Then the line about knowing the world was killing her. It was her dad's favourite Elvis Costello song, the one he'd named her after.

Ali wanted to shrink and fall through a gap in the floorboards. She often felt like she took up too much space, but she couldn't deny that the sound of her name in his mouth set a small furnace going in her stomach.

Ed was leaning over her, rocking forward and back as though to the music in his head. 'And is this your boyfriend, Alison?'

Her eyes screwed shut and her whole face felt like it was made of teeth. She couldn't bring herself to look up at him or at the stranger next to her, but she could feel the stranger shaking his head, probably embarrassed to be paired with her by the man from the TV.

She'd never felt more alone, but she couldn't go home. It was either this or spend the rest of the worst day of her life getting drunker on the sofa and ignoring the unopened envelope on the coffee table.

She sensed Ed's bulk moving away as he ducked under the lights to peer at a new target on the other side of her neighbour. 'So are you his lover?' He pronounced the last word as though French, lowering his mic and glancing back for a second, catching Ali's eye. He winked and returned to his work.

Ali pushed her back against the hard plastic of her chair, looking at her hands in her lap, willing her pulse to slow down.

She wanted to tell someone that she had been someone's lover, even if it was just for three weeks and one day. But then she'd have to tell them that it didn't count because of what she'd done. An unforgivable thing.

As Ed continued to work the room, she risked looking at him again. From her end of the row, she could see him in profile and tried not to stare at the generous round of his belly hanging over his jeans. She'd seen a picture of him in a cardigan in the *Radio Times* at Christmas and imagined how nice he would feel to fall asleep on. God, he looked comfortable.

Even on a warm July night in East London as Ali's thighs stuck to the vinyl-covered seat, she thought about disappearing into his chest, sinking into his flesh, his arms around her, a hug so tight she could only just breathe. She chided herself because she was supposed to be working. But she saved up the look back and the wink, knowing that she would want to think about them again later when the terrible shame had passed.

She wished she could sit somewhere else, but she'd been jostled to the front row as the lights went down. She was not a front-row person, but latecomers didn't get to choose. There was only ice left in the double vodka and tonic she'd drunk too quickly, knowing it wouldn't be enough to numb her. She wished she'd bought two.

With no time to work out what to do with her hands as the lights came up on Ed, she'd wedged one under her thigh and laid the other on top of her leg like she was about to summon a dog. She stayed that way, getting pins and needles, terrified that moving would attract attention.

If the evening had worked out the way it was supposed to, she'd be sat next to Mark, pretending they were a normal couple. What would he have said if Ed had picked on him? 'Is this your girlfriend?' At least she'd been spared that. She imagined the irritated curl of Mark's lip, the moustache stiffening with indignation, his fury at having to define whatever it was they were doing. He'd have lied. 'And do you live together?' God, he'd have been raging.

Ali hadn't met anyone who wore cufflinks since her dad in the nineties. Mark smelled of woody aftershave and dark hairs poked out of his shirt cuffs. She'd never seen him out of a suit, which made her think of teachers; how it's a shock when you see them on a Saturday in jeans. She didn't think Mark owned any jeans, or if he did, he'd wear them with proper shoes.

If she saw Mark out of the corner of her eye, he was hot, capable, nice-smelling.

But if she looked straight at him, he was a furious teacher waiting for a minibus.

When she'd left him at the hotel two hours ago, she didn't look back to see how angry he was.

A whoomph erupted in the room and Ed surfed the laughter deftly into an introduction. 'Ladies and gentlemen, keep it going for our brilliant, amazing next act, she's going to be huge, we're lucky to have her, the absolutely brilliant… Bethan Gill!'

As the applause got louder, a short woman with a brown plait crossed the stage and nodded to Ed as he passed. She began to wriggle the mic stand down.

This wasn't who Ali had come to see. Paul Bonatti would be the surprise headliner, she had it on good authority. She was pretty sure the rest of the crowd had no idea and took a moment to enjoy her privilege.

Her boss, Otis, the MD of Zone Digital, wanted an 'already made it' to front the weekend breakfast show because he had no imagination and loved to collect famous people like cars. He also collected cars.

Paul Bonatti was perfect, in that he was on television and Otis hoped to appear in Paul's Instagram pictures at one of the comedian's famous poker nights. Most of the comedians Ali followed on Instagram had been in one of the poker-night pictures, bottles of beer aloft, a low light hanging over the green baize table.

Paul's features were instantly recognisable, like a cartoon: thick black glasses framing narrow eyes, a dad's softened middle on top of thin legs and a slight stoop at odds with his huge success. He nodded a lot during his act, as though keen to seek consensus from his audience. Ali remembered him playing the flatmate in a sitcom she used to watch hung over at uni. But here he still was, as popular as ever, selling out the big theatres, keeping up with the new talent on the circuit, always happy to mentor and encourage.

On stage, Bethan Gill was launching into a rant, her large, dark eyes and small frame jarring with the deep gravel of her voice. Ali thought she'd sound great on the radio, but Otis looked blank when Ali had mentioned her name.

Ali promised to 'charm' Paul - Otis's word - when a last-minute dinner came up and the boss couldn't be there to schmooze the talent in person. Ali was sure Otis wanted this to come off as some sort of power move, sending a lackey in his place. Otis didn't live in the real world or understand that his radio station was only the centre of his own universe and no one else's.

She tried to make herself concentrate on the new occupant of the stage, but her mind slid back to the hotel room earlier that afternoon, even as she tried to stop it.

Mark had been in the bathroom showering. Ali had shuffled her dress back down over her thighs and started looking for her knickers in the bed sheets. She wanted to wash before she put them back on, but Mark would be a while yet. She'd picked up her phone and looked for an email: the tickets from Paul's agent. She needed to strike while the iron was hot and Mark was still in a good mood. Just a couple of drinks at a comedy club, then back to the room.

Distracted by her phone, Ali hadn't thought to ignore the knock at the hotel-room door. It wasn't the kind of place that did room service but maybe a part of her thought he'd ordered champagne, something special to mark the day. As she turned the handle, she remembered she hadn't told Mark that today was anything special.

Bethan's fist was raised in salute as the crowd whooped and applauded. 'Fuck the patriarchy,' she said, grinning as she replaced the mic in the stand. 'Bye.'

She passed Ed as he came back holding a small glass of what looked like whisky. 'What did I tell you? Bethan Gill, everybody.'

As the last of the applause died away, he reclaimed command. It was like watching a mesmerist, Ali thought. He seemed calm, reacting to the room, but also several steps ahead of it.

Satisfied he had them where he wanted them, Ed let a smile break slowly across his face as he prepared to introduce the surprise guest, allowing the mystery to continue for a while longer as mutters went around the room.

Ali indulged the idea that people in the bar afterwards might think she was important when she greeted Paul. Then she spent the rest of the show worrying that he'd be angry she wasn't Otis and that she'd overcompensate like she always did.

Ed took a step back and raised his hand towards the wings as loud hoots and cheers greeted Paul's entrance. The humble stoop meant he had to lower the mic stand even though Ali guessed, now she could see him, that he was about the same height as Ed.

'Now. No. Come on.' Paul's hand went to his brow, his eyes occasionally flicking up from the ground to take in the sight before him as the noise continued. He shook a couple of hands on the front row as though welcoming high-ranking dignitaries, thanking them for coming. He paused to take in the room again and shook his head, eyes creasing in thanks.

When his stillness brought the room to quiet again, he began, picking up a thought halfway through and immediately taking the room with him.

Ali wondered what Mark was doing. She pictured him in the passenger seat of an SUV, Gemma driving them home in silence as it got dark. She wouldn't leave him, Ali was sure of that. But she would punish him. Maybe that was their thing.

'You've been lovely. I've been Paul Bonatti, good night.' The applause made Ali realise she hadn't been listening, his short set passing while she remembered the hotel room and her sticky skin and how she'd just wanted Mark to get out of the bathroom.

Downstairs in the bar she joined a queue for drinks, glad of the cooler air. She'd get the meeting with Paul out of the way, go to the off-licence near her flat on the way home and pretend it was just another day, another bottle of wine.

She tried to imagine how Mark would've reacted if she'd told him why she was so desperate to go out. She'd thought it was safer to use work as an excuse than to tell him the truth.

She'd shown Mark her phone as they lay on top of the covers in his room, hoping to subtly suggest the gig as something to do 'for a change'. He glanced at it and handed it back. 'A bunch of comics having a cock fight? No thanks.'

'There are ladies too. Look, this one, the Welsh girl.'

He'd glanced over at the picture on her screen and smirked. 'You can say Pakistani. It doesn't make you better, you know, pretending you haven't noticed she's brown. Sorry, "of colour".' He went back to his own screen.

She just needed to get past this and onto him pulling at her underwear. The feeling of him wanting her made her drunk, propelled along on a ride she had no control over. It struck her that she didn't care who was doing the pulling and pushed the thought away.

After the first time they slept together, they mostly stayed in. He brought prosecco from the M&S by the office, she brought crisps and they'd fuck and watch TV in the room. But tonight, she'd wanted just one night out as a normal couple. She didn't tell him why because she knew it would sound desperate and sad and shrivel his dick and make him recoil from her.

None of this had been her idea. He'd kissed her at the Radio Awards when she was hammered on champagne, wearing the black dress she'd worn to her dad's funeral. She'd thought it would make her invisible, but Mark could see her from across the room, swaying. He'd watched her as he pointedly tipped the last dregs of his wine into his mouth and placed the empty glass on the table next to her.

He'd messaged her when he came back to London for work, asking to meet. He kept pouring the wine that took her away from everything and made her float above herself. She reasoned that all she'd done was say yes to the numbness.

She finally reached the bar and a girl with black nails looked at her like she'd already waited too long for Ali to decide. Ali blanched. 'Vodka and ice. And some lime?'

'Single? Double?' The girl looked actively pissed off now.

Ali almost whispered the word double, ashamed, but the girl was still looking at her like she hadn't heard.

'A double,' she almost shouted, mortified.

There was nowhere to sit down so she went to the far end of the bar to lean.

Leaning felt weird, so she stood upright again and studied the posters on the wall.

The room was comfortably dingy; dark red walls, old wooden chairs on their second or third life, some with crosses cut into the back and shelves for hymn books. The round plywood tables were branded with a smiley face like the one on the hand stamp. 'Fun Club' repeated around the table's edge in lower-case letters.

She would flatter Paul, tell him how good he was and tee up a meeting at the radio station. Then she could go. The vodka would get her there.

After a few minutes she realised he might be waiting for her, not wanting to come into the bar where fans would bother him.

Backstage was smaller than she expected as she edged the door open, feeling like a burglar. Paul was sat at a dressing table, smirking at something on a laptop. Maybe he hadn't heard her knock. Over his shoulder was the door to a bathroom, ajar, the toilet inside with its seat up, making her want to look away.

Paul finished whatever he'd been reading and looked up, adjusting his smile to one that said, 'Great to meet you.' He seemed to be waiting for Ali to speak.

'Oh. Ali, hi.' She put her hand out, hoping he'd be a shaker. 'From Zone Digital.

I'm so sorry I'm not Otis. He's gutted but something came up.'

Paul stood and mirrored her, extending the same arm and making a handshake impossible. She hated that there wasn't a single standard greeting any more. It felt like a game of rock-paper-scissors to her and she always picked the wrong one.

As Paul leaned in, the bristles around his mouth prickled, his damp lips connecting with her skin. He smelled of something expensive and herbal and she knew she was turning pink without looking in the mirror. Something in the way he was looking at her told her he'd noticed too, but it passed. She couldn't wipe her cheek in front of him, so it stayed wet.

Paul started putting the laptop and some other things into a backpack. 'Well, I hope you enjoyed it.' He emphasised the 'you'. Ali had always liked watching Paul on TV but something about being in this room with him now made her feel hot and unprofessional.

She started as the dressing-room door opened into her shoulder and a 'sorry' came from the other side. She moved towards the bathroom to make space for the new visitor and turned to see Bethan Gill in the doorway. Bethan looked from Ali to Paul and back and he smiled broadly at her, pushing his glasses up towards his brow. 'Hey, nice work, nice work. Caught the end of yours.'

Bethan stayed where she was, not really acknowledging the compliment.

Unbothered, Paul turned towards Ali again, holding his backpack in front of him. 'OK, nice to meet you, Elly. Otis has blown it, tell him.' Another big grin and Bethan stood aside to let him pass, waiting till he was out of sight. She creased her brow at Ali. 'Are you OK?'

Ali was puzzled. Did something about her not look OK? She came out of the bathroom and pulled the door to behind her, stealing a paranoid look in the dressing-table mirror. 'Yes, fine. You were great, by the way,' she added hoping it didn't sound like an afterthought.

'Thanks. I just to need to get...' She indicated the jacket on a hanger behind Ali. 'Sorry. Of course.' Ali looked down at the floor, scraping at a piece of electrical tape stuck to the floor with her foot while Bethan put her jacket on. Ali's compulsion to fill awkward silences took over.

'I'm not a fan. I mean, I am a fan.' She gestured to the chair recently vacated by Paul. 'I'm a radio producer. We were just... touching base. He might be doing a show with us, so.'

She could see she was losing Bethan's interest. 'And now, my life story. Sorry, I'm babbling, Ali.'

She put out her hand and Bethan shook it, her brow softening. 'You might want a back-up plan.'

Ali didn't understand but tried to look like she broadly agreed with whatever was happening here. Bethan came in and closed the door. 'Your friend,' she looked at the chair where he'd been. 'Not a good choice if any women work at your radio station.'

'Right. Oh.' Ali was nodding. Bethan's face told her she wasn't joking. 'You just did a gig with him, though.'

'I didn't know he was going to be here. Ed hadn't heard the stuff I've heard about him. He has now.'

'What's he actually done?'

Bethan reached for the doorhandle. 'Not my story to tell. Just trust me, it's multiple women, it's not good and I don't think it'll be long before it comes out. Up to you.' She opened the door and held it for Ali to go first.

By the time she got back downstairs to the bar, Ali felt the anger hot on the back of her neck. 'Up to you,' she muttered to herself sarcastically looking around the room at the tables filled with groups and couples, talking and laughing, at ease with one another. Someone knocked a glass onto the floor and a group of lads cheered.

The walls were covered in overlapping show posters lacquered with varnish. Mad faces thrust at her, competing with each other for most emphatic expression. The women looked confused, scared, excited. The men stared down the barrel, disappointed, purposeful, angry. It was oppressive, but sort of comforting. She ordered another drink, not wanting to go home yet.

She looked at her phone, trying to compose a message to Otis, taking sips from her glass, feeling the cold turn to warm inside her, her breath getting shorter the more she thought about Bethan's self-righteous little speech.

The hotel room and Gemma's face rushed up at her like the ground in a dream. 'Fuck,' she said to her phone's screen, the room too noisy to hear her. She stared at the words she'd just typed and deleted them.

The expression on Mark's wife's face had something else mixed with the disgust and anguish. 'Not again.' Of course Mark had done this before. Gemma must have known the signs; how he offered to take the kids to the park or changed his aftershave when he was up to his old tricks.

At the hotel, Gemma had stood at the threshold, car-key fob gripped in one hand, her other holding the strap of her shoulder bag. She took in the sight of Ali with one hand behind her back, squeezing her knees together, saying nothing.

Gemma looked past her into room. The unmade bed brought a

film of tears to her eyes. She cracked when she saw Mark's brown shoes neatly stowed under the chair by the mirror.

'Do...' Ali had nothing to offer, the shame paralysing her.

'I thought you'd be young,' said Gemma, her jaw clenching.

Ali picked up her things and left. A text message arrived a while later from Mark.

Great, now everyone gets hurt.

Ali tried to turn away from the rest of the bar and its ebullience, but there was just the wall to her left, covered in gurning faces, all indifferent to the onset of panic currently tightening its drawstrings somewhere inside her.

She stared at her phone, hammering out a new apology to her boss, reassuring him she'd persuade Paul's people to circle back, praying for the surge to subside.

She counted the seconds, holding a breath in, letting it out slowly. It'll pass. It'll pass. She said the words in her head, simultaneously terrified people could see the words. You're OK. You're OK. She allowed herself one more out-loud 'Fuck.'

A shadow passed over her screen as someone else arrived at the bar next to her.

There was a pause. Jeans and trainers belonging to a man drew level with her feet and she could feel that their owner was looking at her.

Ali lifted her head and found herself looking into the eyes of Ed Catchpole.

Two

She attempted a smile and returned to her phone.

The girl with black fingernails came over and beamed at him. 'What can I get you?'

Ed looked at Ali, wordlessly checking if she was waiting to be served. She held up her full drink in answer, not trusting herself to speak yet, and he asked for whisky.

They stood side by side for a while, Ali pretending to read, him looking at her reflected in the mirror behind the optics. Eventually, he spoke.

'What is that? Surgical spirit?'

Before she could answer, Ed took the glass from her hand and sniffed, never taking his eyes from hers. 'Neat vodka. That's a serious drink. Who'd drink that? Katharine Hepburn?'

She was Katharine Hepburn. Her teeth were trying to escape her mouth again and she pressed her lips together, trying to trap the hysteria behind them.

Ed ran a hand through his hair, lowering his voice. 'So, Katharine, are you OK?' The question was so sincere she felt a breath catch in her throat.

'Yeah, yes.' She pulled herself more upright, realising she'd slumped.

'I'm… it's a work thing.' She made a face, wafting the words away with her hand. His look said, 'Go on'.

'I was just upstairs talking to Paul. I'm a producer. Just on radio, but my boss sent me to, you know. Anyway, I might have…' She couldn't think of an alternative. '… fucked it. And then Bethan. Gill?' He nodded, keeping up. 'She had some… opinions.'

'Ah.' He straightened up too as though paying attention. 'And how did that go?' He was assessing her.

'Not well. Well, well at first and then not well.'

'Wellwellwell.' His smile made two deep furrows from the corners of his mouth to his nose, the stubble darkening in the crevices. Her own face cracked, teeth wet as she laughed.

Ed enjoyed her abandon for a moment. She wondered if he was appalled by her unwhitened smile. He shook his head and his nose dipped into his glass. 'Bethan read me the riot act too.'

Ali tried not to look too curious. 'Right. About Paul?' He nodded, raising his eyebrows.

'Did she tell you what he's done? She was a bit vague.'

Ed puffed whisky breath down through his nose. 'She told me enough. She's got her ear to the ground. If he's on the list,' he shrugged. 'I believe her.'

Ali wanted to ask what the list was but decided it would be cooler to act as though she already knew.

'What are you going to tell your boss?'

She thought about the deleted email. 'What is there to tell? Someone says Paul's a bit dodgy, no, I don't know what he's done and yes, this is all just something someone told me in a green room. Fuck knows.'

'Oh, you've got…' Ed reached over the bar to a pile of napkins by the till and handed her one, pointing to the corner of his own eye. 'A bit of something.'

She looked in the mirror behind the bar and rubbed at the mascara goop, wondering what else she could do to really nail the bad impression she was making.

When she emerged from her tissue, she noticed a tall girl behind Ed. Her short brown hair stuck out in tufts behind each ear and she seemed to be waiting for something. Ed followed Ali's gaze and looked over his shoulder. 'Sid. Sorry, old chap.'

The girl gave him a curt smile. 'I'll get my own drink, shall I?' 'And one for…' He turned back to Ali.

'Oh, you don't need to… Ali. But it's OK, I'm not…'

He turned back to the girl. 'Vodka rocks. Wedge of lime.' Ali's hand went to her hair. 'Thanks. That's… thanks.'

He hadn't showered and there was a whiff of sweat as he leaned in and offered his hand. 'Ed.' It was all she could do not to scream 'I know!' in his face. She thought she saw people look over, curious to see who he was talking to.

A young girl further up the bar was staring from under thick, dark eyeliner. Her pale hair was cut into a bob, the ends blue as though dipped in paint.

Ed exchanged a look with Sid. 'Hold that thought.'

Ali watched him go over to the girl, his back to them. The two seemed to talk for a while but she couldn't hear them.

Ed's tall friend was back with her drink.

'There you go. It was a wedge of lime, right? Not lime cordial?'

'Yes, perfect. Thanks.' They stood awkwardly for a beat, then spoke at the same time.

'I'm Sid.'

'Ali. I was meeting Paul about a work thing.'

Small smiles passed back and forth. They sipped their drinks. Ali tried to decide how old Sid was. She could be a woman in her twenties or a teenage boy. The pale blue veins on the back of her hands made Ali think of cold blood and the grey dungarees and tennis shoes of a kid in a Spielberg film. The black shirt underneath was buttoned up to the top.

Sid's slightness made Ali feel what she always felt when she met someone thin: she's better than me. It wasn't a hostile thought, she just knew it was true. Paper wraps stone, thin beats fat.

Ali spoke first. 'Do you do comedy too?'

Sid shook her head incredulously. 'I just help out.'

Sid saw Ali watching Ed with the girl. 'Number one fan. Well, one of them. He always makes time for them.'

They made small talk about the night, Ali's job. Sid asked questions, listening to the answers, laughing when Ali made jokes about Otis. Her curiosity felt genuine, not just said to fill the space until Ed came back.

The faces on the posters approved of Ali like old friends. She was warmed by the thought that she wasn't just 'a fan' like the girl at the bar. She didn't know how she had crossed that threshold. Maybe Sid thought she and Ed were old friends.

He was coming back. The young girl put her bag on her shoulder and left without looking back.

Ed was holding a brown paper bag, his smile not reaching his eyes. 'Again?' said Sid, looking at the bag.

'Yup.' Ed checked over his shoulder to see if the girl was gone. 'Have you got room in your bag?'

Sid took the package and saw Ali looking. 'Bananas.' She tilted the open end towards Ali. 'He did a bit about bananas curing hangovers. About six months ago?'

Ed nodded, nose back in his drink. 'And now she brings them every time.'

'I do like a banana the morning after. Potassium, magnesium, very good for getting over the drink, but fuck me. Bags of the things. I don't know how to tell her to stop.'

Ali raised her glass. 'Save me one of those.' She wondered if that was too much, laying claim to his bananas after such a short acquaintance.

'Gladly.' He did the wink again.

How did he make that look so appealing, so decidedly un-cheesy?

The sound of a phone ringing sent Sid fishing in the pocket of her dungarees. She answered it and pointed towards the door to the street.

Satisfied they were alone again, Ed's eyes softened. 'Are you OK?'

Ali felt moth wings thinking about what it would be like to be held, pressed against him, her nose buried in his shoulder. His shoulder became her dad's shoulder, the striped pyjama fabric against her cheek.

Ed was looking at her like he couldn't work her out, something he saw in her making him laugh softly, brow furrowed.

She looked down at the scrunched napkin in her fist and felt tears in her eyes. 'God, sorry. I don't know what I'm doing.' She looked up at him and he stopped laughing.

His look was disarming. 'Who does?' Something about the way he was looking at her told her it was safe to go on.

She grimaced. 'I don't cry in bars.' The tissue was a hard ball in her hand. 'My dad died. I'm fine, then suddenly, I'm not.'

. He left space around this like he knew there was more to come. She spoke without knowing what was going to come out. 'When he was dying, he said sorry to me. For not being around enough when I was a kid, like it was his fault. It wasn't, it was hers. Wanting the big house, making him do a job he hated. And I worry I'm so angry at her that I'll forget to miss him. I miss him.' She said the last bit more quietly, head bowed.

Ed nodded like he understood everything. 'Grief. Can't go over it, can't go under it…'

Ali smiled, remembering her dad reading something like that to her when she was little. 'Can't go around it. We're going on a bear hunt.'

He passed her a new napkin. The bar receded and it was just the two of them, smiling at each other.

'We're going for a drink. It's not far. Come with us. I've got an idea.'

Ali nodded, not wanting to spoil the moment by saying anything. She drank the rest of her vodka. She wanted to tell him everything and it seemed like he wanted to listen.

Sid was coming back. She had a muttered conversation with

Ed and then he raised his arm like a falconer, Ali's cue to join them.

She wanted to be swept along like a carrier bag on the wind, to let someone else decide what happened next. The thought made her feel lighter than she had in weeks.

Ed swept her out of the door. Sid followed. He talked about his tour, Edinburgh first, just for a week. No point doing the whole month. Whisky wafted as he spoke over his shoulder, forging on like he was showing her the sights.

She talked about her job, the bleakness of the early-morning breakfast show, how she wanted more, even if she didn't totally believe that she'd ever do anything about it. She wanted him to think she might.

By the time they came to an anonymous door next to an all-night newsagent, she realised she didn't know where they were. It was a street she hadn't been down before, dwarfed by tower blocks on one side, right at the edge of the City.

She couldn't stop talking. 'If you produce a show at four in the morning and no one hears it, does it make a sound?'

Ed laughed at that and she nearly lifted off the ground. She was funny and Katharine Hepburn and halfway to really drunk.

'Hence this other show.' He stopped. 'Would it help if you pitched me?' Ali stopped and he turned to face her.

'What?'

'If Paul is, quotes – a problem – quotes, use my name. I mean, if you think your boss…'

'Are you serious?'

He smiled at her, almost like she'd tied her shoes for the first time without help. 'My agent will be furious, but I'll deal with her. Attach my name, if you think it'll help. Call it a favour. What is it, six weeks? We'll be done before the tour.'

Ali looked over her shoulder at Sid, worried they were excluding her, but she seemed content to follow. 'He loves a new friend,' she said, smiling and holding the door open for them.

They went inside, down black shiny steps and left into a dimly lit room. It was filled with discreet chatter and in the background the low throb of hip-hop. Ed seemed to know where he was going.

People drank cocktails from coupes at small tables, the sound of ice cubes smashing against the inside of a shaker like percussion out of time with the music.

Sid went to borrow a stool while Ali and Ed sat on padded velvet chairs at a table that seemed to be waiting for them.

Ed's face loomed out of the dark, lit underneath by a tea light in a glass. They were talking and Sid must have joined them but Ali was starting to lose track. Lit from beneath, Ed reminded her of a painting. 'Joseph Wright of something. You look like that science experiment.'

Ed didn't hear her. He made a little cough, nodding at a coupe the bartender had put in front of her. 'This drink raises the dead. Corpse Reviver.' He paused, frowned. 'Sorry, too soon?'

She shook her head and he re-joined the thought where he'd left it. 'Corpse Reviver…' Now a pause for effect. 'Number two.'

Had they even ordered? 'Shouldn't we drink the number one first?'

He clinked his glass gently against hers and fixed his eyes on her, waiting for a reaction.

She did as she was told and drank. The zest started at the tip of her tongue, turning to a green wave over her soft palate, burning briefly at the back of her throat.

He looked like a scientist, watching his test tubes. She felt like she was expected to appraise.

'Aniseed?' Ali wasn't sure if she liked it. Judging by his face, she hadn't said the right thing yet. She took another sip.

'That's…' She was nodding. 'Yeah.'

He seemed satisfied. 'Right?' He'd drunk half of his in one slug. 'Absinthe. The green fairies. Feel the life returning. That's the aniseed.'

19

She'd always been scared of absinthe. 'I'll have weird dreams.' The horizon was overbalancing and she knew she was reaching a full tank. The wine from the hotel mixed with the vodka. A thin film of sweat formed on her forehead, a greasy coating of panic on her insides.

The only way forward was with conviction, like believing you can punch through a wall. She did a slow nose breath, taking her time with the exhalation.

'Jump. The fairies will catch you.' She wasn't sure if Ed had said that or she'd just heard it.

He seemed to like schooling her and she was enjoying letting him. What had they been talking about? The conversation bubbled and frothed, he less drunk than her, but catching up.

When he went to the loo, she and Sid gossiped about who Sid had worked with at Ed's agency and which celebrities were awful. Sid seemed to like Ali's questions and the idea of herself as someone who knew things.

She looked at Sid's glass of beer. 'No fairies for you?'

Sid shook her head. 'In the office early. Loads to do before we go.'

'Ooh, where you going?' Ali was becoming aware how drunk she sounded. 'The Fringe for a week. Although to hear him you'd think it was the front at

Dunkirk.' She said this more loudly as Ed returned to his seat and grinned at Ali as Ed made a performative huff. The two women rolled their eyes, Sid taking a bigger slug of her beer. 'No, you two enjoy yourselves. Have another drink. Have two.' She took a hoodie from her bag and pulled it over her head.

Ali liked her benign sarcasm. She seemed like someone who held back more than she gave away, always making room for other people. She thought she seemed a lot wiser than the average twenty-something. Compared to the ones Ali had met at the radio station anyway.

Sid took a last drink and turned to Ed. 'Have you got your

key?' She stood. 'Old chap,' Ed said, patting his pocket in confirmation.

Sid smiled and did an awkward little wave at Ali. 'Mail you tomorrow.' She turned and disappeared up the stairs.

'Bye, Sid.' Ali felt guilty at how glad she was Sid had gone. 'She's ace, isn't she? What key?' Her mind leapt about like a fly on a sandwich.

'I stay at the flat on gig nights. Don't live in London, do I ?' He let the cod-estuary flood his vowels for effect. Ali couldn't place his real accent any more precisely than 'South'. Somewhere south of the middle, but with no particular pull towards east or west.

'Where do you live?' Ali wanted to ask him thousands of questions.

'Village in Suffolk. Horses and fields. You won't have heard of it. Very pretty.' He landed this last word looking into her eyes in a way that made her feel like she was going to drown, but that maybe drowning would be nice.

'What village? What office? Sid works at the club.'

Ed took a smaller sip. 'She's my – I don't want to sound grand and say assistant – but assistant. She techs shows, does my diary. Helps my agent sometimes. That's the office. We don't pay her enough.'

'And landlady?' Ali's filters were gone and the sound of her own questions surprised her.

Ed's eyes widened. 'Sid's dad owns the club. Quite a few clubs actually.' A wave of his hand suggesting a vast empire. 'He set her up in a place in Covent Garden, the turns use the spare rooms. You wouldn't know it to look at her, but she lives in the West End like a lord.'

Ali drank more, starting to enjoy the odd taste. 'I was really proud when I bought my place. I mean, got my mortgage. Mum and Dad came down to see it when my dad was still...' She couldn't start crying again so she focused on a different emotion. 'She looks around – Jean, Mum – clearly wondering where the rest of it is and calls it a 'bedsit'. It's a fucking studio flat. It's a nice studio flat! It's quite big.'

'Good for you, independent woman.'

She made a face. 'Oh, I'm… all right.'

He blew air between his lips like a horse. 'Good job, your own place. You're a catch, mate.' He clinked his glass against hers. 'We can do a bit better than all right.'

'Best I can do is a married arsehole from work.' She couldn't believe she'd said it out loud. The drink was strong and she'd downed it too quickly.

'Oh, mate.' He looked in the direction of the bar and raised his eyebrows. Satisfied that the bartender had clocked him, he turned back to Ali. 'What's all this?'

She shrugged, not sure herself. 'I work weird hours. When do I meet anyone?' She stopped short of telling him she was lonely. Even drunk, she knew that wasn't a thing to say out loud. 'He's got a wife in the country and I'm his city girl. We have sex in rooms with non-opening windows. Well, we did.'

'What did he do to get your attention, this married arsehole?'

'Um. He was interested?'

'That's a high wall to climb there, Juliet.'

She put her head in her hands. 'Now you think I'm one of those people. I'm not. I can't believe I told you. I've never done anything like…'

He held up his hands, looking at her as though it hadn't even crossed his mind. 'What do your friends think of this…' He paused, turning the stem of his glass.

'Situation?'

'My best mate's got babies. Loads of babies. I didn't tell her because of what she'd say. She's coupled up now. I don't really make new friends.'

'Because of the funny hours?'

She blinked. 'Yeah.' She changed her mind. 'No. Women are tricky, you know? Competitive, sizing each other up. They've either bullied me or left me or judged me.' She peered over the rim of her glass at him. 'I don't trust them.'

He leaned his chin on his hand. 'You've got to have friends. Who do you turn to in your hour of need? Men?'

She rolled her eyes. 'Maybe? That's bad, isn't it? I'm like a baby duckling. You know when they're born and they imprint on the first creature they see? That's me when I sleep with someone. I think I love them. Shag. I love you. No quality control.'

She looked at the green puddle at the bottom of her glass, the candlelight quivered by her breath. 'I don't think I like Mark. Like, his personality?' Another thought fluttered across her brain. 'Who was blue girl?'

She was beautifully disorientated; she hadn't thought about her face for hours. 'People can see what you're thinking,' her mum had told her. 'Like your dad. You can't hide what you're thinking to save your life.' It was the worst crime, to let other people know what you were thinking. The thought made her panic often in company. But not now.

'Blue girl?' Ed was looking at her like a puzzle again. 'From the club? Cally with the bananas. Sweet kid. She's been through a lot. We just try and look out for her.'

A bartender delivered two fresh drinks. 'There you go.'

The conversation waltzed on, the two of them swaying in and out of each other's stories, making room for one another. She said she loved train journeys. He used to, but not so much now he was on TV.

'It's not the ones informing you that you're shit. The fans are worse. Wanting to tell you what they love about you and you're trapped with them for the duration. Car's just often easier now.'

Ali pretended not to have thought about the fact she was having a drink with a famous comedian. 'That sounds stressful. I love a long train trip, not a coach, though. I can't read on a coach.'

She remembered a school coach trip to Edinburgh. 'The teacher marched us up Arthur's Seat. I thought I was going to die.'

'Why? Best hangover cure if you go early enough, before all the cunts are out of bed.

'I had a panic attack. I looked down over the edge and saw the drop and the other kids were laughing and pretending to push each other. I've been scared of heights ever since. Guess what my favourite film is?'

He rested his elbow on the back of his chair, taking her in. 'Something with vampires in.'

'*Vertigo.*' She grimaced.

He sat back, looking at her. 'Come to Edinburgh. I'll take you up Arthur's Seat. No, don't cheapen this.'

She was convulsing again. She was laughing too much at everything. She cringed away from the table and was confronted by herself, looking back at her from the mirrored wall next to them. She looked stoned, carefree.

'Stay like that.'

She did as he asked, but looked into the reflection of the room, not wanting to spoil the glimpse she'd had of her face looking almost attractive. Big pupils made everyone look lovely, she thought.

'Head still.' He pulled a small Biro out of his trouser pocket and slid a napkin in front of him.

She kept as still as she could but the lack of motion only under-lined that the world was tipping and slanting.

She didn't know if she had to keep her mouth still. 'Are you drawing me?' She pronounced it with an N, jaw fixed like a ventrilo-quist's dummy.

His eyes stayed on his canvas, occasionally darting up to take in his subject.

'There.' He put the napkin in front of her and it was recognisably her profile, but with something darker and more mysterious about the eyes. He'd flattered her.

'Wow. That's good. I can't draw at all. Look at me!' She held it up.

'If you work quickly, you can trick your brain. Don't give yourself the time to think. Try it.'

'Draw you? Fuck, no. You'd never want to see me again.' She blanched at how that sounded. 'I'd love to be able to do that. You're so jazz.' She made herself laugh. He didn't join in, but he was smiling.

He turned the napkin over and gave her the pen. 'Sixty seconds. Don't think, just draw shapes. Squinting helps.'

She was shaking her head and laughing as she did what he said.

He adopted a serious expression, staring right at her, and didn't flinch for the entire minute. An alarm tinkled from his phone. 'Stop.'

She put the pen down, her other hand covering her eyes, then her mouth, trying to clutch the paper to her chest. 'I am so sorry about your nose.'

He held a hand out expectantly, but didn't try to snatch it. She gave it to him. His face gave nothing away. Then a raised eyebrow. 'Not bad. There's something… vital.' She groaned and covered her face. He took her hand away from her mouth. 'You've got to keep doing it. Every day. You'll get better.'

He was making friends. She wanted to be friends.

He put the napkin back on the table. 'You're ready for bed.'

Ali's eyes widened and he held his hands up in protest. 'I mean you're tired.' They smirked at each other and she pulled herself upright, desperate to show that she wasn't tired, like a child wanting to stay up past their bedtime.

He talked about his divorce. Ali wanted to know everything but kept her questions to a minimum, letting him speak, thinking about him touching her hand.

'We were in our twenties when we met. I invited her to my first gig.' His eyes cast down, then slowly lifted as though he'd decided the bridge was safe to cross. 'Her health wasn't good. Her mental health, for years actually.' He trailed off.

'And you carried that on your own? That must've been hard.'

'I shouldn't talk about her. She was always so private, I couldn't...'

Ali thought carefully. 'Everyone needs to talk to someone.' She met his eyes for a moment.

He looked down at her hand on the table. 'She put it into her art. I didn't do that, out of respect, I suppose. A lot of comics go confessional, but I could never.'

'I suppose comedy is art. If you want to be a ponce about it.' Ali tried teasing again. She wanted to change the subject, feeling out of her depth. Like she'd pressed her face against their bedroom window. 'You're more like a conductor. That's an art, isn't it? Conducting?'

He looked interested, liking the image of himself with a baton, holding the room to attention. 'We're all just waving our sticks around, love.'

She forgot to laugh, concentrating on her thought before it ran away. 'That's what it was like watching you tonight. I felt like we were the orchestra and you were telling us when to fortissimo and when to piano.' She was conducting the air and almost knocked her glass.

Ed thought for a moment. 'My agent got an offer for that conducting show.'

Ali beamed. 'Oh, why don't you do it?'

He flapped a hand. 'It's a bit desperate.'

She felt foolish. 'You'd be brilliant,' she said more quietly, twirling the stem of her glass, sensing she'd said the wrong thing.

'You can put yourself in a rut going that route, reality, pop fac. I can't spend time going sideways, I'm not 30 any more. I'm not fucking 40 any more. It's got to be up. Don't want to be one of those panel show cunts forever. And even there, they need to clear out some of the old white guys. It's not the nineties.'

She rolled her eyes. 'Right?'

'I've seen where those poor bastards end up. Right-wing news channels.' He mimed a noose around his neck.

Ali smiled, watching him intently for clues.

'I want to do something good. Benefits for refugees and rail unions are all fine, and I'll do them gladly. But it's no use if you're not saying something, you know? To a bigger audience. TV isn't the place for that any more. Satire's dead. But it's where I need to be if I want to be heard.'

'And you should be heard. Do you think it's hard for men now? I mean harder.'

He made his hands into a prayer. 'For pity's sake, think of the men. No, I've wanted it to change for them for a long time. The women. They're doing all the best stuff now. Bethan's going all the way this year. Her Edinburgh show, pffft.' He made a gesture by his temple like his mind had blown. 'Happy to give up my chair, if it helps.'

Ali gazed, her eyelids struggling to express admiration, becoming lead.

'Right, down that. You need sleep.' Ali opened her mouth to protest, to tell him that she was just starting to feel at one with the room. She would always drink here now, if she could find it again.

'Promise me something?'

Her spine tingled.

He waited until he was sure she was paying attention. 'We don't know each other well, but I think we will. You're great and you reject every compliment. All of your wit and your wonder – don't waste it. And certainly don't waste it on creepy old men with wives in the country.'

He swept his fringe to one side and looked at her face, softened by candlelight, eyelids drooping.

'OK,' was all she could manage, feeling elated but also really, properly drunk. 'You're a good guy. I'm going to stop saying. Saying? Talking.'

He put the napkin in her hand, their fingers touching and retreating.

He passed some money over the bar on their way out and up

the stairs. Ali thought she hadn't seen anyone pay in cash for a long time, so old-fashioned. So nice.

Her eyes tried to record the back of his head, the way his shoulders moved when he walked. She kicked herself for being so drunk.

Outside, a warm breeze blew the soot smell up the stairs from the nearby tube exit. Ed's arm was already aloft, flagging down an approaching taxi.

'I can get a train. It's fine,' she began, knowing she couldn't really afford a cab.

'Talk to Sid tomorrow, about the show.' He shepherded her towards the car and stepped forward to open the door. She wished it hadn't arrived so quickly.

Why wasn't he drunk any more? He slid his hand through the window and gave the driver something, then turned to her, putting his hand out to steady her. 'Where to?'

She didn't reply, other than to beam at him like the sun. Was this flirting? She thought about toast and peanut butter. She was hungry. He was handsome. Her thoughts were pale green and wouldn't stand in straight lines.

She slurred her address at the driver and turned towards the open door, intending to turn back and leave him with a good impression. Ed caught her waist, just preventing her skull from crashing against the side of the car. She felt his fingers sink into the flesh there and tomorrow she'd keep remembering and wishing he hadn't felt her plumpness.

She turned to look up into his eyes and pictured an epic kiss, synchronised swimmers fanning in concentric circles around them.

Ed hugged her and she disappeared into him, arms pinned to her sides, trying to breathe him in. Just as quickly, she was out in the night air again. They grinned at each other, laughing at nothing.

'Safe home. Let me know you got there, OK?'

It was ending.

'It's my birthday.'

His eyes widened and he took her in with something that could have been sympathy but looked to her more like deep, disarming affection.

'Alison.' He stepped forward, taking her face in his hands. 'Happy birthday.'

The kiss was firm, then soft and only a second long. She felt what she thought was his tongue grazing against hers. A wave of warmth broke inside her.

He pulled back again, letting her go.

She was dazed. 'You going?'

'Gig in Glasgow tomorrow. Have to start walking now.' He waited while she struggled with her seatbelt and closed the door, careful not to catch her clothes as he did.

'Bye, nice man,' she smiled as he pushed the door shut and banged his hand on the cab roof.

Still dizzy, she was moving forward. She looked through the back window at Ed receding, hand raised.

Lights twinkled on the dirty window. She would forget so much of what they'd said. It would go and this epic feeling would go and she'd chase it to the ends of the earth to feel it again.

She closed her eyes to feel the kiss. It was hardly anything, but it was something.

She must've slept. The cab leapt through time, turned into her street and came to a stop. She fumbled for her wallet but the driver said good night in a way that meant 'get out'.

She got herself and her bag onto the pavement. Home. Peanut butter. Everything else could wait.

Upstairs on the coffee table lay one of the two envelopes that she'd picked up from the mat when she got in from work. The other card sat on the mantelpiece, a hand-drawn cartoon from Ava dating back to a stupid university in-joke, inside a promise to buy Ali dinner when she was able to leave the twins. In Ali's head they were still kneeling up on Ava's bed in halls, trying to waft dope smoke out of the window. Laughing through the fog, it was the first time Ali had felt true fellowship, that someone liked her just as she was, liking the things she liked, not the things she pretended to.

Ali turned the second envelope over in her hands. She knew the writing, the careful loops that could seem arty and yet stayed entirely uniform.

Ali tore the thick paper, revealing a pastel-pink cake with candles surrounded by flowers and champagne glasses at jaunty angles. In the middle, the number 40 in gold foil.

She didn't read the greeting. She knew what it would say. She knew what it wouldn't say. 'How can I have a daughter who is 40?'

She took Ed's napkin from her pocket, slid it under her pillow and slept in her clothes.

Three

Ed's face in candlelight, telling her the man on stage wasn't the real him. It was all she could see when she shut her eyes. She rolled over. The smallest graze of his tongue still in her mouth if she concentrated.

'You can see me.' He was looking at her like she might save him. The picture was trapped behind Ali's eyes. She couldn't open them if she wanted to. She never wanted to again.

The morning light prodded through the blinds, threatening to flood the room. The wooden slats wobbled in the draught from the window and the sun teased the far wall, happy to wait. It had all day.

Cloudless skies were not good for Ali's increasingly anxious hangovers. London's thick summers were sent to mock her, luring her in with the promise of sunny wine in pub gardens, then berating her the next day for letting go and enjoying the moment.

This beast needed grey, cold air and light rain.

The voice that gnawed at her had already set to work; she'd talked too much, been too sycophantic. She'd spilled her drink and thrown him off his stride.

Her temples throbbed. She reached for her phone. The message at the top leapt out, sent at 1 o'clock to an unknown number.

You're funny. Have a radio show. This is a contract. Signed Ali
Lauder xxx

She pressed the screen to her chest and only started breathing
again as she remembered Ed taking her phone and tapping at the
screen as though it belonged to him, adding his number to her
memory, sending himself the message.

There was an email from Sid. She hoped Ed hadn't kept her out
too late.

The last line threw Ali. 'Still up for meeting today if you're not
too broken. We can look at his diary and see what works. I can
tell the radio thing appeals.'

She didn't remember making plans, but there was probably plenty
that had dissolved in last night's green haze. Not the kiss though.
She could still feel that.

If she slept first, maybe it would be good to meet Sid. She could
use the opportunity to find out more about Ed. She kept her head
as still as possible and replied.

Later today is good. Where?
Come to a work thing. We can talk after. If you can stand warm
wine and TV people.

The words triggered nausea and she sent a thumbs-up emoji
before putting her phone face down on the bed and closing her
eyes.

She woke two hours later and showered, pausing to look at
herself in the bathroom mirror. Her breasts no longer filled her
bras and her belly went flat when she lay on her back instead of
forming a dome. She hadn't been hungry since the funeral, so eating
was something she did when she remembered to. She liked it.

She couldn't remember her mother ever calling her fat specifically,
but Jean never failed to notice changes in her daughter's shape.

Once, when she was little, she'd heard Jean joke to a family
friend, 'No danger of Alison getting an eating disorder.' Ali had

been licking an ice cream with a chocolate flake, looking at the wind making snakes on the loose sand of the bay.

While her mother tutted and talked, Ali went to the edge of the water and stared at the marks left by her tongue in the ice cream, sculpting it around the base of the flake. She dropped the cone into the sea and watched the white ice bobbing and dissolving as the chocolate bar floated away on the foam like a tree trunk.

When Ali came out of the bathroom, she saw the birthday card on the table. She didn't have the heart to put it in the bin, so she took it to the shelves by the fireplace and slid it between two books.

She made the bed and found Ed's napkin, tucked where she'd left it under her pillow. She propped it on the mantelpiece, the portrait he'd done of her facing out.

Then she lay on the bed and made herself come thinking about him. It gave her a headache.

The TV studios took up the bottom two floors of a tall tower block next to the Thames.

It wouldn't be dark for another two hours, but yellow lights already dotted the trees by the river and the tower's windows glowed fluorescently on all 20 or so of its floors. London was always on, never off.

Ali had walked past the place before. One time, a famous TV presenter had been outside smoking and talking on his mobile. She'd pretended not to notice because that's what people from London did. After 15 years, she considered herself a local, as much as anyone could be.

She could see the brightly lit reception area through a revolving glass door. A woman and a man sat behind a long desk on the right of the doors, dwarfed by a huge vase of flowers. There was a lift lobby with four sets of sliding doors to the left.

Floor-to-ceiling pictures of TV stars' faces covered the walls and Ali recognised the married couple who presented a morning chat show. Above street level, the square, white tower pushed up into a cloudless sky.

Ali's phone was already on silent in case it rang in the studio. She felt a shot of warmth go through her as it started to vibrate in her hand.

> Bran's the big Welsh guy with a beard. You will love him, Don't believe a word he says. x

She laughed aloud in the street. Ed sounded protective. She answered.

> I can look after myself. A beard, you say? Are we talking the full trawlerman?
> You're too pure for him, Lauder.
> You can tell that from looking at me, can you? Aren't you limbering up for your gig?

A queue was building up to the left of the main entrance, curling around the side, where a security guard in a yellow tabard stood listening through his earpiece.

A picture arrived on her screen; Ed with a tea towel tied around his head like Bjorn Borg, puffing his cheeks out and performing a deep lunge.

She almost choked laughing.

> People are staring. Stop it. xxx

Sid emerged from the revolving door and waved at her. 'Ali. Over here.'

They hugged and Sid saw her looking over at the line. 'Production guests this way. You get a wristband.' Ali made an 'ooh' sound.

The giant wall celebrities grinned at each other over their heads, their white teeth the size of paperbacks.

Sid detected her nerves. 'Don't worry. We'll watch the show, then a drink in the green room. Recordings can go on a bit, but Justin's usually motors through. He likes to be home in bed by eleven.'

'The host, right?' Ali had seen countless episodes of *Head Games* on the digital channels that seemed to show little else, but she didn't want to sound like a fan girl.

'Justin Kennedy. Michelle's most important client. Don't tell Ed I said that.'

'And Michelle is…'

'Ed's agent. My boss. Well, my other boss. She's one of those people you really want on your side, because God help you if you have to go up against her.'

Ali smiled, picturing a bad bitch in a power suit and spike heels.

'It'll be a couple of hours, quick bit of housekeeping, then we can drink.' Sid took out her phone.

As they filed into their seats, Ali looked up at the ceiling, a forest of lights and cables above her. Runners with headsets herded people into the raked rows, reminding people to turn their phones off.

Sid nodded at someone standing to one side of the set. 'I'm babysitting tonight.' She pointed. 'Femi Abegunde. I'll introduce you. It's their first telly.'

Ali imagined sitting in front of the cameras and lights, the audience waiting. 'I bet they're nervous.'

Sid laughed down her nose. 'Ha, no.' She went back to her phone.

Ali couldn't work out whether TV studios smelled good or someone in front of her was wearing perfume.

She could see why TV recordings overran. The comedians all had different ways of pulling focus and going off at tangents but Sid was right, it did fly by. She liked Bran's sullen regard of the younger panellists, playing his part, taking his time. She could see what Ed meant.

In the green room, down several flights of echoing stairs, Sid pointed Ali towards the drinks table. A few people were already there, but no one she recognised. Ali felt shy about helping herself.

'Have a drink.' Sid's phone was ringing. 'Back in a sec.'

The cream walls were bare except for a couple of photos of the white tower, taken from different angles. There was a large flat-screen TV where a window should be and 20 or so people scattered on black sofas and padded chairs, bottles of beer and glasses of wine in hand.

Ali put her bag on a chair in the corner. She made herself go over to the table, picking out the fullest glass of white wine. Heading back to her corner, she found Bran there, rolling up a jacket and putting it next to her things.

'You're new.' He already had a beer. 'Did I see you with Sid?'

'Yes. Ali, hi.' She stuck out her hand and he shook it, seeming to find it funny. 'She was just here. She'll be through in a minute.'

He took another drink, assessing her. 'Did you watch the show?'

She'd forgotten her role. 'Yes. You were really funny. The stuff about the farmers. Howling.' She always did this. She couldn't just say nothing, so she gushed and overdid it. It made her want to claw at her own face.

Bran's smile made her uncomfortable, like he knew something she didn't. He raised his beer at someone walking past them.

'Thanks. So, you're a friend of Sid's?'

'I'm doing some work with Ed Catchpole?' She watched his reaction, trying to glean anything from it but he just nodded, a look she couldn't place passing across his eyes.

'Good lad. Wasn't he supposed to be here?'

Ali's chest pulsed even though she knew he was hundreds of miles away. 'He's filming in Glasgow. I think that's why Femi got the gig actually.'

Bran swallowed his beer. 'Yeah. He did all right.'

'Um, they. I think they're non-binary.' She didn't know why she kept saying 'I think', she knew they were. Sid had told her.

'Ah, right.' Bran nodded like 'Sure, if you like' but he didn't care to engage with it.

She followed his eyes as he watched Sid come in and make for the table with Femi. The young comic was drinking water and talking animatedly while Sid listened intently to them.

Bran was suddenly leaning in closer than Ali felt was comfortable.

'Give my love to Ed. See you again.' He headed for the far corner, where Justin was standing with a small circle of people around him, his suit from the recording now replaced by an expensive-looking blue tracksuit.

Ali stood awkwardly, wondering how to compose her limbs in a way that suggested she was happy on her own. A new message gave her something to look at.

> Stop talking to Bran.
> Has he tried to shag you?
> Cone you feel the love tonight?

The last one had a picture attached. Ed pointing up at a statue of a man on a horse with a traffic cone balanced on its head. He must have propped his phone up on the ground to get everything in the frame.

She imagined him setting it up, thinking of how she'd react when she saw it.

She laughed and looked up to see Bran watching her from the other side of the room. He turned back to Justin, who was explaining something energetically.

'Sorry.' Sid arrived. 'You OK?'

'You left me alone. I had to talk to people.'

'What people?'

Ali nodded towards the back of Bran's head. He'd manoeuvred himself around so he was facing away from the rest of the room, trapping Justin in the corner while the rest of the small group broke off into another circle.

Ali supposed Justin was the most famous person there. He sold out huge venues when he toured and almost always had a show on TV.

'Bran?' Sid shuddered and then saw from Ali's face it had been palpable. 'One of the old school.'

'Ed said he would try to shag me.'

Sid looked put out.

37

Ali tried to defer. 'I assumed he'd already had a go at you.'

Sid shrugged. 'And did he?'

Bran had given up his position with the silverback to pick up another beer. He looked at Sid as he passed them. 'All right, Dave?'

She sort of smiled but it didn't look comfortable.

'Dave?' Ali mouthed.

Sid shook her head like she shouldn't ask.

The room was full now. Ali and Sid talked to someone called Helena with strands of animal hair on her jacket. Helena booked the talent for the show and lived in Brighton. She drained her glass and announced she had to catch her train.

The producer, Henry, was in cycling gear and sticking to water.

Sid took Femi over to Henry and talked them up. Femi feigned humility while Henry praised their debut. Judging by the body language, Femi had a good chance of getting booked again.

Ali was happy to listen, seeing how this world worked. It was sort of a party but chillier, more strategic.

Bran circled back and Ali found herself opposite him again, the rest of the group engrossed in their conversations. 'You don't work in TV.'

Ali had drunk enough wine to be bolder this time. 'Is that a question?'

He smiled. It still didn't feel like a generous act. 'If you like.'

'I don't. I work in radio. Producing.' She added the last bit because he was looking at her like she made the tea.

'Ah. And you're working with Ed? What radio?'

She assumed he'd rather be talking to someone else but he'd run out of useful people. 'Nothing's signed yet. We're just talking.'

Bran seemed pleased. 'Fan of his, are you?'

'I think he's funny.' She weighed up the next words, angry that he seemed to be finding buttons to push. 'That's probably a good thing, if we're going to be working together.'

Bran shifted his weight to his other foot and leaned on the back of the sofa next to him. 'Yeah, I suppose it is. He's a good lad. Over-complicates his shows, mind. All that AV and clever-clever stuff. I told him, keep it simple. Jokes.'

She made some noise of agreement. The wine was starting to taste bad and returned to her throat in short, burning waves. 'Is that your thing? Jokes?'

Bran's lip curled. 'It's whatever they'll pay me for.'

Sid joined them, looking from one to the other like she knew what had passed between them. 'Ready to go?'

Bran watched them leave.

Ali and Sid were alone again, sitting in a loud hotel bar just along the river. It was too noisy for proper conversation but it was nearby and they hadn't felt like walking far.

Ali picked up her glass, now filled with properly chilled wine that tasted like butter. 'So why did you give it up?'

Sid pressed her bottom lip with her top teeth, looking into the neck of her beer bottle. 'There are loads of good artists, struggling to get work. I just wasn't good enough.'

'Says who? Have you got any pictures?' Ali looked at Sid's phone on the table and the younger woman picked it up reflexively.

'No. Seriously. I was never any good.'

Ali put her wine down and fiddled with the paper wristband from the studio. 'I've been thinking about doing an art class. I never do anything except watch TV and go to work. We could do one.'

'Like life drawing?' Sid's eyes widened as she shook her head. "I don't go swimming because I might be in the same room as a naked person. I'm not going to stare at muff on purpose.'

'It's art, not live porno.' Ali was trying to be louder than the music but the word porno made the girls at the next table turn around.

Sid laughed, gnawing her lip again. Ali noticed she felt drunk, like the room was happening behind a soft haze. She loved being this amount of drunk.

A conspiratorial look crossed Sid's face. 'It's been a long time since I even thought about it. When were you thinking?'

Ali sensed Sid was seconds from drunk capitulation if she kept up the pressure. 'I promise you I am worse than a child. I can't draw at all. You'll already be better than one person in the room.' She found her phone. 'There's a pub in Stoke Newington that does one on Tuesdays. Don't make me go on my own.'

'I'll think about it.' Sid was grinning.

Ali was enjoying Sid's company, getting all the gossip about other comedians at her agency, people who had done *Head Games* and never been asked back, who was sleeping with the producer to get more bookings. She'd forgotten to ask about Ed.

'I'm just gonna,' Ali pointed towards where she hoped the loos were.

As she reached the door to the bathroom, her pocket started to buzz. His messages arrived in stacks, rather than one at a time, like his thoughts were queuing outside a door, waiting to come through.

Stealth hangover. I just did a two-hour recording trying not to blow chunks on camera one.

I died. You broke me. RIP me.

Not on stage. I was brilliant of course. I mean I think I have stopped breathing.

Wear something sexy to my funeral.

She clapped her hand over her mouth as she locked the stall door behind her. She sat on the closed lid and replied.

I'm drunk again. Have you tried drinking it better?

She came back to see Sid had ordered a bottle. She loved being out with someone who wasn't looking at the time. Sometimes Mark had spent the whole evening with her, checking his phone and then his watch.

The two women drank and leaned together to hear each other better.

Ali felt like confiding in her. 'We're supposed to wait for the divorces, right? And I was. I was waiting. But he just... I was standing there and he just decided it, so I let him. It's never happened to me before.'

Sid nodded, finding her glass with her mouth. 'Almost like he knew what he was doing.'

Ali became more serious, like the reality was hitting her for the first time. 'She looked at me like I was nothing. Like I didn't exist.' The thought made her genuinely sad. 'He just wanted me and I wanted him to.'

Sid rested her head against Ali's for a second, then sat back to look at her. 'Well, I've never made any mistakes. I'm judging you.'

Their laughter was easy, heads bowed over their wine glasses.

Sid's smile evaporated and she became matter-of-fact. 'I spend a lot of the time thinking I'm invisible.'

'Who said that?' Ali grinned, unable to resist the cheap gag but she could see Sid was serious. 'Do you really think that? Sid, why?'

Sid shrugged. 'It just... is. My dad literally moved me out of the way when he re-married. Into the flat when I was 17. New wife didn't like me or more probably could tell I didn't like her. So I was out.'

'I'm sorry.' Ali knew that was inadequate but she couldn't say nothing. 'You're not invisible. I can see you. Ed can see you.' She pulled idly at the wristband but the glue was too strong. She'd have to cut it off when she got home. 'Where does Sid come from? Is it short for something?'

Sid wrinkled her nose. 'Sidonie. French maman.'

'And where is she now?'

'In the ground.' Seeing Ali's shock, she added. 'Don't worry. She's dead. He's cold, but he's not a mob boss. Well, not that I know of.'

'Sidonie.' Ali tried to pronounce it as Sid had done but she was never any good at French. 'She named you that? It's so pretty.'

'It doesn't suit me. Ed shortened it to Sid, now everybody does. I prefer it.'

'You must miss her. You were just a kid when you lost her.'

Sid was starting to look uncomfortable and didn't seem to want to continue down this road. Ali sensed she'd be more at ease out of the spotlight. 'I think I'm invisible to my friends now. The married ones, definitely, which is most of them. It's like one day, the music stopped and everyone had someone. But if you were too slow, tough. Wait for the divorces, get a cat. Take your chances with the mouth breathers that are left.'

'I'm a mouth breather who's left.'

Ali gawped at Sid. 'You're twenty fucking seven.'

'I'll be the same at 37 and 47 and 57. I'm wallpaper.'

Ali was desperate to reply to Ed but it felt rude. What if he thought the silence meant she wanted him to stop?

She blew air through her lips. 'I watched you, working the room.'

'I've never worked a room in my life. I can talk to people, but they get bored. I'm good at quitting while I'm ahead.' Sid didn't seem to be looking for sympathy, just stating a fact. 'Do you think you'll hear from Mark again?'

Ali shook her head. 'Fuck, no.' She didn't feel anything.

Sid was resolute. 'Good. He sounds like a twat.'

'What was Ed's ex like?' Ali hoped it would sound conversational, just idle curiosity.

Sid kept her features blank. 'You've already looked her up.'

'It was… research.' Ali widened her eyes and joined in Sid's laughter. 'Madeleine, 41, artist. Not many pictures of her. She looked thin.'

'She's a size 12.' Ali wondered how Sid knew. Maybe Ed got her to buy underwear for his wife's birthday. Assistants did that kind of thing.

'You'd get on. She's nice. Funny.'

Ali didn't like to think of her being funny as well as everything else. She was mad, though. So there was that.

A knowing look spread across Sid's eyes.

Ali narrowed her own eyes, pointing a witchy finger. 'You think I want to shag him.' She did want to shag him. She thought about him pulling her jeans down, her hands in his hair. 'He's a good friend, isn't he? Really good at making new ones. It's a nice way to be in the world. You know, open to it, to new people.'

Sid nodded and there was still something enigmatic about the way she looked at Ali. 'Yeah. Like I said, he loves a new friend. He goes full lighthouse on someone, you know?' She seemed to want to change the subject.

They hadn't really talked about work but neither seemed to mind. Ali pulled out her phone and put her arm around Sid's shoulders. 'Let's say hi to Ed.' She pushed her hair around her face and lowered her chin. Sid looked shyly at the lens and smiled.

Ali showed Sid the picture and she nodded like it was a good one. She didn't like having her picture taken.

When the wine was all gone, they stood and hugged and Sid made noises about setting up a proper meeting before she headed down the stairs. Ali went back to the loo.

She started to type and saw Ed was online.

Work meeting. Very busy. x

She attached the picture.

After a few seconds, he sent a picture of himself, arm raised in a wave, the same surprised expression as the fan photos. He was on a train, a first-class antimacassar behind his head. The interior lights on the train made a halo around the top of his hair. There was a whisky miniature on the table next to a plastic cup. She looked for other clues reflected in the train window so she could picture where he was going, but the other things on the table were cut out of the picture.

She needed to pee and yanked her knickers down as she sent one last message.

My funeral dress is not sexy unless black smocks turn you on. Please advise. x

His reply came straight back.

Then we'll have to get you a new one. x

Four

Twilight London blurred past the cab window, a faint nuclear glow in the sky, the streetlights and the dark mixing to make a new colour. The only good thing about an early cab ride was the chance to be alone with the city, a theme park before the crowds arrived. There had been whisperings about staff using the tube now it had gone 24 hours, but some women in the office complained.

Ali was glad of the cab's plastic partition and the space to stretch out her legs. It always felt luxurious even if the cab was old and smelled of sweat and smoke. She could imagine it pulled by horses, her petticoats spreading over the seat, a fan quivering at her bosom.

The cab rumbled on through trafficless streets. Ali caught the driver's eye in the rear-view mirror and didn't look away in time.

'Working early?'

She turned her look of crushing disappointment into a yawn behind her hand. He was a talker. 'Yep,' she replied, trying to balance 'approachable' with 'tired'. Maybe he'd pick up the hint.

The cab turned off the main road and down a street of Victorian terraces with pastel-painted doors. No bins overflowed, the few lights in the windows were warm gold, the kind of places Ali knew she could never afford.

But she liked to walk down these roads sometimes, on her

way to the park, picturing herself in one of the large basement kitchens, looking out over a long garden through glass doors. She didn't see children on the lawn, but there were cats: two tabbies with big yellow eyes and short fur. And there was a man, tall and broad, in a cardigan, called Joe or Harry, broad shoulders, kind, bringing wood in from the log store to make a fire. It was always autumn, her favourite season, and leaves crunched under his feet as he crossed the garden, little puffs of breath clouding in front of his mouth.

. She experimented with the idea of Ed in the cardigan, carrying the wood, and felt ridiculous. But she couldn't un-see it.

'What do you do?' asked the cabbie.

Ali knew that telling cab drivers what you did was always a mistake, particularly if your job wasn't a source of joy or pride. But now she was Ed's producer – she liked the sound of that – she wanted to tell everyone she met.

'Radio producer.' She pictured herself sitting across from Ed in the studio, flying the desk while he smiled at her from behind his pop shield.

They'd be one of those on-air gangs she'd grown up listening to in her teenage bedroom, looking out of the window at her housing estate on the outskirts of a town near Coventry. Those voices that sounded like they came from a different planet where everyone shared a joke she wasn't in on.

'Oh yeah? I'll give it a listen. What station?' The cab driver pulled up to a set of red lights at an empty junction.

Commercial drivers were the bulk of Ali's audience. 'Zone Digital?'

He nodded, seeming impressed. Then the penny dropped. 'Not that bird with the lips?'

Ali pressed her own lips together to prevent a smirk. 'Kat Kelly, yeah.'

She remembered Kat on TV in the nineties in tight jeans and a Puffa jacket, running around the streets with a microphone, the camera always behind her, saying 'Back to the studio' through glossy lips.

The 'lips' he was talking about were a more recent thing. A cosmetic enhancement that drew the photographers briefly back to her door but only because it had gone wrong and someone had caught the mutant swelling on camera.

The cabbie was shaking his head gently, as if indulging a child. It made Ali feel weirdly protective of her though they'd never really bonded.

In the year Ali had produced Kat's show, most stations had ditched their early breakfast hosts in favour of pre-records and uninterrupted playlists. But Kat somehow held on, the audience of cabbies and insomniacs loyal to her throaty laugh and false intimacy. Her voice still suggested Jack Daniels and shagging and the Met Bar, even if her face didn't. On air, she knew how to sell it.

Ali guessed Kat would have been in her thirties at the height of it all, the ad campaigns and chat shows. Making hay while the sun shone on her tanned skin, her neat, silky body selling beer and bras.

Kat's plump features and long hair extensions were like modern additions to an old house. Ali caught herself feeling sorry for her as she pouted into the studio window, checking her make-up. According to Ali's mum, women with good looks and nice figures had it all to lose. Ali looked at the seatbelt digging into her stomach and supposed it was some compensation that she'd never been one of them.

On the days when Kat smelled of breath mints, Ali brewed stronger coffee and braced for on-air slurring. The early show wasn't supposed to have a producer, but Kat had never learned to drive the desk and Ali knew management didn't trust her to do the show alone.

Otis had a soft spot for Kat. Ali imagined her posing on a page torn from a magazine on the wall next to his bed at boarding school.

'Have you had anyone famous on, then?' The driver wasn't going quietly.

'Not at that time in the morning. I'm developing something new, though. I can't talk about it yet.' She had always wanted to say that.

'Your folks must be proud, you working in showbiz,' he said, enjoying himself.

Dad's dead and Mum's dead inside, she thought, before filtering. 'We lost my dad this year, but he was. Very proud.' She rotated his signet ring on her finger, the one she used to feel pressing into her palm when he held her hand.

'Ah, sorry. Does your mum live local?'

Ali shook her head. 'The Midlands.' She didn't feel like talking about her.

'We all just want our kids to be happy,' said the driver. 'I've got two girls, for my sins.'

Ali nodded, 'Ah,' like she understood the significance. He went on talking about his daughters while Ali made agreeable noises in the gaps.

She couldn't honestly say her mum did want her to be happy or unhappy. Jean sent emails asking when she was coming to visit, but when she got there, they would just watch TV, her mum assuming their tastes were the same: medical dramas and detective shows interspersed with adverts for funeral plans. They hadn't talked about Ali's dad or how either of them felt about him being dead.

The idea that Ali was thriving outside the womb seemed to confuse Jean. 'At least you've got a job,' she'd say as though that was a compliment, the very most Ali could expect. In all the films and TV shows she'd watched growing up, Ali saw parents hugging their children, telling them to follow their dreams. This wasn't a message Jean had ever transmitted to Ali.

While Ali's dad worked and commuted and washed the car and creosoted the fence, Jean reminded Ali to keep her expectations in check, to be realistic. She underlined the importance of remembering that we can't all be film stars. Ali had never wanted to be a film star, but she did like writing, making things, daydreaming. None of those were jobs, of course.

When her dad had been made redundant, their semi-detached house became a magnolia holding cell for Jean's resentment and his shame at no longer providing for the family. In his fifties and out of work, he'd applied for hundreds of jobs, started dyeing his hair to hide the grey, moving his date of birth forward a few years, but they didn't want him. Jean didn't say anything as the estate agent showed people around her home, stoically adjusting her Toby jugs on the windowsill.

The cab driver was saying something about America: his second daughter was in New York, working in PR. They were flying out to see her in a few weeks, planned to see some shows, do the tourist stuff. 'We always knew she was going places. Like she'd decided it from the start. Ilford was never going to be it for her.' His pride reflected back at her from the rear-view mirror.

When Ali's dad was dying, she and Jean had sat either side of his bed, the conversation stilted as his slow breaths punctuated the still air. The room was vivid in Ali's memory. He lay propped up on pillows, looking at the ceiling, half awake. Ali wiped her nose and balled up the tissue, ready to chuck it in the wastepaper basket in the corner. 'What do you think? Will I get it in?'

'Yes,' her dad replied, through a fog of drugs, his voice hoarse from the dry breath passing in and out of him.

'No,' said her mum, not looking up from a puzzle magazine.

Ali let the ball fly from her hand and it bounced on the edge of the bin, landing behind it.

'See?' said the old woman, smiling to herself.

'Thanks, Dad. You had faith in me,' said Ali at the pale man, whose eyes had closed again. He was smiling back.

'But it was misplaced, wasn't it?' clipped Jean, satisfied.

It had just been her and her dad at the end. Jean expressed

surprise that Ali had 'come all that way' on a whim, but Ali had a feeling in her bones that she needed to be with him. It was a Saturday afternoon and she heard his voice calling her 'Muffin' as she was microwaving beans for her lunch. She left the food where it was and headed straight for the train station.

When she'd arrived at the nursing home, Jean put her puzzle book in her handbag and said she was going home to water the plants. She'd sounded practical, confident in the way that Ali used to take as total certainty as a child. She watched her go, glad it was just the two of them.

Ali pushed two chairs together and lay down next to her dad's bed, watching him for a while, wondering if he was going to wake up and say something. After a while, she put her earbuds in to listen to a podcast as he snored, morphine coursing through him, smoothing sleep over his brow.

She took out one earbud, wondering about the time. He wasn't snoring. Turning to look at her own nose in profile, a triangle of shortbread protruding from a ruddy face, she saw the last, steady breath leave his mouth.

She stood, not knowing what happened now. A nurse came quietly in, followed by another. Ali put her head on the cotton stripes of his pyjama top and let the tears roll down over her nose onto the fabric.

'Hey, Dad,' she whispered, not looking up at him. 'Love you.' His eyes were half-open, fixed on a far-off point.

The cab slid down into an underpass.

Ali's phone vibrated. It was just before four.

It's me, Ed Catchpole. R u up? Y/n?
Yes. Work sad face puke face water pistol emoji.
You type your emojis? Thorough. How do you get up this early?
If I turn the radio on now, will it be on fire?

She could almost feel Ed poised on the other end, tennis racket ready. She dragged her brain back to the game.

Do you ever go to bed? You ARE a vampire. When I next see
Sid, fully expect her to be a milky corpse with two red dots on
her neck.
Advise wearing scarf when we work together. Not good with
bare necks.

The word 'bare' made her shift in her seat.

The entrance to Zone Digital was lit by a red and blue neon
logo. A cleaner's bucket and mop leaned against the glass in the
front window. It was only ever her, an engineer and a couple of
cleaners in this early. Ali liked being in the building before anyone
else and resented the office filling up after nine. After the show,
she'd put her headphones on and take her time editing scripts so
they'd leave her alone.

Ali lifted her chin at the security guard, who didn't look up,
tinny synth music crunching from his phone's speaker.

She poked the up button and sucked in her middle in front of
the mirrored lift doors. She didn't often look up when stood on
this spot because she felt no urge to make eye contact with the
dumpy animal facing her.

She had half an hour before Kat followed her into the building,
huge scarf wrapped around her neck in all weathers 'for my voice'
and dinner-plate sunglasses covering the eyes of the long-term drink
enthusiast.

Kat had moved out to the countryside 'because of the paps' but
kept a little flat in town. How she paid for it was a mystery. She
mentioned her 'good friends' sometimes, men who'd take her out
to dinner and were never given names. Ali was sure she'd read about
some model from that era working as an elite escort. Elite escort
sounded like a car. The lift doors opened.

She was still thinking about how the cab driver had described
Kat: just a pair of lips. She hadn't wanted to patronise Kat with
sympathy and they'd only just started working together, so she
hadn't mentioned it in the studio the day after the photos were

splashed all over the tabloids. In the small room she'd looked everywhere but at Kat's mouth.

'I mean, can she still talk?' Otis had asked.

In the following days, Kat took to wearing the big scarf and only leaving the house in the early hours for her show. She'd bought elaborate sunglasses for her mid-morning exit from the building, but the photographers moved on.

At her desk, Ali opened her laptop and looked at her emails. Two new unread. A smear test reminder and Otis throwing in one of his casual editorial bombs. He'd changed his mind. He wanted two comedians. Two comedians talking was better than one. He'd heard it on a podcast. He asked Ali to come up with some names.

Paul and a woman. Could be good to 'mix it up'. She rolled her eyes at his creative genius and started to think how to introduce the idea of Ed when she knew how desperate he was for proximity to Paul.

The lift dinged and Kat came in, pulling a wheelie suitcase. She swiped the sunglasses up into her hair and looked around the room. The two women acknowledged each other.

They were in the smallest studio, just big enough for a desk and two chairs. Ali and Kat sat opposite each other as Scott counted them in from the booth. Kat removed large hoop earrings and put on her cans. She did her intro in one unbroken drawl, delivered with emotionless precision. She sounded like a conspiratorial best friend confiding in the microphone.

'Goooood morning, it's your old mate Kat here to get your Wednesday party started.' She faded up a Pink track and took a sip of water.

They did actually work well together, despite the occasional lapses in Kat's concentration and stumbles over words. Ali thought she could probably present the show in her sleep. She didn't need much producing once they were up and running. The thought of people listening seemed to put Kat at her ease.

At the end of the track, her eyes returned to focus on the pages in front of her. 'We'll be taking you through the next two gorgeous hours before a sweet slice of breakfast with Gibbo. Sweet,' Kat paused to labour the segue into the next track, 'like chocolate. Here's a chunk of Shanks and Bigfoot.'

Ali's phone screen lit up. Eyes darting down, she saw Ed's name and turned it face down. She forced her attention back to her laptop to scan ahead to the next link, knowing that Kat needed leading firmly through the script, which she still insisted had to be printed on paper in a font size she could actually see. 'Trail off the back of this, then travel.' Ali's brain danced about in her skull. She could relax once the next link was done. Then she'd allow herself to look.

She looked.

Are you writing this? Tell me you didn't write the last one.

She squirmed at the thought of him listening. She'd have made an effort if she'd known he'd be tuning in. She wanted to evaporate. She read the message again.

Her knee bounced under the table as the show crawled to its final track and the breakfast team assembled in the bigger studio across the corridor. Even through soundproof glass they emitted fun. They were so animated. It's what she thought radio would be like when she listened as a child. Not work at all, just mates in a studio, making each other laugh.

Kat cleared her throat as the red light relit on the desk. "That's all from me. The Gibbo Show is on the way, straight after this.' Kat sat back from the mic, fiddling with a hair extension tangled in her headphones.

She waved through the glass at Gibbo – Steve Gibbons, eternally effusive breakfast host – and he waved back, beaming and exaggerating a mimed 'HELLO' through the glass.

Ali could see him say something to his studio gang that made everyone laugh.

Kat pretended not to notice. She steadied herself on the arm of the chair and curtsied at the booth before heading to the ladies where she threw the empty vodka bottle from her handbag in the sanitary bin.

Ali cleared the table of papers and mugs and went back to her desk.

> Gig tonight. Sid'll send you the address. Trying new stuff. Want you to see. Pint before. x

Ali swallowed but there was no saliva in her mouth as she reread the email she'd sent to Otis. She realised most of her job was working out how to tread carefully around men and specifically Otis. But this one would take real subtlety if she was going to make him think that offering the show to Ed was his own idea.

She also knew she couldn't just tell him to swerve a famous comedian because of the gossiping of a bunch of women with absolutely no evidence to back up what they were saying. Better to make Ed seem like the best possible prospect rather than trying to make Otis drop the idea of the other guy. Like tempting a toddler with a biscuit to get him to stop licking the remote.

The breakfast show posse were playing up to the studio webcams. Julie, the travel reporter, was performing dance moves for their social media feed. Ali thought it defeated the point of radio.

She guessed Sid would be there tonight and the idea of the art class returned. She put her headphones on and searched for the life drawing place as the desks around her began to fill with their occupants.

Another message arrived from Ed: a link to the comedy club's location. She remembered him on a show featuring comedians in cars and a plan began to form.

'Catchpole you later,' she said to herself, drinking from the mug in her hand and showering her keyboard in vodka.

Five

Ali finished the glass of wine in front of her and looked around the pub. A girl in a denim apron collected glasses; hers and the tumbler that had contained Ed's whisky. She wished the bartender had left it so she could smell the fumes coming from the melted ice again and think of him leaning over the table to kiss her cheek.

He was over the road now, preparing for his set. Ed had suggested meeting in the pub beforehand 'to avoid the masses'.

She wanted to give off the air of someone comfortable with her own company. She tried to enjoy being this new person who sat alone in bars, absorbed in thought, but it still made her feel like she was painted fluorescent yellow.

The comedy club was the basement of a Victorian pub at the bottom of a steep high street in north London. Ali crossed the road and made her way through the busy bar and down the stairs.

Photos of comedians lined the wall all the way down, mostly men shot in black and white. Ali counted three dead ones: one alcohol, another cancer and a third who'd been in a motorbike accident. She remembered it being on the news.

At the bottom of the stairs, she spotted Bran's picture. He was shrugging haplessly in a cable-knit jumper. That peculiar stare from the green room was replaced with something more benign. He looked harmless, sweet even.

Inside, a young man was on stage, talking to someone on the front row about what they did for a living.

In the low light, Ali couldn't see Sid. She looked at her phone and a message from Ed instructed her to go through the door at the back of the room.

She turned the handle, hoping it wouldn't creak too loudly. The corridor that led backstage was strip-lit and the brickwork was painted dark blue. A hand-written sign asked for quiet during a show and conversations to be saved for the green room. She pushed the door at the far end.

'Lauder.' Ed was sitting on a sofa next to a younger man in a room the size of a small lounge. A sink and a fridge took up one side, two sofas formed an L shape around a rug and low table on the other.

'Catchpole. Hey again.' Why couldn't she just say hi?

Ed smiled but didn't get up and she hovered in the middle of the room. Wanting to look decisive, she sat on the other sofa and took out her phone like she needed to check something.

The man next to Ed had a shaved head and tattoos on his hands. He was staring at his laptop, but he looked up now. 'How're ya?' Hearing his accent, Ali was about to ask him which bit of Ireland he was from, but he'd already gone back to whatever he was doing.

Ed opened a can of beer and, thinking better of it, offered it to Ali. 'You can watch from the side.'

She didn't like beer, but she took it anyway. 'Thanks.'

He turned back to his Irish friend. 'You just need a beat longer after "parasols". A look around the room. Don't get there too quickly.'

The younger man nodded, seeming to appreciate the guidance. 'Yeah, they want to wait. Beat. Then bring it back up.' He nodded as he typed something.

Ed looked at his watch and stood, indicating Ali should follow him and pointing to a sign on the door ahead of them saying STAGE in large black type. He turned back and put the pointing finger to his lips.

She wondered at the etiquette of offering improvements to another performer's work. Maybe Ed could do it because he was senior in this room. Or maybe they just really respected him. He obviously knew what he was talking about.

Ed positioned her at the side of the stage on a stool and stood behind her, watching the MC, a woman called Caroline with long grey hair in high a ponytail. Ali sat still, tasting the sourness of the beer, enjoying the feeling of him close behind her.

He put a hand on her back and leaned in to whisper. 'What I do on telly isn't really what I do live. This is me in a room.'

She felt electric moths down her back. Then he brushed past her and took the mic from Caroline as the applause broke Ali's stupor.

The room warmed to him quickly, beyond the black drapes. Ali clutched the beer and craned to see through the gap to the small stage. Ed stood in front of the mic stand, one hand behind draped over the top of it like it was a perch designed specifically for the purpose.

If she passed Ed in the street maybe she wouldn't notice him. His clothes hung oddly and his dehydrated skin was multicoloured in the harsh stage light. Burst capillaries around his nose escaped onto his cheeks. The pocket of stubbly flesh under his chin wobbled when he became emphatic. In a Hollywood film he'd play the basement-dweller brought in to hack the mainframe, not the lead man. Not even the best friend. But up there, looking down from his pulpit, he was their leader.

'It's like the pedals on a piano.' He'd leaned towards Ali in the pub before the show, about to impart classified information. He drank water from a pint glass. They were waiting for Sid. 'Sorry, is this wank?'

Ali laughed, shaking her head. 'No, your method is very interesting to me.'

He was nudging at the border of real pretension and Ali couldn't help drinking it in, feeling the glow of privilege at being invited behind the curtain. She folded her crisp bag into a triangle while she listened, trying to seem less sycophantic.

'Yeah, piano pedals. Loud, quiet, loud again. You work out a rhythm that's pleasing and it almost doesn't matter what you're saying.'

He'd looked around the pub; a guy played the quiz machine by the door, two women laughed as they poured prosecco into glasses.

'They think I'm funnier than their friends. That's why they pay. The version of me up there is what they want. If they met this guy, they'd be disappointed.'

Ali furrowed her brow incredulously. 'And what do you get? The love you always craved?' She wondered if that was too familiar.

He screwed up his face. 'Muuummeeeee. Why didn't she love meeee?' His hand found Ali's arm and squeezed. He held it too tight and she knew there'd be a bruise there tomorrow.

He let her go and put both hands up. 'I'm filling the unfillable void. I need the clapping.' He drank the rest of his water in one swallow. 'Because it's tasty. Sid!' He held his glass aloft.

Sid hovered in the doorway, saw the empty glass and went to the bar.

Ali wished it could just be the two of them and then felt guilty because she did genuinely like Sid's company.

Sid seemed used to hanging back, keeping the drinks topped up. Didn't it make him uncomfortable, having someone wait on him?

Ali watched her pretending to remove fluff from her sleeve while she waited for the drinks. Another guy arrived next to her and the bartender served him first.

Ed went on. 'Everyone goes home with something.'

As Sid arrived, Ed excused himself.

'Hey.' She put down a gin and tonic in front of Ali and a whisky for Ed.

'Aww, thanks.'

Sid waved a hand. 'Work meeting.'

Ali looked in the direction Ed had gone. 'Cheers. Does he remove himself when it's time to talk business? Does the money sully his art?'

'Pre-gig shit, I should think.' Sid sat down and Ali laughed, trying to push the image away.

'So, mid-morning Saturday and Sunday. What's the slot?'

Ali got a notebook from her bag and pushed the end of a biro with her thumb. 'Saturday nine thirty am. Jason's got a telly, big new Sky series. We don't actually know if he's coming back, but this'll be fixed-term. Six weeks. I figured that would work better for Ed anyway.'

Sid nodded. 'He'd do ten. In the morning. I know what he'll say to nine thirty.'

Ali pictured Otis, recognising Ed from the TV and doing that ingratiating laugh. All she had to do was hint that Paul was tainted somehow and offer him a solution in the same breath. 'Shall we get them together in the room first? Once he's met Ed, I know he'll be open to negotiating all of this.'

She mentioned Otis's email and talk of a co-host. Sid made a face. 'Wait till after. Don't mention it now.'

Ed was coming back.

When it had been time to leave for the gig, Ali was relieved. Sitting with Sid had given her an uneasy sense of standing in someone else's garden. The way she drew a fence around Ed when she spoke about him, knowing his likes and dislikes. She seemed entirely designed to smooth the world before him. He was just Ed, Ali thought. She didn't work for the Pope.

Watching through the gap in the drapes, Ali couldn't drag her eyes away, but she wasn't looking at Ed any more. It was them. A sliver of the audience, faces turned towards him, screwed eyes, skin around their mouths creasing. He'd got them where he wanted them.

A thin shaft of light leaked into the wings and the door closed softly behind her. She turned to see Bethan Gill standing behind her. They both mouthed, 'Hi.'

Bethan peered out past her to look at the audience and took a piece of paper out of her back pocket, scanning the notes on it. Ali wondered at her, apparently calm, about to stand in front of a room full of strangers, mostly glad it wasn't her about do the same.

The audience started clapping and Ed thanked them. Ali made sure she was looking in the right direction when he jogged towards the wings.

He bumped fists with Bethan and steered Ali through the door. She threw a good luck over her shoulder, but Bethan was immersed in her notes.

In the empty green room, Ed picked up a tea towel next to the sink and dabbed the back of his neck while Ali headed for the sofa still clutching the tepid beer. A whisky was waiting for him on the coffee table. He pulled his phone out of his pocket and put it next to the whisky. 'Back in a minute.'

After a few seconds, his screen lit with a message from 'Bones.' Ali craned her neck to see but all she could make out was the name. While she waited, she tried to think of a way to convey enthusiasm for his new material without going overboard. How did normal people give compliments without going fully Uriah Heep?

When Ed returned, he sat on the other sofa and tapped the screen, looking up at her and indicating he'd better deal with whatever he'd seen there. He muttered 'shit' under his breath and started thumbing the screen.

Ali got the feeling that he was about to leave. Why did she feel like he was always on the way somewhere else? She wanted to say something affirmative about the jokes. Good jokes? Jesus, she thought. Say it was funny.

As her mouth opened, he re-joined her in the here and now. 'Sorry, bit of politics. Bones, wants me to play poker. Paul, I mean.'

Ali felt the hairs on her neck lift. 'Why Bones?'

'He loves *Star Trek.*' He looked at Ali as though a plan was forming. 'But I'm washing my hair tonight.' A smile played on his lips.

Ali didn't get it, then she did. 'It does lack both body and shine. Actually, while I've got you, I need to run a thing by you.'

He gave her his full attention. 'Of course.'

'If we could make it work, and obviously if it was someone you absolutely approved first, what about we pitch you and a co-host? My boss listens to too many podcasts...' She trailed off, trying to gauge whether she'd messed up the delivery. 'I think Bethan would be great. What do you think?'

'So me and Beth together?'

Ali couldn't tell if he was happy or upset at the idea. 'Obviously, you could carry it on your own. But they like the gang vibe. It's exactly what you said. You, talking to your funny mates, the listeners get to eavesdrop.'

He turned his head and looked at himself in the mirror by the fridge. Ali looked at his reflection too as the smile came back to his lips. 'Delightful.'

She couldn't help smiling at his hair going in every direction.

Later, in the bar across the road, Sid reappeared and Ed seemed to want to keep the party going. Ali was quietly electrified at the prospect of more time in his company and occasionally allowed herself to think of the kiss when he wasn't looking right at her. She wondered if Paul was pissed off with him for bailing on his poker night and what excuse he'd made.

Bethan joined them and Ali admired the younger comic's ease at interrupting Ed when her joke was funnier than his. They were going to sound good together, which also made her jealous. She said she'd probably have a tour in the autumn but she reckoned her agent could work something out with keeping those weekends clear.

In her excitement Ali said something about stealing Paul's show out from under him and there was an awkward pause. She would kick herself about it for days and weeks afterwards. But the general mood was upbeat.

Ed was holding court, but no one minded. He was reminding Bethan of a gig at a Welsh comedy festival. The home crowd had lapped up her set and he couldn't get them on side. The self-deprecation was adorable, elaborate in its generosity.

Ali turned to Bethan, preferring to direct her naïve questions about being a stand-up to someone who wasn't Ed. 'How do you put yourself through it every night? You don't even look nervous before you go on.'

'I enjoy it, mostly. If I take too long off gigging, it gives me headaches. Real bastards.'

Ali wasn't sure if she was telling the truth. 'Actual pains in the head?'

Bethan nodded. 'It's chemicals. They go up and down and you can actually feel it in your body. Adrenalin to get you out there, then a huge release of whatever it is after you come off. It's like quitting caffeine if I don't do it for a while.'

'You make it sound unhealthy, like you're all addicts.'

Bethan laughed, indulging her. 'Oh, there's all sorts. My high is from an audience, of course. Organic like.' She put her hand to her heart. 'But we've got our fair share of addicts: drunks, coke-heads, sex addicts.' She made air quotes around this last one.

'That's a thing, isn't it?' Ali felt out of her depth.

Bethan puffed out her cheeks. 'They're certainly the magic words when you're caught being a predatory creep.' She exchanged a look with Ed.

Ali nodded sagely. 'Right.'

'The men you know to keep clear of late at night, in the backs of cars. Don't sleep on their sofa after a gig.'

'Why?'

Bethan looked at her like she was a huge-eyed Disney fawn.

'Blow job for another gig. Or, you've missed the last train, stay here. And you wake up with them on top of you.'

'That's just a hazard of the job? Do you work in cowboy town? Doesn't anyone stop them or report them to someone?'

'We do, for want of anyone else. To each other. We keep lists. We've got a WhatsApp group.' She grimaced. 'Lots of WhatsApp groups.'

Ali's eyes widened. 'You keep a list of perverts?'

Bethan sat back. 'Well, not all of us. We're not one big happy family. But we share gossip, if you like. We keep each other safe.'

Ed chimed in. 'And what are the men doing while you're being groped on sofas?'

Bethan smiled at him. 'The good ones keep an eye out. They don't book the arseholes. They listen when we tell them someone's dodgy. Most of them keep pretty quiet.'

Ed rolled his eyes.

Ali wondered if Bethan and Ed had ever slept together. She knew she would wonder this whenever she met a new woman now. Would Ed like her?

Ali smiled at Ed and Bethan sat forward, putting her drink down. 'A woman says "A man did this thing to me", first thing we do is say "Is she lying?" Never "I'm sorry that happened to you." It's all we've got – our wagging tongues.'

Ed tapped the table as though he'd just thought of something and went to the loo.

Sid caught Ali's eye as she watched him go. 'Thank God for the good ones.' 'Yeah.' Ali didn't know what else to say. She felt competitive again and it made her feel itchy.

'How did you end up working… with him?' Ali corrected herself before blundering into 'for him'.

Sid mentally counted. 'It was about ten years ago now. Dad owns a couple of clubs. Ed started doing a night at the Camden one. I used to hang around there and I ended up helping him out. Until it eventually became a full-time job.'

Ali wished she could probe her more but she didn't want Ed to come back and find them talking about him. 'He's not that hard work, surely?' She tried to keep it light.

Sid shook her head. 'It wasn't a fun time in my life. I should have been going to uni but I had… I wasn't well. So, when it didn't work out, Dad told me to find a job and moved me into the flat. Ed offered me a job.'

A young man in a football top came out of the toilets grinning and went over to his friends. The group laughed as he recounted something to them, miming holding his dick in his hands.

Ed was smiling as he walked back to the table, but something had changed. He didn't sit down. 'Can't even take a piss.' He picked up a bag from under his chair, pulled his phone out. 'Ladies, a pleasure.'

He was gone before Ali had a chance to understand what was happening. She felt the loss of him like a change in temperature. His half-drunk whisky sat on the table. No one spoke for a while.

Sid broke the quiet. 'Poker game. I thought he'd forgotten.' She smiled at Ali.

Ali looked quickly at Bethan. 'No, I don't think…' Bethan held up her hand like it had already been discussed.

Sid seemed thrown. 'It's being on all the time. Tires him out, I think.'

Ali wished Sid wouldn't look at her. She wished she could tell her that she knew, because she could see he was tired. But she turned the sting inwards and pushed her new bruise on the tube home.

As she put her keys in the door, her inside pocket buzzed. One message after another, juddering against her chest. And it was like all the blood returned to her body.

Show me drawings. Do it every day, remember?
Forget shading, just get shapes, half-shut your eyes, speed is better. Give yourself three minutes.
What are you wearing?

A picture arrived. It looked like he was in a toilet cubicle, white brick tiles behind his head. He was doing the face again, but it was like he was looking right through the screen and into the back of her head.

Diary. Tomorrow night at the Sides, NW1. I'm on about 7. If you're not sick of me. I'll do something new, just for you.

She tried to jump on the merry-go-round, but it was going too fast.

I'm wearing a coat. Can I take it off first? You OK?
Draw this.

His last message arrived with a picture of a woman in old-fashioned lingerie, her breasts filed to two impossible points like the nose cones of twin rockets. It was an old photo, maybe from the 1950s.

Ali looked at the woman's expression, lips making an 'O', eyes confident, one hand on her hip. Is that how he saw her?

She went to the kitchen cupboard, hysterical, and pulled out two tins of tomato soup. Putting on a woolly jumper, she put a tin in each cup of her bra, stretching the wool over the top and thrusting her chest out. She propped her phone on the mantelpiece on a timer and mimicked the pose of the woman in the picture, kissing the air.

She bit her bottom lip, trying several slightly different attitudes, fussing strands of hair, making herself too hot in the wool.

Sweating and divested of the jumper, she flicked back and forth until she found one she didn't hate and sent it.

What was she doing? She didn't know, but she was laughing so hard she didn't care.

Six

Ali looked at the rail, the dresses and cardigans pressed together, different shades of 'dark' packed so tightly she couldn't see what was there.

She pulled her going-out dress off its hanger. She'd grown out of it before her dad died and now she easily fitted into it again. It tied under her breasts and flowed out over everything else she wanted to distract from. She didn't like the material touching her stomach. Other women seemed to wear things based purely on who they wanted to be that day. She only ever chose clothes for what they'd hide and wondered what it felt like to pick through a rail of colours and shapes, nothing off limits.

Pushing her shoulders back and flattening her stomach, she looked at herself in the bathroom mirror, turning to the side to inspect her silhouette.

She thought about Mark's breath as he'd kissed her between the rails of coats in the cloakroom. That warm, sour waft that came from a champagne mouth. When he turned to the side to see if they were being observed, she could still smell it and marvelled at how his bad breath could go around corners.

She'd drunk and drunk until she couldn't feel anything and Mark had seen her swaying at the side of the dance floor. He'd guided her by the elbow, like he was helping someone who couldn't see.

She took out her small silver earrings, replacing them with big hoops and sprayed dry shampoo into the roots of her hair. Steadying her elbow on the windowsill, she peered into a powder compact mirror and stroked black liner across her eyelids, holding her breath until they were even.

She wondered if Mark would be there tonight. She pictured Gemma's hand clenched around the car keys and the shame washed over her, Gemma's words returning. 'I thought you'd be young.' Ali hadn't noticed herself ageing, but now she peered into the mirror, the skin under her eyes was definitely greyer. The job messed with her sleep and now Ed was keeping her up at night too.

Bored out of her mind in her teenage bedroom, she'd have swooned to think of herself at a party with free wine, waiters circulating with snacks on trays. The reality was lonelier.

Tonight was an event laid on for the advertisers. Ali didn't have to go but she wanted to remind Otis she was a company woman. He only really remembered things when they were right in front of him and she could at least begin the campaign to dislodge Paul Bonatti while the boss was a few glasses in.

'Are you in the Zone, Ali?' Otis had said on her first day at work, narrowing his eyes at her like he'd asked an important question. She didn't know for sure, but she thought Otis's dad had bought him a radio station to give him something to do. He treated Zone Digital like his own personal cult and bragged about reading books on unorthodox management techniques.

'Absolutely,' she'd replied, knowing that making the tea and ferrying competition prizes to the post room did not require this level of religious zeal.

She checked her lipstick. If someone injected her with a truth serum, she'd admit she also wanted to look pretty if she bumped into Mark. She fantasised about him being angry with her, furiously cornering her by the bathrooms, his rage turning to lust as he pushed her against a wall.

She found her 'occasion' shoes on the floor of the wardrobe; silver block-heels with ankle straps. When she pushed out the dents, they looked OK. She'd kept them on when she'd fucked Mark that night to make him think she was the kind of woman who kept her shoes on during sex.

She went back to the bathroom mirror and pulled herself in and up, knowing she never stood like that in real life but that fixing the image in her mind would give her the confidence to leave the house.

Work parties were only fun if you had someone to roll your eyes with, chugging wine and canapés, pretending to find it all terrible. She used to bring Ava when she'd first started at Zone and they'd play spot the minor celebrity. Once, a former boyband singer came over and told Ava he liked her dress and she went all quiet.

Ali used to like how Ava teased her about 'working in showbiz' but now it sounded like a consolation prize for not having a husband and kids. 'You, with your showbiz life.' Ava was trying to be kind but Ali knew she'd rather be dead than still single and living in one room.

The one time Ava had met Mark, Ali remembered the savage side-eye when he'd cracked a sexist joke. He'd sensed the atmosphere and added something about it being ironic but that was all it took for Ava to put someone in the 'no' category. Ali hadn't told Ava when she'd started sleeping with Mark.

Her phone lit and her stomach dropped two floors to the pavement below.

Tonight at 8. When I see you, remind me I need to tell you something. x

'Fuck.' She typed quickly with both thumbs, desperate at the thought of needing to be in two places at once. She was losing track of the days, one blending into the next.

So sorry. Forgot work thing. Good for our show but boring AF.
I will be having the worse time. x

When she came back from the bathroom there was still no reply.
She booked a cab. Work would pay and the shoes were not for
walking in. She poured a glass of wine and her phone chimed.
She'd changed the noise so that Ed's messages made a different
sound to the pizza offers and marketing spam. Ava only ever sent
Facebook messages.

It was a video. Just the empty club stage and spot-lit microphone
in the middle. No audience. Ed's face rose slowly into frame, looking
desolate. Sad string music was playing.

He walked her down to the front row, the camera on his face,
then turned it around and put a drink on the edge of the stage.
Clear liquid with ice and a piece of lime. 'Just in case, Hepburn.'
The camera zoomed slowly into the drink and the video ended.
She played it again.

She drank wine, watching it over and over. She wanted to show
someone and ask them, 'This is flirting, isn't it? Am I imagining it?'
She thought of him getting the drink, planning what he'd say,
filming himself for her. He'd added music.

It was intimate. Their acquaintance could be measured in hours,
not weeks or even days. With every new message she felt defence-
less, like a house with no windows or doors.

She wanted to smoke. She hadn't done that in weeks, not since
Mark said he hated the taste in her mouth. The panic started to
rise. She couldn't believe Ed was thinking about her, writing to
her, like he was whispering in her ear.

She laughed out loud to herself and thought about a reply. She
wanted to let him know she was thinking about him too. A notification pinged; her cab was nearby.

The traffic was solid as they made slow progress through Friday
night streets. The party was in the city, a hotel function room among
the glass and steel of the financial district. Her phone's battery was

already on fifty per cent, one message after another arriving from a comedy club in Camden. Maybe someone at the party would have a charger. She typed, feeling car sick from looking at her screen.

Aren't you supposed to be on stage? Stop looking at your phone.
Give me five seconds.

She giggled, watching the trio of dots on the screen as they caterpillared.

Had to deal with a heckler.

She didn't have time to reply before the next.

What are you wearing? No seriously, what are you, though?

She fanned her dress out on the seat and leaned forward. With the phone high above her, she took a picture and sent it to him. She knew her tits looked good and the angle made her face look thin.

There was nothing for a while and she just looked at where all the life and chatter had been, willing it to come back. She rolled the window further down, tilting her face to get the breeze on her cheek as the car swung down a side road to avoid the jam.

Another chime. It felt like drugs, a hit, something physical happening at the sound of each message.

Alison Lauder. Are you paying attention?

A video was attached. Ed's face in close-up, darkness behind him. He wasn't smiling. She pressed play.

'It's stupid. I warn you now. One of the more stupid things I've said, in fact.

But...' he paused. 'I miss you.'

He thought for a moment, wondering if there was anything else. Then he decided. 'I wanted to tell you.' He made a what's-that-all-about face and the clip ended.

Ali put her hand to her chest, her breathing quickening. The smile almost broke her face and the nausea made her wind the window down further. 'Sorry, excuse me.'

The driver took a moment to realise she was talking to him. He raised an eyebrow in the rear-view mirror, looking concerned. 'All OK?'

The blood was rushing to Ali's head. 'Can I change the drop-off?'

By the time the car pulled up outside the club in Camden, she was losing her nerve.

She looked down at the dress and the silver shoes and wished she could click her fingers and change back to normal, a reverse-Cinderella, but it wouldn't be midnight for hours. She checked herself in the cab window as it drove away. She could go home and spend the rest of her life wondering or she could do the exact opposite of what her body was telling her to do and go inside.

The panic, just beneath the relaxing effects of the wine, could be drowned or at least delayed with a drink. Maybe Otis would find her commitment to the talent impressive. Giving herself no more time to think, she ducked into the doorway and pushed through the crowded small room to the bar. She barely felt the first shot as it went down, ice numbing her lips.

At the top of the stairs, a woman in a red sweatshirt sat behind a school desk with a rubber stamp and a card machine.

'One, please,' Ali said, waggling her card to get her attention.

'You've missed most of the first half,' she said from behind round glasses.

'It's fine,' Ali replied, making the contactless payment, walking away and then twirling on one foot to come back and get her hand stamped. 'Thank you,' she smiled. She was Audrey and Katharine and all the Hepburns.

She lingered by the door, listening for a sign she could slip in unnoticed. As the sound of laughter erupted in the room, she crept in and tried to adjust to the dark, planting herself against the back wall by the sound desk.

Ed was coming to the climax of his set. The laughter dipped as the room sensed him preparing his final run-up.

A ringing phone cut through the carefully crafted lull. Ali looked around the gloom for the poor bastard about to get crucified as dozens of eyes turned towards the back of the room.

The ringing was coming from her dress pocket.

She looked up at the stage. Ed's mouth was open, mic in position, eyes squinting into the dark, one hand shielding his brow from the lights.

Ali groped for the mute button but instead hit receive. 'Why you not here?' slurred a man's voice through the speaker.

As the phone flipped through her fingers and onto the ground in front of her, the voice continued, 'Aliiii?'

In one motion Ed hopped off the front of the stage and made for the light of the offending item while the crowd hooted delightedly around him.

As he bent down to pick it up, Ali thought about running but the nearness of him stopped her.

'Hello? Who's this?' asked Ed, turning to the audience and holding the phone to his mic. He hadn't noticed Ali yet, eyes still adjusting to the gloom.

'You've just fucked my denouement. This had better be good, friend.' Ed's eyes sparkled in the dark and Ali didn't know what to do but enjoy it. She realised she was actually holding her breath.

'You're not Ali…' Mark's voice sounded weedy and childlike over the PA.

Ed made an elaborate show of hanging up to the audience's delight, then swivelled and held the phone out to Ali who had started convulsing.

'He hung up,' he grinned, handing it back.

Ali's hand went to her face as she took the phone. She mouthed, 'I'm sorry' as the audience erupted around her. He was totally unfazed. Back up on his stage, he turned the interruption into a volley of new gags she hadn't heard before.

As the audience filed out, she stood and watched them smiling and muttering to each other, swapping favourite bits from the show, seeing the effect Ed could have on a roomful of people. She followed them, still shaking with adrenalin.

As she waited in the bar, she could still feel the tremors in her chest and arms. He could have turned the crowd on her with a word.

She sat on a stool and waited for the bartender to get to her.

'Are you trying to think of something cool to say?' It was a familiar voice behind her.

She turned around. Ed's almond eyes crinkled at the edges where his cheeks lifted in a smile.

'Yes, yes, I am.'

'What did you come up with?' Ed stood back to take in her outfit. 'Whoa, stand up.'

She cringed and did as she was told. 'Were you this tall before?'

She lifted a foot to indicate the cause and put it back down again before she lost her balance.

'Well, thank you for dressing up nice to ruin my show.'

She winced again. 'I'm so sorry.' She opened her eyes to see his were full of fondness. She gestured at her outfit. 'This was for the work thing.'

He nodded and laughed like he didn't believe her. 'Stop it.' She basked in his teasing. 'It was for work!'

'No, it's flattering. Honestly.' He brought her in for a hug.

When she pulled back again, Ed was looking up as though listening for a far-off sound. 'What day is it?' He pulled his phone out. 'Thursday. Give me five minutes.'

He went back upstairs and left her beaming, trying to turn down the smile, like this was average for her. She smoothed the fabric of her skirt and tried to breathe like a normal person.

When Ed came back, he had his bag and his face looked different, more flushed.

'Walk with me.' He gestured towards the door.

The shoes had already started to cause a dull ache in the balls of her feet, the leather rubbing at the tops of her little toes. There would be raw little wounds there tomorrow. 'Are we going far?'

'About…' he calculated, 'ten minutes.' He noticed her limp. 'Stop stop,' he said, sitting her down on a low garden wall and grabbing one of her ankles. 'It seems a shame because they are lovely feet, but they'll have to come off.'

'Are you going to hack the heels off with your machete?'

Ed stared at her, not comprehending.

'Michael Douglas and Kathleen Turner. *Romancing the Stone*. Are you telling me you don't have a machete?'

'I do not,' he said, quite seriously.

She concentrated on the feeling of his fingers on her ankle, close to the bone. He pulled at the buckle and freed her from the first leather strap.

Now three inches shorter and carrying her shoes, she felt more vulnerable than she had tottering on heels. She reverted to child-hood, avoiding pavement cracks, looking for smooth patches between the hardened chewing gum and cigarette butts.

She looked up at him. 'Are we nearly there, ye… Fuck. Fuck.' Her foot stung suddenly, coming into contact with something hard and sharp. She put her hand down to feel for damage and it came back wet and red. 'Oh, really fuck.'

'What have you done?' Woken from his reverie, Ed was looking at the red hand held out to him. 'There's been a murrrr-derrr,' he exclaimed, putting on a ridiculous Glaswegian twang.

Ali laughed, pained. She hated her shoes and her blood but most of all she hated herself. For wearing the stupid things and not being able to walk in them and ruining everything.

'So much blood. Here.' Ed pulled a napkin from his pocket.

She leaned on a garden wall and wrapped it around her foot. 'Where do you live, Lauder?'

'Well, my flat is…' Her bed covered in laundry and the sink full of dishes taunted her in a dirty montage.

He looked into her eyes and fixed on them until he was satisfied she was locked in too, steady again. 'We need to clean it. Arm round me. Let's find a cab.'

Ali looked at her clean, bandaged foot propped on a cushion and then over at Ed, who was in the kitchen, opening cupboards. She was grateful to whoever had broken the beer bottle on the pavement now. He had seemed untroubled by the mess, ushering her into the bathroom and sitting her down on the closed loo seat so he could turn the shower on her foot. Ali bundled toilet paper in her hands while she watched the water splashing his jeans.

He came back to the sofa with wine and two mugs. 'No clean glasses.' He wasn't disapproving, just practical. But the shame burned all the same.

'Where were you taking me? Before all of the blood?' 'So much blood,' he said, giving it his best Bela Lugosi.

Their hips were close on the sofa and her stomach flipped.

'Doesn't matter. Another time.' He put his feet on the coffee table, on top of a pile of magazines. It was strangely proprietorial.

He looked around at the books on the shelves, the lights round the fireplace. His eyes settled on the poster for Hitchcock's *Vertigo*. She worried it was a bit student halls, like she was a teenager who hadn't grown up.

He fixed her with a serious pout and did a new accent. 'Oh, I've been understanding since I was 17. And the next step is, if you're going to see me tomorrow, why don't you stay the night?'

She beamed at him. 'No way.'

'The tawdry brunette. You'd make a good Kim Novak.' He took a drink, looking at the figures on the poster, a man and a woman, falling endlessly into the pupil of a giant eye.

She ransacked her brain for another quote, ignoring the fact she looked nothing like a woman in a Hitchcock film. 'If I do what you tell me, will you… will you love me?' She simpered, trying to match his accent.

'Yes,' Ed growled, now-Jimmy Stewart, trying to be heard above the roar of the waves. He broke character and shook his head. 'And a Hitchcock nut?' He swished the wine around his mug.

'Of course.' She basked in the implied praise.

He got up, seeming entirely at home, drinking from her Zone Digital mug, browsing her books.

He stopped to look at her lying there. 'I'm giddy. Are you?' He wasn't waiting for an answer, more delivering an address.

She listened, not knowing what was coming. He could literally be about to say anything.

He knocked back the rest of his drink and placed it down. 'We haven't talked about the thing that we haven't talked about.' He sat back down. 'I feel like I can say this to you. I feel like I could say anything to you.'

She managed a quiet 'Of course' as she fought with her mouth to keep back the torrent.

His eyes were full of apology and kindness. 'I am a mess, Ali. A mess and a car crash. And a bin on fire. And you and I. There are feelings, aren't there?' Again he didn't wait for an answer. 'Put on some music. I find it helps.'

She scrolled through the music library on her phone and hooked it up to the Bluetooth speaker on the mantelpiece. She set the *Vertigo* soundtrack playing, forgetting it started with a frantic police chase across the rooftops of San Francisco.

Ed was laughing. 'It this supposed to put me at my ease?'

He took her phone and scrolled down further. 'Ah.' He'd found what he was looking for. '"Scène d'Amour". The doomed love affair reaches its end.' He tapped the track and gentler flutes and violins washed into the room.

He flicked off the standard lamp by the sofa so just the fairy lights glowed in the fireplace. They sat together in the half-light, sipping. Not talking.

She didn't know what he'd meant by the 'doomed' affair. They weren't having one. He looked far away, lights catching in his eyes.

She followed his gaze to the same spot and squirmed at the napkin portrait still propped on the mantelpiece. She didn't want to think any more.

The strings built towards the bit she loved with the sea crashing on the rocks and the kiss, Kim Novak's cream scarf carrying on the wind as Jimmy Stewart holds tightly onto her.

They looked at each other and she closed her eyes as soft lips, edged with stubble, brushed her forehead and he wrapped his arms around her.

Despite the blatant encouragement from the violins, the kiss didn't come. Why did he choose this track? She smelled his neck, skin mingling with a trace of perfume, maybe his deodorant.

She stayed there, her arms around him too, feeling like she was going mad but that she would like to stay there forever. The music ended and she could only hear the thump of his heart. A real, stabbing pain came from her chest, a hot fire of longing burning there.

They left their mugs on the table and she followed him to the bed.

When they were both lying on top of the covers, they stayed side by side, not touching. Ali waited, following his lead. Why did she feel paralysed around him, like any movement would be un-natural or too startling? Every muscle contracted.

A hand reached towards hers and she let his fingers tangle with hers. He squeezed for a moment and looked at her. She didn't dare do anything but look back, letting him decide what was next.

'I can't stay.'

She already knew. There it was again, the man on his way some-where else, which made the having of him feel more special.

They lay there for a while and talked. She asked him about his life, travelling around, performing. Wasn't he lonely? He talked about the end of his marriage, how it was right but that it still hurt.

It was after two when he put his trainers back on and looked around for his bag.

She sat up, trying not to stare at him as he came towards her and sat on the edge of the bed. He looked down, as though taking a run-up to speak. 'Can I see you sometimes?'

She pretended to understand what he meant. 'Sure. See me sometimes.'

He seemed satisfied. 'I'll message you.'

'I might come to Edinburgh. The last week? I'm owed holiday.' The second she'd said it, Ali wished she could take it back.

He smiled and ruffled his hair. 'We'll be hectic, but yeah. Shout if you're in town.'

It sounded dismissive and she felt foolish. Of course he'd be busy. He wouldn't have time for her. It must have registered on her face.

He met her eyes again. 'Let's go for a walk. We'll do Arthur's Seat.'

He got up, shouldered his bag and touched the back of her hair, kissing her forehead again.

The door closed and she was alone, still burning.

Seven

Ali threaded her way through the people outside in the busy garden, squinting over drinks in the low evening sun, lighting cigarettes for each other. She stepped into the almost empty pub and paused to enjoy the shade inside, her skin goosepimpling in the cooler air. As her eyes adjusted to the low light, she looked for the stairs through a door to the left of the bar, her pocket vibrating with messages as she headed for the first floor.

In a lighter room at the top of the stairs, next to a bleachy-smelling bathroom, chairs were set out in a semi-circle. The handful of people already there had sketch books on their laps. The more serious had spread palettes and oils on the seat next to them. One woman in a headscarf sharpened a pencil. The man next to her assembled a wooden easel. Three large cushions covered in Indian fabrics sat in the centre, unoccupied.

Sid was early and sat on the far right as Ali came in, knees pressed together, pint gripped in one hand. She looked uncomfortable.

Ali wondered if she was smiling too much. 'I'm not late, am I?'

Sid shook her head. 'I'm early. I couldn't be late if I tried. My whole personality is… early.'

A short woman with tomato-red hair in a bob walked to the centre of the room and took off her kimono in one swift motion, turning to drape it over an empty chair and causing her eye-level nipples to form a dual sunset on Sid's unavoidable horizon.

Sid put her pint on the floor and unzipped a pencil case on her lap. She looked for something in it for a long time, until the woman moved away.

A crimson tide broke over Sid's face. Ali, already giddy from her continually vibrating hip, bit hard on her lower lip to stop laughter escaping.

They looked at each other and Ali made her mouth into a shocked oval.

Sid laughed quietly, shaking her head. 'Bowls of fruit, you said.'

The model, Letitia, sat down on the cushions with her back to them and fluffed her hair. Ali marvelled at her ease, her body so matter-of-fact in the middle of the space.

'OK, an hour of tits, then a drink?' Ali stuck a pencil behind her ear and stole a look at her phone.

What are THEY wearing? Are you surrounded by nake…

She suppressed a delighted snort.

'Are you sure you've got time for tits?' Sid was looking at Ali's phone.

She made a show of turning the screen off and pocketing it.

As she opened a large sketch book to a fresh page, Ali imagined herself kissing Letitia on the cushions in the centre of the room while Ed watched, smiling from behind an easel.

'Ali.'

Sid had asked her something but she hadn't heard. 'Sorry. Say again?'

'Do you want my sharpener?'

Ali took the pencil from behind her ear to see it was blunt. 'Oh.' She accepted a small wooden tool with a short blade, looking at it like it was a mystery.

'Here.' Sid took the pencil and blade and began to carve at it while the woman running the class came to the front and welcomed them.

The teacher, Clare, held the end of her long beads with one hand as she spoke. 'We'll do three short poses. Three minutes each. Then break. We like to put everyone's work on the floor at the break, so we can see what we've got.'

Ali crossed her eyes at Sid.

Clare's eyebrows were raised as though in question but everyone else in the room smiled and made happy little grimaces as though she'd twisted their arms.

Sid handed back Ali's sharpened pencil.

Ali was impressed. 'Skills.'

She grabbed her phone for a last look and typed quickly.

Wall to wall melons. Gotta go. xxx

His answers multiplied across the screen. She couldn't understand how he typed that fast.

You enjoy yourself. Have a lovely evening. Leave you to it.

This was followed by a further torrent of prodding and poking, teases, insults, GIFs, declarations of affection.

Tell me how to stop thinking about you. You look sweet when you're asleep.

She couldn't remember going to sleep that night. They'd stayed on their own sides of the bed, she following his lead. He drifted off and she stared at his profile until he rolled onto his side away from her. His back was broad and warm and she thought of his body surrounding hers.

You're precious to me, Ali. x

From the safety of his screen, he seemed to want to tell her everything. All Ali wanted to do was read and reread.

Clare looked over pointedly and Ali slid the muted device back into her pocket, readying her pad and pencil to start.

As she drifted off again to the place in her head where Ed was all the time, smiling and beckoning, Letitia took up a pose on the cushions. She lay on one side, curled into a foetal scroll. Her dyed red hair flopped over her lower shoulder, revealing the curve of her neck on the other side.

Ali held up a pencil like she'd seen artists do on TV, measuring her subject, closing one eye. 'Don't think. Just squint. Go for the shapes.' It was like Ed was standing behind her.

They sat quietly, making tentative marks on paper, Ali looking at the bend of Letitia's spine, resisting the urge to copy each bump of her vertebrae, trying to see the bigger form like Ed had told her. She imagined him chiding her for shading before she'd finished sketching.

Letitia's bottom pointed directly at Sid, an embarrassment-seeking missile.

The rest of the room regarded Letitia's body as though it were a vase or a chair. Ali was already thinking how she would tell Ed about the man sitting across from her whose neck went pink every time he looked at his subject.

Letitia's stomach, even curled over, was flat like a skateboard, slightly creasing at the sides where she articulated. Her breasts were small but pointed directly out. Ali wondered why she was doing this. She scanned her body for signs of her inner life. No tattoos. She wondered if Ed had tattoos.

'Thirty seconds then,' said Clare with the beads. She lurked around the room's edge, peering over shoulders, offering encouraging nods. She hadn't made it to Ali's side of the room yet.

Ali liked the big, confident pencil strokes she'd started with, but then she ruined them by switching to colour and trying to add facial features and a splash of red hair as the clock ticked down. A nude Ronald McDonald ammonite stared back at her from the paper as Clare rang a little bell.

Ali leaned back in her chair but Sid had already turned the page on her sketch book and was waiting for the next pose.

Ali tilted her paper to show Sid what she'd done. 'Um.'

Sid stifled laughter with her hand, then changed it to an awed gasp. She looked, then began to nod. 'Beaker from the Muppets: foetal, dynamic, unflinching.'

The two of them became hysterical. No one else in the room was louder than a mutter and the more they tried to stop, looking away from each other, the stronger the impulse to cut through the silence with their helpless cackling.

Letitia stood and turned to face the window, wrapping one hand around her arm, which she let hang down by her side.

Ali could just see her pubic hair was a spruce triangle and her thighs bore no sign of irritation from whichever hair-removal method she used. Ali's thighs were blotchy from waxing or shaving when she was out of wax strips. All other women seemed to just achieve hairlessness without pain or ugliness. Her hair clung to her, leaving scars when it was reluctantly parted from her. In the last of the evening sunlight, Letitia's skin was the same calico all over. Ali was glad that Ed was somewhere else and not looking at the woman with the jutting shoulder blades. Maybe Letitia wasn't funny. Or a vegetarian.

As the last short pose ended with Clare's bell, Ali closed her pad so no one would see her sketches and picked up her bag. While Clare's back was to her and people started to place their pictures on the floor for inspection, she stood up, careful not to scrape her chair and slipped out onto the landing.

When she reached the bottom of the stairs, she took out her phone and sent Sid a message.

No WAY I'm letting those people see the shit I drew. Meet me in the Rose & Crown, back towards the station. x

Ali was sitting at a garden table outside the pub an hour later when Sid showed up. She put her phone down. 'You actually stayed.'

'I really enjoyed it.' She sounded surprised.

'Being eye-to-nip with a bare lady? Who knew?' Ali pushed a cold pint towards Sid.

Sid looked around the garden. 'Some of us just aren't mature enough.'

'That was your fault. Now I'm the child who couldn't be serious in naked art class. Oh God, don't tell Ed.'

'Ed?' Sid stiffened and looked at her. 'Was this his idea?'

'No. Well, not really. He was just being nice, encouraging me to take it up. But my god, I'm really actually bad. Let's see yours.'

'Did you tell him we were going together?'

Ali said she couldn't remember mentioning it. 'Come on, let me see.'

Sid pulled her sketch book from her bag.

Ali ran her fingers over the badges on the flap of Sid's canvas bag, enjoying the smooth, round buttons under her fingers. One caught her eye. 'What's this? A band?'

'Not really. It's Bethan's thing. I just did the logo.'

'This is yours?' Ali looked again at the white lettering on the shiny, red badge spelling out Scold's Bridle.

Sid nodded and laid her sketch book on the table.

Ali opened the first page. 'Oh my god, Sid. These are amazing.'

She was looking at the kind of confident line drawings you'd find in a school text book. She turned the page and several smaller sketches were spread across the space, some in different pigments.

On the last page was a large portrait, recognisably of Letitia leaning back on her hands, her legs stretched in front of her.

'Hans lent me his inks for that one.' Sid was looking at it too, lost in the markings she'd made.

'You made friends with the congregation?' Ali was almost more impressed at this than the drawings.

'They were nice.' Sid picked up her pint.

Ali took her phone and turned her back to Sid so she could get them both in the photo with her picture. 'Let's show Ed. He'll be so impressed. Does he know you're an art genius?'

'No.' Sid went to close the pad and cider sploshed from her pint onto the page.

Ali pulled her sleeve over her hand and tried to mop the liquid away but the ink began to bloom and blur.

'It's fine.' Sid shook the liquid onto the floor and closed the book.

'Your lovely drawing.' Ali could see she didn't want to talk about it.

They sat and drank for a while, talking about Letitia and the alien concept of public nudity.

Ali wondered why Sid was so unwilling to take compliments for her work. 'You could earn money doing that.'

'What, stripping? You're all right, thanks.' Sid grimaced into her pint.

'No! Why haven't you drawn for ages? Why don't you want to show people? If I could do that, draw like that, I'd want to show everyone. Actually, can I send a pic of one of yours to Ed and tell him it's mine?'

Sid smiled and then chewed her bottom lip. 'I don't know. They're not that good.'

'Um, well they are.' Ali folded her arms. 'It's OK, I won't tell anyone.'

They didn't say anything for a while but Sid seemed to relax again.

Hours later, lying on her stomach, poring over her laptop, Ali searched Ed's name again. 'Ed Catchpole wife' still turned up no new pictures of Madeleine. A couple of him standing next to other women she recognised, but none of the mysterious wife. 'Ed Catchpole interview' returned dozens of results, videos of him at the Edinburgh Festival, sitting at a pub table or in a radio studio. He gave long answers to questions, deviating, talking at speed.

Ali thought it must do strange things to you, being constantly asked about yourself.

Someone had cut together his best moments from his panel show appearances. The comments were a mixture of fans swapping favourite jokes, women adding him to their guilty crush lists and men saying they wanted to punch him.

As she scrolled through his mentions on Twitter, she saw a tweet from an account called @nowaycarrykay; 'He's a prick. #edcatchpole' She looked for the rest of the conversation it was replying to, but there was nothing there. Ali clicked on her profile. She was young, in her 20s, flat brown hair with a blonde streak over one eye. An Irish flag emoji sat alongside green and pink love hearts and a unicorn. A filter gave her white cat ears.

She enlarged the profile picture. The girl disapproved of the world. Maybe she was obsessed with him and thought this was a good way to get his attention. Ali felt sorry for her and returned to Ed's messages.

Eight

Ali stood by the revolving doors, watching delivery riders going in and smokers coming out. It amazed her how many people in the Zone Digital building she didn't know.

Scrolling down to check the email from Otis's assistant, she tried to read back over their conversation, struggling to navigate it on her phone, Otis interjecting sporadically with 'mad thoughts'. It had been agreed that Otis would meet Ed. Ali knew he watched *All Night Garage* religiously and Ed was a regular on it. She could use that.

Then she'd set about planting the seed that the new show should sound like a podcast, something Ali had taken from Otis's earlier email. Better with two voices. Bethan would be perfect. She'd line up a meeting. She was on her way to the very top, she assured him.

Bethan was due in first and Ali thought it wise to prep her for a face-to-face with someone she was sure Bethan would instantly dislike. She'd done a whole bit in her set about entitled posh boys. It was like she'd already met him.

During that morning's show, Ali had spent too long staring at her phone. Ed had gone quiet after the art class. She scrolled through old messages, looking for echoes of the hit she felt when she first read them.

Her wonderings about Ed's wife grew to fill the gap left by his silence. Ali found her online shop and browsed the bowls and mugs, but she didn't seem to have any other presence. Ali didn't understand people who stayed away from social media. She envied their restraint and also wondered what they were hiding.

When she tried to picture Madeleine and her life with Ed, she imagined someone slim with big eyes and brown hair, in a long nightdress, brandishing a candle. She realised most of her ideas about 'mad women' were formed from repeated readings of *Jane Eyre* as a teenager. Had Ed realised how odd it was that he shortened her name to Maddie?

Sid rounded the corner in the same dungarees and black shirt Ali had seen her in before. Ali thought she lumbered rather than walked, like her bag contained something heavy; a bowling ball or someone's head. Ali pretended not to see her, turning to look the other way as though scanning the street for her. Eye contact now would be uncomfortable and would have to last for too long. She was doing them both a favour.

When Sid was a safe distance away, she turned, 'spotted' her and raised her chin in salute. Sid looked like she hadn't slept.

'Hey, the walking dead,' Ali said, opening her arms to offer a hug. They'd hugged before, but drunkenly. This time was stiff and brief. Neither knew what to say but both were aware that the silence needed filling.

Sid got there first. 'You get the monkey today, sorry.'

Ali shook her head, indicating she would more than do. 'No Bethan yet.' That was obvious but she suddenly couldn't think of any words that weren't 'Where's Ed? How's Ed? Have you seen Ed?'

'No.' Sid scratched her arm.

'Do we want coffee? Or will Bethan want a drink? How is she in meetings, because I think Otis is going to set her teeth on edge.'

Sid shrugged.

'Let's do The Dolphin.' Ali began to feel a knotting in her guts.

'I see you've met my agent.' Bethan came towards them from the other direction.

They laughed, grateful for a talkative third.

'How's it going?' Ali decided to keep it general until they were sitting down. Bethan answered, assuming this was directed at her. 'Less than a week till Edinburgh? Like I want to throw up and have a fight.'

Ali nodded like she knew what that was like. 'Are you up for the whole month too, Sid?' She felt a pang, imagining them all there without her.

Sid wobbled her hand. 'Back and forth. I'm directing a friend's show.' Ali stopped and turned back to her. 'That's amazing!'

Sid finally looked up. 'It's a first show and the venue's basically a cupboard. I don't know if anyone will actually find it, let alone see it.'

They turned into a mews with small terrace houses, mostly Victorian, broken by a clutch of modern ones at the far end. The street was cobbled. She loved these kinds of streets. Squinting away the satellite dishes, she could be in the London from Ealing films. She'd watched them with her dad on Sunday afternoons, avoiding the washing-up after Sunday lunch, hearing the huffs and banging pots from the kitchen next door, enjoying their truancy.

The Dolphin looked as it had done 50 years ago: dark wood walls, low red stools gathered around small tables, the once-bright swirly carpet muted by brogues and boots. Their refusal to install a TV meant no passing sports fans, just serious drinkers and committed time wasters.

Sid and Bethan sat at a corner table while Ali hovered. The place was empty except for a young man with a backpack, sitting near the door.

'I can see if they do coffee…'

Bethan was unequivocal. 'Oh, let's have a drink.'

Ali brought the drinks and sat on a stool facing them. She lowered her face to the meniscus of her pint, tucking her hair out of the way.

'Good show?' Sid said.

Bethan joined in. 'I've heard it a couple of times when I couldn't sleep. Kat's got a hot voice. Is she hot?'

Ali thought. 'She's an old pro. She used to be known for her hotness, for sure.'

Bethan seemed satisfied with that. Ali didn't know if this meant Bethan was gay or she was just making conversation.

'How's Ed?' Ali didn't like the sound of her own question but she craved information. 'Are you up to your eyes in previews?'

Sid wiped her mouth. 'He's nearly done with previews. One more before the off.'

Every time Sid talked about spending time with Ed, Ali wanted to compete with her. She wanted to ask about the girl on Twitter who hated Ed but she knew it would make her sound like a breathless fan girl.

Ali didn't like feeling so out of her depth. 'So, radio. This show is pretty fluid. They'll ask for "a format" but, confidentially, Otis has no idea what he wants until he hears it.'

Bethan grunted. 'Otis.'

'Tell me about it. But I think you'll be a good balance, the two of you. It won't take much to sway him away from Paul but leave that to me. Our job is to sell this. You and Ed. I know neither of you usually do double acts, but I've heard you talking. It's a nice rhythm.'

Bethan nodded, drinking. 'We'll fall into it. He's not one of those pricks who'll talk over me.'

'Oh, you're more than capable of keeping him on track.' Ali was warming up. She liked the feeling of knowing her stuff or at least sounding like it.

Bethan's phone started to ring and she indicated she'd take it outside.

Sid's cheeks were rosy. 'You're smart, signing her up now. She'll be in LA this time next year.'

'Really, that fast?'

'She'd be mad to stay here.'

Bethan came back. 'Meeting's off. That was Michelle.'

Ali checked her own phone but no message. 'Half an hour's notice? Fuck. I'm so sorry.'

Bethan sat down. 'Boss man's been called away. Maybe he's changed his mind.' She looked pissed off.

Ali soothed. 'You're one hundred per cent doing the show. Otis has the attention span of a fish. Something shiny will have gone past the window and distracted him. I'll sort it.' Ali had no idea if she actually could, but she was furious at being made to look like an amateur in front of her new friends.

Bethan finished her pint. 'No point going home, got a podcast later. Might as well have another?' She didn't wait for them to agree and went to the bar.

They drank, pushing into the afternoon, tables filling and emptying again after the lunch rush, blurring the hours. Ali decided to take on the character of a producer having a pointless meeting while the suckers went back to their carpet-tiled offices. She congratulated herself on getting paid for this.

She checked her phone and a drop of lead settled in her stomach at the sight of no new messages.

'Fucking prick.' Bethan was looking at her own phone. Her face was thunderous like she was taking a run-up for a fight but one she was looking forward to.

'Who?' Sid looked at her, concerned.

'Tom Weissman. He's doing two nights at the Playhouse. Fastest comeback yet.'

'Tom Weissman at the Fringe? Already?' Sid's lip curled in disgust. Ali didn't recognise the name.

Sid could see she wasn't following. 'American comedian. Creep.'

Bethan snorted, 'Narrow it down.'

'He groomed teenagers he met at his gigs, showed them his willy on the internet. Not taking no for an answer during sex. Two girls said he raped them. He denied the illegal stuff, announced he was going away to think about what he'd done, but I make it about six months?"

Bethan put her phone down on the table. 'And all the little bitch boys will be so glad to see him back. What is wrong with people? He's an abuser. More than twenty women aren't wrong.'

Sid was shaking her head.

Bethan lowered her voice. 'We should have a meeting. Make a plan.'

'Make a plan to do what?' Ali saw them exchange a look, then Bethan went on.

'Some women have formed a group. Scold's Bridle. Follow us if you're interested.' She corrected herself. 'Them. Follow them.'

Ali looked down at the badges on Sid's bag, remembering the red and white logo.

Bethan leaned forward. 'The Scolds is just a name for a bunch of us who are going to actually do something about the shit state of our industry. But Michelle doesn't want me to talk about it while I'm promoting my show.'

'Why not? Will it make you unpopular?'

Beth puffed out her cheeks. 'Depends who you talk to. But with some people, yeah.'

Ali found the Instagram account and followed it. 'Done.' She thought it sounded like the kind of thing women like Bethan did, but not women like her. Ali didn't see the point in trying to change things when they'd always been the same.

She sensed Bethan was on the turn and decided to give her something else to get her teeth into. 'If you do this show, you'll actually be doubling our female DJ quotient overnight. Otis doesn't live in the same world we do. He only hired Kat because he fancied her in sixth form.'

'Oh, I can suck it up to get past the gatekeepers. I've got to work.'

'He said you were, quotes, "an interesting mix". His tourism knows no bounds: race, class. Whatever dumb shit he says to you when you do eventually meet, I apologise. You're going to have to hold your nose.'

Bethan's volume went up. 'Interesting mix. I'm not a fucking Müller Corner. Get over yourself, Lord… fuck.'

'But obviously take his money when the time comes.' Even hammered, Ali didn't want to ruin the deal. 'Promise you'll still talk to us after you win all the awards and castrate all those men in Edinburgh.' Ali was slurring now.

Sid was smiling.

'Right? You've gotta keep it quiet.' Bethan looked at Ali seriously now. 'I mean it. Right… wait.' She fiddled with her phone. 'Look at that. It's not live yet.'

Ali took the phone from Bethan. The browser was open at a black web page, the red logo from Sid's badge in the centre. Ali waggled the phone at Sid. 'You did that.'

'I'm just artwork. I leave the activism to her.' A hint of a smile passed across Sid's face.

Ali turned the phone towards Sid and Beth grabbed her hand, turning the phone back around to face Ali. 'This is where we're publishing it.'

'It?'

Bethan's eyebrows shot up as the volume of Ali's question. None of them could tell how much noise they were making. She leaned in closer, indicating the need for caution.

'We need people we can trust. If you're up in Edinburgh, we're planning something. Not till the last week.' She looked back down at her phone and tapped rapidly with her thumb. 'That's when he's there. This could actually be perfect.'

Ali read the page and handed the phone back, nodding to Bethan. 'If I can get the time off.' She thought of Ed's face when she'd suggested meeting him there and how stupid she'd felt. If she was busy with someone else, maybe it wouldn't look so desperate.

'If you're serious, I'll message you when we've got a meeting set up.' Bethan raised her drink.

Ali couldn't really afford Edinburgh in August if it was just her. She used to split the hotel room with Ava, taking the overnight coach when they were students, switching to the train when they got jobs.

They did a few days at Edinburgh every year, seeing shows and falling into drunken sleeps at three in the morning, until Ava started IVF. Then she and Andy moved to Kent and she swapped fancying comedians for 30 plants a week and mindful drinking. To Ali, Ava's growing up had seemed almost aggressive, like she'd started to judge every glass of wine Ali drank when she came to visit.

The last time they'd seen each other was at the funeral. Andy hovered in the car with the twins so she could still feed them and Ali sat between Ava and Jean, numb and staring at the wooden box with a bunch of white daisies on the lid. She'd brought them because she knew Jean wouldn't have done flowers.

Ali and Bethan chased the last of the cider with whisky, giving in to the soft edges of the afternoon. Sid just looked at hers, too drunk to function.

Bethan was on a roll. 'Heels. The patriarchy, stopping us running away from them. Underwire. The Patriarchy. Fucking...' She thought what else she could add to the list. 'Everything. The Patriarchy.'

Sid's slight frame had absorbed the alcohol less well and she was almost mute, occasionally coming round to agree. 'Don't even own any heels.' She was a couple of beats behind. 'No one wants to rape me anyway.'

'Any man would be lucky to rape you.' Ali clutched at Sid's leg. Bethan looked around for her stuff.

Drunk Sid was softer and smilier. She looked pretty, Ali thought. She felt bad for thinking what one of those men who tell you to smile would think. But it was true.

Bethan picked up her empty whisky glass and put it down again. 'I'm done.' She was up and trying to remember where the door was. 'Fuck the radio.'

She got to the door and came back towards them, lowering her voice. 'Obviously not fuck the radio because I want the money. Never been more broke in my life and my show is not ready and I want my mum. OK, later guys.' Satisfied, she headed for the door.

Something Sid had said swam back into Ali's head. It could have been just then or the first time they met, but it suddenly felt important. 'What did you mean when you said "lighthouse"? "He goes full lighthouse on someone"?'

'What?' She blinked, ransacking her tattered memory for clues. 'Oh.' They were back to Ed again. 'With new friends. He goes full beam on you. Casts his light, you know.' She did the last bit waving her hands like beams of light were coming from them.

Ali tried to suppress a smile, tucking her lips over her teeth and squeezing them together. 'He's good at making friends.' Ali hoped hard that Sid was drunk enough not to read the subtext leaking through.

'He's coming out of his shell again. I can tell. Last year was tough for him, with Maddie and moving house.'

Ali just nodded as though she knew what Sid was talking about.

'Fucking messy at the time.' Sid seemed more confident now Bethan was gone, or she was sobering up. 'The woman he had the affair with was fully nuts.'

Ali leaned forward. So that's why he was divorced. He'd alluded to 'mistakes' when they'd talked but this was new information.

'She wanted him to leave Maddie, then Maddie found out.'

'And what happened to her? The woman?'

The bartender approached and reached for Sid's glass. She let him take it, the whisky still in it.

Sid became more animated. 'She was mental. I said that. She threatened to kill herself. But then she didn't. I don't know where she is now.'

'Someone on Twitter was all "He's a bastard". Is that something to do with her?' A ball of tension built inside Ali at the thought of these women, desperate for Ed. But he didn't look at them the way he looked at her.

Sid continued. 'Was she Irish? There was an Irish one not long ago.' She seemed to notice her glass was missing. 'I think because he looks so approachable and cuddly, some of them get the wrong idea. You'd be surprised how many women try to meet him after gigs. He says no thank you, they turn nasty sometimes.' She started to unroll her coat. 'You working early tomorrow?'

Ali pocketed her phone. 'Yep. But I plan to do a lot of sleeping before then.'

It felt nice, being on the same side. This is what he'd meant by 'see me sometimes'. He just liked being around her because she wasn't making demands on him. All she had to do was hide how she felt.

Sid stood, uncertain whether to hug or not.

Ali threw her arms out wide and held onto Sid, somehow surprised by how insubstantial she felt.

Lying on the sofa at home, eyelids heavy, Ali searched for Scold's Bridle and found old illustrations from a history website of a head contraption made of iron and attached with leather straps, a metal plate fitted into the mouth and pressed down on the tongue to stop the wearer from talking. In one drawing, a man held a rope attached to the back of a bridle, walking his wife like a dog.

She found the site Bethan had shown her, the red logo sitting at the top, and tapped around the screen, but there was nothing to click on.

Notifications began to tile across the small screen. Message, message, message.

Ed was ready for another game.

Her arm hair stood on end and she felt wide awake. She boiled the kettle for coffee and began to read.

Nine

Ali woke up where she'd fallen asleep, on the sofa. A panic sat on her chest until she'd done the complicated work of understanding where and when she was.

She held her phone to her and it was warm where she'd left it plugged in. When she shut her eyes she could see his face, peering through the screen at her.

If she looked for the messages again now, would they have burned away to nothing? Most of her night had felt like a dream, the afternoon cider mixing with coffee. Then coffee with vodka. She was drinking too much but decided to allow herself to because of the grief.

She swiped up and tapped the thread, stretching back through the night. She'd turned her alert sounds back on, desperate not to miss his next communication, afraid she might fall asleep mid-sentence.

When he finally let her go, she dreamed about him, the same image repeating; he tilted his head, swept the hair from her face and came towards her, their faces never quite connecting, turning to smoke.

The car would come soon to take her to work. She scrolled down to her favourite part, wanting to savour it again. The part where they'd agreed they should be friends.

So we're never going to fuck then.

No question mark, but it was implied. The rush was intense, the second and third and twentieth time she read it. He'd said it. He'd thought about them having sex.

She was drunk and hung over, excited nausea filling the hollow where food should have been.

Her reply to him hung in space underneath.

Never?

Then a gap of nearly half an hour. Maybe he'd regretted it as soon as he'd typed it.

She scrolled further back. The drunker they got, the more incoherent. They ended up lost in YouTube, hitting 'Play' on video after video, taking turns to show each other things that made them laugh.

It felt natural, hurrying to type out the same favourite line, drinking between gasps of laughter. Laughing so hard drink spilled down her chin.

She stank of whisky. Why did she stink of whisky? The half-empty bottle on the coffee table answered her. He'd told her to go to the 24-hour shop and buy some. She sent him a picture, pretending to swig from the bottle. It was her dad's drink. Had she told him that?

He told her to drink it with two cubes of ice. He was right. It tasted better after the ice had melted slightly.

Then, the green video icon flashing next to his name. She was exposed, adrenalin flying through her like spooked bats through a cave. Not wanting to answer in case her real face destroyed the idea of whoever he thought he was talking to.

She rolled onto her front and arranged her hair over one eye, propping the phone up against some cushions. When the call connected, she could see he was lying back, unselfconscious as his chins bunched into the logo on his t-shirt. A band she hadn't heard of. She made a mental note to look them up.

'Hello.' He was smiling easily and his voice had a late-night growl that made her want him.

She rested her chin on one hand, knowing the angle flattered her face. 'Why are you awake?'

He grimaced like she'd asked a stupid question, huffing air out through his nose. 'Why is the earth flat? Why did they fake the moon landings?'

She didn't understand.

'I'm not awake. I'm calling you in my sleep. Haven't you got to work?'

She looked at the clock. 'Three hours. Who needs sleep?'

His smile broadened. She could see his gums and felt suddenly disgusted and thrilled by looking at something inside of him.

'I like this hair. Should I have said that?' He dipped his head to one side as he asked the question.

'That my hair's nice?'

'No. Not that.' He waited.

She wished she could hear him say it, but she knew he wanted her to. 'The thing about us never fucking?' Ali felt bold, enjoying the word in her mouth.

He said nothing but looked deep into the lens of his phone camera. It only occurred to her later that his pupils didn't flicker up and down during video calls, switching from her face to his own, like most people's did. His gaze felt like a beam of black light pushing into the back of her eye sockets.

She asked where he was, trying to sound playful. She knew a sliver of cleavage was visible where her shirt opened.

'Hotel.' He gave nothing else away.

It didn't look like a hotel to Ali. All she could see behind him were curtains and a painting of the countryside. The wall was cream and textured, more like a bedroom in a house.

She looked at the curve of her cheek as she turned her face slightly to the right.

She always did this in photographs, conscious of her own lack of symmetry.

In a thin, angular woman, someone French with a fringe, it would be an appealing quirk. In herself she saw only charmless imperfection arranged around a sharp nose.

Every time she made him laugh, she felt more beautiful. As she lay there looking into the dark of his room, trying to make out detail, it occurred to her that he could ask her to do anything. She thought it matter-of-factly. She would do whatever he asked.

He was still smiling. 'If we can't. Could we... talk about it? What it would have been like.'

She breathed in and tried to get her bearings. She'd felt like this a lot in the months since her dad died. A brief feeling of not knowing where she was or what was real. She was never going to see him again.

She fixed back onto Ed's eyes. He was waiting for something.

'It's not against the law to talk.'

The idea of talking filth to someone had always seemed embarrassing to her. Surely one or both of them would laugh. Did he want her to say something disgusting? She tried to guess what would make him want her but the thought of saying anything out loud crippled her with shame.

Looking into his eyes, she didn't feel like laughing. He dipped his eyes and brought them back up to meet hers. 'What colour is that? I can't see.'

'I thought we were just talking.' She tutted, then pulled her shirt collar to one side so he could see the strap of her bra. 'What colour do you think?'

He looked for a while, putting a hand to his chin.

She felt foolish. 'Show me your bra first.'

He laughed from his throat but continued to assess. 'Mauve. Lilac?'

'Very good. I'd just have said purple.'

'So, we're talking. I wish we could... what's your favourite hotel?'

She held eye contact as though not bracing herself against a wind tunnel of her own raging lust. 'In London? Claridge's. I mean, I like the bar. I've never actually stayed there.'

He was locked in. 'We're in the bar at Claridge's, I've bought you a third martini. There's a room.'

There it was again. The knowledge she'd do anything he wanted.

She'd never had sex on a phone. She didn't want to have phone sex now, like this. It was forcing her to hover above herself, shuddering at every possible combination of words, the self-consciousness was too much. But what if she did let go of control? She wondered what it would feel like to be that free.

His voice flattened. 'Show me.'

Fear engulfed her. She couldn't do it, even though she wanted to.

He looked back down the lens again, removing all the hunger from his gaze. 'Sorry. Don't do anything you don't want to.' His face softened and his eyes rounded to muddy pools.

She loved his face. 'I'm a big girl.'

He put his hand over his mouth as though preventing a cheap joke from escaping. They laughed again. The awkwardness passing.

'Let's talk about how sad I am that I'll never get to see you like that. Not even a photo.' Back in the wind tunnel, her chest thumped and she could feel her blood moving around her.

She drank from the glass by the bed. Room temperature whisky, hardly tasting it.

If they were in the same room, talking like this, what was the difference? They stood either side of the line, neither crossing it. This was what he wanted, for it to be impossible.

She wanted to see the admiration reflecting back at her as she undid her buttons and lowered the straps of her bra. She wanted it so much.

'Never?' she said again, daring him to push her further.

'Stop tempting. Go to sleep.' His eyes creased in the corners, the regret flattening his smile. 'I'm going to dream about us in that suite.'

'It's a suite now? How much is Otis paying you?' She tried to reverse out of the cul-de-sac, but all she could do was want him. She didn't want to stop but she had no idea how to go forward.

The second alarm squawked across her remembering. She was still in underwear and a shirt and the car was outside. She looked for a dress, running deodorant over her armpits, feeling dizzy and drunk and like her insides were alight.

In the kitchen she plugged her phone in and tapped the last thumbnail in her picture gallery. He'd gone to bed and she'd stood in front of the bathroom mirror, wired, trying out poses, angling her chin down, sucking her stomach in.

She'd deleted all the pictures, except one.

In it, she was looking at her reflection, one arm wrapped round her middle, the other holding the phone up for the best angle. It was cropped from the waist. Her breasts were pale like the rest of her and gently pushed together. Her mouth was open a little, but the eyes weren't committing, nervous doubt sabotaging her attempt at seduction.

He wouldn't be looking at her eyes.

She opened the message thread, selected the picture and pressed 'Send'.

Ten

Ali sat on the white sofa outside Otis's office, watching his assistant, Monica, chew gum. Monica kept her mouth closed, her tight ponytail announcing absolute confidence in her own bone structure. She stared at a laptop, her hand motionless on the track pad.

Men's voices came from behind the frosted glass either side of Otis's door, but Ali couldn't make anything out.

The executive floor had a different feel from the rest of the building. If you came out of the lifts on this level, you'd think Zone Digital was a candle-scented laboratory of creative innovation, not the open-plan, carpet-tiled oubliette that Ali had languished in, five days a week, for the last eight years.

The celebrities and money people were brought straight up from the lobby to sign contracts overlooking the London skyline. It was a place for successful people and their pressed clothes and good hair. The toilets were called bathrooms and smelled of expensive hand soap.

Ali didn't know what to wear to meet both her boss and the first person she'd shown her naked breasts to since Mark. She could see Ed had read the message, but still no reply.

Sitting to attention on the edge of the pale leather, she realised she was in the same thing she'd been wearing when she first met

Ed. What did he call it? Her smock. She remembered the way he looked at the fabric. 'You're secretly hot under that. I won't tell anyone.'

Perhaps it would look like she hadn't tried, which was actually cool when she thought about it. Today was work. Maybe he'd offer her some small sign, but they would be professional. She was Katharine Hepburn and she had work to do.

The lift bell dinged and an older woman in slim jeans and a dark blue jacket emerged. Ed was behind her, looking at his phone.

The thought that he might be looking at her picture flashed across Ali's brain and made her legs go weak. Stand up. Do the job.

They walked to Monica's desk and she smiled at them, her ponytail swishing as she spoke. 'Hey. How are you doing?'

The older woman, Michelle, took off her sunglasses and rested them on her head. 'Ed Catchpole for Otis.' She touched her heart. 'Michelle Gladstone.' Michelle's reading glasses hung on a long gold chain around her neck. Her jacket looked like silk.

Ed still hadn't looked up from his phone. He was different, wearing some sort of designer trainers Ali didn't think were very him. She stood, wondering how to get his attention without looking like that's what she was doing.

He looked up briefly, then turned to Michelle, who smiled maternally back. 'Let's get you a coffee, tired boy.' Michelle looked at the pod machine in the corner and grimaced.

Ali stood and put her hand out. 'Hi, Ali Lauder.'

Michelle was on a train of thought. 'Do you mind going downstairs to the Italian place? Two Americanos with cold milk. Do make sure it's cold, thank you.'

Ed grinned at Ali like they'd never met. Something behind his eyes was aggressively cheerful.

She mouthed 'Hi' but couldn't tell whether it had registered. His eyes scanned the room, hovering over Monica at her desk. The long-necked PA smiled at him in a way she'd never smiled at Ali.

'Cold milk. Absolutely,' Ali said over her shoulder, rolling her eyes in a way she hoped would convey patient forbearance even though this really wasn't her job.

As she got to the lift, she turned to see the office door opening and Otis's large, tanned hand holding it open. Another similarly dressed man came out; pressed jeans, slip-on shoes, open-neck white shirt. Otis greeted his new guests and, with a whoosh of mountain air, they followed him inside, Otis in full autograph-collector mode. 'Love your work on *All Night Garage*. I've actually got that model Tesla.'

'Ah, thanks, man.'

The lift doors slid shut, cutting her off from the air conditioning. She let out a desperate laugh. He'd seen her boobs and now he was meeting her boss and she was getting him coffee. This was mad. This wasn't how it was supposed to be. She should be in there, impressing them. She wanted Ed to see her in full flight, firing off ideas, not shuffling in with hot drinks like the help. She looked at her hands and saw they were shaking. She rested her forehead on the mirrored wall and breathed through her nose, making little puffs of mist on the glass with her nostrils, trying to calm down.

As she waited for the coffee order, she tried to picture herself walking into Otis's office, joining the conversation. Future Ali spilled coffee on the white rug.

No, she'd bamboozle them with her research on demographics, thoughts on Bethan, ideas for brand sponsorship of the inevitable podcast, which she could totally produce, of course. She needed to find out how to do that.

A sob still bulged in her throat. She needed to be back in there but not until she'd stopped herself wanting to cry.

The barista was new and worked slowly. When they finally arrived, the coffees were pushed into a cardboard holder and one had 'Alley' scribbled on the side.

On her ascent to corporate nirvana, she checked her eyeliner in the lift mirror, swallowed the last of the cry and stepped out of the doors.

Her heart stopped. Otis stood in front of Monica's desk, clapping Ed on the back, kissing Michelle on both cheeks. Monica and Ed exchanged a smile. Ed was leaving.

'Oh, thanks.' Michelle took the coffees from her as she approached, dumb. Michelle took a sip of one, handing the other to Ed. 'Mmm.' She turned back to Otis. 'Let's help each other. I think we've solved your problem, no?'

'Cold milk,' Ed said, smiling, like he was surprised she had remembered.

Her mouth hung slightly open, her jaw at a loss whether to go up or down. She looked around the room as though searching for an ally and caught Otis's eye.

'Great stuff. Ali, Monica can drop you a line, get you up to speed.'

Of course, Monica had been in the meeting.

Ed and Michelle were heading to the lift. Was he actually going to leave without talking to her? What was he doing? She wanted to fall down the lift shaft and just keep going.

As the lift doors slid together, she looked straight at him. He must be able to see her, surely. He winked and then Michelle turned her back, standing in front of him. He was gone.

'Actually, Ali…' Otis's head emerged from his doorway again. He went back inside. She followed, feeling like ambulant roadkill.

Otis never sat still. He probably thought a restless body indicated a brilliant mind because he'd seen someone clever do it in a film.

He turned and strode to the black chair behind his desk, spinning it to face the window. Then he knelt up on the seat and regarded her over the headrest like a sniper behind a wall. He pushed off from the desk and the chair started to revolve. He continued the conversation revolving slowly, pushing the desk whenever he lost momentum.

'Did you float the idea of working with the Welsh girl? Good voice. I like the idea of them together but who is she? What's she done?' He thought for another 180 degrees. 'She's not well known enough really. But maybe better banter. Better. Ban-terrrr. You say she's going places? You're my comedy sherpa.' He played with the words as he turned.

'Yes, he... sorry, what did you talk about just now? Did you go through it with Michelle? She reps Bethan too.' Ali didn't know why Otis had his job. Except, of course, she did.

'Just getting a feel for the guy. Not every stand-up can do radio. He'll be good. We'll have a think about her. You want to produce.' It wasn't phrased as a question but he left a gap. Still twirling.

'We need to rearrange the meeting with B... oh, yes. I've got ideas.' She held up her notebook but the merry-go-round wasn't stopping. He possibly couldn't even hear her, like she was reading in lines for a scene he already knew. She kept going. 'I'm happy to move on from the early show. Or work something out with...'

He put his hand on the desk to stop for a moment. 'Ah, Kat.' He didn't elaborate for a moment, then brought the chair to a stop. 'All good things and all that. It makes sense for you to move to weekends. As a trial. Early breakfast must, I fear, go the way of automation.'

'Automation.' Ali's brain sped towards an understanding of what he was saying. He was telling her she was losing her job but giving her a new one. A trial. She nodded, her breath stuttering in her neck as she tried to form words. 'OK, so you've spoken to Kat?'

'I'll take her for lunch.' He started spinning again, untouched by the consequences of anything he was saying. 'Right. Piece of paper on the table. That's how much you'll be paid for the trial period. Knock it out of the park. Six weeks with Catchpole and...' He groped for the name.

'Gill.' Ali was almost squeaking.

'Yep. And maybe the move to weekends becomes permanent. Let's see. Let's see. Shame to lose you.'

He nodded towards the front of the desk where a small white piece of paper sat, folded in half. He was slowing down, clearly starting to feel dizzy.

While his back was to her, Ali read it and swallowed down a

surprised noise, making it into a little cough. It was a pay rise, but temporary. She didn't know how to feel.

Ali nodded as Otis turned around to face her again. He formed his hands into two pistols, aiming them at her head. 'Let's make a show.' He fired, both barrels. 'I did like Paul, but sounds like choppy waters ahead. We're best out of it. Can't be too careful with hash tag me too.'

Ali sensed her audience was over. 'Cool.' She walked to the big door, reaching for the brushed-steel handle.

Otis jumped off his chair and walked in a straight line to the sofa, arms out to the sides as though proving sobriety to a police officer. Satisfied, he smoothed his fair hair with both hands. 'He asked for you.'

She turned, taking a minute before she comprehended. 'Ed did?'

Otis was already halfway to a door at the other side of the room; his bathroom, Ali assumed. He held his hand aloft, thumb up in answer, as he disappeared.

Ali's head lifted off her shoulders, sailed through the open window and out into the bluebird sky.

Eleven

The hangover was waiting for her when she got home, like she'd been followed for miles by a shadow with a grudge and now it stood at the top of the stairs, swinging a hammer.

She slept in her clothes until early evening, then moved to the sofa to flick through the guide on her TV, not settling on anything. The current programme played, an antiques show. She let it.

He'd asked for her.

Whatever that was earlier – the winking – he was playing it cool. Of course he was thinking of her, making sure she was in line for the job.

She didn't want to think about his eyes lingering on Monica or Michelle's maternal fussing.

He still hadn't mentioned the picture. She moved it to her deleted folder, but she couldn't wipe it from her mind. In her whole life she'd never sent a naked picture of herself to anyone. She remembered when a film star's phone had been hacked and pictures she'd sent to a boyfriend multiplied all over the internet, strange eyes suddenly intimate with her body. She thought how different it was from seeing the same actress naked in a film, how truly naked she looked. Then she felt bad for looking at the pictures in the first place. And she knew in that moment that she'd never be so stupid. Never take a picture like that.

She opened her laptop. An email from Bethan apologised for getting shitty over the meeting cancellation. She sounded depressed. The fact Otis had dismissed Bethan so easily, in a way he'd never have done with Ed, confirmed everything she'd assumed about 'those men'. But still, she was sorry.

Ali wondered where all of Bethan's anger came from. The way she let it rip like it was always just beneath the skin. Those men she'd talked about, the ones they warned each other not to be alone with, Ali tried to picture what they were like and why Bethan hated them so much, but all she could feel was hot and a sort of guilty excitement.

Bethan said she would think about the radio show after Edinburgh. She was panicking about the Fringe and having no money and not feeling ready.

It was still light outside but heavy summer clouds had rolled in, lowering the ceiling of the city and making Ali's head hurt.

She put on the TV and found a yoga video, moving the coffee table to one side.

Ali had been at the bottom of a deep well and now the end of a rope ladder swung just above her. Two men looked down at her from the fresh air above, holding onto the top of the ladder. Ed's smile was encouraging, promising her he wouldn't let go. The other man was Otis. At any moment, he might forget why he was standing next to a well and follow a girl in tight shorts walking past the well. But, for Ali, escape seemed possible for the first time in years. This really could be something. Not just another desperate leap to a similar job that would 'do' because the current one was ending. A step up. A step towards something she actually wanted.

She thought about phoning her mum. She would find a way to characterise it as failure. 'You're losing your job?' Or there'd be something else it wasn't quite as good as. Ali was always impressed by the speed at which she could do that, take a good thing and squash it with a throw-away sentence.

Her phone lit silently. She'd turned off the vibrate alert now too. It was the cause of too much hope. She could see it was from Ed and that it was short, which was almost worse than not hearing from him at all. But the small burst of warmth still fed her.

Away for a few days. Pic delightful. x

She put her hand to her throat to stop the surge of angst. He was somewhere else. Even though she didn't expect to see him, the knowledge that he wasn't in the same city made it hard for her to swallow. Away where?

And the picture was an afterthought. Like a parting shot thrown over his shoulder on the way through the boarding gate. 'Delightful'. Something about the word repelled her and made her want to put her phone on the gas hob and ignite it.

She scrolled to her deleted pictures folder and looked at her pale body. It was so obviously fear she saw in her eyes now.

She wouldn't send any more pictures. Even if he asked her to.

When she thought about it, he hadn't.

She was drifting into sleep when her phone lit the darkened room.

Lauder. Wake up.

She laughed, sitting up and touching her hair like he could see her.

The messages flew back and forth again. She sat at the kitchen table. The bed was too comfortable and she didn't want to fall asleep.

He was bored with hotels. The receptionist had recognised him and asked for a selfie and he said OK but he wasn't in the mood and wished he could say no without looking like an arsehole.

Ali sympathised, soothed. She liked being the one to make him feel better. He said she understood him in a way that made him homesick. She gazed at the words, reading them over and over till a new note arrived.

Before I forget, tickets. Check your email. Edinburgh will sell out.

She sucked her cheeks in.

So I'm coming to Edinburgh now? I might be washing my hair. x

Ali loved it when they teased each other. It felt familiar and like she had permission to cross a line that other people didn't.

This is work. You need to be here. I need you here. x

She read it again and again. It wasn't a wish or a hope any more for her either.

Twelve

The weekend was a lonely stretch of hours. Ali had nothing planned and nowhere to be and all she could think about was him.

The messages had stopped at two in the morning and now all that remained was a vacant pain whenever she looked at the end of the thread, arrested and un-growing.

She had to get out of the flat.

She put on a t-shirt and a denim pinafore and pulled on her trainers. The windows were streaked with rain but she didn't look for an umbrella. It would be more dramatic to get wet.

The drizzle dotted the material of her dress and began to darken her red Converse, her hair starting to frizz. She wandered in the direction of the high street, feet squelching, until she reached the supermarket.

The refrigerated cheese and yoghurt aisle was a relief from the sultry damp of summer in London. She picked up a tub of butter and looked at the cooked meats, pink and livid in their plastic packets. The circles of pink and speckled red, sliced and fanned out, flat flesh from an unspecified source.

She flicked through a TV magazine on the news stand and found a picture of Ed smiling behind three seated comedians on the set of a panel show.

He was leaning in, one hand on the shoulder of the woman sitting in front of him. She was leaning back ever so slightly, like she was enjoying it. Ali put the magazine back, feeling too sensitive to every small change in mood.

She kept walking, past baked beans and self-raising flour, feeling sick and desperate. Like if she didn't hear from him soon, she might stop breathing. She held her breath from cleaning products to ice cream and frozen vegetables to see how it would feel.

The basket handle dug into her forearm as she walked and she saw the bruise had faded almost to nothing. Maybe she'd dreamed all of it. She wanted to make a new bruise to remind her.

She had to wait. She imagined calling him and then feeling like a fool as his answer message began. He wouldn't answer. He screened his calls. She'd seen him peering at the number or name but never picking up, preferring to talk or text when he was ready.

She was powerless.

Her phone rang, suddenly and loudly. No one called any more. It seemed indecent to answer in a public place. She hit the volume button to silence the ringing and saw the caller's name. Why was Sid calling her?

Excitement tightened her throat as she accepted the call, unable to wait. 'Hey. Everything OK?'

There was no sound on the other end of the line. She was just about to end the call when a strange noise came out of the tiny speaker. A sniff or paper tearing.

As the reply finally came, Ali could hear the words being forced past a blocked nose. 'Hi. Can you meet me? Today?'

'Oh, sure. I'm at the supe—'

'Bar With No Name at four?' This wasn't Sid at all, so decisive and direct. She didn't call the shots or even suggest things. She followed and complied.

'Yes, OK.' Ali waited a beat. 'Are you OK?'

'See you there.' Sid hung up.

Urgent drums pounded in Ali's head as she paid for the shopping and emerged onto the street. The sun was back and people were straightening up again, pulling down their hoods and closing umbrellas.

She tried to imagine what would make Sid call and kept coming back to Ed. Had she worked out that there was something going on?

Ali squirmed at her own excitement as the bus rumbled slowly towards Islington.

Her clothes were mostly dry by the time she arrived at Angel and she ducked into the cinema toilets to stick her head under the hand dryers.

The bar was down a side street lined with cream-painted houses, blue and red doors flanked with stone pots and trimmed greenery. She wondered why Sid had chosen this place. There was no sign outside, just the street number in large black numerals over the door. Sid was pubs and pints, even though Ali assumed she could afford to drink in much nicer places. Ali waited in the doorway until a bartender in a white jacket approached and pulled back the bolt. They were just opening.

The tables were black squares, just clearing her knees when she sat down. It was quiet and dark, one couple sat already at the bar like they knew the owner. The bartender was pouring them shots from different bottles to try.

Ali ordered a vodka martini and a bowl of almonds. The drink came in a delicate coupe, frosty, with an impossibly thin stem. After two sips, she was settling in and enjoying the decadence of a 4 o'clock cocktail in a dark corner, wondering what mystery awaited.

She wished she could send Ed a picture of her drink, captioned with something smart alluding to an old film, to remind him of their first meeting. He always got the reference, never not knowing which film she was quoting from.

The waiter returned to the table as Sid arrived. He looked at the dungarees and trainers and showed no judgement. Smiling, he poured two glasses of water and set down a menu.

Sid looked wide open, like whatever fence usually surrounding her had blown over in the wind. 'Sorry about the...' She wiped her nose with her hand and sat down.

Ali went first. 'So something's up.'

Sid interrupted. 'This is weird. I mean, this is going to sound weird.' She looked pale, more so than usual.

'OK,' said Ali. 'Do you want to wait till you've got a proper drink?'

'Yeah.' Sid straightened the silver ring on her index finger and asked the waiter for a beer.

'What have you been up to?' Ali filled the silence, feeling it was her job this time.

Sid looked spent. 'Cleaning the flat. I don't know why I do that. I've got a cleaner. Dad pays for her. I clean before she arrives and then leave before she gets there.'

'No. It's... I get it. Weird being on your best behaviour for some stranger.' It had never occurred to Ali to get someone else to clean her flat.

Sid was nervous. It made Ali feel strangely warm towards her. 'I love this bar. Someone plays the piano at weekends, I think, in the evenings. I didn't know you knew it.'

Sid shrugged. 'I don't. I just remembered you talking about it. Actually, I remember Ed talking about it because you told him about it.' She looked around at the other tables. 'It's nice. Quiet.'

Sid's drink arrived and they sipped at the same time, mirroring one another.

Sid's next question seemed to erupt from somewhere deep inside. 'Is something going on with Ed?' She looked almost surprised by her own query.

Ali found her face spreading into a smile even as she tried to stop it. It was a nervous spasm. She smiled at difficult moments, her muscles uncontrollable. Funerals, hearing bad news, a stupid smirk compelled her mouth to bend and she couldn't do anything to stop it.

'No. Well, sort of no. Probably not what you think. What makes you ask?' Ali felt pinned to her seat, thrilled the subject had turned to this so quickly.

She kept talking, seeing Sid needed more. 'He just wants someone to talk to, I think. I've been told I've got that kind of face. People tell me things.' She wasn't ready to give up all of her secrets.

Sid took a breath. 'Are you sleeping with him?' She didn't wait for an answer. 'Because I am. I am sleeping with him.' She picked up her glass again but seemed unsure whether taking a drink now would look like crowing. She was shaking.

Ali sat up in her chair as the words hit, bracing herself. 'But…' Ed and Sid, having sex. She couldn't even summon the image.

She sat back again, like changing position would help it make sense. 'I thought you were in love with him. Maybe. I thought you were going to warn me off.'

Ali stared at the table, rearranging the furniture in her brain, trying to make it look like this new reality. A smiling Ed looked on as her insides crumbled like the floors of a building folding in on each other in a film about earthquakes. 'Why are you telling me this?'

It didn't appear to have given Sid any satisfaction to say what she'd said. 'Maybe I am trying to warn you off.' Ali had never seen anyone look so defeated. 'I didn't think he'd do it to you. He doesn't usually go after my friends.' She said the last word uncertainly, like she was embarrassed to declare it.

'Do what to me? Shag me? He hasn't.' She tried to pull herself in. 'He told me he was stopping himself, that we should be friends. But then he messages all the time and talks about it.'

Sid's expression said everything, like she already knew.

'You sleep with him?' Ali kept going, pushing past the despair because it was too big and too awful to feel now. She wanted to know everything. She felt high, everything raced, her pulse joining in. 'When did this start? You said you met him when you were a kid.'

Sid looked at her drink. 'We were friends for ages. Months. He never looked at me like that. Then, one day. One night. He stuck his tongue in my mouth after we'd been out, back at the flat. He said he wanted a drink and then... from nowhere. No flirting.'

Ali watched as another couple came in and sat at a table nearer the bar.

'You worked for him, Sid. How long has it been like this?'

'I don't know. Years?' Sid's eyes rose to the ceiling as she tried to count. Her eyes widened. 'Nine years. Ten.'

'You've been sleeping with him for ten years? When he was married? Now?' Ali could see the fear in her own eyes, cradling her breasts with one arm in the picture. Everything went cold.

Sid looked stricken. 'I couldn't believe he could see me. No one else could. It's not just me. Ali, there are so many.' She tried to regain control of herself. 'I knew something was happening with you. It was the drawing.'

Ali wasn't keeping up. 'What was the drawing?'

'It's how he tests the water. Try this. Cook this. Wear this. Take up this hobby. He uses the art thing sometimes. It sounds encouraging. He tells you you've got talent.'

Ali looked at her, pressing the hollow of her throat. The waiter came past and she asked for 'two more', not caring which drink they brought.

She re-focused. 'Why now? If you've watched so many others fall for this. Why me?'

Sid's lip quivered and her eyes welled. She lowered her head, a dam threatening to burst. 'Because I like you.' She took a deep breath and tried to draw herself in. 'I've never told anyone about him. You're the only person.'

Ali put her hand out to touch Sid's arm. It felt awkward but some show of solidarity was needed.

Sid wiped her nose on a napkin. 'Something's happened and I've got no one else to tell.'

Ali was high on the drama. It was better than feeling what she knew she would when this was over. Whoever Sid was talking about bore no resemblance to Ed. She wanted to hear about this new guy and the dreadful things he'd done. She felt like she'd never met him. She tried not to do the nervous grin. 'What happened?'

'A girl in Ireland, Deirdre Callan. She's dead.'

She said it so flatly, Ali just waited like Sid was explaining the plot of a soap she didn't watch.

Sid looked for the right words. 'They were together.'

'I thought she was a fan. You said she was nuts.' She tried to picture Ed's face and suddenly couldn't get the features to arrange themselves, like he wasn't loading.

'I say a lot of things. Throw up distractions for him. He does what he does and I stand next to him, making sure people don't see. Fuck me, I'm Rose West.' She looked distraught.

Ali put a hand of reassurance on the table. 'This isn't on you. What happened to Deirdre?'

'He sent her money. A couple of times he flew her to where he was staying on tour. I think he paid for stuff. Sent her presents.' Sid crumpled into a sob, her mouth contorting. 'She's got a kid.'

Ali passed the napkin from under her drink and Sid covered her nose and mouth with it, composing herself.

'Ed's kid?'

Sid shook her head.

'What's it got to do with him? How did she die?' A light flicked on in her head but this still wasn't a real person she was talking about. 'Did she kill herself?'

Sid's head shook again silently. She wiped her nose and gripped the tissue in her fist under the table.

'She went to Turkey.'

Ali remembered the internet was right there and flipped her phone over, hoping to give flesh to the name. 'Sorry, go on.' As Sid spoke, she searched Ed's Instagram followers. There was only one called Deirdre.

There she was, making a peace sign at the camera, her dark hair parted in the centre, framing thick, arched brows.

'He did what he always does. Back to the hotel after a gig. Then he takes it long-distance, phone sex, asking for pictures. Then it changes. It's subtle, like you wouldn't notice at first. But he starts to find fault. "You'd look great if…" Like pulling the wings off an insect. You get so desperate, you'll do anything. He lets you work it out for yourself.'

Ali scrolled down and down through dozens of pictures, most of them selfies, Sid's words not really landing. 'She can't be more than mid-twenties.'

'She'd had a baby. A toddler now. And he'd got on at her about her stomach. It doesn't just ping back after you've had it.'

'How do you know this? Does he talk to you about them? Jesus, Sid.'

Sid shook her head again, shamed at hearing this out loud. Seeing what she really was in someone else's eyes. 'I messaged her friend when she started slagging him online. Carrie. She told me to fuck off. Then nothing. Then, two days ago, Ed was suddenly going to Ireland, changed his schedule. Carrie messaged and told me Deirdre was dead. She sounded so weirdly calm.'

The pieces of information swirled in front of Ali, refusing to take any recognisable shape. 'I'm still… she went to Turkey and died?'

'For surgery. An operation on her stomach.' Sid finished her drink and swallowed hard. 'The anaesthetic killed her. She was allergic.'

Ali couldn't feel anything at all. None of it was real.

Looking back down at her phone, Deirdre's name brought up local news sites. 'Dundalk Mum Dead in Botched Op'. She tapped through to the story. 'Body flown home by family' was captioned under a picture of 'Deirdre (24)'.

Deirdre looked different in this one, presumably supplied by her family. She looked her age, wore less make-up. Her hair fell in soft waves around her face and she was in a short summer dress, black with white polka dots, thin straps sitting in the grooves left by her bra.

Further down the article was a more recent picture; the young mum holding her little girl. The toddler was squashing her nose and laughing while she screwed up her eyes and opened her mouth, pretending dismay.

Ali put her phone down. 'You think this is Ed's fault? That he made her do it?'

'No, he never makes anyone do anything. That's his talent. But… he gave her money. Carrie thinks he helped pay for the operation. He'd have got a kick out of it. Her cutting herself up for him.' Sid stopped talking, seeming to focus all of her energy on breathing.

Ali recognised the fear in her eyes. 'Just slow down. You're OK. Breathe.' She put a hand out to Sid's under the table until they were looking at each other. 'In through your nose. It's OK. This is going to pass. Don't worry. Slow down.'

Sid followed her instructions like a child, keeping eye contact, willing Ali not to drop her. Her breathing slowed again. The bar was quiet and no one seemed to have noticed them.

Two new drinks arrived.

Sid still looked grave. 'Has he asked you for photos?'

Ali's insides turned to lead. She swallowed and looked up at the single deep furrow between Sid's brows. 'No,' she lied. 'I guess I was lucky.'

The humiliation turned every cell of her to shame. He'd probably looked at the picture and felt pity, not lust. She wanted all the oblivion this room could give her and drank half of the cold vodka in one gulp. It worked quickly.

She looked down at the paper menu on the table, curling it at the corner, rolling it between thumb and finger.

Sid had tears in her eyes but she wasn't crying. 'I watch it happen. Over and over. I've walked around London at night, knowing I can't go back to the flat, my flat, because he's there with someone.' She looked down. 'But I get him sometimes, when there's no one else.'

'You know about all of these others and you let him? Just... let him?'

Sid sniffed. 'He owns me.'

'He doesn't own you. That's ridiculous. If he's made you feel that way, that's...' Ali couldn't find the word. Maybe she wanted him to own her too. 'It's bullshit, Sid.'

'He tells you everything you want to hear, can't leave you alone. Then he goes quiet and you panic. And when he comes back the relief is... it's like drugs. You've never felt so good.'

Ali just nodded. She already knew that feeling. The flood of relief when he got back in touch after an absence. The hollow time when she couldn't reach him and he didn't try to reach her.

'He starts to ask for things. He says it's because he's lonely. Because he's homesick. He misses you. What he wants, at first, it's flattering. He makes you really like yourself, see yourself through his eyes. Then it changes.'

'Changes how?' Ali wanted every detail, like this was her favourite true-crime podcast.

'If he can't have what he wants, he shuts down. Leaves you gasping like a fish on the riverbank.'

Ali was disgusted and simultaneously trying to hide her fascination. 'What does he ask for?' She wanted bodies, placement of limbs, every dirty word he'd ever said to her.

'Depends what you're willing to do. You get an email address. He plays games, making you guess. I've seen him looking through the pictures and videos like it's the Argos catalogue.'

'You make porn for him.' She wanted to tell her to get some self-respect. That it shouldn't have taken a dead girl to wake her up from this.

Sid's eyes said yes. The two of them sat there, steeping in private baths of shame, not speaking.

'He didn't kill Deirdre, but she wouldn't be dead if she hadn't met him. He pulled her apart like a bored kid, picking at wallpaper. Until she felt ugly the way she was. He never causes the damage. He just sets you up and watches you do it to yourself. He enjoys it.'

Sid's head bowed. 'You stop eating to look better in the pictures. But he's already bored, looking for a new one. I've made myself sick, bought slutty underwear. I can see the disgust in his eyes sometimes. He doesn't hide it. But still, it's not nothing.'

'Why didn't you say no, if it made you feel that way?'

'I have said no.' She paused, weighing up whether to go on. 'He asked me to do things I didn't want to. And when I wouldn't, he went cold.'

'Are you going to tell me what he asked for? I feel like you owe me that. You lied to me, Sid.' She was being mercenary now in her desperation to know.

Sid looked as though she didn't know where to start. 'A three-some with a girl called Summer. He brought her to the green room at a TV recording. I knew she was the new one. We can smell it on each other. He kept calling us "my girls". She looked as embarrassed as me.'

'You meet them? Did the two of you talk?'

Sid shook her head. 'I know he's asked some of the others to film themselves fucking a guy. Like, hide the phone on a shelf and do it for him.'

'Jesus.' Ali didn't have much else. She wondered what she'd have done to pass his test.

Sid wasn't sure Ali understood. 'Nothing happened. After that night at the TV recording, he didn't speak to me for a month. Michelle said she needed me in the office, to steer clear of the club for a while. He stopped coming to the flat. It's like I was erased.'

'Because you wouldn't fuck this girl? Jesus, does Michelle know?'

Sid shrugged. 'She doesn't ask the right questions. It's just how it is. For some of them anyway. They're on tour a lot, away from home. It's not Michelle's job to monitor who he's sleeping with.'

'I can't believe you and this Summer girl didn't talk to each other. When he went to the loo or something. Does she live here?'

'No, Liverpool. He's got them all over.' Sid could see Ali was getting involved in the reconstruction currently being staged in her head. 'No one says it out loud. You just know. Everything is designed to make you feel it, the competition. I didn't compete. I couldn't if I'd wanted to.'

Ali crossed her arms, glad he hadn't seen all of her. The flab on her thighs, the silvery stretch marks around her stomach.

'Deirdre was in love with him. She went to Turkey and her family brought her home in a bag. He didn't kill anyone. But he plants the seed and he helps it grow.'

Sid put her hand to her mouth, a greyness washing over her skin. She moved quickly, boots bashing the stairs as she ran up to the bathroom.

Ali stayed where she was, paralysed by the weight of information. For a while, nothing happened. It was surreal. Like Sid had never been there. She could go home and pretend it was a bad dream and everything could return to how it was.

She had felt it. The jealousy for every woman Ed had mentioned. When he'd started to make suggestions, hint at the underwear he liked, a thing she should cook, she had already begun to feel her hands slipping from the wheel and how much she'd liked it. Not deciding anything any more.

When Sid came back, sweat glazed her forehead and chin. She sat back down and drank all of her water.

'It's OK. We'll go.' Ali turned towards the bar where their waiter was already picking up a tray and moving smoothly across the room.

'Just the bill. Thanks.' Ali nodded.

When it came, she paid without looking. The space in her mind usually taken up with worrying about money was filled with this now.

She didn't feel drunk enough and she wanted to be. 'We'll go to mine.'

Thirteen

At the mini supermarket around the corner, Ali waited in line behind two girls talking about their plans for the evening. They were young, long bare legs under short dresses. She stared as they strode to the counter on heeled boots, holding bottles of wine and crisps.

When it was Ali's turn, she asked for a pack of cigarettes and a bottle of vodka. She bought matches because she always imagined there were no lighters at home. There were at least six disposable ones in her bedside drawer.

Outside on the pavement, Sid looked like a ghost, translucent in the evening sun.

'We'll get a cab.' Ali put her arm out as one drove straight past them. If they'd had long, tanned legs and short skirts he would've stopped, she thought.

She was coping, making sure Sid was OK, finding transport, being practical. She was good at this. She could absorb the pain and shock and grief of others as easily as a kitchen sponge. It made her feel good to be useful.

As the minutes passed waiting for another cab, Ali worried Sid would want to leave and the story would leave with her. Ali stepped out onto the road and raised a hand again, making it impossible for the next cab to pass.

Sid slept on Ali's shoulder during the short journey. While she dozed, Ali searched Ed's social media for the women she'd mentioned, trying to remember names through the fog.

Deirdre's Instagram page drew her back. There were pictures of her smiling with girlfriends at a festival. A toddler in pink dungarees poking her tongue out at the camera. The last picture she'd posted made Ali's mouth dry.

Tanned knees were pressed together at the front of frame revealing slender thighs like two brown hot dogs and beyond the view from a sunny balcony. The sea covered in heat haze led out to the horizon and another peninsula beyond, crowded with rooftops and towers. The location tag said Izmir. Ed had liked the picture.

Ali looked at the legs, thinner and smoother than hers and for a moment she envied them. Even as she imagined them laid out on a metal table, a tag looped around one painted toe.

The flat was in darkness by the time they arrived. Sid followed Ali up the stairs and stood limp while Ali fumbled for the right key.

Not wanting to startle her with bright lights, Ali moved around the room, switching on a table lamp and the fairy lights in the fireplace. It looked romantic, like when Ed had been there.

The thought of never doing that with him again caused a cramp, the first sign she might actually feel something tomorrow other than sick. She went to the kitchen counter and took the vodka out of its plastic bag. If that was sadness descending, she wasn't ready for it yet.

'Sit down.' She pointed towards the sofa and put ice into two tumblers, leaning against the kitchen counter for support. Her body was drunk, even if her brain wasn't.

'Sit,' she repeated. She got the feeling she could tell Sid to stand on her head and she'd do it.

Ali set the glasses down on the coffee table and poured vodka over the ice like it was water. Pulling the cigarettes and matches out of her pocket, she tossed them on the table. She opened the big sash window behind the bed and sat by Sid on the sofa, crinkling the plastic off the cigarette packet.

'What are you going to do?'

Sid looked as though it hadn't occurred to her. 'I don't know.'

They lit cigarettes and Sid breathed hers in, her eyes following the thin cloud as she blew the smoke out. 'I think that was it. My relationship history. Beginning, middle, end.' She inhaled again and something fell into place in her mind. 'He won't want me now.'

Ali couldn't hide her amazement. 'You'd go back?'

Sid looked at her like she'd just thrown her a lifebelt. 'He doesn't know I've told you. Are you going to tell him?'

Ali thought about the radio show and the rope ladder and the sadness began to grow.

Sid was staring at the wall opposite the window. '*Vertigo*. He made me watch that.' She made a face like everything made sense now.

Ali put the glass against her cheek. 'He said it was one of his favourites. He quoted lines from it.'

Sid laughed, shaking her head. 'He was doing his homework.' A thought occurred. 'He's been here.'

Ali figured she might as well tell her. 'He stayed the other night. He didn't even kiss me. If he's such a shagger, why didn't he do anything?' She'd never felt uglier.

'Different games for different people. Maybe for you it was making you wait. Knowing he can have you is enough if he's got someone else to actually fuck. Which he always does.'

Ali looked at the *Vertigo* poster and wanted to rip it down. 'This is not how I thought today would go.'

'Are you going to tell him?' Sid tipped her glass, watching the vodka trickle over the rocks.

'What would I say?' Ali imagined his face as she cried and pleaded. The disdain.

'If he knows I've done this, that's it. I'm gone.' Sid's knuckles went white around the glass she was holding.

Ali wasn't listening. 'Tell me about Summer. Is he still seeing her?' Ali crunched an ice cube in her teeth, picturing Ed kissing a blonde woman in a meadow.

'I don't know. She's still all over his social media. He was probably getting bored. Hence.' She nodded at Ali.

Again, Ali's heart leapt at the idea he'd dropped someone else for her. She was a trained poodle, standing on her hind legs every time he threw a treat. She didn't recognise herself. But also, she did.

'He doesn't ever really end things. I mean, he ignores me. Says horrible things to me, but then he comes back like nothing's happened.'

'What horrible things?'

Sid thought. 'One time, I was going through a really bad depression. I was low. I messaged him, asked if I could see him. I knew he was just back from a tour. He said sure, come to my gig. Afterwards, he came into the bar and we got drinks and I told him I was struggling, that I couldn't pick myself up. Some guy recognised him. Ed lit up, put on a show. "Thanks so much, man." Took a selfie with him. I just sat there. I must have looked upset? The guy walked off with his selfie and Ed looked at me, just total contempt on his face. He said, "Don't be a cunt all your life," and walked out. He left me there, crying.' She didn't cry now, just looked up at Ali blankly.

'How can anyone do that? Who is he?' Ali spoke softly, feeling more in control again. She didn't know how she was going to feel about Ed tomorrow, but right now, she hated him. She tried to store up how it felt for when she needed it.

'Who else do you know? We should talk to the others. Let's do it now.' Ali felt like running through the streets, shouting through letterboxes.

Fear passed over Sid like a shadow. 'No. It's bad enough I've told you.'

'We have to talk to them. Message Summer. What's her last name?' Ali reached for the laptop, spilling vodka on her leg.

'No, don't do that. Promise me you won't.'

Ali stared at her. 'You told me. So tell her.'

'I hardly know her.'

Ali looked at her like she was mad.

Sid panicked. 'She's on meds. Anxiety and depression, I think. I don't know how she'd react. She knows about me. She'd have to have been an idiot not to see what he was trying to do that night. But I don't know what she... how it'll affect her if I just drop this on her.' She was like a porcelain figure, stiffening with fear.

'You're protecting him. He doesn't deserve that.'

'I've ruined things for him with you. That's enough.' She rubbed her temples. 'I need to work out what to do.'

'No, it isn't. We should stop him. If what you said about Deirdre is true...'

Sid's breath heaved in her chest like she couldn't get enough air into her. 'I told you to stop you. I don't know if Summer's still seeing him. Please.' She looked ashen.

Ali thought of Otis, revolving. She was going to lose her job. She poured more vodka, lit two more cigarettes.

'Surely it's too much effort to be like that; calculating, tricking people and covering your tracks all the time.'

'I think I need sleep.' Sid held the cigarette Ali had just given her. 'Sorry, I can't.' 'This can't be it, Sid. We need to work this out. What are you going to do?' Ali stood too, holding a burning cigarette in each hand.

The younger woman picked up her bag and ran a hand over the back of her head. 'I shouldn't have said anything. Can you just... give me a minute?'

Ali could see she was losing the battle. 'OK. We'll take some time.' Sid was moving towards the door.

Standing outside on the street, they hugged. Or rather Sid let Ali hug her while her arms stayed by her sides.

'I'm sorry.' Sid really did look like she was.

Ali stood in the doorway. 'I know that took a lot. You told me for a reason. It's too much to carry on your own.'

Sid turned towards the lights of the high street.

'I'll get you a cab.'

Sid pretended not to hear and kept walking.

Fourteen

Ed flicked a piece of fluff from his cuff and pressed the doorbell. His jacket buttons strained against his midriff but he wasn't buying a new suit for this.

The other men at the house would be in suits. In his peripheral vision, a white net curtain moved in the window, discreetly put back in place.

He saw his face in the rippled glass panel of the door. Serious, but warm. Approachable. His 'in the provinces' face.

A man with yellow teeth had recognised him at the airport baggage claim. 'I know you.' He accompanied this with an unpleasant grin. Ed cloaked his disgust in a smile and continued on his way to the taxi rank.

The woman who answered the door was younger than he'd expected. Early forties maybe. She wore a black dress, a v-neck showing the beginning of her cleavage, the material fitted around her waist, looser on the thighs, but he could make out the shape of her body. Her hair was dark and to her shoulders, dyed to cover the first grey roots. The green eyes he recognised, smiling out of a different face.

She smelled of cigarettes and perfume. 'It's so good of you to come. Bronagh, Deirdre's mam.' She was uncertain, like she was greeting an alien, reaching her hand towards him.

He took it in both of his. 'I'm so sorry, Mrs Callan.' He paused. 'Bronagh.'

She looked into his eyes, a spark of warmth lighting in her own.

Ed turned and raised a hand at the car waiting on the other side of road. The driver opened a newspaper.

He turned back to her, still holding her hand in his. 'I'm so sorry I can't stay for the service. I couldn't go without paying my respects.'

Her face crumpled. 'Sure, come on in.' She stood to the side and indicated the hallway. He wiped his feet and she closed the door behind them. 'Through to the kitchen, Ed.'

He walked straight ahead through a carpeted hallway into a bright room with pine cupboards and a pine table against one wall. She watched him go, somehow impressed that he could be here in her house, despite the occasion.

The sun caught the leftover fog from a recently extinguished cigarette. The table was covered in Clingfilmed plates of sandwiches. Cardboard boxes underneath contained bottles of wine and cans of beer.

'Can I get you something to drink? The kettle's on. Something stronger?'

'No, thank you. You're kind. How are you coping? Sorry, that's a stupid question.'

She pulled a pine chair out from under the table and indicated the one across from it. 'No, it's a good question. I don't know, Ed. I just don't know. None of it seems real.'

He sat, unbuttoning his jacket and straightening his tie.

'Jack and his brother had to fly her back fr…' She broke suddenly. She stifled sobs into her hand.

It wasn't quite 10 o'clock and Ed was already wondering when it would be OK to leave. He took the hankie from his top pocket and pressed it into Bronagh's hands. Not yet.

A bottle of whiskey sat on the table.

'Come on.' Ed opened it and poured a little into a glass for her. She sipped it, calming down.

134

Footsteps thudded on the stairs above their heads and a girl appeared in the doorway, carrying a toddler. 'Are there more nappies, Auntie Bron?' She noticed Ed and became self-conscious. There was an awkward pause as she took in the scene.

Ed smiled blandly. 'Hi. I was a… friend of Deirdre.' Perhaps some tears here, he thought, rubbing an eye with a knuckle until it looked suitably red.

The girl was visibly impressed. 'She loved you on that show.' She looked guiltily at Bronagh, like she'd realised this wasn't the time or place to talk about TV.

Ed smiled, beneficent through moist eyes.

'Under the sink in the bathroom.' Bronagh wiped her nose with Ed's hankie and smiled at the toddler.

The kid wriggled, her fingers tangling in the girl's long hair. 'Mummy.' It wasn't so much a question as a statement. She had stopped asking where her mother was now, but she said the word often, soothed by its sound.

'We're all going now, aren't we?' Ed demurred as though he shouldn't be the one to be crying here.

The girl made a face as the toddler's fingers tugged too hard on her hair. 'Right, OK.' She headed back upstairs.

Ed could smell the shit in the departing baby's nappy. 'She touched a lot of lives. She did.'

Bronagh reached for a cigarette packet on the table. 'Do you mind?'

Ed blinked back dry tears. 'Please.' Anything to cover the smell of shit, he thought.

She lit one and sucked at it between phrases. 'It's so good of you. We didn't expect… It's good of you.'

Ed performed his best self-effacing smile, closing and opening his eyes slowly to emphasise the sincerity. 'I couldn't go without passing on my sympathies. Is there anything? I sent flowers to the church.'

She shook her head. 'It's enough you're here. It would have meant so much to her.'

They sat in silence for a moment. She tapped the ash from the end of her cigarette into a saucer. 'Would you… like to see her?'

He didn't understand for a moment. Of course. An open casket. He was filled with revulsion. The body was here. He took a deep breath, containing his excitement. 'Would that be…? I don't want to intrude.' He wanted to see.

She scraped her chair back, stubbing out the cigarette and smoothing the dress over her thighs. He liked her tits. They were bigger than Deirdre's.

He imagined the dead girl in garish make-up with a push-up bra under her dress, so she looked less like a child. He'd always liked her legs and the way she started wearing shorter and shorter skirts after he'd pointed them out. He liked the way she wore her glasses in Instagram posts after he'd told her they were sexy.

He thought about a video she'd sent him, undressing in her bathroom mirror, the cheap fabric of a shiny red slip falling to reveal small breasts. She'd rested the glasses on the bridge of her nose and sucked a dildo, slowly, like he'd asked.

He solemnly followed Bronagh back towards the front door, hands clasped, the first traces of an erection brushing against his boxer shorts.

They turned right into a darkened dining room. The curtains were closed and two candles flickered on the sideboard. Instead of a dining table there were two trestles with a dark wood coffin laid across them. As he'd hoped, it was open.

He took Deirdre in from the feet up, like a camera panning up a starlet's body on the red carpet, saving the face till last. She wore black ballet pumps, tan tights and a blue dress that stopped just below her knees. Brown beads were wrapped around her fingers, clasped over her stomach.

Ed looked to Bronagh, who said nothing but squeezed an arm and left him alone with her daughter.

His eyes reached Deirdre's face. Her brown hair was fanned out on a white silk pillow and her cheeks were pink. Aside from that, she could be lying in bed next to him any of the times they'd fucked. Her skin was tanned. He guessed the high neckline of the dress was chosen to cover the grey of the flesh underneath.

She still had those fat painted nails, scarlet and shiny. She'd sent him a photo of the colour choices at the salon. He always chose something lurid in pink or red.

He couldn't stop looking at her, wondering at the techniques used to keep her seemingly alive. A small gold cross on a chain nestled at her throat. He'd never seen her wearing it before but it suited her.

He leaned forward until his nose was almost touching her ear. She was wearing the same perfume as always. The one he bought her at the airport. 'Such a shame.'

He turned, hearing Bronagh come back through the door.

'It's so surreal. Seeing her like this. She came to see me in Galway last year. We ended up drinking sambuca.' He laughed as though lost in the memory.

Bronagh nodded, joining him there. 'That's our Deirdre.'

Suddenly stricken with the reality of the dining room and its contents, Ed seemed to collapse. The dead girl with the red nails finding her place in his conscious mind. This was Deirdre.

He started to cry and turned to the curtains, covering his mouth and nose with both hands.

Bronagh put her hands on his shoulders. She moved her hands up and down the tops of his arms. It felt maternal and arousing at the same time.

He turned around and rested his head on her shoulder. 'I'm so sorry,' he choked the words out.

His agent didn't put him up for enough acting work. He'd done one regional tour of a Shakespeare but he was always pigeonholed as the stand-up. Not right for most of the parts he wanted to play. He was 43 and fat. Defined jaws and hard abs trumped talent when it came to the kind of parts he saw himself in.

He patted her back, indicating it was time to let go.

He composed himself, still allowing his voice to wobble. 'She was a lovely person. I don't know what made her want to... do that to herself. She was perfect as she was.' He let the tears come again. Or rather, he closed his eyes to indicate that they were newly flooding.

'It was after the baby. She used to laugh when Amara prodded her tummy. "You used to live there."' Bronagh dabbed underneath her eyes with Ed's handkerchief, careful not to smudge her mascara. 'She got it into her head that it had to be flat. All the exercise, the diets. I bought her, you know, those pants.' She touched her own stomach. 'Nothing made her happy. Then she says she's going to Turkey. Asks me to take Amara for the week. I thought it was just a holiday with Carrie. That's her friend.'

She opened out the handkerchief and re-folded it, looking for a dry patch.

Ed didn't say anything. He just looked at Deirdre's face. The pink and white flowers lain alongside both her arms. The quilted fabric lining the coffin lid. Such a lot of set dressing for an empty vessel. 'I know there's nothing I can say,' he said, building up to say it anyway. 'But you'll all be in my thoughts. She's going to be so, so missed. Galway won't be the same.'

Bronagh dipped her head. 'You must be so busy with the TV and such, it meant so much for you to come.'

They hugged again and this time he was sure she could feel his erection. She didn't move away. She felt warm and her breasts pushed against his chest, firmly resisting the pressure. She was in good condition for an old model.

He imagined pushing her down on the floor and having her next to the coffin. His cock got harder. He pulled back and took her face in his hands. She wasn't stopping him. He was high on the transgression. He was certain she was imagining the same thing. He kissed her, firmly, for a second too long. He tasted the whiskey and cigarettes in her mouth. He felt her whole body pulse in response before he let her go.

The front door was opening. Men's voices burbled in the hallway. As a group of four or five in black suits filed past the door, Bronagh turned to face the far wall, holding the handkerchief to her mouth. They weren't seen.

Ed turned back to the coffin and rested his hand gently on its edge. 'God bless her,' he said, taking a last look as though a vicar who'd just given the last rites.

He paused to contemplate a bright future lost to tragedy, sneaking a look at the watch poking out from under his shirt cuff. 10.15 exactly.

Bronagh looked over her shoulder, her expression somewhere between horror and disgust. Was she going to say something? Her mouth was open.

Time to go. He adopted the formality of a pallbearer, clasped his hands low in front of him, gave a small bow in Deirdre's direction and made the sign of the cross on his chest. He'd always wanted to do that.

He turned, made for the kitchen and nodded goodbye to the assembled men. He didn't introduce himself. They knew who he was. They could all gossip about it later at the wake. How the famous comedian had come to their house.

And Bronagh would say nothing. Maybe not even at confession. He headed for the door, checking his watch again and removing his jacket so he could drape it over one arm, shielding his hard-on. He turned the latch, ruffling his hair, forming his features into tortured sorrow, then he stepped out into the porch.

Bronagh's hands shook as she stroked her daughter's hair, hardly believing what she'd done.

Ed lingered briefly on the doorstep, shutting the door behind him, making a pantomime of checking his phone and looking up and down the street.

On the opposite side of the road, next to a postbox, a young man took photographs with a phone camera while pretending to look at something interesting on the screen.

Ed didn't acknowledge him, appearing lost his in own thoughts. 'Visibly stricken,' the caption would say.

Once he was in the car and clear of the housing estate, he unbuttoned his jacket and took off his tie. As the car joined the slip road to the motorway, it began to rain. The grey vastness of the M1 slipped past his window. They were Dublin-bound.

He pulled his phone out and read a newly arrived message.

What time and where? S x

He smirked and texted back.

Staying at Brooks. 4 o'clock. Find a pub nearby. Don't wear knickers.

Fifteen

The quiet of the streets was disturbed by the occasional passing night bus. Ali was wide awake and walking. She'd fallen in and out of sleep all day. Sid wasn't answering her messages and Ali's imagination played out a whole scene between her and Ed, arriving back from wherever he'd been.

In her daydream, Sid pretended everything was as it had been, made him dinner, stripped to red underwear and knelt at his feet to suck his cock while he looked at porn on his laptop. Daydream Ed's lip curled as he scrolled, his head on one side, concentrating on the women in the videos, watching as they did as they were told, humiliating themselves for him.

The self-hatred had forced Ali outdoors, even though work didn't start for two hours.

She cancelled her cab to the office and kept walking. It would take her that long on foot and she needed to get away from home and herself. Exhaustion hummed through her like a current.

She wanted to persuade Sid to tell her who the other women were so she could message them and make friends with them and ask them what he'd done to them. But if she felt this crippling shame, they would too.

When she looked at her phone again, she'd been walking for an hour and she was lost somewhere near the edge of Camden. Still, she reflexively checked to see if he'd been in touch. Still the same chemical dip when there was nothing.

She'd strayed off the main road at the sound of young men shouting up ahead and now the streets were unfamiliar. Terraces with painted gates had given way to estates of grey concrete, high balconies punctuated with bikes and laundry. The buildings rose to dwarf her.

It started to rain. She could've opened Maps on her phone but she just walked, letting the tears mingle with the drizzle, feeling contentedly tragic with her dead dad and her toxic love and no job.

Looking up and down, she made for the nearest bus stop. Everything was an effort. Where was her travel card? She leaned against the corner of the shelter and searched in her bag.

She didn't notice it at first; a muted thumping sound coming from the patch of dark just off to her left.

She lifted her head halfway, not wanting to look directly at the source of the noise, buying herself time. She could make out rapid movement, in time with the thumps.

The possibility of someone nearby became suddenly real and she looked up, straight into the eyes of a young man in a green, hooded coat. He couldn't have been more than 25 but he had old, hard eyes. He looked put out, a snarling lip beneath an unwavering stare. The zip on his combat shorts was open and his thin penis poked out of his fist. The thumping continued.

He wanted fear and she gave it to him, a gasp of air rushing from her mouth as she stood upright and threw herself away from him. She started to run, the adrenalin almost lifting her off the ground. She resisted the urge to look behind. Why did they stop, the women in horror films? She felt like she would never stop running. In another minute or so, she was breathing hard and slowing to a walk.

When she got to the next bus stop, an older man stood under the shelter, lit by an advert at the far end. He wore an orange tabard over his clothes and a black woolly hat. If he noticed her breathless arrival, he didn't show it.

She looked past the man at the advert. A naked girl on a beach, over-exposed in white sunlight, wrapped her limbs around her body, crouching on the sand so her nipples and crotch were hidden. An orange tube of fake tan displayed to the right of her.

Ali was glad not to be alone and closed her eyes, her wheezing turning to crying in her mouth.

The man in the woolly hat tapped his phone screen with a dirty thumbnail.

Ali wished the advert would change, and it began to roll upwards, about to be replaced by the next picture on the roll. The scrolling mechanism stuck, so the model's thighs hung above a picture of a burger, lurid ketchup running over the edge of the bun.

Ali stood just inside the shelter, making a thousand small judgements about the safety of the man and whether she was better to keep moving. Only then, she looked behind her. There was no sign of the green hood. She wanted to stay near her new protector but the awkwardness paralysed her. She rummaged in her bag, her pulse thumping in her temple.

The man looked up from his phone and paused, wondering whether to make contact. 'Are you OK?' he said finally, angling his body out towards the road, looking to the right as though scanning for a bus.

She nodded, still looking in her bag, driving her top teeth into her lower lip. 'Uh huh.'

He pulled a packet of tissues from his pocket and passed her one, careful to stay at arm's length. She could feel his caution.

'Thanks.' Her whole body shook as she took it. It smelled faintly of tobacco. Maybe he kept it in the same pocket.

She wiped her eyes and thought about her dad and the smell of the pipes he used to smoke when she was small. She wanted to see his estate car pulling up to the kerb, the passenger door opening. She was never going to see him again.

The man with the tissues returned to his phone, looking up once or twice but never directly at her. She wished she could throw her arms around his neck and cry into his high-visibility shoulder.

They didn't say anything else to each other. When the bus came, he stood aside to let her board before him. Inside the empty bus, he watched her turn left up the stairs and took a seat on the lower deck.

The bus meandered along the quiet streets, waiting occasionally at empty stops, keeping to the timetable. By the time it dropped her in Trafalgar Square, the sky was starting to brighten.

She walked along the wet pavement feeling like she was made of concrete, puddle water splashing her ankles, until she reached her building. The door lock clunked as she bumped her bag against the entry panel, her Zone Digital ID card in the outside pocket. Once inside, she felt jelly replace her leg bones and sat in one of the colourful visitors' chairs by the window. It was deserted as usual, but the lobby smelled of bleach. The cleaners had already been. She was late.

Inside the lift, she pressed 'five', leaned her back on the railing and shut her eyes, remembering Ed stood on the same spot, winking at her. The doors closed and then opened again.

She raised an eyelid to see Kat stepping in and hitting the button for the fifth floor. 'Just in, are you?' She stood against the adjacent wall, smelling of a dense perfume.

'Morning.' The tiredness drenched every part of Ali. She knew she looked like shit and waited for Kat to notice.

Clearing her throat, she nodded and pulled down her sunglasses to get a proper look at Ali. 'Late night?'

Ali faked a laugh. 'Too old for this shit.' She was nodding like a dog on a dashboard, wanting this to be over. From somewhere above them, metal scraped and groaned. The lift stopped.

'No no no no no no no.' Ali was instantly at the panel of buttons, looking for the emergency bell.

Kat seemed unbothered. 'There won't be anyone at the desk yet. Call Mike.' Her lack of panic made Ali uneasy, her own angst now all the more conspicuous.

'Worst comes to worst, Kwame can cover. He'll be thrilled. They don't let him broadcast in daylight.'

Ali tried to steady the panic in her voice as she left Mike a voicemail. Kat sat on the floor, legs in skinny jeans out in front of her, and brought out her tobacco tin.

Ali hung up and stared intently at her phone. There was nowhere to look in a small box made of mirrors. She was exhausted and filled with lead. The need to collapse and give in to everything took her over. She thought of the man with the tissues and slid down the wall opposite Kat. She sat, head in hands, and cried, embarrassing the air with her noise.

Kat's hand reached over, offering a thin, brown roll-up.

Ali shook her head, too ashamed to look up. 'No thanks.' She gulped and tried to breath in something that wasn't snot. 'Sorry.' The tears came again.

'Can you see a smoke detector?' Kat leaned back and lit the roll-up. She put her sunglasses on her head and looked at Ali. 'Talk about it. If it helps. We're not going anywhere.' She inhaled and watched the trail of smoke as she blew it back out.

Ali felt like she was made of smoke. She let the limpness wash over her like all of her cells were giving up, one after another, in a Mexican wave. She knew everything was going to pour out of her and she didn't care.

'A guy just wanked at me at a bus stop.'

'Just now? Did you get a look at him?' She jabbed her cigarette at the air. 'You've got to report it. Seriously. That's a slippery slope.'

'After the show. I will.' The sneer of his lip stayed in her mind's eye. 'Are you OK?' Kat took another drag. 'I don't just mean today.'

Ali didn't know what to make of Kat's interest in her. Maybe she was bored and looking for gossip to pass the time.

Kat sucked again on the roll-up and spoke as she exhaled. 'I do notice things. The bags under your eyes. The hangovers.' She ignored Ali's eyebrows raising at mention of her drinking. 'You look like you're not sleeping. Or eating. Is this your dad?'

Ali didn't want to go through it all again, to see how pathetic she was in someone else's eyes. But the gates were already open.

'No. Maybe.' She took a breath and looked at Kat to avoid looking at her own reflection. 'There was a man.'

'The lawyer?'

Ali's eyes bulged. 'How did you know about him?'

'Oh, babe, everyone knows about him.'

Ali couldn't take it in. She was the office invisible. Had they been talking about her?

'He's gone back to his wife?'

Ali let out a laugh. He seemed like such a long time ago. She breathed in, letting some of Kat's smoke in. 'Actually, can I have one?'

Kat started to roll another.

'This is a different one; a comedian.'

Kat rolled her eyes but didn't make any judgemental noises or jokes about revolving doors. 'They're as bad as musicians. I could have told you that.'

'He was so… interested in everything I said.' Ali wanted to feel every particle of stupidity in her, falling for charm and smoke and mirrors. 'He wouldn't leave me alone and I didn't want him to. And then it turns out this is his full-time job: making women love him so he can get them to do whatever he wants.'

Kat was listening now.

'He made me feel so good about myself. And none of it was real. I'm literally one of those magazine stories in the supermarket, holding a photograph of the fucking boat hire guy who took my savings.'

Ali looked at Kat, expecting to see pity or incomprehension. But Kat was nodding.

The older woman passed across the new cigarette with the lighter, warming to her theme. 'And you feel like he sucked the life out of you and left you with nothing. Every time you saw him, you'd be high as a kite and then have a headache for days afterwards.' She pinched the end of her cigarette and dropped it into the tin. 'They go all in at first, like they'd die for you. Then cold and unreachable once they've got you. And you try harder and harder to please them and they let you, watch you squirm. And it annoys them, how hard you're trying. Disgusts them.'

Ali breathed in the first smoke from her cigarette and imagined it flooding her lungs like a medical diagram.

Kat sat back. 'That's a narcissist.'

'A narcissist?' Ali pictured Ed peering at his reflection in a pond, combing his hair, rolling a hand over his belly. 'Aren't they supposed to be beautiful?'

Kat cleared her throat. 'No. They don't love themselves. If anything, the opposite. They dump all of their self-loathing onto you. Into you. It's like being poisoned. But it tastes amazing, so you keep going back for more.'

Ali straightened her spine against the wall, clenching her stomach muscles. 'I don't understand. Why?'

'Show me a man with a queue of women, waiting their turn and I'll show you a narc. My ex-husband was one. Mack.' She looked to her left, checking her eyebrows in the mirror.

'You were married? I didn't know that.' Ali was looking at her as if for the first time, imagining her in a white dress on a beach, hair blowing in the wind.

'Five years. And another five back and forth. It was like getting off smack.'

Ali crossed her legs, putting her bag on her lap. 'Was he beautiful?'

'No. He was short and thinning on top. But he was… the same thing they all are. Good at putting on an act. They only care about how they can get what they need from you. You're there for round-the-clock adoration and ego-massage and sex. Even though it'll never be enough.'

'Enough to what?'

'To drown out the truth. The person they really are underneath; bitter, needy, weak liars.'

'He cheated?'

'Aaaall the time.' She pre-empted Ali. 'And I stayed, for ten years.' She smiled weakly at the older woman. 'Jeez.'

'I've done all the therapy. If I knew then… You think about yourself. You know that you're a mix of good and bad things combined, right? They only see good and bad. Nothing in between. You're a good producer. You don't like yourself much, which is why you get overlooked here. Your eyes are beautiful. You can't dress for shit.'

Ali couldn't believe Kat had noticed anything about her. They sat in that studio morning after morning, Ali taking the shades and the body language as a Keep Out sign. She didn't know how to feel about this.

'First show we ever did together, you covered for me. I cocked up the links. I was a mess and you smoothed it over, convinced Otis I'd be fine.'

Ali thought about Otis's face when Kat's name was mentioned. She wondered if they'd had their lunch yet.

'And you take all manner of shit from Mike, I've watched you. From all of them. The way they speak to you sometimes, because they know they can.'

Ali blew upwards, making her hair flutter. 'Oh.'

Kat went on. 'Narcissists can't see themselves as a mix of good and bad. They don't have the software. They see brilliant or terrible. In themselves, in other people. They don't get that people are both,' she held out her palms, one high, one low. 'You're either beloved, angel, perfect or worthless trash. Nothing in-between. Because that's how they see themselves. Like a child.'

Ali had never heard Kat talk with this much actual content before. She was expert at filling the air with weightless prose, burbling manufactured warmth into the mic without ever actually saying

148

anything. She should do this on air, Ali thought, her brain starting work on a new show.

Kat looked at her, weighing up whether to get further into this now. Ali appeared to her like a kid learning the truth about Father Christmas. 'At the start, they take your breath away. Mack sent flowers every day. Filled hotel rooms with them. If you saw it in a film, you'd think it was romance. But it's demented.

Pathological. It's too much. In a week, he loved me, couldn't live without me.'

Ali eagerly swallowed the idea that Ed thought he loved her. Even for a minute.

'He wrote me songs. It was overwhelming.'

Ali thought of the sketch book and pencils lying on the kitchen table that arrived the day after the art class. A note to encourage her, telling her she had something special.

'Messages, all day every day. Such earnest interest you almost want to tell him to chill out, but of course you don't, because it's like sunbathing.'

Ali looked down at her lap, remembering the feeling.

Kat's phone chimed briefly then stopped. 'That's how it was for me. You know the giant National Lottery finger, pointing down from the clouds. It's YOU. He was in a band. He saw me coming a mile off. I dropped friends if he didn't like them, stayed home while he went on tour, not seeing anyone. I needed him for everything. I couldn't make myself happy without him.'

'But what do they want? Why can't they just let us love them?' Ali sucked a big breath in through her nostrils and released it slowly, feeling the panic starting to encroach in the closed space.

'Control. They're kids. We're toys. They need us to do what they want or we spoil their game. They're tired children who won't sleep. Mack would come home from a gig and be awake most of the night.'

Ali's stomach tumbled. 'Ed messages at odd hours. Not every night, but I can see when he's not sleeping. Liking posts on social media in the middle of the night, leaving messages for when I wake up.'

'And you probably felt guilty for missing them. And they warn you. "I'm a mess. Don't get mixed up with me." Because they know it's catnip. We think we'll save them. They make you feel they can only be themselves with you. But they aren't being themselves with anyone.'

Ali's face registered despair and Kat paused, not wanting to grind salt in the fresh cut.

'They construct this shiny personality to hide the snivelling mess underneath. Like I said, I did a lot of therapy.'

'And become comedians so they can spot easy targets in the crowd.'

'Don't be hard on yourself. They're the fuck-ups, not us.'

'So what am I?' Ali didn't want to know the answer. She suspected it was just gullible.

'He picked you because you have all the things he doesn't.'

Ali laughed. 'The squint from childhood? The way my thighs chafe in summer? My overdraft?'

The older woman shook her head. 'You can feel. You can love. He doesn't have the nerve endings.'

'Oh.' Ali wasn't convinced, but she hadn't expected that.

'Self-pity. They can feel that.' Kat took her sunglasses off the top of her head and replaced them in her hair.

'How did you find out about Mack?'

Somewhere above them, a cable tensed and the lift started moving upwards again. Ali wanted more time. If the lift doors opened, the spell might break and she really needed the counsel.

Kat looked up. 'He kept a notebook. A diary of everyone he'd slept with. I found it. Maybe he wanted me to. And you start to question why you're the one treading on eggshells. Your default is to watch what you say. Watch your tone. Anyway, I rumbled him because it turns out they're not very bright. I left, but I went back. More than once. He said he'd kill himself. Spoiler – he's not dead.'

Ali could see herself, drunk on her bed, messaging Ed to feel that surge of warmth again. What would she even say to him? Why did you lie? She wished she was stronger or that he was easier to resist. 'I want everyone to know who he really is. But also I don't, because then I'd be that woman, shouting about a bad man.'

Kat raised her eyebrows. 'Bad idea.'

'He's hurt so many women. What if I could stop him?'

'You want revenge.'

'If I told everyone what a monster he is...'

'What? He'd mend his ways? They'd all turn their backs on him? What's your end game?'

Ali rubbed her temples. She didn't have an answer.

'Dozens of Mack's friends know what he did to me. To all of us. It didn't change a thing for them.'

The lights on the panel reached the fourth floor, then the fifth.

Kat tucked her tobacco tin back into her bag. 'Play dead. For now.'

'For now?'

'Bide your time. He'd enjoy you crying and yelling as much as all the worship, trust me. Don't give him anything.'

They got themselves up off the floor, Kat more slowly. Ali reached out her hand and Kat took it, mugging as she got to her feet.

They regarded one another for a moment. As the doors slid back, an irate Mike was standing just beyond them, looking at his phone. He held open the glass door into the office, his headphones hanging around his neck. 'I've cued up some tracks and an ad break.'

Kat looked at him sourly. 'We've got time for coffee. Ali?''

'I'd love one.' They were smiling, which only enraged Mike further. 'Stick an extra track on. Ali's had a shock.'

'Take all the time you want, of course.' He muttered something else under his breath as he followed them in.

An urgent burst of synth music announced the 7 o'clock news bulletin and Ali pulled her headphone jack from the desk. Kat waved a hand when she started to clear up. 'Go on. I'll do it.'

Ali fast-walked to the bathroom and shut the cubicle door. She sat on the lid and looked at a sticker on the door asking that only toilet paper be flushed down the toilets. She read it to herself three times, feeling the panic ease. When it came, she mostly knew how to ride it out. She needed to be away from people, so they couldn't see her face. A locked cubicle was safety.

When she came back to her desk, Kat stood next to it, looking at her phone. She handed her the receiver from the phone by her keyboard. 'Call it in. I'll stay.'

Ali listened while the operator on the end of the line said they'd check the CCTV at the bus stop, maybe send a patrol. She wrote down a crime number on the back of an old script, thanked them and hung up.

Kat rubbed her back awkwardly, then stopped. 'I hope they find him and slice his wiener off. Hand it back to him if he likes holding it so much.'

Ali tried to find it funny but the image of his sneer stayed at the front of her brain any time she tried to picture anything.

She looked around to check no one could hear them. 'What am I going to do about Ed? I just talked Otis into giving him weekends.'

'So it's the guy you're leaving me for?' Kat was smiling but a trace of hurt lurked under it. Otis had taken her for lunch then.

Ali went to say something but Kat continued. 'You can't go steaming in, saying he's a wrong 'un. Legally that puts you on the sticky end. If you start throwing around accusations, stop Otis employing him, he could sue you. Wait here.' Kat returned with a piece of paper. 'Tell him it's off the record – use those words - but get his advice. Say I sent you.'

Ali looked at the scribble. 'Lloyd Appleyard?' The email address was from a newspaper Ali recognised. Not one her dad would have read.

'You don't have to do a kiss and tell, it's not the nineties. But there are other ways of hurting them. What's-his-name will be waiting for you to make your next move.'

Ali furrowed her brow. 'He doesn't know I know. Someone else told me.' 'You haven't been in touch with him?'

Ali shook her head.

'That's good,' Kat thought, eyes roaming Ali's desk as though for answers. She slid the journalist's email towards her. 'Put that somewhere safe.'

'I'm not selling a story on him. There's no way I'm going to be one of those women.'

Kat made an 'Oh really' face and Ali felt bad.

'You've got ammo. What about the others?'

'What about them? I don't know them.'

'Don't tell me you haven't started stalking them on social media because you definitely have. They make us nuts. It's a self-fulfilling prophecy. Find the cast-offs. They'll be as angry as you.'

Ali thought about the pictures, the ones she'd posted, thirsty for attention, hoping he'd like them.

She looked at Kat. 'Thanks. For being nice. I don't think I've ever felt so stupid.'

'Not stupid. Naive. Live and learn, sweetheart.' She pronounced the last bit like she was in a gangster film. 'That look. The one you're sure is flirtation, they all have it. They're not suddenly disarmed by your beauty. They've just spotted another mark.'

Her mum was right. Everything Ali had ever felt was carved into her face. Ed could have spotted her through a brick wall.

An email from Monica arrived. Otis had been informed about the bus-stop incident. Ali could have compassionate leave and counselling on the company if she wanted it. They were all over pastoral care since a male sports reporter got suspended for inappropriate conduct the year before.

Kat diverted to Ali's desk on her way out. 'While you've got them where you want them, have that holiday. You go to the festival, don't you? Have my Edinburgh place if you want.'

A crackle of adrenalin shot along Ali's breast bone. 'Would that be OK?'

'Brandon was going to be there but he's staying in Berlin with the new girlfriend.'

'Brandon?'

'My son. He's a musician, like his useless dad.' She cast her eyes up to the ceiling tiles. 'I'll send you the code. It's a key safe. Go. It'll only be empty.'

She knew she couldn't afford a hotel in Edinburgh in August but the gratitude wouldn't assemble into any useful sentence. 'Thanks.'

'Not another word.' Kat patted the skin under her eyes' looking into the black of Ali's monitor' and headed to the lifts.

Ali thought about asking her for a drink some time. She wondered if Kat drank socially, or just on her own. The moment passed.

Sixteen

Ali looked at the email she'd just written and saved it as a draft. She imagined Lloyd Appleyard in a dimly lit newsroom, suit jacket on the back of his chair, nicotine fingers, poring over its contents, an ashtray overflowing on the desk.

The idea of telling a stranger what Ed had done made her feel sick. The idea of losing her job made her feel sicker.

If she sent the email, Sid would never forgive her and she would be 40, single and unemployed.

Her laptop lay open on the bed, browser tabs fanned across the screen, one for every name she could remember from Sid's unburdening. One for Summer, another for Sid (although she didn't really post much), another for the dead girl. One for her friend's Twitter post about Ed being a bastard. A woman in Derbyshire who looked almost old enough to be his mum. Another in Birmingham who seemed to be in a relationship with a woman.

Everything was blurring now, like a shopping list in a puddle. She couldn't remember distinct details from their conversation in the bar or after at the flat. Just a sense of rubble and exposed wires, smoke clearing after an explosion.

The warm pulse of hope she felt every time she thought of his name appearing on her phone screen was lifeless. She planned to fill the void with this. She needed an evidence wall with photos of the women, string wound around pins in maps. No crimes, but so many victims.

She scrolled through grids of pictures of people she didn't know, unable to stop. She tried to remember scraps of new information Sid had given her, knowing she'd be more reluctant to talk again now, struggling to keep information from slipping through the holes in her memory. She saw it in Sid's eyes on the street outside. The regret of burning Ed's house down, knowing it was her house too.

Ali thought of Jackie Kennedy trying to scoop JFK's brains off the back of the Lincoln Continental and return them to his blown skull. Such an honest reaction to shock. That instant impulse to put everything back as it had been.

She clicked on Summer's tab and scanned her photos for interactions. Ed had liked some of them, but nothing in the last few weeks. Was he getting bored with her, like Sid had said?

She guessed Summer was in her thirties but it was hard to tell from a picture. Her eye make-up was dark and framed by jet-black brows.

She'd just posted a new photo of a tattoo on her hand, Medusa with one of the snakes slithering down her finger. She was online.

Ali began to type.

Hi Summer.

She deleted the 'Hi'.

Summer,
We don't know each other but I think we have a mutual friend. Well, two. This is difficult to get into over messenger but I think you've possibly had the same experience as me. With our mutual friend. And I would really like to talk to you about it.

Hard not to sound like a bad spy novel without going into specifics. But if you know what I'm on about and you do want to talk, please get in touch.

I think women should talk. All the best,

She deleted 'All the best'.

Ali x

She deleted the kiss and pressed 'Send'.

For a while she read and reread the message, hating every syllable a little more each time. What was she doing? What would she actually say to her if she did reply?

She fell asleep next to her keyboard and woke again an hour later, greasy from a bad dream. Her subconscious had dressed her in a long, white nightgown, candlestick in hand, running through an endless attic, trying to set light to un- burnable curtains. Every time they caught, a window would open and a breeze would blow out the flames. She couldn't see him, but she knew Ed was behind one of the doors. She didn't know what she'd say to him if she found him. How she'd explain all the little fires.

She pulled herself upright and tapped the space bar but the power had died while she slept.

She lay flat again for a few minutes, thinking about looking for the cable. When she finally brought the screen back to life, she lay still next to it, gathering herself. It had been a gargantuan effort, hanging over the edge of the bed with her eyes shut, feeling for the plug on the floor.

Sitting up again, she could see a message waiting.

Hi,
I don't know what this is about. Don't mean to sound rude but what is it you want to talk about?
Summer

She felt idiotic but she could taste hope in her reply. She wouldn't have replied at all if she hadn't been a bit curious. Ali had to compose the next message with care or risk scaring her off for good.

Hi again,

No, I'm sorry. That'll teach me to be all cloak and dagger.

I think we have been involved with the same man. I'm sure we have and I think, if you feel like you could, we should talk about it because he's not at all who I thought he was and now something serious has happened.

Are you on the same page with this? Maybe you're not and this will make no sense or you already know all about him and I'm coming across like a nutter.

No worries if not, but I think we have a lot to talk about.

Ali x

The kiss was too emphatic but she left it this time. She read it back. It still sounded like a freely associating child who struggled with basic sentences.

Maybe Summer would find it charming and her heart would go out to Ali. She'd embrace the guileless vulnerability and the two of them would swap messages, comparing notes and saying supportive things to each other about how they both deserved better.

I don't want to continue with this.

Ali clicked on Summer's profile picture at the top of the message and the screen filled with white where the pictures had been.

She'd blocked her.

Seventeen

When Ali woke again it was getting dark. She lay on her back and felt the ache in her empty stomach, stretching the fabric of her pyjama trousers over it, enjoying its alien flatness. She hadn't eaten properly for days and she wasn't hungry now. She wondered how long she could stay this way, just existing.

The memory of Summer barged in on the stillness and she sat up. Her mouth tasted bad and her neck hurt. She pulled the window up and felt the breeze on her closed eyelids.

Looking in the bathroom mirror at the grey fish skin under her eyes and the redness of her nose, she looked 40. She imagined Ed looking at the picture of her naked breasts. She'd taken it in the same spot with just a candle lit next to the sink. She'd tried it with the light on but it was too harsh.

The thought occurred that Summer would tell Ed about the strange, desperate woman contacting her. Then he'd know. She didn't want him to know.

She wanted to contact Summer some other way and beg her not to say anything. She was poisoned by the realisation that she didn't know who he was any more, or what he was capable of. And he had her picture. He was carrying it around in his pocket.

She stood in front of the open fridge, thinking about what the few things inside would feel like in her mouth. She didn't want any of them and began to feel a sense of control returning.

Sitting at the kitchen table, staring at her phone, she flinched as a message arrived. She'd turned notification sounds back on as Ed's contact became less frequent.

It was him.

Eighteen

As the last stragglers took their seats, Ed put his earbuds in and closed his eyes, hoping the two seats next to him stayed empty. He wasn't usually anxious on planes but he needed to block out the world and retreat. Being "on" exhausted him more the older he got.

Ireland had worked out the best it could, but he clenched his fist when he thought about the inconvenience that girl had put him to. She was trying to fuck everything up, dragging his name through the mud. Still, the story in tomorrow's paper would heal it all over like an old graze. It was a memory. He needed to look to the future. Michelle had suggested he go all out and offer to be one of the pallbearers. It would have made for better pictures, but all those hours with sobbing relatives, making small talk over sausage rolls. No thanks.

He went over the story again in his mind in case some journalist came digging for extra dirt. This kind of thing always stirred the pond. Deirdre was a fan who'd become obsessed. He'd just wanted to help her and her little girl, but he didn't know she was going to use the money for something like this.

When he deleted his side of their conversations it did look remarkably like a crazed fan trying to get his attention with nude photos.

Deirdre had been a good girl and deleted all the pictures and videos he'd sent her of his dick. 'It's probably better to get rid,' he'd said, knowing that would be all it would take for her to obey.

Everyone knew what the groupies were like. How they offered themselves to him in a way that turned his stomach. Sometimes, they'd just offer him sex, like they were showing him a menu. And he'd look at them, waiting for them to realise how unappealing they seemed to him. He liked to watch them crumple, their confidence evaporating. How dare they think he wasn't discerning, just because he was fat.

The story in the paper wasn't a lie exactly. Michelle put them off by threatening to deny them access to Justin Kennedy. They'd agreed to a deal.

Ed promised Michelle he'd stop drinking for a while. It clouded his judgement and made him overly generous, which he could see was a problem.

A member of the cabin crew drew level with his row and dipped her head inquiringly. He looked up, waiting.

'Anything to drink?' The stewardess hadn't recognised him, which annoyed him. He took out one earbud and looked at the trolley. 'Why not? A couple of those.' He pointed to some whisky miniatures and she passed them along with a plastic glass of ice and a white smile.

He liked her neat, red lips and imagined them around his cock, her eyes turned upwards, begging, the lipstick smearing. Best not flirt. Someone on the plane might join the dots when the story came out about the dead girl. He offered her his warmest expression of silent thanks and plugged back into the sound of himself, talking animatedly to a young female comedian on her podcast.

Naomi had begged until he agreed to do an episode. She laughed too much at his jokes or when he put on a funny voice. Their chatter was intimate, pauses suffused with unspoken tension. He'd gone over to her place and she'd set up two microphones on the coffee table in front of her sofa. They'd sat close together, not touching. He could have turned and kissed her at any point. She was desperate for him to.

He opened his emails and tapped out a message.

Listening to the pod. God, we sound like we're in bed. x

Bored, he switched to messenger and tapped the conversation labelled 'Lauder'.

She would flush at the arrival of his message, the three little dots underneath it, leaping into life as she rushed to respond.

Taking off soon, coming home. I missed you. What are you doing? x

Nineteen

Ali looked into the toilet bowl and tried to retch, but nothing came up. She stayed, crouching on the bathmat for a while, thinking of the words in the green bubble on her screen.

She spat, reached for the flush and sat back on her feet.

The first feeling that came was wanting him. Not disgust, not anger. Like her mind wasn't her own. She knew she was going to reply before she'd pulled herself up on the edge of the bath and wiped her mouth.

She reached for her phone and made a call.

'Sid can't come to the phone. Leave Sid a message.'

Ali hung up and sat on the loo seat to type.

Can you call me? Please. x

She looked up at the extractor fan whirring weakly overhead, little grey wads of fluff glued to the grill covering it, wishing it would draw her up into the ether.

She started to type another message to a number she'd never used outside work.

Sorry if this is weird. But can I ask, when you went back, why did you? Ali x

She pressed 'Send' before she could overthink it. Kat's reply came straight back.

I went back because I didn't know how to be without him. I didn't know myself. I only knew myself with him. You ok?

Her hands shook as she replied.

Cold turkey. I'm getting the itch. Sorry, you're not my sponsor.
What does he know? If it's nothing, keep it that way.
He thinks everything is normal. He 'misses' me.
Good. Think tonight, reply tomorrow. OK. x
Get some rest, kiddo. x

Another message arrived.

I asked you not to contact her. She's having a fucking meltdown.
I'm dealing with it.

Sid's tone was uncharacteristically forthright. Ali's mind ran wild with thoughts of a tear-stained goth threatening to throw herself off the Liver Building.

I'm so sorry. It's mad that we're not all talking to each other, though. Is she OK?
I've explained. I think so. It's just a shock, actually having it spelled out. I'm calming her down.
Please tell her I'm sorry. I didn't mean to freak her out. Good that you two are talking. x

She was desperate to know what they were saying. She couldn't sit down. If this girl would talk to Sid, maybe she'd talk to her.

She opened the browser on her phone to distract herself. Scrolling through her saved videos, the first thing that caught her eye was a clip of *All Night Garage*. There he was, in a blue checked shirt, seatbelt stretched across his middle, laughing generously at something another comedian was saying, slapping his knee.

She stared at his features, looking for signs of the real Ed under the joviality. All she could see was him, smell the whisky breath, feel the arms around her.

With every ounce of resolve she had, she held down the power button on her phone, like a pillow over a desperately importuning face, until the screen went black.

She threw the phone, ceremonially, into the laundry basket by her desk. And it went right in.

Twenty

When she looked at herself in the bathroom mirror at work the next day, there were cheekbones hinting behind her usually rounded flesh.

Another coffee would replace breakfast, but it would also bring back the sick feeling in the pit of her stomach. She looked through the drawer in the strip-lit kitchen and made mint tea.

Sitting at her desk, playing and replaying a potential face-off with Ed, Ali became aware of someone approaching her chair. She knew who it was without lifting her head. She recognised the aftershave.

Mark was furtive, like the paps were behind him. 'You OK? I'm back for a couple of days.' He looked around the office, trying to keep it casual.

She had no idea what to say to him. 'Yeah. You?' Ali wanted him to go away. The knowledge they'd been the subject of office gossip made her wish she could teleport out of there.

Mark looked tired and, unusually, clean shaven. Gemma didn't like his stubble.

'Fine. Better. We're going to counselling. I'm relieved in a way.' He trailed off. 'I just saw this and thought, if you hadn't seen it…' He put a newspaper in front of her, folded open at a story.

There was a grainy picture of a man holding a jacket, standing on a doorstep next to the headline. 'TV funny man pays respects at tragic ex's funeral.'

She tried to keep a blank expression as she recognised Ed. She nodded as though all was as it should be.

Mark waited a couple of beats. 'I've been drawing up his contract for weekends. Might be worth checking out, though. It sounds a bit suss.' He waited for something but didn't seem to get it. 'I know you were with him that night, Ali.'

She stiffened. 'What night?' The irony of the married guy suspecting her of sneaking around made her want to laugh out loud but she sat on it.

'Whatever. It doesn't matter now. Just thought if you hadn't seen…'

She looked back at her screen, feigning indifference. 'He's been to a funeral. Not exactly news. We talk about work.' She left the tabloid where it was and pretended to check over an email. 'I had you down as a *Daily Express* man.'

His laugh was humourless. 'Well, it sounds like you've certainly made friends.' He sounded sad rather than sneery. 'We're OK, aren't we? I'm sorry, about everything. Not my finest hour.' He was still looking for something, a crack in her resolve.

'Of course.' She gave him a bigger smile, designed to infuriate. 'No hard feelings. I really hope it works out with… everything.' She couldn't say his wife's name without recalling the look in her eyes.

His hand squeezed her shoulder quickly and he was gone. He'd only come to check that she was devastated, maybe throw a little salt on top with the article. Mark was a prick.

She kept looking at her screen until she was sure the lift doors had shut behind him.

She read the story properly now, feeling the bile return. Ed looked unusually smart, his hair swept over to one side. She desperately wanted to hoover up every word in front of her. Could anyone see what she was doing?

Allowing herself a few seconds to scan the page, she could see there was another picture in the bottom corner: Ed grinning from the passenger seat on *All Night Garage*. In a small box-out was the picture from Deirdre's Instagram with the toddler's face pixellated out. It was horrible, seeing them next to each other; Deirdre and Ed. Ed and Deirdre.

Her eyes skipped along the lines of the story, looking for subtext. 'The two dated for a short time after the TV star's split from his wife.' He paid for white lilies to go on top of the coffin, her mother was quoted as saying. 'It would have meant a lot to her,' added Bronagh (45) from Dundalk.

Ali hated the dead girl for being so special. She would always be perfect now.

There was no quote from Ed and the pictures looked like they'd been taken from a distance. He was looking down at his phone. In another, looking up the road, she could detect a slight redness around his eyes. She felt jealous of the corpse. Ali wondered if he'd be devastated if she died.

At midday, she came out through the revolving doors with the newspaper folded in her bag. She lit a cigarette. It tasted disgusting. She took one more drag and dropped it on the ground, squashing it under her boot.

Turning, she almost walked into a bike courier coming out of the revolving doors. For a moment she saw the sneering lip and sallow cheeks and thought it was the wanker. She shook like an earthquake as she walked towards the bus stop.

Then she changed her mind. Home was the last place she wanted to be, vibrating with energy and overcome with the urge to email Lloyd Appleyard, telling him everything she knew about the man from the TV.

She walked towards the park. Lunchtime office workers dotted the grass, eating salad from cardboard tubs, sitting on spread-out jackets. The sun made her forearms tingle. She sat under a tree, escaping the heat and looked around the green expanse fringed by oaks and plane trees. She breathed in as though in the countryside or by the sea, hoping the outside air would bring her to the present again. The grass underneath her was parched and spiky, poking her skin.

She pictured Ed in a suit, following the coffin into the church, brushing away tears. No, he wouldn't cry, but it would all be in his eyes. The grief-stricken boyfriend. 'It was complicated,' he'd say at the wake. 'But she meant a lot to me.'

She felt like crying again and closed her eyes, leaning back on the trunk behind her. She felt like a psycho and thought about buying wine.

She searched Twitter, looking for Deirdre's friend and the tweet where she called him a bastard but she couldn't find it. She hadn't posted for a few days, not even after her friend's funeral. Why wasn't she saying anything?

Ali made a call. When Sid answered, she sounded awkward.

'Hey, I just wondered if you had some time today. I could come to you? At the flat?' Ali knew how to bulldoze her.

'Yep, mm hmm.' A pause. 'Yes, OK, sure.' Sid sounded like she was having a different conversation.

'So, what time today? Is he there?'

'Haha, yeah. OK, I'll give you a call. No, I'll let you know. Bye.' The line went dead.

Ali looked around at the other people on the grass, eating sandwiches, staring at their phones.

Ed was back and Sid was acting like everything was the same. But she'd played along with the phone call.

Ali trembled at the idea he'd been standing a few feet away. She looked up the funeral story on her phone and a couple of other papers had picked it up. But there were no new details as she scanned the text.

She felt like she was chasing Orson Welles down a moody sewer tunnel. Harry Lime was the most beautiful-looking thing she'd ever seen when she'd watched *The Third Man* in her teens. But the bit where Trevor Howard explains who Harry really is always spoiled it for her. When he tells Joseph Cotton how Harry diluted penicillin for the black market and that the sick children who took it died or went mad. She couldn't still fancy him after that. Except of course she could. And Mr Rochester and Jareth the Goblin King and Maxim de Winter. And Dracula.

Ali's phone beeped in her hand and a little burst of something warm and delicious swept through her, the chemicals still having their effect.

I've missed you. Can I see you? x

She hadn't replied to his last message. Maybe he thought she'd have seen the story of his trip to Ireland by now and some explanation was needed. Did he see her number come up on Sid's phone?

She was in turmoil. It felt amazing. Her phone buzzed again.

You're precious to me, Lauder. x

She read the words to herself. No one was close enough to hear. He might've been a bot designed to churn out sentiment for lonely women. Isn't that how hypnotism worked? If you're described as 'a good candidate', it just means that you really, really wanted to be hypnotised.

She took out an apple and bit into it, thinking of people she'd seen on TV magic shows, hypnotised to eat an onion like it was a Granny Smith.

The apple would do for lunch. Her underwear, stretched by years of bloating and wine, was starting to hang loose on her. She'd ordered new pants and spent too long wondering if Ed would like them. She put the rest of the apple on the grass and put a hand on her stomach, feeling it ache.

She looked at his last message, still unread but hovering in preview. She paused in mid-air over it and then both thumbs tapped out a reply, like tiny fists against the glass.

Sorry for your loss.

As she pressed 'Send', another message interrupted her.

Sorry I blocked you. I've been trying to put this behind me and your message made it all raw again. I understand you were coming from a good place, but I've got a lot going on. If it's not presumptuous of me, get as far away from him as you can. Because everything he says is empty.
Summer

Ali tried to stay calm. To not say everything in one go. Summer was keeping her at arm's length, which was understandable, but she wasn't saying 'Go away.' Not entirely.

A reply wouldn't over-step the mark if she kept it short.

Sorry for the clumsy approach. I'm glad that you and Sid are talking. What he did to her made me so much more angry than what he was trying to do to me. A x

Another hour passed with messages going back and forth; Summer cautious and Ali letting her new pen pal set the tone.

They agreed that the way he'd treated Sid was the worst, making her watch, making her complicit, not able to tell anyone. They were more angry for each other than for themselves.

The messages continued for a while as though the two of them were making their way across from opposite sides of a minefield.

Summer said she was ashamed of the things she'd done. The things she could never take back. She just wanted to move on. She was trying to. This had opened everything up again.

Ali knew she meant the pictures and videos but she could only wonder at the specifics.

I'm sorry. That must feel horrible. Does he keep it all in one place?

Ali wondered if she'd pushed too far.

Just on his laptop. He's not that careful. He names the folders
dull things. Vat receipts. Invoices.

Ali imagined a warehouse, filing cabinets full of naked women.

I'm tired. Took a sleeping pill. Thanks for getting us talking. I
don't know that I feel comfortable talking to you about this yet.
Is that OK? Sorry.

Ali felt the implied chill in the air.

Absolutely. No need to apologise. If you do ever want to, I'm
here. x
OK. Closing thought. You never felt him go cold. Whatever you
do, don't get sucked back in.

She looked at Summer's pictures again, the usual mix of cheerful
social groups and selfies taken from a high angle. Ali liked her face.
She could see something of herself underneath the dark eyes and
heavy fringe. The same uncertainty behind the smile.

She wondered if Ed had played the same game with Summer,
making her wait. She had so many questions, maybe so she could
torture herself with the answers.

She thought about what Kat had said about him watching her
squirm. All of those times Ali thought she was hiding it well, how
much she wanted him. But he could see it.

It wasn't her decision to want him at all, even though she still
blamed herself. But she was also starting to blame him.

Ed wasn't giving up.

I want to tell you the truth. Can I do that? x

She had to reply now. She didn't want him to give up yet.

I don't know. Can you?

No kiss. She knew he was going to ask to meet and she knew
she wouldn't be able to say no.

Another green bubble.

Sat in a bar in Dublin yesterday, Elvis Costello song starts playing. Realised I was smiling like a fool. x

'Bastard,' she whispered, letting the waves of lust and revulsion break over her.

Twenty-One

Ali didn't know what she was doing. The flat was tidy. Smoothing the pale blue duvet cover, she looked at the results of her stress cleaning. The room looked weird and Ed would know something was off straight away. She kicked a few shoes back onto the rug, dropped a towel by the bed, punched a pillow and lit a cigarette.

She looked back at the last message Summer had sent her, making sure she had the details memorised.

Look for folder called VAT REC 18-19. In Documents.

She reasoned that she was 'gathering intel', to which Summer sent back an eye- roll emoji. She could tell they were both as curious as each other to see what he'd harvested from the other women. She'd never be able to wallow in the details like this with Sid, but Summer was actively egging her on.

She looked at the towel and the shoes and tidied them away again.

She dropped her phone on the bedside table and leaned over to lift the sash window.

Kneeling on the bed, she let the smoke coil from the end of the cigarette and out into the warm evening air. Inhaling, holding it in her mouth and blowing it out slowly, calm returning.

She thought about how she used to smoke when she was younger, little shallow puffs like a dragon in training. A girl called Nicola Cleaver in sixth form stood outside a nightclub on the high street, holding her cigarette by her cheek, big hoop earrings glinting in the streetlight. 'Don't you inhale?' Nicola demonstrated how she kept the smoke in, letting none escape from her maroon lips.

Leaning on the windowsill, blowing smoke into the branches of a silver birch, Ali tried to imagine what the evening would be like.

He never stayed long. Always on his way somewhere, carrying that bag on his shoulder. The laptop went everywhere with him. Even if she could get at his computer, she'd have to wait until he was out of the room. There was only one room in her flat. What if he didn't need the loo?

She needed a plan and remembered the trick with theme parks and salty chips. Didn't they add salt to make people buy more fizzy drinks? Did she have any laxatives? She could sprinkle something into his wine. Didn't they take hours to work?

She tried picturing Ed walking to the door on the street below, messing his hair and pushing the buzzer. The anticipation of the sound made her hands shake; her stomach skydived as she thought about reaching for the intercom to let him in. You have to invite them in, she thought, like vampires.

She distracted herself by watching a pigeon that had come to rest on a branch a few feet away, oblivious to her smoke. London pigeons were so unbothered by all the dirt and pollution, she thought. The pigeon's lungs probably looked like Nicola Cleaver's, two blackened sponges. Ali wondered if pigeons could cough. She imagined their insides turning darker and blacker until they were just feathers around soot.

She felt sorry for it, living in such a filthy place in a way she never felt sorry for herself, breathing the same air. Did it know there was a lush, green land without chimneys and cars if it just kept flying?

The pigeon glided down to the pavement and pecked at fried

chicken in a discarded box. Ali withdrew, not wanting to watch the cannibalism. Her hand stayed outside, a futile attempt to keep the cigarette fumes from sinking into the sheets.

The physical symptoms of wanting Ed were still close to the surface. With a bit of concentration, she could summon them: the churning inside, hot hands, presenting just the same as fear. Her body was either in mortal peril or it was looking forward to seeing him.

She wanted a scene, something from a film. Her hand flying towards his face, him grabbing her wrist in mid-air, pulling her to him. They'd end up on the bed, kissing. This had never happened to her in real life but she could imagine it happening with Ed, like he'd join her in the fantasy, acting it out, playing along.

The pigeon was back, a string of flesh hanging from its beak. She clapped sharply, sending it flapping. 'Gross.' Ash snowed onto the clean pillowcase as she shut the window.

When the intercom buzzed, Ali didn't feel anything. But she noticed she was unsteady as she got to her feet. She leaned her hip against the kitchen counter, staring at the handset on the wall. It buzzed again.

'Hey.' She was holding the receiver and talking into it, not remembering the journey there.

'Hello.' His reply was without energy. Before she'd have been desperately trying to read it for signs, pre-empting how to behave when he walked in. He didn't sound playful. Tired maybe.

Her face would give her away. What was she doing? She wouldn't risk the laptop. The reality of it was terrifying to her now.

She pressed the key button and left her door ajar. Then she went to the kitchen and stood looking in an open cupboard dumbly, wondering what she should be doing when he arrived.

She felt the plastic pen drive in her dress pocket and shoved it in the fruit bowl on the side, under the apples. Why hadn't she thrown it in a drawer? There were three drawers just under the counter.

The latch clunked as he came into the hall, feet trudged up the stairs, his steps slowing and his breathing getting laboured as he neared the top. She was frozen, too afraid to move the small plastic block now.

He'd complained before about the lack of a lift. She'd been embarrassed to make him climb up two flights of stairs, sorry for the trouble she'd put him to. Now she could hear why it bothered him. He was heaving and panting like a dog.

She took a wine bottle from the fridge and drank from it, taking a second to gather herself. If he was two people, she just had to pretend not to know about the other Ed until she'd worked out what to do.

As she closed the fridge, a knuckle rapped on her door, pushing it open. 'Anyone home?'

She lost control of her face and he greeted whatever it was doing with a frown.

'I'll go, shall I?' He smiled, then stopped, waiting for her invitation.

She let out a kind of snort, shaking her head and standing aside to let him pass.

He handed her a bag. 'Open it.'

A bottle of wine was wrapped in paper from the wine merchant near the tube. Most of their bottles were over 20 quid. He was showing off. She made a noise as though impressed he'd pushed the boat out and he seemed satisfied.

He looked shorter somehow. And wider. As he turned and headed for the bed, she could see extra flesh gathering above his waistband, rounding out his back, a grey t-shirt she recognised more stretched over his trunk than before.

He unloaded his shoulder bag; a khaki canvas thing that could have been carried by a soldier in a war.

She screwed the metal spike into the wine's cork, trying not to look too closely at the contents of the satchel as he took things out and laid them on the bed.

He looked at her and she looked at him and, as though pre-empting her, he spoke. 'Pour us some of that, then we can talk.'

She remembered she was supposed to be pissed off with him. She was making it too easy.

Her phone whistled on the bedside table. Her stomach jumped and she stayed where she was, working the cork out of the bottle. It would be a message from Summer, wanting to know if he was there yet, wanting details.

Ed held it out to her without looking. His Mac Book was open and he was absorbed in something on his own screen.

She handed him a wine glass, took the phone and walked around the bed to sit on the other side, legs still shaking.

Is he there?

Had he seen the name on her lock screen? She felt like she was leaving her body, watching herself in a film.

'I need to ask you something.' She sat on the opposite side of the bed, wine in hand. She tried to look assertive, knowing her character would want to know what his character had been up to.

He raised his head from his emails. 'There's something I want to talk to you about too. You saw the paper?' He waited, gauging what she knew.

She took a drink, feeling in control of herself again, nodding once, smoothing her hair. He was going to lie and she was going to believe him.

'You never mentioned her. The girl in Ireland.' Ali pretended not to have her name immediately to hand, even though it was scratched into her brain like graffiti on a desk. Deirdre. Deirdre RIP. Deirdre with the dates after her name.

Ed looked contrite. Was there a hint of moisture at the corners of his eyes already?

She thought about Summer and what she'd said. 'He'll cry. He'll definitely cry.'

Ali had never been able to muster tears from the ether like that. She wondered what he thought about to make them come on cue. Another comedian getting a chat show?

Did he cry yet?

She checked again to ensure her phone wouldn't disturb them and put it face down.

'Hey,' she said, reaching out a hand and putting it on the bed between them. It was instantly awkward. She withdrew it and drank nervously. 'Talk about her if you want. I don't mind.'

He wiped at his eyes with a sleeve and took a drink. 'Of course. Because, well.' He gestured towards her, implying something admirable. He checked to see that he had her and went on. 'We saw each other a few times, when things with Maddie were bad. Her head was.' He gestured a little explosion next to his ear. 'I went to Dublin for a few weeks, for a show. She was just a nice kid. Persistent.'

He allowed himself a smile at the memory, then let it break carefully into a silent cry. He bowed his head.

Ali took it in: the total victimhood. It looked so real. His chins concertinaed, pushing his stubble out at angles, Velcro catching on itself. This terrible thing had happened to him.

Ali crawled across the bed, moving his laptop onto the pillows. She knelt up and held him, his head to her chest. 'It's OK.' He let her for a moment. It felt wild, being close to him again. Not arousing but like every cell in her body was on alert.

Her arms around him could hardly contain him. Where he'd once felt soft, he now seemed to her like a sausage bursting its skin, its contents too much.

Pulling himself upright, he gave her a brave little smile and looked out of the window, as though remembering something beautiful.

Ali sat back, making room for his important recollection.

'I should have told you, but it was over in a few weeks. Madeleine and I split. I told her, of course. You and I didn't know each other. And then by the time we did, I heard what happened to her. I'm still in shock, I think.' He blinked. 'And I didn't know how to…'

A tear broke free of his bottom lashes and rolled down to the stubble by his mouth, pooling there.

She was impressed. Maybe Michelle should put him up for more serious acting work. He had talent.

She picked up her wine and watched the red liquid cling to the inside of the glass, viscous and glossy. She remembered how she'd bought these glasses in a box of six from a department store on Oxford Street to impress him.

She drank some more and tried to picture Deirdre's tanned face, the older, paler man standing next to her, the same age as her dad, an arm around her waist.

She told him he shouldn't blame himself and changed the subject. She asked him about Edinburgh. How his previews had gone the week before, working hard to make everything normal and pleasant, realising she hadn't noticed the effort of this before. He worried about the technical aspects, didn't trust the venue to get it right. Sid would be there to keep an eye on it.

Ali soothed his doubts and laughed at his jokes and it was like everything was how it should be.

She relaxed and drank her wine like she was at a show. The second glass was bigger. She thought about what it would be like to kiss him but her body didn't answer. No wild leaping of gazelles in her stomach.

He was looking at her, trying to work out where to go next. 'You're probably wondering what we had in common. Deirdre and me.'

Of course, he thought she was brooding on Deirdre. Or he wanted her to. She shrugged, leaking a little of the real jealousy she'd felt when she first heard her name.

'It's not what you're thinking. Maybe? She was an old soul. We joked about it. Her old lady name.' He feigned a nostalgic smile, tiring of this performance and thinking about jerking off to a porn clip he'd watched earlier, set in a funeral parlour.

Ali stayed still, looking at her wine. He was forced to work harder when she gave him nothing. It seemed to agitate him.

'I want you to know that that's not me. The guy you clearly

think I am. One in every town. Ali?' For a micro-second his eyes darted to his laptop, open on the pillow, then back to her. She had to give him something now or he might cut his losses.

'There was a girl on Twitter.' She looked into her wine.

He kept his gaze steady.

'She was angry, saying stuff about you. I think she was friends with…' She left a gap, wanting to see the name on his lips again. How easily he could enunciate it now she was in the ground.

'Deirdre?' He nodded, showing no sign of surprise she'd brought it up. 'Sid mentioned. Just looking for someone to vent at, I suppose. Who can blame her?'

Ali wasn't blaming her.

'It's senseless. I saw the family obviously; they're devastated. I did what I could for her mum.' He let that sit, his kindness, despite everything.

He looked so humble, so unassailably servile, putting his wine down as though he didn't deserve it. Another micro-glance at the laptop.

Ali wanted to keep him talking. Why wasn't he drinking? 'Hold on.' She went to the kitchen and came back with a bowl of crisps, putting it on the bed between them.

'Crisps for dinner.' She smiled and watched his fingers dip into the yellow pile. He was clearly going through one of his eating phases. All the excess made sense now. Drinking too much. Stopping drinking. Eating everything. Going on a diet. He didn't have another setting. Just on and off.

When she looked back, he was sucking salt from his fingers and reaching for more. 'No impulse control.' Kat said it was a narcissist thing and that with Mack his had been drugs and drink. In it goes, into the emptiness, not even touching the sides.

Maybe Deirdre's death had got to him. She hadn't seen Ed like this, feeding himself like a starving man.

She watched as the bowl emptied. 'I'll get more.'

He wiped his hands on his trousers. 'Back in a sec.' He was up and crossing the room. The bathroom door closed behind him.

Ali was alone. She put the glass down, splashing wine onto a book. The lid on the laptop was open. His confidence that she was back in harness not even a conscious thought to him. Why hadn't he tried to hide his inner life, all sitting there in emails and folders and internet search histories. Was it a test?

A loud, staccato fart punctured the silence and she waited for a moment, feeling hysterical. Nothing.

Her hands shook as she ran a finger over the track pad, looking for the finder, clicking through the little blue rectangles until she found Documents. She was wild with adrenalin. Tripping on a boot sticking out from under the bed, she stubbed her toe brutally, not making a sound. She sprang across the room to the fruit bowl and retrieved the pen drive.

Then she froze, listening for signs of life beyond the bathroom door. There was a clank as his weight shifted on the toilet seat. Then nothing. She looked back at the laptop open on the pillow. There was no time. As she got back to the bed, the faint sound of piss on the toilet bowl bought her seconds to scour the screen. She emptied more crisps into the bowl, careful to provide sound effects for what she should be doing in case he could hear her through the door.

Her fingers shook as she typed, 'vat rec 18' into the search bar and hit return. There it was, a blue folder, a list of other 'vat rec' files underneath, stretching beyond the bottom of the search window. She shuddered as she plugged in the pen drive and dragged the folder across.

A noise from the bathroom. The flush. A small rainbow beach ball spun in place on the screen. She thought about yanking away the USB stick, but something made her wait. She couldn't believe what she was doing.

After the flush, the noise of the water could cloak the sound of him finishing. She guessed he'd be looking at his phone, checking in with his admirers, but there was no way of knowing. She imagined this is how bungee jumping felt, just before you let go.

The squeak of the toilet-roll holder and a tear of paper. She heard a splash and felt disgust and relief simultaneously. She looked back to the progress bar as the last files transferred. It was taking too long.

The sound of weight shifting again, the loo-roll holder, a second flush. He was moving. She had as long as it took for hand washing, drying, checking his hair. How long was that?

There was no sound from the boiler. Why wasn't he washing his hands? She grabbed for the pen drive and shut the finder window.

The door opened and Ed stood there, lit by the bright bulb behind him. 'You look like you've seen a ghost.' He wasn't smiling.

'Sorry, for a minute there… doesn't matter.' She bent her startled expression into wistfulness, knowing what he'd read into it. That she wanted him. She tried not to think about his fingers touching shit.

He tilted his head and softened. 'Let's kill that bottle.' He came back to the bed via the wine, leaning forward to fill her glass. When she turned around to retrieve it from the bedside table, he checked the laptop and stole a look at her.

She watched him pour, mustering old flirtation from somewhere far inside. 'You're trying to get me drunk. Finally.' She pressed the hard, square end of the pen drive into her palm with clasped fingers, too scared to put it down.

He dipped back into the crisp bowl until they were all gone. She wanted to bleach the bowl.

Ed decided he'd give her a little more, then be on his way. He knew how to keep the fire glowing.

'Are you drunk? You don't seem it.' He sipped his wine and looked into her eyes, pushing beyond the flirting glister, deeper in. He wanted her to think of him penetrating her, pulling her hair.

She let herself flirt with the other Ed, had more wine and felt herself relaxing again as the adrenalin subsided. She could still play this part because somewhere deep down, she still wanted it to be true. She wanted to absorb all the generous looks and disarming flattery like a junkie with a favourite drug, even knowing it was killing her.

'Sorry I can't stay longer.' He looked longingly at the pillows next to them. 'I wish I could.' Back to her eyes again, making sure all that meaning landed squarely on its target.

She reddened and smiled. 'Don't.' She made sure it sounded like 'Do.'

'No no, I didn't mean "stay". You know what I mean. I just like being with you.'

Ali was nursing her wine, not wanting it to run out yet. The end of the bottle would be his signal to go, breaking the spell. If she offered him more, he'd say no. She still hated the idea of him saying no.

His phone chirruped in his pocket. 'Ah.' He read whatever it was, brow knitted like it might be important, then he reached for his glass, drained it and replaced it on the bedside table. He started to pack up his laptop and she pretended not to look.

'I know it seems silly, but maybe this is enough. We can do this, can't we? I'd hate to lose it. Our time together. You're good for me, Ali.'

She held his gaze. 'Like bran.'

He laughed but it was mirthless. He was on a different train of thought. 'Come here.' He stood and pulled his bag onto his shoulder.

She walked around the bed obediently, slotting into the gap left for her. His hug was too tight. Too much. Just how she liked it. She took one more second to feel the big arms closing around her.

He kissed her forehead and looked at her. 'So Edinburgh? Come to the show. I've sent you tickets.'

She nodded, smiling at him. 'Sure. I'd love to.' She was thinking about his fingers again.

He got to the door, turned and looked at her like she was food and he was starving. She raised her glass and drank with a similarly thirsty look and he was satisfied.

'Lauder.' He opened the door and turned back to look at her. 'I should have told you. I should have known.'

'What?'

'That I can tell you anything.'

Ali felt a smile creep over her lips. She looked down.

'Hey. Thank you.' His sincerity was turned all the way up to man-of-god.

'See ya.' She stood still and listened to his footsteps, followed by the clunk of the front door downstairs. She went to the window to watch him disappear, phone already in hand, texting as he walked.

When she was alone with the quiet again, she opened her hand and saw the metal edge of the pen drive had pushed into the base of her thumb, leaving a deep, red dent. It hurt.

Running a fingertip over the new scar, she picked up her phone. The words were sent before she had time to think.

I'll be in Edinburgh. I'm in. Who do I contact?

Bethan's reply came back a few minutes later.

DM the Scolds Twitter. Tell them I sent you. You'll get instructions. Welcome aboard. x

Twenty-Two

She and Summer spent the rest of the night messaging. Sometimes Ali thought they were competing again between the lines, unable to break the patterns they'd been in with him.

Summer released small parcels of enlightenment because it was late and she was drinking Jack and Coke. Ali responded in kind, saying something even more appalling about herself to defuse Summer's embarrassment.

Summer was starting to let her in. Ali liked that she was cautious one minute and then some completely ungoverned truth would just splutter out of her. It made Ali feel safe with her.

She told Ali that Ed liked to be naked. When they shared a hotel room, he'd move around, order room service, eat, never bothering to get dressed. They sent each other puke emojis. Ali told her about Ed not washing his hands and how he'd left skid marks in her toilet.

It was past midnight and Ali could hear sirens wailing in a nearby postcode as she looked down at her street, the shops shuttered and lights extinguished in the flats opposite. A fox padded down the middle of the road, not even bothering to use parked cars to shield himself. He stood under a streetlight, poised, his fur tinged green in the light. Ali watched him turn the corner onto the main road and disappear behind some bins.

She knew she wouldn't sleep until she'd seen what was on the drive, but how would she feel if a stranger had the same access to her, naked? Ed's wine glass was still on the bedside table.

Maybe just a peek to see if she had the right folder, then she'd decide what to do with it in the morning.

She put her laptop on the kitchen table, facing away from the window and moved the chair around so no one would be able to see her screen from outside. Her hands were sweaty. She felt like an old man in a dirty trench coat.

Once, when she'd first moved in, a bus had passed the window and some people on the top deck saw her coming out of the bathroom with a towel just around her waist. She'd kept the blinds closed since then, mortified by the exposure.

Even if she never saw any of those people again, they'd seen her. Sometimes she woke up thinking about the brief flicker of a smirk on one boy's face as he looked from the bus window.

She could remember her first time as a sex object like it was yesterday. Builders had started work on the land behind her parents' house. She had been suffering the self-consciousness of starting secondary school, being made to shower with the other girls all at different stages of puberty. Some of them had started wearing bras and using tampons with a confidence that terrified her. The apparatus of womanhood felt alien, like it didn't fit her. But that morning, she had got up and pulled her Betty Boop nightdress over her head. She had looked for a clean vest in the drawers by the window and heard a shout. Looking back at her was a man in a hard hat, 20 feet away. He was standing on a digger bucket, waving at his mate in the cab, telling him to raise it higher so he could get a better look.

She'd dropped down beneath the level of the windowsill, shame beating out a rhythm in her chest. The curtains were still open and she could hear the man laughing. She'd curled into a ball, hating herself and her body, crying as the innocence left her.

When she'd walked into the village after school to buy *Look-In*, she saw him. The man in his overalls and hard hat, crossing the road towards her. Her insides had frozen, but he didn't notice her in her school uniform.

That was the day she knew men would be looking, even at her. That they were thinking about bodies under clothes, working out the shape of you, x-raying you as you waited for the bus. Thinking about your holes and what they wanted to put in them. Everyone was checking everyone out and she could see it now, like someone had flicked a switch and revealed the real world to her.

Plugging the red plastic lozenge into its dock, Ali shivered. A grid of small thumbnails spread across the white finder window like the stained glass at Coventry Cathedral. The pictures were too small to see detail, but the palette of peach tones told her she had found what she was looking for.

She scrolled and stopped at a series of photos that turned out to be all of the same girl. Something heavy dragged in Ali's insides as she opened the first picture.

The same desperate plea in the eyes cloaked in manufactured lust, white lace underwear, mouth open as though about to accept a cigarette. One hand rested on her hip, the other holding out the phone towards the mirror. The bathroom mirror. Is that where they all went to act out their shame, because it had a lock on the door?

The girl had flat, blonde hair just past her shoulders, and freckles on her chest. The arm that held the phone up was covered in monochrome tattoos from shoulder to wrist. She looked flushed, like she'd just downed a drink or run from another room. But so much was the same as her own photo. Maybe this was her first one too, the one he casually mentions he'd love to see, but no, we mustn't.

Ali couldn't believe what she was seeing and also knew this was exactly what she'd find. She clicked through more pictures from the set, the same girl posed in front of white tiles. A wooden shelf on the wall behind her displayed three small cactus plants next to a lucky cat, waving its golden paw.

In a later picture, the girl pulled at her bra strap and bit her lip. Ali kept hitting the arrow to the right. The girl's expression changed and the angle did too. She leaned forward over the sink, dipping her cleavage and sticking her backside out. She must've used a timer. Her hands were on her bum, edged in matching lace. She looked into the camera like she wanted it to fear her.

In another, one hand plunged inside the cup of her bra, her eyes closed. Then there it was, the picture he would have waited impatiently for, pretending there was no pressure, not if she didn't want to.

The girl was naked from the waist up, one hand tangled in the back of her hair, the other trailing at her side. Her pose was bolder than Ali's, but she was younger. Maybe by ten years.

She checked the date. The pictures were from a year ago. Perhaps he was bored with her now or maybe she hated him, realising what she had given away and to whom. Maybe she found out he'd lied about it being only her he wanted.

She scrolled on, wondering what she was even looking for, needing to see more.

Had she copied the whole folder or was this just some of it? The screen was a palette of cream, pink and beige, a meat counter of different cuts, breasts and legs. She couldn't see any skin darker than that and wondered if he was a racist too.

The shape of the women's bodies stopped meaning anything as they flickered past, dark nipples on small flat breasts, hair sprouting from armpits, legs opening to show pink, glossy crevices, goose pimples where hair had been plucked, unwilling.

She couldn't stop. Piercings, tattoos, fat rolls, stubble, tender meat prickled with irritation. Stretch marks, loose skin draping, stomachs spilling over elastic, bones jutting from hips.

She stopped at a familiar face frozen, the cover image for a video. It was blurred but she could make out the same fair hair and 'fear me' expression. She clicked 'Play', now unable to stop, promising herself she wouldn't look at anything after this.

The darkness was broken by a sense of movement, then the camera swung to find the girl's face. She was looking up into the lens. As it pulled out, Ali could see she was kneeling on a cushion, red knees pressed into the dark fabric. Her underwear was white, as before. Muscles flexed in her thighs, holding her upright.

'Better?'

Ali's system flushed at the sound of Ed's voice on the video. The girl nodded. She looked cold or scared. It was hard to tell. 'Go on.'

The girl smiled up at the man holding the camera and reached behind her back to unhook her bra.

'Bite your lip.'

Ali closed the window. She wanted to see what he did to them, but she couldn't. It felt like taking something that didn't belong to her. Like standing in someone's bedroom in a ski mask and hearing them come home.

She dragged the folder across her desktop into her cloud storage and watched as the files synced. She ejected the drive and put it in a kitchen drawer, under the tea towels.

All of those faces, peering out, wanting him to want them, so nothing else mattered. She imagined him lying back, laptop balanced on his stomach, browsing.

Rows of shelves, jars filling every horizontal, in each jar a specimen bobs, eyes blinking. He walks to the shelf with a new jar and puts it with the others. Ali looks out at the room, trying to make out shapes through liquid. The lights go out. She feels her neck and finds sharp little flaps, gills.

Ali woke with a gasp at the kitchen table.

Twenty-Three

The breakfast show gang burst through the office doors, their laughter rupturing the quiet. The two hours between the end of their show and Ali's liberation from the office were the worst. Like being back at school while the popular kids loudly expressed an ease and confidence that made Ali want to evaporate.

She was miles away, unable to focus on the script she was supposed to be writing. She reached for her headphones and closed the browser she'd been staring at. Dozens of pictures of Ed Catchpole disappeared, replaced by tomorrow's running order.

She waited till the noisy interlopers were back at their desks, sank into her seat and opened the email from Lloyd Appleyard. Kat had been in touch with him and he hoped it was OK to drop her a line. No names had been mentioned and she was under no obligation.

He said he'd be interested in having a chat but that he completely understood her nervousness about talking. She thought of Sid and how angry she'd be. This stranger in an office block somewhere across London, knowing what had gone on in hotel rooms and flats and dressing rooms and parked cars.

He said Kat had kept it vague, described 'wrongdoing' and numerous victims.

He said that if she had any evidence, whether or not she decided to go ahead with a story – emails, messages, pictures – she should keep them somewhere safe for now. She thought of the pictures and videos of impossibly private moments that were never supposed to be seen by anyone else.

Lloyd finished by saying Ali could speak to a 'female colleague' if she didn't feel comfortable talking about something like this with a man.

She read that part again and tried to imagine what the female colleague would be like, but she saw the same dirty fingers and overflowing ashtray. She watched too many old films.

She imagined her words in print in the red-top Lloyd wrote for. The picture of the woman clutching the photo of the boat-hire guy who stole her life savings. She knew she'd never go through with it. But what if there was no picture? Lloyd cited a recent broadsheet story in which dozens of women accused a TV producer of drugging and assaulting them, pointing out that none of them had gone on record using their names. He could guarantee anonymity, he said.

If no one ever found out it was her, she could hurt him, embarrass him. Everyone would see the real him. The total humiliation of Ed was something she had started to imagine a lot since his visit.

She marked Lloyd's email as unread and picked up her phone. The message thread between her and Sid stopped a few days ago, the last few from Sid non- committal and short.

Ali didn't ask direct questions about Ed. But she fed on every scrap and detail Summer leaked, imagining herself in the situations Summer described; lying on the kitchen counter in underwear, tied to a bed in a hotel room. That was the worst feeling; her revulsion for him mixed with residual lust and the idea of not being able to get away. She thought about this one the most.

She picked up her phone and messaged Summer.

Time for a chat? Want to run something by you. x

The reply came back straight away.

Working this eve. Before 5? x

A few hours later, at home, Ali lay on the floor, the coffee table moved to one side, as the soothing voice of an Australian woman encouraged her to inhale and exhale slowly from a video playing on the TV.

She stretched her hands over her head and slowly brought herself up to a sitting position, her lower back tensing with pain. Her fingers reached towards her toes as she leaned forward but got nowhere near them.

The Australian woman on the video was folded flat like a wallet, nose touching her thighs.

Ali's phone warbled. She got herself up and propped the phone on the mantelpiece.

Summer's inky fringe filled the screen. She sat back and composed herself. 'I wasn't sure if you were calling me or I was calling you.'

'Hey.' Ali waved.

'Are you exercising?' Summer leaned back to get the draft from a fan on the table behind her. 'In this heat.'

'I've invented a new thing. Bikram Pilates.'

'And how is it?'

'Yeah. I think I'm going to puke. Good.'

There was an awkward pause as the short burst of laughter died out.

'So.' Summer blew her fringe and angled the fan towards the back of her neck.

'Yes, sorry. It's not a big thing. Just something I've been thinking about.' She weighed up how to proceed. 'I was talking to a friend at work. She knows about these things.'

'What things? This is an Ed thing?'

'Kind of. Anyway, I was talking to her – no names, obviously – but she said there was someone who might be able to give us advice. He's called Lloyd. He's been really helpful.'

Summer looked blank. Ali couldn't tell how this was coming across. She went on.

'He deals with these stories all the time and he says there's a way to do it without any of us being identified.'

Summer's eyes darkened. She wasn't blank any more.

'You've spoken to a journalist?'

'No. Well, yes. But I haven't done anything. We just talked, well, emailed. We haven't actually spoken yet.'

Summer swallowed. 'No. The answer is no.'

Ali put a hand up, trying to put the words back into Summer's mouth. 'I promise I wouldn't do anything to identify you. But if we got together...'

Summer butted in. 'Ed's got videos of me doing the worst things. Do you understand?' She started to cry. 'Stuff I never want anyone to see. Do you think he'll do nothing if we go to the papers? He can ruin my life if he wants to.'

'How can he without incriminating himself? Anyway, revenge porn is illegal. He wouldn't be that stupid. The point is...'

'You don't know what he'll do if he's got nothing to lose. It's all right for you.' She couldn't catch her breath between cries.

'Summer, I promise I won't do anything. There's no story. We just talked. I haven't given him anything. I was just angry. I can't believe we just sit here while he carries on as normal.'

Summer was shaking. 'I can't stop you. But I'm asking you. Please don't.'

The call ended.

Ali tried to call her back, but she didn't answer.

Twenty-Four

The train emerged from the dark of the tunnel into low, bright sunshine. Ali stared at her phone, waiting for a signal to return so she could send the email she'd just written.

She read the explanation again, making sure it sounded convincing: her anxiety had worsened since the incident at the bus stop. She'd need compassionate leave for a few days, until she could see a doctor. She copied in Otis and Kat.

In truth, Ali hadn't felt anything since the incident. She'd dreamed about the thin penis in his fist, a skinny sausage coming out of a machine. It kept coming, metres of it, coiling into a limp pile on the floor.

The train rumbled north out of London, tilting on bends, dropping the horizon to the bottom of the window and making Ali feel nauseous. She wanted to sleep but she was too full of purpose. She closed her eyes and listened to a podcast.

Bethan and the host, another woman, talked about creeps in the comedy industry. They were funny, recounting times they'd been alone with the wrong man in deserted green rooms, a hand on their leg in the passenger seat of a late-night lift home. The anger just beneath the jokes was thrilling. Bethan didn't say anything about Scold's Bridle.

It was getting dark when the train pulled into Liverpool. Ali knew she had crossed the line into obsession, but she didn't care any more. She had to talk to Summer.

She stood on the steps outside the station, looking out over the city, trying not to lose whatever energy had brought her this far. She needed a hotel. Then she'd find the club.

A tall, square building just down from the station had a familiar logo over its door. It was more than she could afford, but she put it on her credit card and went up to her room on the second floor. She wondered if this was where Mark stayed when he visited Zone Digital North.

It was a characterless box with a single green cushion in front of the white pillows and a matching fabric strip wrapped around the bottom of the duvet. The grey padded chair by the desk had a rip on one arm but otherwise there were no signs of previous habitation. That was a hotel's job, Ali thought. To make you forget that other people had pissed and fucked and picked their noses there just before you.

She had the same thought now, anticipating meeting another one of Ed's women face to face.

She wished she could tell Sid what she was doing. That she wasn't sitting back and taking shit from awful men any more and neither should she. She knew the truth was that Sid would think she was crazy. She felt crazy.

The street was still warm, despite the dark. A tepid wind licked at Ali's ankles as she turned right past the concrete cathedral. It looked dystopian; a vast grey crown balanced on top of a circus tent, lit theatrically, threatening to take off and return to its home planet.

The club was in the basement of an arts centre further along the street. At first it looked closed, the blacked-out glass along the ground floor concealing the interior. A wooden board propped outside said 'Live Comedy' with an arrow pointing down. When Ali opened the glass door, the sound of muffled music and voices broke the quiet of the warm night air.

She had thought the city would be busier, wanting that feeling of getting lost in something bigger than her. Perhaps there was another part of town where more people met to drink and eat and dance. In London, it seemed every inch of space in zone one was in constant use.

Ali tried to imagine the least alarming way to approach her. Summer had told her she worked at Fun Club Liverpool and Ali was pretty sure there was only one.

It felt like an idealistic gesture, boarding a train on a whim. The kind a guy would make in a romantic film and somehow the heroine would receive it with delight rather than horror.

Ali's feet were carrying her down the stairs, her brain still working on an opening line.

The other side of some double doors at the bottom of the stairs, a room bustled with talking and jazz music, a saxophone noodling and drums pounding out an irregular beat over speakers.

Summer was behind the bar. Her black t-shirt was branded with a large white Fun Club logo, tucked into a full skirt that seemed to start straight under her breasts. Her black fringe was perfectly straight, covering dark brows.

Ali thought how different they were. She liked that Summer wasn't thin. If she'd been thin, she would have been intimidated by her.

When Summer saw her, she just stared, seeming to get even paler than her usual ghostly shade.

Their eyes met and Ali's insides lurched as she walked towards her, sliding between the groups of talking patrons, apologising as she squeezed through gaps.

The two women looked at each other.

'Have you just come from London?' Summer was shaking her head. 'I'm legit scared of you.'

Ali stood at the bar, Summer on the other side behind a row of beer taps. She wore thick, black liner over her eyes, finished in fat, pointed wings. Her arms were folded, a pair of black roses climbing up towards her elbow.

Ali tried to convey sanity and humility. 'I know, right? Should I have brought flowers?'

Summer was still taking it in, someone going to all this effort to speak to her. She had a sort of embarrassed smile as she absorbed it.

A man came towards Summer, holding an empty glass and she directed him to one of the bar staff, glancing over her shoulder to steal another look at Ali as she spoke to him.

Summer glanced at the clock above the bar and turned her back, picking up something Ali couldn't see. The music dipped and Summer's voice came over the speaker. Ali could hear a faint shaking as she spoke. 'Ladies and gentlemen, welcome to Fun Club. The show starts in fifteen minutes. Come and get your plastic glasses. No glass inside the venue. Fifteen minutes. Thank you.'

She turned back to Ali. 'I'll come and get you when they're inside. We can talk in the office.' She disappeared through an arch at the back of the bar.

Ali ordered a pint of cider and stood under the air-conditioning vent in the ceiling, the sweat drying on her face as she tilted it up to meet the breeze.

The bar area had the same branded tables and old chairs as the London one. The same grimy feel and sticky floor. There were posters in frames behind the bar advertising comedy, burlesque nights, a séance evening. Two flies took it in turns to land and launch from a metal dish of lemons behind the counter. Ali wondered about Sid's dad and how much money he'd made from dark, sticky rooms dotted around the country, filling them with bored people looking for entertainment.

Ali watched the audience file slowly through the door to the venue, decanting drinks into plastic cups held out by the woman checking tickets.

When Summer came back, she seemed different. She'd redone her lipstick.

Ali saw her talking to another woman behind the bar; the woman looked over and then back to Summer. They talked some more. The woman moved off.

Ali took this as her cue to go over.

Summer stayed where she was. 'Erm.' Her throat was flushed, one hand with silver fingernails touching it as she gathered herself. 'This has been a shock. All of it. You might need to give me a minute. Are you still here in the morning?'

Ali swallowed. 'Sure.' The word croaked out.

'I appreciate you came a long way. Just, give me tonight to, you know, take it in? I'll meet you tomorrow somewhere. We'll talk then. I'll message you.'

It was so odd, looking at her now, standing stiffly when the two of them had confessed so much to one another. Ali tried to seem less desperate than she was. 'How about half ten outside the cathedral?'

'Which one? Paddy's Wigwam?' Summer pointed up and in the direction of the concrete church.

'Perfect.' Ali put her pint on the bar and raised a hand. 'Tomorrow then.'

Summer nodded. Ali was aware Summer's friend was standing at the other end of the bar watching them.

Sounding a little too upbeat she added. 'Cool!'

Back at ground level, she walked at speed away from the club, not caring where she was going, until the ground under her changed from tarmac to cobbles. Her feet had found the old part of the city, where tall Georgian houses lined long, wide streets. Old lanterns like the ones from Christmas cards dotted the pavement.

A waiter came out of a wine bar on her left, holding a tray of glasses. He set them down in front of a group of women sitting at a table. Ali moved to the next restaurant along, where the outside terrace was quieter. She sat on a wooden bench and picked up a menu.

Of course, Summer had been in shock. It was good that she was taking the time to think. Ali considered the possibility Summer just wanted to get rid of her and was planning to ghost her in the morning. It made her feel sick.

A waiter stopped at Ali's table as she lifted her head. 'Um.' She scanned the drinks list quickly. It was cheaper than London.

'Glass of Viognier, please. Large,' she added, pre-empting his question. She couldn't look him in the eye.

She took her phone out, more conscious of being alone than ever. She wondered if Ed was at home. He always messaged more when he was on the road. Ali took a picture of her wine and then realised she was doing it to send to him. She put her phone back in her pocket and thought about how accustomed she'd become to sharing everything she did with him. It made her feel less alone, sitting in a restaurant or at a bar, talking to her invisible boyfriend.

She promised herself she wouldn't look at her phone and would just try to sit there to enjoy her new surroundings. Maybe someone would pass by and start chatting to her. Northerners were friendlier than Londoners, weren't they?

A loud ping came from her pocket.

Where is she and what is she doing? x

She told herself she had to reply to keep up the pretence but she didn't really know what for any more. Even if the newspaper story was anonymous, it would lose Ed the show and she would lose her job. She wondered how it would feel to add 'unemployed' to her already pathetic CV, watching her self-respect circle the drain.

She thought about her dad's eyes in a Christmas picture they'd taken in front of the tree when she was eight or nine. The three of them posed for the Christmas card photo, just after he'd been made redundant. He was suffering 'exhaustion'. That's what Jean had told people when he spent weeks in bed. Sometimes at night Ali could hear him crying, but no one said anything. 'He works too hard,' Jean had said. Even then, Ali knew he hated his job and he wanted it all to stop.

She knew he'd tell her to jump now, don't wait to be pushed.

Why was she thinking of him? He'd played Beatles records to her in the attic, where he kept his old record player, and showed her the guitar that lived up there in a soft case with worn handles. Now she thought about it, he never brought his life, his things downstairs.

She looked at her phone, Ed's message hovering. She replied.

In Liverpool for work. x

At great speed, a reply came back with a picture. It was of a bigger-than-life statue of the Beatles cast in bronze, standing in a row like they were walking towards something. Ed on the end as though he'd just joined the line-up.

Ali you need is love. x

A Liverpool tour bus was visible in the background. Ali couldn't work out how he'd found it so quickly. She felt the lead of panic, wondering if he was here too.

Had she just missed him at the comedy club? She looked up and down the street, expecting to see him smiling back. Another message came through.

Give the place my love. x

She put down her glass, hand trembling, and fumbled in her bag for her purse. She left money on the table and walked back towards her hotel, suddenly feeling afraid.

Unable to even think about sleep, she filled the small, plastic kettle at the bathroom sink and turned the TV on. Changing from channel to channel, she knew she couldn't keep the panic at bay indefinitely. It had started to disperse into her like the brown stain from the tea bag into hot water.

She left a painting competition running on the screen in the background, the volume low, and picked up her phone, searching for a thread to lose herself in.

She wanted to run but she didn't know where to. Home was far away and the idea of getting back there was insurmountable.

She was thinking about her dad's coffin entering the flames, the guilt of leaving him on his own to burn overwhelming her.

She had to talk herself through it. She could go to the station. The last train to London would have already left. Better to wait here rather than a cold station bench. There's no one at home. The hotel room is as good as home if you have the TV on and look at the internet.

She tried to think about her breathing without thinking about it. If she thought about it, she would have to acknowledge that she was panicking. Her phone shuddered in her hand and the sensation instantly soothed her.

Are you in a hotel? I am. Folk piss in the kettles, they say. Statistically, your kettle is a piss kettle.

It often felt as though Ed could see her from miles away.

Ali needed distraction. She replied, hardly focusing on the words or what they meant.

Maybe I won't have this tea.
Why aren't you out carousing? It's not even midnight.

He still hadn't asked her what she was doing there. He was simultaneously engaged and without curiosity. She hadn't noticed before.

She foraged in her bag until her hand closed around a small cardboard box. She took one of the Valium from inside.

Feeling shaky. Grief is fun. Just trying to peel myself off the ceiling. #valium

The honesty of her own reply surprised her. There was a longer pause, then a flurry of messages.

You've been through so much. Take it slowly.
Are we breathing? Start there. Slow breath in through your nose.
Longer breath out through your mouth.

He sent the same messages on repeat for a while. She waited till the follow-up message to exhale, comforted by the company and the simple instructions.

How's that now? x

The hollow feeling in her stomach was all that remained of the panic, the ghost of it lingering in her body.

Thanks. Better.

She felt dirty, like she shouldn't have let him.

What are friends for? Get some sleep. I'll check on you in the morning. x

She turned the TV down to almost nothing and left it on. Rolling onto her side she slid her feet under the duvet and let the effects of the pill wash over her.

Twenty-Five

Ali didn't feel like she'd slept but she must have because she became gradually aware of the hum from the extractor fan in the bathroom.

The TV had put itself on standby. The pillows were still smooth on the other side of the bed, plump and white like snow. All of the beds she slept in looked the same, dented on one side. She pulled one of the untouched pillows to her and held onto it.

She cried for a while, thinking about her dad. She wished they'd come here together and done all the tourist things, a picture next to the Penny Lane sign, Eleanor Rigby's grave. Everything felt like a pilgrimage now.

She boiled the kettle again, checking it for yellow stains. She imagined the boiling water would at least sterilise it.

Get down the docks, send me a picture. Go to the Tate. You'll love it. The Chagall is extraordinary. x

She tried not to think about how Ed had helped her while she was spinning out, holding her hand from far away and seeming to care. She wanted someone to treat her like that so much, but now she felt like she did standing opposite Gemma at Mark's hotel. Sticky thighs.

'And he fucking knows it.' She pushed her face into the pillow and let herself cry again.

Straightening up, she picked up a sachet and sprinkled coffee granules into the scalding water, prodding them until they were all under the surface.

The sky was entirely blue as Ali approached the cathedral. Colourful banners flapped in the breeze, lining the way up to the stone steps that tapered towards large glass doors. The entrance was flanked by grey, brutalist panels, concrete chunks carved with abstract shapes.

It was past ten and visitors were already making their way inside, stopping on the steps to look up at the designs chiselled into the stone frontage. A row of bells hung at the top, each nestling into its own square nook above the door.

Ali wondered if Summer would show up. She tried to put herself in the same position, ambushed by a strange woman she'd talked to online. She wasn't confident.

She looked at her watch again and followed the people inside, wondering if it was free to look around while she waited.

She didn't visit churches enough, she thought. The overwhelming quiet in such a large space always made her feel something, even though she didn't believe in God. She'd never thought about why cathedrals were on such a grand scale. It's not like they were packed to the rafters with worshippers. It was to humble the faithful, a reminder of their insignificance before the Lord.

When she was a child, Ali had imagined God as the helmet from a suit of armour, floating on a cloud, like something from Monty Python.

Ali wondered if Catholic girls were Ed's speciality because they were already used to abasing themselves before a greater power and feeling guilty about everything all the time.

Everywhere she looked, she thought about the pictures she would have taken to send to him. The joke she'd have made to impress him, not dispatching it until the beats of the joke worked to her satisfaction. On a different day, Ali would have admired the stained glass and tried to capture the intense blue light pouring through floor-to-ceiling panels at regular intervals around the circular room, trying to get herself into the frame in a way that didn't make her chin look huge.

The cathedral was beautiful, but her brain kept making it the backdrop to a Technicolor porn film; Ed dressed as a priest, Summer and Sid kneeling in bras and wimples.

When she came back out into the light, Summer was sitting on one of the concrete blocks at the bottom of the steps, her back turned to the sun. Ali swerved left across the stairs so she didn't approach her from behind, hoping not to startle her any more than she already had.

Summer took off large cat-eye shades and looked up to see Ali walking down towards her.

'I was just having a look inside.' Ali pointed her thumb back where she'd come from as she negotiated the last few steps.

'And you didn't burst into flames? Good going.'

Ali laughed. 'Do you want to walk? Or coffee?'

It felt like a first date.

'It's hot, isn't it?'

Summer nodded. 'Yeah.' Ali was sure she could detect a hint of sarcasm that she'd opened with weather chat.

As they walked, Ali talked nervously about the podcast she'd listened to the on the train. 'Tom Weissman is doing two nights at the Playhouse. Do you know him?'

Summer shook her head. Then, 'Oh, the dick guy? Is he back already?'

Ali nodded. 'There's a protest at his show. Do you know...' She thought better of mentioning Bethan and steered around it. 'There a group called Scold's Bridle.'

'Yeah, I follow them on Twitter.'

Ali continued. 'They're picketing his show. I'm thinking of going and waving a banner. Are you up for the Fringe?'

'All my friends are, so probably. I go most years.'

'Up for a bit of placard waving? It's in the last week.' Ali realised the idea of going alone filled her with fear.

Summer shrugged and said 'Maybe', leading them down a narrow street. 'Are you surprised I turned up?' She was looking at the pavement ahead of them, giving nothing away.

Ali looked sideways at her. 'Yeah. Not gonna lie.'

They stopped and looked at each other now, Summer screwing her face up, acknowledging the madness of the situation. 'There's a coffee place down here.'

Sitting opposite each other a few minutes later, they drank iced coffees in plastic cups at a small table outside. Summer had ordered first, then Ali copied her.

'Why don't I drink this all the time?' Ali sucked the cold, milky coffee through a straw.

Summer flicked her fringe between her fingers, keeping it away from the sweat on her forehead. 'Sorry about last night. I was just upset.'

Ali knew eye contact was needed. She needed Summer to trust her. 'Of course. My fault, honestly. It's a mad thing to do, just showing up.'

Summer's lips parted, then pressed together again, like she was blotting lip balm. 'Bottom line: I don't want to be in the papers. Everyone pointing at the angry woman.'

Ali sucked a shard of ice. 'No, of course not. Neither do I. There's other ways of doing it. This journalist…'

'Journalists want stories. They'll say whatever it takes, reassurance, guarantees. But someone would know, word would get round. We'd be roadkill. The women never come off well in these things. I know we said we'd get the dirt on him, but we were drunk. I didn't get as far as what we'd actually do with it.'

Ali pulled back the lid of her drink and put another ice cube in her mouth. 'Why did you?'

'What?'

'Meet me? I wouldn't meet me. I've clearly lost the plot.'

'Curiosity? I wanted to see what his new one was like in the flesh.'

Ali stiffened. 'I'm not his new one. He was just winding me up for his own amusement.'

'Oh no, he'll think he's in love with you. A few more weeks and he'd have been telling you. I can't live without you. Did he get really interested in the things you like? Like too interested?'

Ali's face answered the question.

'His life is littered with "friends" who introduce him to stuff. It took me months to work out what "friends" actually meant. Vaginas.' She smiled, just with her mouth.

Ali choked on the sudden use of the word. 'I don't think he wanted to visit mine. He pretty much friend-zoned me. He said he just liked being with me. When we were together, we just talked.' She thought about it. 'On the phone he was different.'

Summer was shaking her head again. 'I bet he was.'

'He never even tried to kiss me. I took that as a strong "please do not show me your vagina" signal.'

'No FaceTime calls with zero warning? No stealth wanking videos?'

Ali's eyes widened.

'He was still reeling you in, I guess.'

Summer's smirk made Ali uncomfortable. Were they competing again? She liked it when they were on the same side, and she couldn't work out whether this was that or territory being marked.

'I'd get them from all over. Once from the hotel bathroom when they were on holiday. Wife sleeping in the next room.'

'Oh, God, why? Why do that? Does he think it looks nice?'

Summer shrugged. 'It's "I'll show you mine", isn't it?'

Ali lowered her voice. 'I sent him a picture of my tits.' She grimaced and Summer feigned shock. Ali continued. 'I don't do that. Ever. He barely even noticed. When we're together it's so different. He wants to talk about films and music and his divorce.'

The levity left Summer as quickly as it had arrived. She flattened the straw and started to wind it around her finger. 'That's nice for you.'

'Yeah, not really.' Ali felt the temperature drop.

'I never got that guy. The friends guy. He just came on to me. Looked me up and down at the bar and asked for my number.'

'Bold.'

Summer let the end of the straw go and watched it uncurl. 'I obviously looked like a sure thing.'

Ali could feel her thighs sticking to each other. 'Obviously, he's a monster, but it doesn't stop me feeling bad, him not even trying to sleep with me.'

They sat in silence for a beat, then Ali spoke, hoping to give Summer back the floor. 'What was it like? Being in a relationship with him, hardly seeing him?'

Summer thought for a minute. 'Intense.' She described it like someone reading out a shopping list. 'We'd meet for sex, sometimes he'd take me for a drink first. I'd lie there, waiting for it to start. Like a sex doll.' She widened her eyes and gaped vacantly, holding her arms robotically in front of her.

Ali creased up and looked around to see if anyone was overhearing them.

Summer lowered her voice. 'He was OK at sex. Sometimes. When he wasn't off his head on something or he hadn't had a bad gig. But sex was always a game, never straightforward. Always on his terms.'

'Off his head, like drunk?' Ali didn't think of him as someone who ever really looked that drunk, even when the whisky seemed to keep coming.

'Coke. Sometimes he made me fuck him on E. I never really took anything before him. It makes me too mad. He's always got coke on him.'

Ali hadn't seen him take drugs and the more she thought about it, she'd never even suspected it. No extended trips to the bathroom. She could have been describing a totally different person.

'Do you miss him?'

Summer chewed her lip. Ali noticed her doing it when she was stalling. 'It was three years. Of course I miss him. I don't love hearing you talk about him, your time with him.'

'We didn't really have…'

'This is what he does. Sets us against each other. He'd have us fighting hand-to- hand if he could, while he watched from a fucking throne.'

'In a paddling pool full of jelly.'

'In a paddling pool full of jelly,' Summer repeated. They were laughing again, the relief washing over them both.

Summer lifted her fringe and wiped her forehead with a sleeve. 'Goths in hot weather.' She put the cup to her neck.

Ali liked her. She was funny. They didn't know what to say for a while, then Ali thought of something. 'You've got amazing skin.'

Summer stroked a ghostly arm and rolled her eyes. 'And a lovely personality.'

Ali could see she didn't know what to do with the compliment but there was a trace of a smile on her lips.

'It doesn't cope well with this.' Summer pointed up at the sky. 'I prefer dark basements. Yeah, Summer. I know, the irony. It has been pointed out.'

They drank more.

Summer came to some kind of resolution. 'Look, I am embarrassed that he's got the stuff I sent him. I wish I'd never done any of it. Now. He says it's all gone, but that's bollocks, isn't it?' She didn't phrase it as a question.

Ali took a second to catch up. 'You've spoken to him?'

'Yesterday.' Summer saw the panic in her eyes. 'He doesn't know anything.'

Ali breathed in through her nose, parting her lips to let the breath slowly out again.

'It's the first time he's called me in months. I still get messages.

Not many.' 'What did you talk about?' Ali searched Summer's face.

Summer shrugged. 'It was just normal. Like he'd never been away. It's always that way when he's been quiet. He asked how I was. How's work? Boring stuff.'

'Took his dick out. Had a quick wank.' The corners of Ali's mouth lifted into two dimples.

'Not this time.' Summer was smiling too, albeit uneasily. 'I said I was worried about something happening to his laptop. Asked him if he'd definitely deleted all my stuff. He said it was gone, but we know he's lying.'

'Can't we just get the police to raid his house? Take the laptop?'

'For what? Having porn?'

They were quiet again. Then Summer looked down at her drink. 'You know what I thought when I saw you yesterday?'

Ali shook her head.

'She's thinner than me. Of course he wants her.'

Ali barked involuntarily. 'That is the first time anyone's said that about me. To me. This is so fucked. Thank you?'

Summer shrugged. 'I knew early on that there were other girls, but you just don't let yourself actually believe it. If you don't have the evidence, maybe it's not true. How thick do I sound?'

'You don't.'

Ali wondered again how far down that road she'd have gone if Sid hadn't said anything.

'You really don't,' she said, meaning it this time. 'I feel like Sid's beating a retreat. I think she regrets telling me. Like, it did the job, she got me to back off and now she's got him to herself again? Kind of.'

The skin on Summer's collarbone was going pink in the heat. 'She just doesn't know what to do without him. I think she'd put everything back to how it was if she could.'

'But you wouldn't?' Ali tried not to make that sound like a direct challenge.

'I was actually doing OK. Got me beta blockers. I was getting through it an hour at a time. I thought I was getting over it. But it's all there, just under the surface. Thanks for digging it up.'

Ali didn't know what to say.

'Jokes. I was kidding myself. My friends, the couple I told, watched it all happening, despairing of me. Jake – that's my best mate – hooked me up with someone, you know, to talk to. A therapist. He nearly shat when I asked him. He's studying to be one and he said he'd been desperate for me to do therapy, but that I had to want to do it for myself.' She rolled her eyes again.

'Therapy. Wow. That's amazing.'

'I'm learning to have boundaries.' She raised her fingers, quoting the air. 'That's what I was doing last night when I told you to do one. Having boundaries.' She smiled, pleased with herself. Ali nodded, agreeing it was impressive.

'What about you? Seen a head shrinker?'

Ali thought about a room with plastic chairs and a stranger. 'Therapy? I don't know what I'd say. I am sad my dad's dead. Here's fifty quid?'

'Fifty quid's not bad for London. Mine's only £45. Welcome to Liverpool.' She raised her cup, smiling.

'You don't seem like someone…' Ali thought carefully. 'Someone who doesn't have it all together.'

Summer narrowed her eyes, nonplussed.

'I mean you run the club, deal with punters. Your eyeliner is always perfect. I'm not getting "basket case".'

Summer shook her head and rolled the straw into a tight drum. 'A madwoman has to be streaked with mascara and cutting up shirts? Throwing paint on his car? It's the meds. I'm a basket case all right. Under here.' She pointed to her fringe.

'Did you ever meet his wife?'

Summer's eyes saucered. 'No. Why the fuck would I?'

'Sid has. She said she was funny. Like, she liked her.'

'He's never mentioned her to me. I just pretended she didn't exist. Like the others. It's like she's not there, no pictures on Instagram. The wife who never was.'

Ali noticed her own eyelid was twitching.

Summer folded her arms. 'What do you think we've all got in common?'

Ali shrugged.

She unfolded them again. 'He can smell it on us. His type.'

Ali didn't understand. They couldn't have looked more different.

'There's a test, early on. He does something or says something and we rush to make it all right, to sweep it under the carpet. He doesn't have to ask, we just do it. That's how he knows.'

Summer put the remains of her straw on the table. 'I never used to sleep when I was with him. A couple of months after I met him, we woke up in a hotel room.' She thought for a second. 'In Edinburgh. And he said I'd snored all night. I was so ashamed. And he patted my stomach and smiled. 'It's the weight.' So I didn't sleep after that. Or eat for a while.'

Ali thought about the hollow feeling in her stomach and how much she liked it. 'That's awful.'

Summer leaned forward. 'Did you love him? I think I did. I know that's fucked up, but it's as close as I've come.'

Ali felt like telling the truth. 'I wanted him to love me.'

Summer looked like she understood. 'What are you going to do with the smut?'

'I don't know. Nothing? I put it on the shared drive. It's your smut too. I just want people to know what he's like. I thought it would be easy to tell people. You know, "He's a creep." Why is it so hard?'

'You know he's not on there? The pictures and videos. You never see his face, he's careful about that. But all of us? Easily identifiable. He's on top of the admin, I'll give him that.'

The caffeine buzzed through Ali's limbs and the sun reflecting off the coffee-shop window was starting to bake her skin. 'Can we walk?'

They made their way back up the hill towards another, bigger church, its stern stone tower incongruous against the cheerful sky. It looked ancient, the occasional arched window the only visible curves on its austere front. God's brown fortress, high on a rock.

They followed a steep path down the side of the building to the gardens below through a tunnel carved into the rock. The walls of the short passage were lined with gravestones, grey teeth sticking up from mossy gums.

'Some of those things, I did want to do them. I liked them.' Summer's voice echoed and she seemed more comfortable talking when they weren't facing each other. 'I'm not a prude. Just not the…' She caught herself. 'I didn't want to be filmed. He was obsessed with filming it.'

'Did he ask you?'

'Like he'd ask, "This OK?"' But right in the middle of it so you couldn't say no. He'd sulk, not call you for days if you ruined it. I gave ground every time. Learned not to ruin it. Because I'm fucking desperate obviously.'

Ali's throat was tight. 'Why do we do this? Take the blame for every shitty thing he's done? He ruined us. How are we the stupid ones?'

Summer blew her fringe. 'For believing him? He'd say he never forced us to do anything and he didn't. There was no gun to my head. I just knew someone else would take my place.'

They emerged into the light again, the park opening up in front of them, high brick walls rising to shelter it on three sides.

Ali stopped. 'We're not in the wrong. That voice is so loud, it's deafening. That it's our fault. It's not. It's his.'

Summer took something out of her pocket. 'Do you smoke?' They walked down onto the lawn, dwarfed by the cathedral above.

Summer stretched out on the grass in the shade of a wall and lit a thin joint. Sweet smoke floated where she'd puffed it, the lack of a breeze leaving it hanging above them.

Ali sat cross-legged next to her. 'Let's try to stop blaming ourselves.

Homework for next time. God, if you'd asked me a month ago whether I'd go on an angry women march, I'd have laughed at you.'

Summer smiled and passed her the joint. 'Last week of August?'

Ali nodded, pressing her lips together to keep the smoke in.

'I might be there then. I'm not waving a placard.' She took her shades off.

Ali inhaled. The sun hitting the cathedral turned its morose walls rust orange. She felt like she had walked into a postcard, the colours polarised and vivid. She exhaled. 'I'll message you.'

They passed the spliff back and forth for a while, not speaking.

Ali's phone buzzed on the grass next to her. Like trained poodles, they both looked down at the same time.

Where's the art? What have you seen? Proof, Lauder. Proof. x

Ali smiled involuntarily and wished again she had more control of her face as Summer pretended not to notice.

'Fuck sake.' Ali tried to show Summer her screen, but the pale girl was concentrating on stubbing the joint out on the grass. 'He wants pictures of me doing tourist stuff. You know, pointing at the Liver Birds.'

Summer brushed grass off her calf. 'Yeah. He's got the same ones of me.' She got up and put her sunglasses back on.

Ali stood up too. 'I probably won't send them. Keeping this up is getting stupid.'

Summer was different. 'So stop.'

'Well, what are we going to do? We need to decide that first.'

Summer shrugged. 'Maybe you're not ready.'

Ali started to babble. 'No, I am. We just need our ducks in a row. I'll be happy never to see the fucker again. I was going to ask, I mean if it's OK, we should tell the Scolds. They keep a list and he needs to be on it.'

'The Scolds? What, so they can picket his show? No fucking way. I work in comedy, for fuck's sake. I'm not shouting down a comedian. This is my living.'

'I don't think that's what…' Summer's weight shifted onto her back foot and Ali knew she had work to do. 'Look, no journalist. It doesn't have to be that. But it's about sharing information. We need to talk to each other, Summer. They get away with it when we don't talk. I just want him to stop.'

'Sure.' Summer wasn't looking at her any more. 'I need to get going. You know your way back to the station?'

'Yes.' Summer turned back up the slope and Ali followed. 'Look, you came to meet me. You wanted to talk. I'm not asking you to go public. I don't need to mention your name or where you work. Just let me talk to the Scolds. Please.'

Summer stopped and turned to look at her. 'And you're sure that's why you're doing this? The sisterhood? Or are you just getting off on the drama?'

Ali shaded her eyes. She was looking straight into the sun. 'I don't—'

'He'll be waiting for his pictures.'

She watched Summer disappear back into the darkness of the tunnel.

Twenty-Six

August brought hammering rain and blackened skies to London. A dark, oppressive weather system pressed down on the city, making Ali's head throb. She leaned forward on her office chair and looked out of the window. On the street below, shop fronts were lurid with summer sales, buses and cabs unloaded their passengers.

Ali was supposed to be listening to new releases for a playlist meeting. She drifted back to her browser, looking for mentions of Ed's name on forums and social media sites, hungry for new information.

Kat passed by her desk and squeezed her shoulder before disappearing into the kitchen.

Ali could hear her singing to herself, 'Ruby Ruby Ruby Ruby'. It seemed to be the only bit of the song she knew and she sang it over and over as the kettle boiled. She didn't need to be in the office after the show, but she often stayed behind, answering emails, not seeming in a hurry to go.

The repetitive humming loops used to drive Ali nuts and she'd usually hide under headphones, but she was glad of it today. The monotony soothed her.

She searched her emails and found what she was looking for.

The title should have read as a joke but now it just made her cringe. 'Bring a sexy friend.'

He'd attached two tickets to the last night of his Edinburgh show.

It felt like a summons. Not 'Are you free?' or 'Which day can you come?' Just instructions to be followed.

Ali went back to her slack-jawed browsing. A pop star had dumped her boyfriend for sleeping with her teenage fans. She found out he'd been picking them up at her gigs.

An email arrived from Kat. Ali looked over to her desk but her back was turned.

It was short. 'Did you talk to Lloyd?'

The mention of the journalist's name made Ali feel cold. She wanted to see Ed's bloated face on the front of a tabloid, doorstepped carrying a four-pack, sweating. She could picture it. The panicked phone calls to Michelle. 'I don't think I can make this one go away.'

She wanted to sit in a bar and talk to Kat about narcissists. She found herself obsessing about them, looking them up online, definitions, case studies, debunking of theories. YouTube videos, usually presented by Americans, advising on how to live with a narcissist. How to leave a narcissist. How to work with one. How to cope with a narcissistic parent.

Her wrist ached from the repetitive strain of scrolling. Bad men and why they hurt us. How to grey rock a narcissist. How to tell if someone has narcissistic personality disorder.

Ali thought carefully before replying to Kat. 'We've emailed. The others won't talk, so I don't think it'll fly. Not going down that road if it's just me. Still thinking. But thanks, I appreciate it. x'

Desks began to fill around her.

There was a message from Otis, his goldfish brain returning to thoughts of the show with Ed.

What have you got for me? Need to nail down format. Ding Monica for a slot next week.

He would forget the request not long after sending it, but that only bought her a day or two before Monica chased her. She read all of his emails for him and kept up the pretence that he knew what he was doing.

Ali was getting her period. The lava pulse in her lower belly confirmed it.

She imagined herself as the kind of person who could quit something. Just fill a box with her desk junk and walk away, a houseplant sticking out of the top. There was always a plant. But the image wouldn't stick. Or she tripped and the junk went everywhere, sprinkled with soil and broken pot. She even failed at daydreaming.

She ground through preparation for the next day's running order, dry-swallowing ibuprofen capsules at her desk. She knew the second one was going to get stuck before she put it in her mouth.

When she got to it, the water cooler was cupless. Always cupless.

Mark leaned around the kitchen partition, the same shifty look as before, holding a mug. 'Need this?' Had he been waiting for her, watching from behind the kitchen door?

She took it and swigged the tepid water, dislodging the pill. The mug tasted of dishwasher. 'Thanks,' she croaked, turning to go.

'Hey. Hello?'

She looked at him. He was wearing his version of summer clothing; an open-necked shirt. She'd always liked the dark hair under his Adam's apple. 'Hey.'

'How are things?'

She smiled, but her eyes stayed out of it.

'Jesus. Do you want to talk? I know, not to me. But… we were friends.' He looked sort of desperate, which she enjoyed.

'Were we?' She smiled to take away the sting, unable to be mean to him even now.

'Well.' He demurred. 'Here if you need me.' He shoved his hands in his pockets and headed back towards the lift.

Whatever that was, she didn't have the energy to decipher it.

She guessed the wheel had turned, he was bored again and he was too lazy to try someone new. By the time she'd sat down, an internal message had popped up from Mark.

'Can you turn down the smile? Your unfettered happiness is distracting and I'm trying to work. x'

A pull of the pigtails to see how she'd respond. Where was the dignity? She ignored it and promised herself never to sleep with someone so unfunny again.

Once outside, she looked at the small patches of blue appearing between the thick greyness overhead. The rain had stopped, leaving big cartoon spots on the pavement.

It was a couple of hours until the meeting. The idea of coming face to face with the women from Scold's Bridle terrified her. It felt like a test and she always felt sick before any kind of test.

Bethan's text was brief: just a time and place and instructions not to discuss it outside of their messages. They'd need to meet her before the last of them headed up to Edinburgh.

Ali assumed that 'they' meant everyone in hoods around a fire pit. The way the women of Scold's Bridle talked on the WhatsApp group, Ali couldn't be 100 per cent certain they weren't planning violence. She tried to imagine hitting someone and what it would feel like. She imagined hitting Mark and blood bursting from his nose. He'd definitely cry.

Maybe there'd be an initiation before they'd let her join, like throwing eggs at a politician or fire-bombing a Rotary Club.

All she could really picture was an Alcoholics Anonymous meeting and group sharing and it made her want to run in the opposite direction.

Twenty-Seven

She was surprised to see Sid sitting alone at the table in the pub's basement room and Sid obviously felt the same.

'Just us, is it?' Ali didn't sit down. 'I didn't know you'd be here. It's good to see you.'

Sid acknowledged her with a weak smile. They were alone except for some people Ali could hear but not see, outside the double doors on a smoking terrace.

'Can I get you one?'

Sid shook her head and Ali went back upstairs to the bar. She could just run. The others weren't here and it wasn't too late to make an excuse. This didn't feel like her thing, women plotting in a basement. She was surprised it was Sid's.

When she came back with a drink, it was still just the two of them.

She watched Sid pull her sleeve over her thumb, stretching the knitted grey fabric to a point.

'Have you joined the fanny army? I thought you just did the logo.'

Sid looked relieved as a woman Ali hadn't seen before arrived. Ali didn't know whether to stand. It felt too formal, so she stayed sitting.

'Hi.' Don't say anything stupid, Ali told herself. 'We haven't started without you.'

Cass introduced herself, putting a red cycling helmet on the table. She looked like someone with important things to think about. Her auburn hair was pulled back in a ponytail and Ali tried not to stare at her earlobes, stretched with black circular plugs so you could see fresh air through them. Ali guessed she was in her early thirties.

The small talk didn't last long. Cass turned her attention to Sid. 'All good for printing tonight?'

Sid nodded. 'Kim's waiting till her manager goes home. She'll put it through as another job for cash.'

'Thank you, Kim,' said Cass, taking out her phone. 'Let's dial in Bethan. Ali, right?' She looked at Ali, finally offering her something like a smile. Maybe she could tell Ali was nervous.

'So Edinburgh. Has she given you the dates?' Cass talked while the video call connected.

Ali was about to answer when Bethan's face appeared on the screen. Ali could see white kitchen units behind her and she was chewing.

'Hiya. How's it going?'

Ali was reassured to see a friendly face.

Cass propped her phone against a tin holding cutlery. 'Good. How's the show?'

'Yeah, OK, I think. Some nights are selling out.'

Ali ventured: 'That's amazing' and instantly felt she was being too gushy.

Bethan ran her tongue along the inside of her top lip. 'Sorry. Fucking starving. Are you guys all set?'

Cass talked about plans for the final week, the build-up to Tom Weissman's show and the night of action, which Ali gleaned was where she would come in. Cass seemed to defer to Bethan. 'Obviously, do what you can. But we know you'll need to keep it on the downlow.'

'Thanks. I've got to go in a minute actually.' Bethan was on her way somewhere else and Ali knew it was now or never to say something.

She glanced at Sid. 'Before you go, the new information I mentioned. I wanted to talk about someone who I don't think is on your list yet.'

Cass was paying attention now. Ali needed to do this while Bethan was present. 'It's difficult because it's a friend. But that's no reason to... right?'

Sid's chair scraped. 'I'm meeting Kim. Good luck, yeah.'

'See you, Sid.' Cass was concentrating on Ali and Bethan looked like she needed to hang up.

'Listen, yes, of course. Cass, have you got time to take details? I'm really sorry, I've got to go. Car's coming.' Bethan gave an apologetic wave and disappeared.

'So this is first hand?' Cass was opening the notes app on her phone, ready to transcribe.

Ali felt frozen. The opportunity was here to talk and she didn't know how to say it without sounding mad or stupid or both. She'd never felt more like a victim. She felt pathetic.

'Kind of. It's Ed. Ed Catchpole?' Now she'd said his name, every piece of her wanted to shrivel and die.

Cass was tapping with her thumbs as she listened. She stopped. 'OK.'

Ali didn't know where to start. 'I know you're focused on sexual assaults and... absolutely. Those men are dangerous. But I think he is too. In a different way.'

She didn't mention Sid or Summer by name. She tried not to rush, aware that she was desperate not to be saying this to a stranger and of her subconscious wanting to drag her quickly to the end and out onto the street.

By the time Ali's story was running out of steam, Cass had made few notes. Her face gave nothing away. Ali had no idea how Cass felt about what she'd told her, which made Ali think she doubted her entirely.

'I've talked a lot, sorry.'

'Don't be. Look, I'm sorry this happened to you.' She put her hand on the table like of course, that was the first thing she should say.

'Not just to me.' Ali was aware that her time to talk was up.

Cass put her phone down. 'What we usually do is corroborate what women tell us. So it's absolutely not that we don't believe women. We do. But to make us water- tight, we need to back it up. Numbers, basically. A number of voices are louder than one. Would any of these other women speak to us about him?'

Ali looked at the table and thought of Lloyd Appleyard. 'No.' She couldn't say Sid's name, even though this was probably Cass's roundabout way of asking if she knew what Ali knew. 'I mean, I know of others, but I don't think they'd speak up.'

'It's hard enough to prove physical assault. Rape even. You wait three years and if you make it to court, you've sat with the trauma for all that time. No wonder women don't bother. That's why we do this. We gossip. But if it was just gossip, they'd destroy us. It has to be more than that.'

Ali drooped. 'Of course.'

'Emotional abuse, obviously, leaves trauma behind. Have a think about others who might come forward. It's not a no. OK?'

'Yeah. I will.' Ali could feel the leaden defeat filling her.

Cass was gathering herself to leave. 'Look, thanks for coming. We really value your support. Keep an eye on the WhatsApp. All the details of where, when, what will be there. Don't worry. We're not torching anything.' She smiled.

Ali hated that Cass could sense her inexperience but the news genuinely reassured her.

They went back up to the ground floor together and out into daylight. The pub entrance was nestled under a railway bridge on a cobbled side street, just south of the River Thames.

'I'm going to get something to eat. The market's just up there.' Cass pointed up the road. She hung her bike helmet on her handle-bars as she unlocked her bike from the railings.

Ali wasn't sure if she was inviting her but assumed she was just being polite. 'I had a big breakfast,' she lied.

'OK, see you in Scotland.' Cass wheeled into the dark under the bridge, Ali's eyes adjusting slowly from the bright sunlight to see her go.

She turned the other way and started walking, not knowing where she was going, not wanting to bump into Cass again at the traffic lights.

Twenty-Eight

At the bottom of the narrow street, hoardings stretched along one side of the road, concealing building works. London was never finished. The wooden barrier was painted and printed with a time-line, dates stretching back to the twelfth century. Underneath the graphic were photographs from an excavation; a woman in a hard hat combing the ground with a trowel, skeletons bent around each other encased in dirt.

Ali followed the years along to the present day. The hoardings gave way to high railings, hundreds of coloured scraps of fabric, ribbons, crochet and baubles tied to vertical bars. The ribbon ends fluttered, a living wall of colour interrupted by an official-looking sign, dedicated to The Outcast Dead.

The sign announced an ancient graveyard, preserved in concrete between the new tower blocks and old terraces.

Red flowers in dark foliage grew from a small trough attached at the far end. As she looked closer, she could see names were written on the ribbons with dates afterwards. Some from hundreds of years ago. Dedications to murder victims Ali had seen on the news, a homeless man who died in the winter with his dog.

Flowers in graveyards had never made sense to Ali. Buying carna-tions for dead people who'd never see or smell them was a waste of money. She could even remember saying this confidently in conversation. But it wasn't her. It was her mother's voice tutting over the news coverage of Princess Diana's death and the floral tributes left at the gates of Kensington Palace.

'And who's going to clear it up? All the plastic and rotting plants.'

Ali moved along the railings, reading the tributes, and felt a hard cry in her throat, pushing out her breath in front of it. The lump rose until she was unable to stop the sound coming out of her in an indecent swell.

Through the railings she could see a garden but there was no way in. She muffled herself with a tissue, pretending to blow her nose, and followed the boundary of the garden until she came to an open gate.

A covered wooden bridge, like an upturned boat, started just beyond the gate, leading her round a bend into the green space beyond. The garden was quiet chaos. Broken concrete paths spread out around tumultuous flowerbeds. Strange statues and shrines protruded from the weeds. Not a formal garden, but someone was keeping an eye, watering and pruning. The tallest plants were just high enough to make Ali feel like she'd left the city and arrived somewhere out of time.

Pairs of metal folding chairs were dotted around the bare patches of ground. She chose one in the shade, looking up at a statue of an angel with spiked wings. Someone had made an offering of apples and herbs at the statue's feet.

The ritual seemed to be whatever you wanted it to be. Teddy bears and lanterns and plaster models of geese dotted the ground. She didn't know what it all meant but it was reassuring; small signs of devotion and tenderness. People thinking about people.

'I close the gate in ten minutes, dear.'

Ali squinted up to see an old face, haloed by pale sun, the two middle teeth missing from her broad smile.

'Oh, sorry.' She made to go.

The woman extended a dry hand, soil under her nails, and

placed it on Ali's shoulder. 'I'll get you when I'm closing up. You stay put.'

She began to fuss the knot of a red neckerchief at her throat. Ali watched her for a minute and then stood without thinking. 'Let me.'

Outside on the street, she wouldn't have dreamed of touching a stranger. But here it didn't feel strange at all. She used her fingernail to pull out the fabric at the heart of the knot.

The old woman raised her chin to let Ali work. 'Fingers can't do knots now.' The woman looked at Ali as she set the end of the material free.

'There.' Ali pulled it gently from her neck and handed it to her. 'Whose garden is this?'

'It's my garden.' The gap reappeared in her smile. 'Yours too, seeing as you're here.'

The woman wiped her forehead and looked at the hedge that she'd appeared from. 'Powdery mildew. Just needs more water, I think.' She rubbed one of the leaves between her finger and thumb.

Ali nodded as though agreeing with the diagnosis.

'Come here for a cry, did you?'

The question startled Ali. Her hand went to her face thinking she must have cried make-up down her cheek.

'Good place for it.' The woman walked off in the direction of a tool cupboard that hung open on the far wall, garden implements stored on its red metal shelves.

As though given permission, Ali did start to cry again. She leaned forward on the chair and let the tears come for a while. When she sat back, she looked at the strange, small statues, the sun playing on the grey ground, a tall, drooping evergreen in the centre that looked like a sad Christmas tree.

Cass's reaction was just what Ali had been afraid to see in someone else's eyes. Her own stupidity looking back at her. She got a strong feeling that Cass thought she was a dickhead, but she always thought other women were judging her. Maybe she was just expecting them

235

to. Her mum would gape in horror if she told her she was going on a protest march, wondering how any daughter of hers could want to do something so vulgar, so public. She realised she was laughing.

The woman was coming back, wiping her hands on the scarf. When she got near enough to cast a shadow, hers joining with Ali's, she looked up at the statue next to her, its wings spread as though about to take off.

'You've had a loss?'

Ali instantly felt guilty that she wasn't crying for her dad. Maybe she had been.

She nodded, feeling self-conscious. 'Dad. It was months ago'

'Months ago. Now. Same difference, isn't it? You loved. You still love.' She nodded to herself like that was about right and took some keys out of her pocket, feeling the weight of them in her hand.

A train rumbled over the bridge above the garden, drawing Ali's eyes up to the silver city skyline beyond. A church bell was clanging somewhere in the distance.

'Sorry, you've got to lock up.'

'Help me get the chairs in.'

Ali was glad of something to do. As she went around the garden, folding chairs and bringing them to her new friend by the tool shed, she looked at the little altars to whoever. 'To all the suicides' said one, making her shiver.

She stood for a moment, looking at one handmade sign leaning up against a wall. A painted red board lettered in black that read 'Don't fuck with the geese.'

'Which geese?' Ali asked, remembering the little plaster figures under the statue.

The woman was laughing. 'You're standing on them.' She watched Ali's face, delighted to see her consternation.

'Winchester Geese. They weren't allowed in consecrated ground because of what they did for a living, so they buried them here,

long time ago. Their customers, of course, sent to lie with God.'
A little whistle escaped through her teeth when she pronounced
her S-es.

'Why geese?'

The woman considered for a moment and cocked her head.
'Something to do with the clap. Bitten by the geese.' She pushed
a grey strand of hair behind her ear and squinted up at another
train passing overhead.

Ali thought about a beak lined with hard little teeth. She felt
shy, thinking of going back out into the world but the woman was
locking the cupboard and turning towards the gate. Ali followed
her. 'Thanks, for somewhere to sit.'

The woman pulled the neckerchief from her pocket and draped
it round her neck, holding either end as she walked. 'Come again.'

Ali noticed a brown skull on a plinth by the entrance to the
bridge. She dropped some coins into the slot under its chin and
hoped the woman would see, but she had turned to pull the heads
off some dead flowers in a nearby bed.

Ali thought about a flock of angry geese as she walked back
along the street, heading towards the river.

Twenty-Nine

The redbrick mansion block was half in shade by the time Ali's walk brought her to Covent Garden. Peering through the blue iron gates from the street, she took in the courtyard beyond.

The flats rose up on all four sides, preventing the rest of the city from seeing in. Four low flowerbeds surrounded an iron gazebo in the centre, a matching metal bench underneath.

She tried to picture Sid and Ed sitting there together. Had they held hands and kissed? She couldn't see it.

The entry phone buzzed, jolting her back to the present. She pushed the gate and made for the door on the other side of yard.

The brown remains of a dead clematis held onto the struts of the gazebo, parched but clinging on.

The balconies and windows crowding above the garden were anonymous; only a few plants and ornaments to suggest occupation. One tattered rainbow flag faded in an upper casement. Ali tried to imagine having enough money to own a London property and not live in it.

Her feet echoed on the stairs as she climbed to the first floor.

Sid opened the door to her flat in jeans and a jumper. She always looked cold, even as the city baked.

'Hi.' Sid's body language said the opposite of hi.

Ali followed her down a corridor to a room with smooth, pale floor tiles. Shiny grey kitchen units glistened down the left wall, black leather sofas and a giant TV dominated the other side.

Just off centre, a large kitchen counter cut the room in two, low pendant lights dangling over a worktop. Sunlight poured through tall glass doors on the far wall.

There was nothing to identify who lived there except Sid's bag hanging on the back of a kitchen stool and a laptop open on the glass coffee table.

'This is nice.' Ali wasn't getting anything from Sid. 'So tidy.'

'You should see my room.' Sid tried to sound friendly, but her tone was brittle.

Ali walked over to the glass doors and peered through. 'Oh, posh.' She opened one of the doors and poked her head outside.

Sid stayed where she was. 'I wouldn't.'

Ali looked over her shoulder.

'It's rusted. Dad's been saying he'll get it fixed for the whole time I've lived here.' She finished with a flat smile. 'It's just for show.'

Ali closed the door and came back to the counter. Sid had positioned herself on the other side. Ali pulled out one of the stools and sat opposite her. 'I'm sorry about earlier.'

Sid looked at her. 'No, you're not. Tea?'

'I didn't mention you. I didn't use names. Cass wouldn't do anything unless there was a bunch of us anyway. Which is fair enough.'

Sid looked at her hands and repeated the question. 'Do you want tea?'

'Thanks.' Ali felt the weather change but continued. 'I'm going to channel the rage into helping them with whatever they've got going on. They might not be able to stop Ed, but better than doing nothing. You're doing something too.'

Sid pulled both sleeves over her hands, pushing one inside the other so her arms became a single loop. 'Nope. Kim can do the printing. I was helping because I like Bethan and she liked my logo. I'm not an activist. This has nothing to do with me.'

Ali opened her hands on the worktop. 'Neither am I. I'm not a militant, but I feel like I've got to do something.' Ali wondered what it would take for Sid to say how angry she really was.

Sid got milk from the fridge and mugs and kept moving while the kettle boiled, making sure she wasn't a sitting target.

'I'm coming up to Edinburgh. My friend loaned me her flat. Maybe I can see the show you directed.' Ali watched as Sid put tea bags into mugs, draping their strings carefully over the sides. She shrugged. 'I'll email you the details.'

The kitchen worktop was marble with sparkling specks running through the grain. Ali wondered if it was the one Summer had lain on in her underwear while Ed ate her out.

'We could get a drink if you're not too busy.'

'I'll be working.' Sid watched the kettle as it began to steam. They didn't say anything for a while.

'I saw Summer in Liverpool.' Ali let that hang in the air between them until curiosity made Sid look at her.

'Did you?'

'Sort of ambushed her. Not my best idea, but she wasn't answering messages. Anyway, I wanted to talk to her about what we do next. What we could do.'

Steam from the kettle misted Sid's glasses and she took them off to wipe them.

'I found pictures and videos on his laptop. Summer told me where to look.'

Sid kept her face very still.

'There's proof. That he's collecting us.'

Sid put down her glasses and concentrated on her task. 'And how are you going to prove they didn't give him that stuff willingly?' She picked up the kettle. Some water splashed onto the work surface as she poured.

Ali was looking right at Sid, getting nothing back. 'I would argue that they didn't know who they were trusting. That it's not consent if it was tricked out of them.'

'What are you doing, Ali?' Sid put the kettle down now, finally showing some emotion. 'Going through people's laptops? Wild goose chases to Liverpool. Christ, you're not in a film.'

'You want it to go back to the way it was. Before a girl died?'

Sid dabbed at the spilled water with a tea towel.

'And why don't we pretend we don't know about all the other women? Summer, his wife, the ones in every town he's ever been to, hating themselves just enough to let him, sending him pictures. All the women having panic attacks and on meds because of how he…' She trailed off.

Sid's hands were shaking as she picked up the mugs of tea.

Ali had nothing to lose. 'There's a journalist.'

Sid put the mugs down again, top teeth pressing into her lower lip. It looked like she was smiling. Ali had never seen anyone look so angry.

'I know. Summer told me.'

This floored Ali. 'Why didn't you say something?'

The groove between Sid's brows deepened. 'It sounds like you've made up your mind.'

'I'm not doing anything without you. It needs to be all of us.'

'What all of us?' If Sid looked directly at her, Ali imagined electric bolts would fly from her eyes. 'There is no all of us.'

Ali's voice trembled. 'You started this. You told me and I can't do nothing, Sid.'

'I told you because I wanted him to leave you alone. I wanted to stop you because I liked you. That's it.'

'Right. Because you didn't want to see me end up in the same mess you were in.'

Sid was pulling at her sleeves again. 'Just walk away. I've stopped you now, so it's over.'

'It's not over. He's still doing it. He's just carrying on as if nothing happened. How can you stand it?'

'It's more complicated for me. This is my life.' She looked around at the bare flat, the milk carton, the teaspoon in front of her. 'And I'm fine.'

'Sid. You're not fine.'

This seemed to snap her to attention. 'If I am or not doesn't matter. No one appointed you CEO of my problems. I'm an adult. I can make my own choices.'

'You're also my friend and I care what happens to you. The longer you stay with him, the more damage he does. Sid, every day he tells you you're not worth any better.'

'That's up to me though, isn't it? You can walk away, but you don't seem to want to. I wonder why that is?'

'I told you, I want him stopped. I want people to know.'

'Right.' Sid transmitted sarcasm with her eyebrows.

'What?'

'You only wanted to be friends with me to get close to him.'

Ali's pulse raced. 'You just want me gone so you can have him to yourself again.'

Sid did look at Ali now. A vein pushed against the thin skin of her temple. 'And there it is.' She looked almost pleased. 'My life has fuck all to do with you.'

Ali wanted to congratulate Sid for finally sticking up for herself. 'Ten years, Sid. Your whole adult life so far and you've never even…'

'What?' Sid's eyes burned into her now, daring her to say what came next.

'That's not a real relationship. That's not love.'

Sid's arms folded, defiant. 'Stop replying to him. He'll get the message. He'll get bored. He probably already is.'

The fact it was designed to hurt, so specifically tailored to gouge where Sid knew she'd feel it most was more appalling than the thing itself. If there was one magic phrase Ali could say to make her listen now, she couldn't think of it. The tears were coming and she didn't want to cry them here.

'It's all in the cloud. Everything I found. I sent you the link.'

Sid pretended not to hear and stared at the marble. 'I don't think we have biscuits.'

Something about the use of 'we' told Ali everything. They were back to where they'd been at the beginning.

'Don't worry about the tea.'

Ali kept the tears in until she was outside on the pavement.

Thirty

Ali cried because nothing was stronger than shame and Sid's shame could uproot trees and bring down buildings.

The street was busy so she slipped down a side alley into a small play park. When it was quiet and no one could see her, she found the tears wouldn't come any more. Numbness returned.

Back in her usual position on the bed, she stared at the blue folder on her desktop, the default wallpaper of patchwork green fields behind it. She opened a browser window and searched for the view from her childhood beach, the one she could see from the castle on walks with her dad. She set it as her new background and got lost in the green rocks poking out of a black turquoise sea. Her dad's hand holding hers, the gold signet ring on his little finger with the black stone, pressing into the pad of her palm.

The still city air hung outside the window, the smell of engines and cooked chicken seeping through the gap under the sash.

'Why collect us? Whole internet full of porn, but he keeps us.' Ali talked to herself sometimes, living alone. But now she held a daily dialogue with herself, sometimes interrogating witnesses, sometimes addressing a fellow detective, showing them her findings. And almost daily she opened the blue folder and stared at the tiny thumbnails, not wanting to expand them, thinking it somehow more decent to just peer at shapes and colours, the boxes keeping her company.

She scrolled down to the very bottom row and noticed another blue folder next to the last image. It bore the generic title 'New Folder'. She hadn't noticed it before. She double-clicked it and opened a short text document with a single paragraph at the top. It was a list of email addresses.

Drawn back to the thumbnails, she was about to close it when she saw the top of another line of text on the page below. She scrolled to find a shorter list of email addresses with small groups of letters and numbers next to each one. Every address ended with the same suffix - shhhmail.com

She opened the browser and searched for the shhhmail login page. A few seconds later she was looking at a stranger's inbox, stuffed with unopened spam. The subject lines were full of XXX and references to horny step sisters. Ali scanned the titles but could see no theme to indicate the user's taste. Just sex with non-blood relations.

She tried the second address. Another inbox similarly full, but every few messages, the contents had been read. She opened a thread of messages with an address that caught her eye: dembones123. They seemed to be a person rather than a bot.

Short emails went back and forth, some with attachments that hadn't downloaded, just icons where the file should be.

She stopped scrolling to read one. 'What can I do for you?'

'My favourite redhead. Fat bitch. I want to see her slap her arse and make it wobble.'

Another further down the thread: 'Not the ugly boyfriend. Tell her to fuck a stranger. Call him Uncle Bones. I'm a little slut, Uncle Bones while she chokes.'

She thought about Paul Bonatti's thin legs, wide eyes peering through rectangular glasses, Ed always calling him Bones. She imagined a skeleton fist around a skinny, white penis, pumping away.

Ed and Bones, naked at either end of a woman, like a threesome with Laurel and Hardy.

She followed the thread down to the reply: 'Delightful.'

Ali moved the laptop off her stomach, not wanting to touch it. She felt her breath shorten and her heart bunch in her chest. She hated that word and how he used it. 'Delightful.'

She began to take screen shots but she didn't know what for. She thought of Lloyd Appleyard poring over this electronic cesspit at his desk, fingers wiping over the track pad.

If these were Ed's emails, Ali wondered if he could tell that someone else was reading them. She shut her eyes and saw the word again: 'Delightful' and she knew it was him.

She picked up her phone with shaking hands and made a call. She looked in the bedside drawer for tablets to quell the acid in her throat as the line rang out.

'It's Summer, leave a message.'

Ali hung up. What was she going to do? Leave a voicemail casually inquiring if Summer knew that she was probably being passed around to other men?

She thought about what Summer had told her in Liverpool, about the other comedians he'd introduced her to at clubs. 'They knew. He didn't try to hide it. He'd bring me to a festival and it was obvious who I was to him. His friends, other comics, looking me up and down. They knew.'

Ali lay on her side and thumbed open the messages from Ed, zooming up the screen and stopping at each picture: Ed holding a pint of Guinness, a close-up of his face in a dressing-room mirror just before he went on stage, looking sad at the airport. She looked at his eyes and tried to imagine them deadened and browsing, bored by the acres of skin. There was something behind the penetrating gaze and elaborate sincerity that was sour and absent now. How had she not noticed it?

She closed her laptop and thought about packing warmer clothes for Scotland and what a relief the cool air would be.

Thirty-One

A group of girls in their twenties were opening canned cocktails and blocking the aisle of the train as they unpacked for their journey, apologising cheerfully to people trying to get past.

Ali watched them from behind her book, envying how comfortable they looked, arms around each other, sharing earbuds. One girl with long cornrows showed her friend a video on her phone. They had their hands over their mouths, laughter escaping their fingers. The two girls opposite them were laying out supplies on the table: drinks, snacks, magazines.

Ali had never had a group of friends like that: girls who moved in inclusive packs, doing your make-up for a first date, lending you a tampon. This was the train journey she and Ava would do every summer, until she met Andy. They'd tried to do the Fringe once, the three of them, but they never wanted to see the same shows and no matter how hard Ali tried, she couldn't help resenting Andy's presence. She'd felt more like a child on holiday with her parents as they organised the cooking and snubbed the late comedy shows for staying in.

When she tried to imagine herself on a protest, carrying a banner, Ali still wanted to die of shame. What face do you even do when you're protesting? What if she started laughing because people were looking at her?

She tried to imagine what she looked like to the group of young women. The dry, light brown ends of her hair sitting on her shoulders, a dark patterned dress loose, politely declining to describe what was underneath. Hooded eyes that had started to lower like roller blinds as she got to the end of her thirties. Did she look old to them? She thought about buying clothes more fitting for a 40-year-old woman when she got paid next month and then changed her mind, remembering Jean's little digs about 'dressing your age'. There was probably a cut-off for dressing like a student and she suspected it was already behind her, but she didn't know how to be anyone else.

If that was going to be her last pay cheque for a while, she might as well spend it on something she actually liked. She'd bought the train ticket to Scotland, not looking at her account balance, trying not to think about what would happen to her job in the autumn. What if she just carried on, did the show with Ed, pretended not to know who he really was. Other people in her industry did it all the time. Why should she be any different?

She picked up her phone and found a message waiting. She'd turned off her alerts, the idea of her phone making a noise and disturbing the rest of the train mortifying to her.

There's being a sell-out, then there's selling out!

It was accompanied by a picture of a blackboard covered in coloured chalk writing, a large blue and red Sold Out emblazoned in the middle. She zoomed into Ed's name in green chalk and 'All Mouth' written next to it in pink.

She looked out of the window, dredging her mind for original responses. She thought about not replying at all and how transgressive that would be. Just leaving him hanging there, waiting for the expected praise. Turning off the tap while he held his cup out.

He sold out! Nice. x

But he was already onto the next thought.

Too good for these cunts. Ignore me, low energy day. Don't know how I used to do this for a whole month oh wait yeah I do drugs. x

He sounded sour, even when things were apparently good. Or maybe she was imagining it.

London's rubbish-strewn railway sidings had given way to countryside, baked fields interrupted by the pulse of trees and industrial buildings, beating out a code in her peripheral vision. Trains always made her want to sleep, but shutting her eyes put her whole body on alert.

She was still holding her phone, the conversation left open uncomfortably like a fridge door.

On my way up. Let you know when I'm Scot-side. x

There was no reply. Just enough talking to coax her out and then nothing.

The volume of the girls opposite had risen as the drink relaxed them, making them forget their neighbours.

Ali must have been staring. The one with the long hair leaned over and offered her an open bag of crisps, brows raised in question. Ali shook her head shyly and went back to her book. She'd tried to smile with her refusal but the girl's reaction suggested she'd failed. The group passed looks between them and their conversation restarted.

Ali knew what they thought about her. They were probably right.

Thirty-Two

The walk up the ramp from Waverley train station was Ali's tradition. The escalators were busy and thrust you straight into the bustle of the main street, bagpipes squawking and tourists filling the pavement with wheeled suitcases, looking for their hotels.

The ramp from the concourse was quieter and gradually revealed the city to you as you climbed, the gloomy spikes of the old town's Gothic roof line prodding into the sky on the left and the blackened spire of the Scott Monument like a rocket on a launchpad over to the right.

The wall to the gardens opposite was lined with posters for shows. Mad, clowning faces took up every spare space, gurning for attention. Ballerinas in a row with their arms crossed in front of them, witches hunched over a cauldron, someone in a mortar board, eyebrow raised at a piece of chalk.

Ali looked up at the unexpectedly bright sky and followed the jumble of turrets along to the sulking stone of Edinburgh Castle, high on its mound. The old volcano forced its way out of the ground like a prehistoric creature, turned to stone as it arched its back towards the daylight.

She realised she was smiling. She pulled her suitcase over the tram tracks and through the throng towards a large square, where the mood was less frantic.

The crowds thinned. Refugees from the madness of the final week in August lazed on the grass under a huge monument in the centre of the lawn, like the pigeons had picked up Nelson's Column from Trafalgar Square and dropped it in Scotland. A few people queued outside a hut selling coffee. The trams ran alongside, stopping to open and close their doors, scooping up tourists with shopping bags.

The occasional yelp of seagulls reminded her how near to the water she was. The skyline was so much to take in, but the site of the glistening sea at the end of the road always brought her to a stop. A beautiful afterthought. She wondered at the romance of the men who'd decided to build a city on a dead volcano by the sea. Maybe if she hadn't moved to England as a child, if she was here every day, she'd be over it by now, inured to the brushstroke skies and cobbled streets. But it felt like a beautiful rush of new and old, every time she came back.

She looked at the water and the hills on the other side of the firth and remembered the same view from the beach along the coast where she'd played. She'd been scared of the gulls when they landed near her on the sand, their enormous, yellow beaks and hard, black eyes like something from a Harryhausen film, eyeing her chips.

Ali sat on the grass and looked on her phone for directions to the flat. She thought about Ed. It didn't feel real that they were in the same place again. The hairs on her arms were standing up. Somewhere not far away, he was sitting, probably searching the internet for gushing praise from the audiences who'd seen his show. Or maybe he was with someone, last night's girl walking around the flat wearing his t-shirt, bringing him coffee.

Kat's place was on a wide terrace in New Town. The building had three slate-grey storeys, a pair of tall windows on each level. Ali looked up at the imposing door painted the same grey as a battleship. At the top of stone steps lined with black spiked railings, she paused to look at the street. On the other side of the traffic, high hedges concealed a large private garden dotted with tall trees. Ali loved these grand Edinburgh rows and crescents, the high ceilings and wide, timber-floored rooms yawning with space that could never be filled. Ordinary furniture looked pointless in the vastness of the rooms.

Ali found the key safe and punched in the code, shouldering the door open and pulling her case over the threshold. Hot and out of breath, she reached the top landing and looked down the stairwell to the chequered hall below, feeling the blood rush to her head. She wondered if Kat ever came here. Edinburgh didn't strike Ali as a very Kat place.

She used the last of her energy to push herself and her case through the door into a light hallway. She was glad of the cream walls. In front of her was a sunburst mirror over a teak sideboard. It wasn't lived in. She looked at herself, hair sticking to her damp forehead, skin blotchy from the exertion of the climb. The flat made her want to be a better person, the kind who could live here and pad around in bare feet, using the complicated pod machine to make professional-looking coffees, drunk out of large Scandinavian mugs.

She left her suitcase where it was, pushing open the doors off the hall until she found a bedroom and flopped onto the clean, grey covers, careful to let her boots hang over the edge. Her face pressed into the cotton.

Rolling onto her back, she looked at the white paper shade hanging from a plaster rose above her. She could smell furniture polish and fabric softener. She wished she could stay forever.

A short buzz in the small of her back told her she'd rolled onto her phone.

Thinking about you. x

Again, it felt like Ed was watching her, knowing her every move. She thought about him typing out the message while the girl wearing his t-shirt lay next to him on a large bed.

She rolled onto her side and looked at the small, green bubble of text.

See you soon. x

She was still trying to bait him, giving too little away. Some part of her still wanted him to chase. But the thought of what he might do if he caught her made her go cold inside.

When she opened her eyes again, it was overcast and rain was splattering the window on the far side of the room.

She decided to explore her surroundings. She went from room to room, muttering to herself about how much it must all be worth, falling onto a giant, blue sofa, enjoying its proportions, higher and wider than anything she'd sat on before. The kitchen was undisturbed calm, no sign of previous cooks or water marks on the taps. Gloss black panels hid every appliance apart from a chrome and black coffee machine with a wicker basket of pods next to it.

It was 9 o'clock and Ed's show would still be in full swing. She got an anorak out of her case, put up the hood and went out for groceries. As the first drops of rain hit her hood and she bent forward, she remembered what Sid had said about chasing drama. Or was it Summer?

It was two days before the end of the festival. The rows of posters along the railings were hanging on. Stapled-on strips of paper announcing star ratings flapped in the wind. She made for the lights of a supermarket next to a tall, thin church. It was getting dark.

She couldn't decide what she wanted to eat and eventually turned for home with a bag of apples, a block of cheese and a bottle of Picpoul swinging in a cloth bag.

As she walked, lightning illuminated familiar features, fusing her boots to the pavement. A line of posters emblazoned with Ed's face were, side by side, creased with damp, the eyes boring into her. 'All Mouth,' shouted the show title across his chest in Gothic black letters. He was just a head and shoulders, dressed in a dinner jacket and bow tie, pink rouge on his cheeks and a thick black line drawn down from either side of his mouth. His eyes stared, a dummy threatening to come to life.

The picture had been taken before the comfort eating of the last few weeks had started to make its way under his chin, padding his jawline. Ali remembered how much she'd laughed when he'd shown her the contact sheet. In each picture he was trying out a variation on the same empty expression, always looking directly down the lens. They'd talked about a film she loved that featured a creepy dummy that came to life and killed people. Or the ventriloquist was mad and it had been him all along.

Ed had been so engaged as she spoke, marvelling at what she knew and how much he loved the same things. So weird that they were so similar, they'd agreed.

Every picture of him looked different now. Like someone had re-arranged the window of a familiar shop.

Ali became self-conscious, staring at his face. She lowered her head and made for the flat, quickening her pace. The sharp clang of a bell pulled her up just in time to see a tram swing around the corner and fill the road in front of her, the lights and faces in the windows bombing past at speed as thunder rumbled somewhere above the castle, like the volcano was waking from its sleep.

In the hallway, leaning against the inside of the front door, Ali's pulse felt like it was escaping her neck. She ran up the stairs two at a time and spilled the contents of her shopping bag onto the dining table, holding the back of a chair. The glass bottle clanked against the glazed top of the table and for a moment she thought it had smashed.

Behind one of the panels in the kitchen, she found wine glasses, the substantial kind with a flattened bowl on a thin stem that people drink out of on TV shows. She put the cheese in the fridge and the apples in a bowl on the dining table and took her enormous drink to the enormous sofa as slowly her heart rate returned to normal.

Her phone battery was about to die. She wondered if Summer

was in Edinburgh yet, or if she'd stay away to avoid her. She wanted to call her and invite her over to get pissed and talk about Ed. She realised with a pang of self-loathing that talking about Ed was still what she wanted to do. She couldn't think of a single other subject that interested her.

Plugging her charger in, she began to text.

Just got in. How was the show? x

Ed's reply arrived a few minutes later. She'd turned the TV on to a property programme. A blonde woman was guiding a couple around a Spanish villa, her sandals clicking on the terracotta floors.

Who knows? They laughed. I can't settle. Your kind can predict the weather – is the storm going to pass? x

She pictured him huffing around the flat. Would Sid be there? She'd be staying out of his way.

My kind?
Witches.

Ali tried to remember what she'd have said in the before times. Something about spells, some reassurance about the show. She'd tell him that he was no judge of his own work. She started typing, tingling as she persisted with the lie.

I'm sure you were great. Sorry you're feeling odd. Check out my giant sofa. Feel like a Borrower. Wish you were here. x

She pointed her phone camera at her legs stretched out in front of her, toes painted red, proving they didn't reach to the far end of the enormous couch. She didn't feel like herself, like they were someone else's legs. The owner of the legs seemed to be making an invitation. Running towards the tram tracks with her eyes closed. She refilled her glass while she waited for a reply.

Wish I was too. Early interview tomorrow. Sleep well. x

She knew she wouldn't sleep for hours.

He was putting her off because he had other plans tonight. Sid was right. The game was to keep her burning. It wasn't even 10 o'clock and he had one week at the Fringe. His evening was just beginning.

She checked WhatsApp, desperate for distraction. The Scolds were quiet but she supposed they would start talking tomorrow. Nothing to do tonight but wait. Ali brought up their website in her browser. It was still the red text on a black background but now red digits appeared in the top right corner, silently marking the hours, minutes and seconds.

The clock counted down to midnight on Saturday.

Thirty-Three

Ali had decided to brave a café in broad daylight. When she looked at the breakfast menu, she knew what Ed would have told her to order. She asked the waiter for a boiled egg and soldiers instead.

As she wiped a stub of brown toast round the yolk streaks on her plate, congratulating herself on eating a meal alone, in public, without Ed for company on her phone, she watched the door of the café.

She thanked the waiter too profusely when he came back for her plate. 'That was so good, thanks. Delicious.'

He smiled politely and turned to walk away.

'Actually, could I get another flat white, please? A friend's joining me.'

He nodded an acknowledgement and Ali went back to her phone.

She searched for reviews of Ed's show. Half a page of results appeared, a couple of three-star ratings. One three point five. That would drive him mad. Mediocrity. At least if they hated him, he could console himself it was personal.

Bethan was peering in from the other side of the glass, hands cupped around her eyes. She spotted Ali and raised a hand.

As she came in, a couple sitting by the door stopped her to say something, smiling bashfully. Bethan dipped her head as she took off her headphones, seemed to thank them and made for Ali's table. 'Hey, all right?'

Ali got up and Bethan gestured her back to her seat.

'Friends of yours?'

Bethan put her headphones round her neck. 'Oh, no. Just…' She wrinkled her nose.

'Oh, fans. You'll have to get used to that.' Ali worried it sounded patronising. 'I mean, I'm sure you already are. Congratulations on the nomination.'

Bethan smiled and sat down. 'Thanks. Listen, I can't come. I've got a photo thing before the awards. Cass knows you're coming. The others are nice, I promise.'

Ali sat back down. 'Oh, no worries.' She tried to look breezy about it. 'So do we know who is going to be there?'

'Cass. You know her. And probably a few other Scolds who haven't got their kits yet. They'll take you through everything. The pub's right on the harbour, you can't miss it. Don't look so worried.'

Ali was deflated she wasn't styling this out. 'I haven't really marched or, you know, fought the power before. Jesus, how old am I?'

Bethan grinned. 'It's just a couple of petrol bombs. Joke.'

Ali widened her eyes. 'OK, I'll be fine. Go on, go. And good luck with the massive awards. Will you get a real gold trophy?'

Beth pocketed her phone and puffed her cheeks out. 'Real gold plastic. It's all bollocks really.' Then she thought better of it. 'No, thank you. Thanks. My promoter was loads better this year. People could actually find the show. I'm gonna break even, I think. I hope.' She mimed showering the table with fifties like a casino croupier.

Ali could see she was pleased.

Bethan's body language suggested imminent motion. 'Oh, take a bag with you. Like a backpack. Have you got something?'

Ali nodded. 'Yeah. Back at the flat. You probably need to…'

Bethan's phone was beeping at her. 'I do. Sorry. You'll be fine. Thanks for this.

More the merrier.'

'Of course.'

The waiter set the cup down and Ali was alone again. She prodded the milky picture in the top of the coffee with a spoon and thought about how Bethan hadn't mentioned Ed and neither had she. The delicate beige leaf swirled into something like a face. It looked like it was screaming.

The waiter brought her bill. 'Could I have this to go, please?'

A few minutes later, Ali was on a tram, tingling from too much caffeine and heading towards the sea. Sitting on the shady side of the aisle, she looked out through the window at passing shop fronts topped by flats the colour of dirty envelopes.

They passed the theatre, a billboard of Tom Weissman's giant American head hanging over the main entrance. His gigs had sold out as soon as they were announced. The comedian's comedian was too good at his job for permanent cancellation. Ali tried to think of a man who was permanently cancelled but couldn't come up with anyone.

In the Scolds' WhatsApp group some had alluded to 'direct action' but Ali didn't know what it meant. A montage of window-smashing and paint-throwing played in her head and she tried to place herself in it, scarf tied around her face. She couldn't imagine herself earnestly pressing flyers into people's hands either. Activism just seemed so humourless.

The wide streets and looming cranes as they got near to the docks reminded her of London. She didn't usually go north of Leith Walk when she came to the festival. The tower blocks of Leith were always at a distance, a whole part of the city she didn't know.

The tram reached its terminus and Ali followed Bethan's directions along the seafront. Fishing boats were corralled into a walled marina on her right, a small white lighthouse on the sea wall stood to attention like the shepherd who'd herded them there.

Ali stalled as she caught sight of the pub and ducked into a small, sloping park opposite the entrance, hoping she wasn't visible from the windows. Being early would just give her more time to lose her nerve.

She walked up the grassy slope to a row of benches along a path that overlooked the water. A woman sat on the middle of three in a plastic rain hood tied with white straps under her chin. She raised her head as Ali approached, nodding towards the space next to her.

Ali found herself sitting, not wanting to look rude.

'All on your own?' The woman was fussing something on her lap wrapped in a white napkin. She lifted a corner of the fabric and reached into her pocket for a small, glass salt cellar like one from a café table.

Ali resented the question. Maybe this hooded woman was a warning from the future to hurry up and get a life or she'd end up on a windy seafront, begging strangers for scraps of conversation.

The woman held the now unwrapped object out to her. It was a boiled egg, peeled and denting where her finger and thumb pressed into its flesh.

Ali shook her head, eyebrows raised. 'No, thanks. I've literally just had one.' She looked out to sea, focusing on the black strip of land beyond the water, one continuous cloud loitering over the low hills of Fife.

'I've got another. You sure?' Satisfied she'd done all she could, the woman shook salt onto the top of the egg and took a bite.

Ali thought about the women in the pub. The prospect of seeing Cass again made her feel small and stupid and she thought about going back to the tram stop. Just hiding in the flat, telling them she was ill.

'Are you thinking of going in?'

'Sorry?' Ali realised the woman was still talking to her.

'Going in?' She gestured at the harbour with her egg. Little crumbs of white had settled in the bristles on her top lip.

'Oh, no. Bit cold for me.'

'You'll not want to take a dip round here anyway. Mucky water, all of it. You'll catch something. Portobello's where you want. You go there.'

Ali smiled her thanks for the information and thought about how best to leave without causing offence.

'Malcolm was in every day. This is years ago, of course. But summer or winter, in he went.' She was looking at the water, her blue eyes moistening. It could have been the wind.

'Is that your husband?'

She nodded. 'Was. I'd watch him, bring him his flask. When it was warmer. In January he was on his own.' She laughed to herself.

'You must miss him.' Ali felt bad for wanting to go.

She thought for a moment, like she was checking with the sea that they had their story straight. 'He could be an awful pain in the arse.'

She bit into the egg again, dried yolk falling onto the cloth. 'Everything his way.' She was squinting at the water as though he was still out there. 'No talking with yer mouth full.' She let out another short, sharp laugh.

Ali nodded, not sure if she was supposed to agree that Malcolm was, in fact, a bit of a tyrant.

'He didn't like my friends coming round to the house.'

Malcolm sounded like a bastard but Ali decided it was politer not to say so. She made a show of looking at her watch and tutted.

'I'd actually better…'

The woman rolled the salt cellar up in the napkin. 'Yes, I need to be going too. Coffee with the girls. We call ourselves the Scottish Widows.' She was laughing to herself again.

Ali stood and looked towards the pub and back at her bench companion.

She was fiddling with the straps under her chin and removing her hood. 'It's stopped raining now, hasn't it? Not going in, then?'

Ali looked confused, then the clouds parted. 'Oh. Not today.'

'You do what you want. You're free as a bird.'

Thirty-Four

Inside, the dark snug bar opened out into a larger room overlooking the sea. Wooden models of galleons lined the windowsills. One table at the far end was occupied by three people but otherwise it was quiet. It was only half an hour after opening and the serious drinkers hadn't surfaced yet.

Ali recognised Cass, and the woman next to her was Mo Graham, a comedian Ali had seen on a couple of panel shows. The third had her back to Ali, her blonde hair in two tight buns like teddy bear's ears. They were deep in conversation, so she got herself a drink — a half of shandy, mostly to give her something to do with her hands. She hated introducing herself to strangers.

'Hey.' Cass nodded towards the empty chair. 'You made it. This is Mo, Steph.' She turned to her companions. 'Ali's a late addition. She's going to help us with some decorating tonight.'

They both nodded and smiled.

'Decorating. Right.' Ali scraped her chair forward and tucked both feet underneath. 'As in...'

Cass didn't answer the implied question. 'When did you get up to town? Yesterday?'

Steph was already talking over her. 'How many altogether tonight, then?'

'Thirty-two on flyering. Most of them have their stuff.' Cass pulled a black messenger bag onto her lap and began taking bundles of coloured paper out and laying them on the table. 'Crew of three on the Playhouse. Everyone needs two of these, a list and a map.' She slid two fist-sized bundles of coloured paper secured with rubber bands towards Ali.

Ali used her sleeve to wipe the table where her drink had left a wet ring and moved the glass away. She flicked through one of the bundles. They were stickers, sharp-cornered red eyes with yellow corneas and black pupils. Some the size of her hand and a few sheets of smaller eyeballs staring out at her.

The other pile were yellow squares in a red frame, a black QR code printed in the middle.

'OK, so two eyes on each face, obviously. Then a QR code on the mouth. Try to use whatever size best fits the poster.'

Ali thought it better to ask now, rather than continuing her policy of pretending to know what she was doing and feeling stupid about it. 'And these are for where? The posters all over town?'

Cass was still taking things out of her bag. 'Got it in one. Names on the list refer to the posters we're hitting.'

Ali looked at her list and quickly saw there was no Ed. 'How will people know what this means?'

Cass clasped her hands on the table. 'Social media saturation since day one of the festival. We've established something is happening on Saturday at midnight. Everyone up here knows.'

'Right, the countdown.' Ali didn't trust herself to pick her drink up yet without her hand shaking.

Steph leaned in. 'They're expecting stage invasions. The management at my venue are shitting it. They're talking about extra door people at some shows.'

Mo was playing with a silver hoop hanging from her right ear. 'Most promoters are trying to pre-empt what we're doing but they have no idea. They're probably picturing women gluing themselves to stages.'

Cass pushed bundles towards Steph and Mo. 'They're looking the wrong way.' She turned to Ali. 'Three Scolds and a ladder—'

Mo interrupted. 'The new sitcom coming soon to ITV3.'

Cass resumed. 'Three of them are climbing up the front of the Playhouse and giving Tom Weissman the same treatment, only bigger. More visibility. The press will be tipped off. Then we'll hit the rest of town while everyone goes to get a selfie with the giant predator.'

Ali nodded, finally feeling relaxed enough to swallow again. She picked up her beer. 'This is great. And the QR code takes you to the website?'

Steph and Mo exchanged a look that would normally have sent Ali scurrying back inside her shell, but she wanted to be part of this. 'You're publishing their names on the website?'

Cass was nodding again. 'A list of names. Some of them aren't faces obviously, the promoters, others the public won't recognise. But their names will be there too, with the word CREEPS in red at the top, nothing else. We talked to a lawyer. It's basically low abuse. Predator, abuser, groomer, they're all actionable. But they can't sue us for calling them a creep.'

Steph interrupted. 'We've harnessed our greatest power.' She looked at Ali, inviting her to guess.

'Multi-tasking?'

Cass's laugh in response felt generous.

'Gossip,' said Steph.

Mo had been looking at her phone and now put it back in her pocket. 'We've been here for a month, dropping bombs. Spreading the word. When that list comes out, when every fucking creep in town is a marked man, they'll know why. Everyone will know why.'

Cass finished the water in front of her. 'Don't share that list with anyone. No leaving it in a bin afterwards, OK. Take everything with you.'

Steph and Mo put their bundles into bags under the table.

'Your section is highlighted in yellow on the map. Stick to those streets and those names. You'll liaise tonight with one of us before the off. Any questions?'

Ali could feel the muscles relaxing in her neck. They weren't setting fire to anything. 'So just stickers on posters? Eyes, mouth.' She held an eye and a neon gag over her own face.

'Yeah, best put them away.'

Ali felt stupid. 'Sorry.'

Cass gave her a reassuring smile. 'It's OK. We've done a lot of groundwork. This bit's the icing. Let's get it right, yeah?'

The other two were getting up.

'Ali, happy?'

Ali nodded. She really was.

'It shouldn't take you more than an hour. Go straight home. Don't hang around drinking with this stuff in your bag. We're being over-cautious but this only works if they don't know where it's coming from.'

'Absolutely.' Ali grinned.

Steph and Mo signalled they were leaving. Ali and Cass walked back towards the tram stop together.

'Word of mouth is obviously key. So, Sunday morning, feel free to spread the word, any pictures, RT, use the hashtag. I saw this. Who are Scold's Bridle? Amplify, yeah? As long as you don't say specifically who it's coming from.'

Ali thought about the contraband in her bag. She needed to calm down. 'No worries. I'm going to walk along the water for a bit.'

'Good luck tonight. We'll be in touch on Sunday.'

Ali walked along the harbour wall to the lighthouse, clutching her bag like it contained thousands in cash.

The wind slapped at her face as she watched the dark green water roll and toss under her feet for a while, the tension leaving her shoulders and neck.

As the gulls wheeled and dived in the distance, she realised she was looking forward to this.

Thirty-Five

The shutters were down on the bars and food trucks around George Square. A rubbish lorry made its stately procession down the cobbles as teams of people in orange jackets removed the flyers and food cartons from around the overflowing bins.

Ali hovered at the entrance to the underpass. She lit a cigarette and leaned her bum on the railings, trying to look like she had a reason to stop.

Ed's venue was just beyond the exit to the tunnel. He'd been there just a few hours ago. She felt like he was haunting her, or she was haunting him.

Every cell of her was broadcasting guilt. Cass assured her that defacing posters wasn't a crime, but Ali clenched every time she heard a siren.

She'd been pulled over by the police once, driving through the Warwickshire countryside late at night with a car full of hammered friends. They'd only invited her to the party because she offered to drive them home.

When the police car pulled up in front of them, Ali's arms shook and she had to grab the wheel tight in both hands as the officer approached her window. He told her she was driving with sidelights and she needed to put the headlights on. The memory of it still made her want to curl into a ball.

Footsteps from the other end of the tunnel made her look up. There were two figures walking towards her. Ali couldn't make out their faces until the tunnel light illuminated them.

Mo's silver hoops flashed in the gloom and she was followed by a shorter figure in a dark woolly hat.

'All right? Nippy, isn't it?'

Ali recognised the vocal fry of Bethan.

'You're here!' Ali's voice was too loud. She mugged, her hand over her mouth, then took it away and mouthed 'Sorry.'

'I wouldn't miss this. Their fucking faces tomorrow. Where are you doing?'

'Other side of the underpass down to Drummond Street.'

'Did you go to the picket?'

Mo answered. 'Not as many as we'd hoped, but we made a noise. The bigger names didn't go in through the front. Someone tipped them off. Tom Weissman is getting his make-over as we speak.'

Bethan scratched her head under her hat. 'We've got one man out with us tonight. And thirty women.'

'That's depressing.' Ali didn't want to lose the buzz of optimism she needed to keep her going. 'But this feels like something. Right?'

'Talking of which.' Mo wanted to move.

Bethan raised an imaginary cigar to her mouth. 'OK, good luck. It's gaggin' time.'

Ali watched them go, her legs twanging like they wanted to run and keep running. Every sound made her start as she began the walk towards her first designated street. She turned onto Chambers Street and looked at her map, following the yellow highlighter pen line to the right of where she stood.

She checked the list, looking at posters on the hoardings outside a big venue on the other side of the street. A suave man with shoulder-length brown hair watched her, frozen mid tie-adjustment, his two-dimensional image repeated over several of the hoardings as she walked along.

She peeled the backing off her first sticker and smoothed it over one of his eyes, flattening the air bubbles with her thumb. When she was finished, she admired the gagging effect of the QR code slapped over his mouth.

The people walking past didn't seem to notice her. Just another flyposter covering the city in paper.

She moved onto the next, a skinny, younger guy in a white boiler suit, running away from the camera, looking over his shoulder. She hadn't heard of him. The stickers didn't quite work. His body was too small and his head was at the wrong angle. But she told herself this wasn't supposed to be art.

She got quicker, less precise with the placement, taking satisfaction from the sea of red and yellow dotted along the railings down Drummond Street.

Forty minutes later, she was picking her way down the hill towards the Pleasance, the cobbles slippy underfoot from the morning dew. Another team had done the main road, where larger posters advertised some of the big names on the railings opposite.

Ali froze as a police car drove slowly past, quickly turning towards the wall and looking down at her hand as though it were a phone. Once the car was gone, she crossed the road to the gates of the courtyard, now locked for the night. A few Scolds stickers dotted the boards around the entrance, the pairs of angry red eyes turning their wearers into tetchy lab rats. The ones who were smiling looked particularly deranged behind their muzzles.

Ali felt the rumblings of anti-climax as the adrenalin began to drain from her. 'What if no one notices?' She realised she'd said it out loud to the empty street.

She turned and leaned on the wall to pull her sock out of her boot where it had bunched up. Her eyes drifted to the railings opposite. Bethan's face beamed back at her under her show's title, *'Bethan Gill: Dragon Lady'*. She was draped in a Welsh flag and yawning a plume of fire over a blackened landscape. A triangular yellow panel stuck to the top right-hand corner announced her as Best Comedy Show nominee.

Ali smiled, then she saw the neighbouring poster. A pair of mean, red eyes stared out from the face of Ed Catchpole.

She put both hands to her mouth. 'Fuuuuuuck.' She took it in some more. 'Shit. Shit.'

She whispered as though with an accomplice, new adrenalin carving its way through her like a knife. 'He's going to fucking lose it.'

She grabbed her phone, took a picture and ran, stifling shrieks as her feet pounded the cobbles back up the hill.

Thirty-Six

Jumping up and down in the kitchen of the flat, Ali wheezed and laughed and caught her breath.

She tried to compose a message to Bethan but autocorrect and her vibrating thumbs kept thwarting her.

Pleasant railings! PLEASANCE fucking hell!!!

She walked to the middle of the room and stood there, not sure what to do with the twitching in her limbs. 'What's the wifi?' She twirled around, looking for a router or a visitor's book. 'What's the wifi?' she shouted again.

When she was finally connected, she sent the picture of Ed in all his red-eyed glory to Summer and Sid on their long-quiet message thread. They'd want to know, even if they weren't talking to her any more.

She sank into the giant sofa, breathing, arms limp, legs tingling. Bethan's reply slid onto Ali's screen.

Had some big ones left over. x

Ali couldn't find the letters fast enough.

This is mad. Thank you.??????

Summer replied to the picture.

Fuck offfffff. Is this real? Did YOU do it? At Fun Club flat. Where u?

Half an hour later, Summer was thudding up the stairs towards Ali's front door, holding a bottle of tequila by the neck.

'Shhhh.' Ali mimed at her from the doorway, nodding at the flat door opposite. She hadn't seen anyone go in or come out but the echo down the stairs made her self-conscious.

Summer put a finger to her lips and tip-toed the rest of the way. When she got to Ali's landing, she mouthed 'Oh my God' and they went inside.

They sat on the sofa and Summer turned to her, something important to say. The smell of sweet grapes was on her breath and she was looking Ali straight in the chin, one eye squinting slightly. 'I'm sorry. I was a priiiick.' She elongated the vowel sound to make her point.

Ali was nodding and laughing. 'It's OK.'

Summer took the cork out of the bottle and they sat side by side, buzzing and taking sips as early-morning light filled the room.

Ali had never liked tequila. It made her think of worms and dirt, but she felt like she was tasting it for the first time. It was sweet and sharp and something else she couldn't place.

Breakfast news was starting as they turned on the TV.

'Why isn't it the top story?' demanded Summer, waving the bottle towards a newsreader with shiny brown hair and sharp cheekbones.

She went to the window and fiddled with the latches on the sash, heaving it up and ducking underneath to get the breeze.

Ali hadn't noticed the tattoo on the back of Summer's leg, a delicate spiders' web, a dagger tangled in it.

Summer rolled a cigarette on the windowsill as she spoke 'When you came to see me, you freaked me the fuck out. I was still... the feelings haven't gone. I hate it, hearing what he's like with the others. It still makes me sick. I'm working on it.'

'I know. I mean, I can imagine.'

'Your brain still goes, he's mine. Which is nuts because he never was and who'd want that fuck anyway? But my therapist says I'm trauma-bonded?'

'Like a kidnap victim? Is that Stockholm syndrome?'

'Yeah, no, not that but like that. He made me depend on him, on his approval.

Now I don't know how to live without it. Like drugs. But I will.'

'You will.' Ali thought about the far-off longing in her own stomach. Its sharpness was lessening, definitely. It got weaker the more time she spent with people instead of constantly living in her own head.

Summer leaned out of the window, fag in her mouth and announced to the street in a stage whisper, 'I will! You fucker!'

'Shhhhhh.' Ali put her hand out to Summer. 'Look.' She turned up the volume on the TV.

The camera panned from the Edinburgh traffic to the front of the Playhouse. Tom Weissman's expansive forehead dripped with red paint and huge red eyes now covered his. The Scolds' gag on his mouth was the size of a dinner table.

Ali was on the edge of the sofa, feeling the cushions, plunging her hands down the gaps. 'Where's my phone? They put the fucking code on the TV. Get your phone.'

Summer dropped her cigarette out of the window and picked up her phone. 'Oh my fucking God.' She pointed her camera at the TV and waited.

The Scolds' website loaded on Summer's screen, the expanse of black now covered in red text, the countdown clock all zeroes.

'It's updated. Fuck. They're all there.' Summer was serious now, intently focused on the words in front of her. 'Rob Tapper, Tom Weissman, Paul Bonatti fuck!' She ran her finger down the text.

'That's my old boss at Smirkhouse. Alistair Watson.' Summer pointed a matt black nail at the last name.

The newsreader was talking over footage of theatre staff looking up at the hoarding. She said activists had targeted the theatre overnight, but that Tom Weissman's second performance would go ahead as planned.

'The group, calling themselves Scold's Bridle, covered the city in their trademark evil-eye motifs in a bid to draw attention to abuse in the comedy industry. None of the comics whose posters were targeted were available for comment.'

'I bet they fucking weren't. Is that national?' Summer started rolling another smoke.

Ali studied the screen. 'No, local. But still.'

As the city woke up, the Scolds hashtags #markedmen and #gagged began to trend. They scrolled through photos of defaced posters. It was mostly women talking to each other, the men saying nothing.

Ali and Summer lay back with their feet up, toasting the names on the list as they read them out, taking it in turns.

'Ed Catchpole,' said Ali. They leaned together, heads touching, the alcohol forming a soft membrane around them. Summer put the bottle to Ali's lips and poured a slug.

Summer put the bottle between her knees and turned to her, tilting her head like she was trying to see her better. Then they were kissing, Summer's tongue inviting itself into Ali's mouth. Ali didn't move away. She thought about Summer's lipstick spreading over her face like jam.

It lasted for a few seconds, Summer's hand moving to the back of Ali's head, a buzz travelling up Ali's neck.

When they stopped, they both started laughing, Ali following Summer's lead. She hadn't kissed a girl since university. Summer's lipstick was still perfect and Ali wondered for a moment whether it had even happened.

Summer reached for her phone on the table. 'Wait, just got to film this for Ed.' She made her eyes huge like she was daring herself to do it. Ali grabbed Summer's phone and slid it across the floor, laughing hard.

She fell back, leaden drunk, like she couldn't move off the sofa now if it was on fire. 'How do you still have perfect lipstick? Look at it.'

Summer smirked over her shoulder as she crawled to retrieve the phone. 'You're a good kisser. Sorry.' She shook her head and kneeled up, cupping both hands around her mouth as though shouting down a canyon. 'I have no boundaries.'

Ali pretended to be checking her face for lipstick, blotting with the back of her hand, but she was still tumbling through the air, the things on the shelves opposite swaying gently as she looked at them.

Summer crawled back to the sofa and crossed her legs under her, putting a subtle distance between them again, swaying with the shelf ornaments. 'This is so me. I like you, so I must also fuck you. My therapist is going to have a field day.'

Ali was dizzy, still aware of the sensation in her body. The feeling of being wanted was so powerful, she wished it could go on and on. If Summer had kept kissing her, she wouldn't have stopped her.

Summer went back to the window to smoke a new roll-up, things returning to normal but somehow more intimate than before.

They both agreed they liked sex more than they thought was usual, the high it gave them, that they felt the need to chase it. They used it to blot out sadness. They knew that's what Ed had liked about them, that they were looking for what he was selling, that it hadn't been difficult to get them hooked.

Ali's phone lit up on the coffee table and Summer turned to look. 'Jesus, does it send up a bat signal every time two women get off with each other? Right now there's an alarm sounding in his nuts.'

Ali tapped the screen.

I need to see you. Today. x

'He needs to see me today.' She looked at Summer's phone on the sofa. 'Three, two, one…' It remained a dark shape, no activity. 'Just me?' The tumble dryer reactivated in Ali's stomach, fear and excitement falling over anticipation and dread. And lust. Still lust. But maybe that was Summer's tongue.

Summer steepled her fingers and furrowed her brow. 'And how does that make you feel?'

Ali watched the black-haired girl covering her envy with a joke. It still stung. 'How does that make YOU feel?' That's so like her, Ali thought, enjoying their familiarity.

Ed's message sat between them and Ali resented it for interrupting whatever this was. He didn't wait for an answer.

You're the only one I can talk to.

Ali didn't show Summer that one. A final message stacked on top of it.

1 o'clock at Arthur's Seat. I'll drop a pin. x

Ali read the last one out loud and Summer arched an eyebrow. 'He knows. He's going to push you off the top.'

'He can't know. It wasn't even us, not his posters anyway.'

Summer stubbed out her cigarette on the windowsill. 'He knows.'

Ali's phone lit up again. She looked down and tears unexpectedly filled her eyes.

She passed it to Summer. 'From Bethan.'

New info came in.
We believe you. x

Thirty-Seven

They slept in Ali's bed, Ali resting her head on Summer's shoulder until the dark-haired girl was asleep. Then she rolled away to find a cool section of pillow.

When she woke, Summer was already up and it was just past eleven. She looked at the reply she'd sent Ed, drunk.

OK, see you there. x

She regretted adding the kiss.

She came out of the bathroom with wet hair and checked the time.

Sitting on the edge of the bed. she googled 'Arthur's Seat deaths', scanning the headings while she applied thin, black eye-liner, finishing in little flicks. She landed on the story of a young couple who'd eloped from Germany in the 1970s. When they arrived in Edinburgh, the boy had taken the girl for a walk up to Salisbury Crags and pushed her off for the insurance money.

Summer stood in the doorway, her pale face round like the moon and scrubbed of make-up. 'Masking tape.'

Ali took the brush away from her eyes. 'Huh?'

'That's how I get the flicks sharp. Masking tape. I've always got a roll in my bag.'

Ali gawped at her like she'd invented the wheel. 'Amazing.'

Summer watched as she went back to work, checking that her eyes were even.

'I know a guy in Bootle who could get you a gun, but it won't be here in time.'

Ali didn't laugh. 'Too risky. Someone'll hear.'

'You don't have to do this, go halfway up a mountain just to tell him to go fuck himself. I'll do it now if you want. Pass me your phone.'

'It's a volcano.'

Summer rolled her eyes. 'We were rancid last night. You still want to go?'

Ali turned to her, screwing the eyeliner brush back into its barrel. 'The Scolds never act on a single tip-off. It's not just us now, there'll be others. If we could get in a room with them, persuade them to talk to this journalist, guarantee they'd be anonymous, I really think we could make something happen.'

Summer's top lip reiterated her doubts.

'Harder for people to work out who we are if there are loads of us. It's anonymity or nothing.'

This seemed to satisfy Summer. 'I could still come.' She came over and took a thumbnail to the corner of Ali's eye, gently scratching away a crumb of mascara.

Ali let her. 'He'd run if he saw both of us. Don't worry, you won't miss anything.' Ali waved her phone. 'I'll record it.'

Summer grimaced. 'What's he going to say?'

'I don't know. Let's find out.' Ali wasn't Ali any more. She felt superhuman.

'Fine, if you want to play spies.' She went to the kitchen. Ali could smell coffee. How did everyone else know how to work the pod machines?

She knew why she was going to meet him. She wanted to watch the show and know it wasn't real. She wanted to see him now his camouflage had been stripped away, the helpless jelly inside the Dalek.

Summer returned with a coffee mug and held it out. 'Be careful then.'

Ali closed the laptop and gave a salute.

'Hey.' Summer came closer. 'Look at me.'

Ali blew on her coffee, looking up at her friend.

'You've killed it with that liner.'

It was quarter to one. The sun was out following a brief hammering of rain and the park was beginning to fill with tourists and locals on their lunch break. Ali's eyes traced the path running through the grass where it criss-crossed with another route on its way up the slope.

She waited for a coach of school children to pass and crossed the road, thinking of her own classmates when she was 12, gathering on the pavement, swinging their bags, teachers counting heads. She wished she could meet Ed somewhere else, but she knew why he'd chosen here. A single piece of information she'd forgotten as soon as she'd said it. She'd told him she was afraid of heights.

She checked her phone. No pin yet. If she made her way up to the crags now, she wouldn't meet him while she was panting and red-faced. She wasn't fit and she'd need time to catch her breath.

The steep paths took walkers up into the mossy inclines of the volcano. Most people forked left up broken stone steps poking out of the gorse to reach the view at the summit. Ali watched them disappearing around the bend, spreading their hands to balance and laughing as they negotiated the rough ground.

It looked different from how she'd remembered it. Standing at the foot of Arthur's Seat, looking up, to Ali it had never felt more like a mass concealing seismic activity. It was officially extinct, but Ali only ever thought of it as sleeping.

The grass was greener than she'd remembered and a strong breeze wrestled with the longer clumps, the ground thrashing in front of her. She knew it would be gustier the higher they climbed. She never had understood how walkers took it so easily in their stride, how they weren't clinging to the unforgiving ground in fear.

A woman in flip-flops passed her on her way down, swinging a carrier bag, as though coming back from the shops. Ali tried to find the sight of her nonchalance comforting, pulling her cagoule tighter around her.

She followed the dirt path up until it split and took a trampled grass route to the right, following a couple in matching blue waterproofs with a small dog. She distracted herself from the thinning air and brisker wind, playing out her meeting with Ed. She wondered if he'd look different, like he'd removed a mask to reveal a different face underneath.

Her legs began to power her up the slope, past the blue couple, who had stopped to look over the city. She slowed as the ground levelled off slightly, opening out to a large green expanse with irregular, brown stones poking through the soft grass near the first sheer cliff to her right. She focused on the casual expressions of people nearby, how unremarkable they found their current situation. She would find it unremarkable too.

She didn't look beyond the grass to the rooftops below, preferring to pretend she was just in a park nearer to the ground. The long grass rippled amiably by the edge of the turf, studded with yellow and purple flowers, a terrible, cheerful juxtaposition to the sudden nothing beyond.

She stopped and tightened the lace on one of her trainers. She wanted to check her breathing and remember the plan. She felt her phone in her inside pocket.

'Ali.'

She stood up too quickly and almost overbalanced.

Ed stood, squinting in the high sun, taking both hands out of his jeans pockets as though about to greet her. How long had he been there? Did he follow her up? Light stubble covered his chin. She didn't remember him wearing white before but his t-shirt looked brand new. It didn't suit him. A grey hooded jacket flapped at his sides.

'You're early.' She instantly became aware of her face and what it might be giving away.

'So are you.' The muscles around his jaw remained tense as he smiled, then relaxed in a way so affecting he looked as beautiful as he had done that first night, just for a moment. 'Thanks for coming.'

She nodded and he gestured up the slope. They made slow progress up the path, his breathing heavy. It seemed to irritate him, the exertion. But he wanted to go higher. He wanted her to go higher.

She stayed a few paces behind, wanting to be able to see him, and he let her. The ground opened out into another clearing and he headed off the path away from the cliff edge.

'Shall we sit?' Ed looked around for a suitable piece of ground and laid his jacket down for her. 'Feeling OK?'

Ali nodded and walked towards the jacket, sitting a few inches away from it. His smile flattened and he picked the jacket up, sitting where it had been. Now she was sure he knew something was wrong.

She felt unexpectedly calm and reminded herself again that he'd brought her here to unnerve her, to put her on the back foot. He was a prick. She didn't need to be nice to him. He would take her presence as a sign that he could get things back the way he wanted them and that she still wanted to be hypnotised.

There were people nearby; a mum and dad coaxing a reluctant child and two older women with backpacks. No one was in any hurry. Ali liked their proximity.

They sat on the grass, facing each other. His face was shiny, like he was digesting a meal. He struggled to cross his legs, she tucked hers underneath her dress and smoothed the fabric over her knees. He looked like he always did, but perhaps less sure of himself. She resolved to stay still like the rock under her, to give him nothing at all to go on. She had practised impassive faces in the mirror but she was a terrible actor. Best to just clear her mind and think dull thoughts.

'So.' She fought the urge to do something with her hands. 'The show's nearly done?'

She could see him trying to work out how much she knew. He didn't answer, tilting his head, looking at her like she was asking the wrong question. This wasn't their usual vibe. She wasn't saying enough and it made him uncomfortable.

If she brought up the Scolds' protest, maybe he'd cut the crap and tell her what he was really thinking. She felt like she was removing the first brick from a wall, careful not to disturb the other bricks. 'I saw… I mean I think everyone saw the posters.' Nothing from him. 'Bit of a shock.'

His expression finally changed, eyebrows rising, a small shake of the head. 'A bit, yeah.' He glowered at the grass between them. 'Not my best day at work.' He breathed in through his nose and then out through his mouth, performing the full length of the sigh. 'I'm on their side. All I tried to do is help and now I'm the bogey man apparently.'

If she asked him a question, Ali was sure he wouldn't give her a straight answer, so she sat with what he was saying, neither agreeing nor pushing back. The wall of nothing was starting to trouble him, she could see it in his eyes and it felt good.

Ed wiped at his eyes with the heel of his hand. 'I wanted… honestly, Ali? I wanted to thank you.'

She kept her gaze steady for a moment, then looked down at a bit of dead skin on her cuticle. She bit into it, until it gave way and chewed it between her front teeth, nodding as though a therapist, encouraging him to expand. 'What for?'

He held his hair out of his eyes as it whipped the side of his face. 'For seeing me, I suppose. The real me. For this.' He shook his head as though he had water in his ear. 'I know I'm a mess. I make a mess wherever I go. Can't seem to stop making them. You don't let me get away with it and I need that. So, thank you.'

She was surprised by how much she wanted to believe him. It sounded so flattering, like she'd passed a test that no one else had.

His forehead twinkled in the sunshine and she thought she caught a whiff of spices and meat, maybe Mexican. A quick burrito before the interrogation? No need to miss lunch. Maybe he'd done a couple of selfies with the fans while he ate, smiling good-naturedly, a little eye-roll to the waitress, dismissing the sideways looks as just the usual people in awe of his celebrity.

Clouds rolled across the sky, occasionally blotting the sun and changing the grass from bright to dull and back again.

He was warming up. 'I think you've always seen. It's a story. That guy, the good guy who looks out for people, the always-has-time-for-his-fans guy – I made him up. This cunt,' he pointed at himself, which Ali felt was unnecessary, 'lies and cheats and smashes everything. Lets everyone down. Hurts the people he really, he really…' His voice cracked, his teeth sinking into his bottom lip.

It would have passed muster in a 1980s soap opera, the ridiculous pause for effect, the haunted look. She could see him, red-eyed, staring meaningfully into a mirror surrounded by lightbulbs, willing the tears to come.

He continued, adding sniffs as punctuation. 'I see other people going about their days, not fucking over their friends and the people they love and… I don't know. I don't know how they do it. I only know this.' He started to cry.

Every cell in her body responded to crying the same way. Become the sponge, absorb the distress, throw herself on top of it. It felt strange not to, but she stayed where she was. He was looking at her like he didn't understand, but kept the sobs coming, committed now.

Looking around at the other people nearby, Ali wondered if they could see the man from the TV sobbing his guts out on a hill. It was bold of him, she thought. He cried like no one was watching but also like everyone was watching. She imagined the scene ending up in the papers. She'd be described as 'a friend' because she wasn't hot enough to be mistaken for a 'mystery woman' or 'unnamed brunette'.

He wasn't breaking character. She almost admired his commitment to the role. She wondered if he was thinking about his poster, the red eyes sneering over his public, blowing his cover.

'I'm sorry.' He let his hair go, making eye contact again.

'What for?' She tried not to enjoy how confused he was that his usual moves weren't working.

'I should have told you. About… all of it. I should have seen with how you were about Deirdre, that you'd be kind. That you'd understand.'

It was like he'd brought her a chewed slipper, eyes brimming with hope.

'Deirdre and? Who else? You might as well tell me now.'

His head was shaking back and forth, suddenly emphatic. 'I made a lot of mistakes, I know. But that's it, Ali. I swear.' More tears came. He lifted his t-shirt to blot them away. The hair on his belly was going grey against the white of his skin. It was like he was literally exposing himself to her.

Better to cover new ground, she thought. 'And how about now? At the moment, how many?'

Now he was paying attention. A glimmer of rage was there and then gone, his face in profile darkening visibly. When he turned towards her again, his eyes were black like a seagull's. 'Ali, come on.'

She decided it was now, the whole wall, time to send the bricks flying. 'I made a new friend. She's called Summer, do you know her?' She watched him closely as the new information was filed.

He looked out over the sea, searching for something in the hills beyond. 'Right.' His answer was devoid of reaction. 'OK.' He was nodding now and Ali felt like she was watching a film. She could be sat at home, holding the remote, it was so unreal.

'She certainly knows you.'

He was going to say something and his expression suggested it was something from the very core of his being. She wanted to turn the sound up, to get closer to the screen.

'It's sex addiction, Ali. I'm talking to someone about treatment. You think addiction is funny?' He could see she was smirking.

'It's a thing, is it?' She was tilting her head for effect.

'According to my psychiatrist it is.' He was indignant now, holding out a note from his mother, disgusted that she'd question its authenticity.

She doubted entirely that he had ever willingly met a psychiatrist, but time spent trying to win points was wasted. She needed him to talk.

'Say something real. Something you actually mean.'

He looked at a group of people coming up the narrow path. They chatted amongst themselves and a couple looked over, but they didn't recognise him. He pretended not to care, lost in his own troubled thoughts.

'I thought I was.' He tried a small smile, a shot of warmth, a treat for her.

'Try again. Why all of these women? Why all the lying? What's wrong with you?' She was getting stiff but she needed to stay where she was, still and in control.

'I fell off the wagon. I'm a fucking idiot, Ali.' He tried to demonstrate his self-disgust, hunched, jeans straining at the crotch. He was doing his best to look pathetic.

'Fell off the wagon? This is where you live all the time. You meet someone, tell her she's special and then drain her of everything she has. But why? It's not love. Or sex. Is it hurting them that gets you off? Do you look forward to it? The crying? The confusion?'

She breathed to force a pause, to slow herself down, checking the volume of her voice. 'Say an honest thing.'

She sat back, supporting herself with both hands on the grass behind her, letting her legs stretch out in front of her.

'I've missed you, Ali.' He reached forward and his hand connecting with her knee sent electricity into her bones. She moved away from him. It felt dangerous, him touching her. She smoothed her dress back over her knees.

'Have you? I think you've been too busy.'

He bowed his head, buying time, changing tack. 'I know what

it looks like. I'm…' The words stopped again, like it was a great effort for him to heave them from his heart to his mouth. 'I'm addicted to painkillers. I'm trying to get off them. I haven't taken any today. You're the only person I've told.' His expression suggested he'd almost surprised himself with this revelation.

It felt like misdirection, like he was palming a card while she looked at the coin he'd just pulled out of her ear.

A Monty Python sketch drifted into her head, the one on the harbour wall with the two men taking turns to hit each other with a fish. She laughed and realised she was doing it out loud.

'Sorry. That wasn't at you.'

Ed's brow knitted into the first real question, but he was reluctant to ask it. He adopted a wounded-but-I-deserved-that countenance that made her want to slap him, just to remove the ingratiating little pucker from his mouth.

'You're a good influence on me. I wanted to be better with you. All that small talk, checking in with each other, saying good night, it seemed like nothing. But it wasn't to me. I think it was good for both of us.' He clasped his hands together. 'I hate myself for destroying it.' In anguish again, he raked a hand through his hair.

'Both of us?' She rolled it around her brain, admiring it from every angle. A good thing in our lives. How did he do that? Insinuate that she was losing something too, like a building was collapsing on both of their heads.

A flutter of panic, the hairs on her arms rose. She shrugged. 'What happens when you stop? All the drink and drugs and sex and humiliation?'

He came to a stop, somehow the grass around him freezing in place as the wind dropped. 'I have to face up to the person that I actually am. And I hate him. So much.' He cried again and this time the sound of his sobbing caught the attention of two teenage boys coming down the path with cans. They looked over and back at each other, talking under their breath, looking over their shoulders.

He struggled to his feet. 'I'm sorry. I can't…' He turned and moved surprisingly quickly up the path away from them.

When she caught up with him, he was sweating and out of breath. Dark patches soaked the front of his t-shirt and bloomed at the armpits of his jacket. As he panted, she thought about how much she had wanted him when she met him, the idea of it now producing no reaction in her.

He turned and faced her, still breathless, arms open as though showing her what she had brought him to. They looked at each other and she tried to imply confusion rather than the anger that had begun to grow at the back of her throat. If she unleashed it, he'd won.

'Why do you put so much effort into hurting people? Aren't you tired?'

A smile began its progress from his eyes to the corners of his mouth. He shrugged, like a kid asked to explain why he'd stamped on a spider.

Ali could see the artifice stripping away from him, the cruelty underneath, the will to hide it leaving him. 'Did your wife find out who you really are? Is that why she left you?'

He darkened again. 'Don't talk about her.'

He was somewhere else, unwilling to be in the same place as these questions.

'Did you tell her everything? Or just what you thought she knew?' She thought about Sid and Summer and dead Deirdre, the shelves of specimens. How if they broke into a roar in unison, it would deafen him.

He looked past her to some distant point again, his eyes glazing as though the film he was watching was suddenly in French.

'Hey, screensaver.' She looked at him with pity. Not that she felt it, she just knew it would cause the most insult, drawing the self-loathing out of him like a tapeworm around a stick. 'Tell me about the pictures and videos. You've got quite the archive.'

His lipped curled. 'Look, lord knows I've been quite the cunt in my time. But all of those relationships were equable. All of them.'

The possibility of winning her over seemed to be dwindling and he tired of the effort.

'Equable? Interesting word.' She took the tone of a bored middle manager explaining a spreadsheet. 'What you do is abuse. You're the man from the telly, they're fans. Nothing equable about it.'

He shook his head as though someone was trying to teach him how to tell a joke.

Ali was feeling bolder. 'You manipulate women, train them and you hide what you're doing. Because if anyone – your showbiz friends – knew what you really were, how you bring women low for kicks, they'd run the fuck away from you.'

His incomprehension was the most believable part of his performance.

'What would they think? All those nice, decent people that you like to stand next to in photos?'

'Oh, they're not all decent, believe me.' This escaped his lips and she was sure he hadn't meant it to.

'True. The ones you talk to on those private email accounts aren't what you'd call gents, are they? Some of the things they ask for.' She was buzzing now, daring herself to get closer to the edge. She wanted to see the fireworks.

His eyes burned into the ground, working it out. When he raised his head again, he wasn't pretending any more. 'My laptop.' His smile was sickening. 'That night at your flat?'

She nodded slowly, aware that no one had passed them for a while. 'I didn't know what I was looking for. I found them by accident.'

'My posters last night?'

'Not guilty. I guess you don't have everyone fooled.' She wanted to conjure multitudes, to give the impression that she came as ambassador from a vast power. Just a word from her and they would rain down burning arrows.

He looked at his fingernails. 'It hardly matters. They'll be forgotten about by tomorrow, your little student protest. Sorry you went to all the effort.' He got to his feet and brushed himself down.

Ali stood too. 'It's all over social media. Women and their stories. Maybe they just needed a push, a sign that it was safe to start talking. Who knows where it might lead. Is your ex-wife on Twitter?' That was probably too much.

He turned towards her. 'She hates all of that.' He sounded almost proud, like she still belonged to him.

The wind gusted strongly again and Ali's concentration faltered, the ground tipping under her. The edge of the cliff was feet away, she couldn't fall. But what if the wind took her legs out from under her? They were too high. The ground was moving again, an eruption or her inner ear playing tricks. She wanted to go back down, to finish this on the ground, but there was no way to go back now without looking weak.

He stayed where he was, looking out at the city, as though it still belonged to him too. Eventually, the quiet became unnatural and he seemed to notice, reviving as though some background task had been completed and he could return to the moment.

He looked over his shoulder, brightening. 'I thought we'd go to the top.' He grinned like they were out for a pleasant walk.

She tried to keep him talking where they were. 'You're angry.' She tucked her hair behind her ears, the trepidation giving her delivery a shrillness.

His eyes changed. 'You're scared.'

She swallowed and maintained eye contact. 'OK. Up it is.' She knew she had to follow even as her body screamed at her to get low to the ground, to hold on for dear life. 'If you want.' She plunged her hands into her coat pockets so he couldn't see them shaking.

He looked at her for a minute and then turned towards the path, putting his hand out like a signpost.

'After you.' Ali waited for him to move off and followed.

The sky grew morose and spots of fat rain began to fall around them as they climbed. She couldn't feel where horizontal was any more, like her first trips down the long escalators on the London

Underground. A travel sickness swamped her and she wanted to sit down, to get low and burrow down to where she'd started. She needed to feel gravity pulling at her, but the floor seemed to be trying to throw her off.

When they reached the top of the crag, she crouched, hiding the panic under her hair as she pretended to tighten the laces on her trainers. Putting a hand down to steady herself, she dug her nails into the dirt.

She thought of the young German girl, arms spread like wings as she looked up at the man she loved still standing on the cliff, watching her fall.

When she tried to remember what Sid had told her that night, how cruel Ed had been and how deliberately and easily he'd inflicted pain, it turned her hands to fists. She wished she could overpower him, force him to feel something. She imagined sliding a skewer into his flesh and no blood coming out, like the trick with a balloon and a knitting needle.

Ali could feel everything. The wind and rain on her face, her dad's signet ring pressing into her palm, Summer's hand on her cheek and the thrum of energy coursing through her when she saw Ed's red rat eyes staring back at her from the railings. She wasn't alone now, she was part of a swelling chorus.

She looked down at people in colourful anoraks on the path below, toy cars circling the roundabout, the gaps in the clouds casting pools of light on the greenery of the park. The clouds began to clear again, revealing patches of blue, grey smudging the white, gulls returning to their circling patterns near the cliff edge.

Ed turned and came towards her, just a couple of steps. 'So this is it. How does it feel?'

She felt unreal, standing on top of a volcano, face to face with whatever he was, thunder rumbling in the distance, the storm on its way somewhere else. 'I'm OK.' She checked in with her breathing, her body, her heartbeat steady in her chest and repeated it to herself. 'I'm OK.'

Ed was still out of puff, feigning disinterest, pretending to be fascinated by the view again. 'So what now?' When she didn't answer, he turned back towards her.

She looked into his eyes, his pinprick pupils hard and polished, like a stuffed animal. 'I think we're done, aren't we? I think that's it.'

She dropped her eyes and took him in from the ground up, taking her time, landing on his shiny, bloated face. 'You'll be wanting to get back to your laptop.'

He looked pained. 'No, Ali. I can't. Not after this, not after you.'

She scooped her hair away from her face, took a breath of clean air and turned back down the path towards the foot of the hill.

He caught her arm and turned her towards him, his expression pained. 'I just see your face.'

She laughed. It was like he'd given her permission to find him truly and finally funny. She looked down at the hand on her arm like it would leave a stain.

His expression hardened into something cold and rancid. He wiped his mouth, smoothing his stubble down with his palm in a stroking motion like he was considering a deal. He pulled her closer. 'I thought you were different. I really did. But you're like every other desperate… well, you're hardly a girl. What are you, 40?'

She kept her eyes on his hand as he came closer to her ear.

'Hanging around after gigs, offering it up on a fucking plate. All I do is say yes, occasionally, because I'm bored. I'm bored. Why not help myself?'

She didn't move.

'I stand there, looking down at Kev from accounts and Dave who lives with his mum. My audience? I fucking hate them. They think we'd be mates, if we met. And they find me after the show and they talk inanities at me while their fat girlfriend tries to eye-fuck me. They disgust me. Every single one of them. They get an hour. They pay. Like I'd do it for free. Rows and rows of them, all over the country, desperate to spend time with someone who's funnier than their dull friends. They're not my people. I'm this close to Saturday night, a TV screen between me and them so I don't have to smell them any more.'

Ali listened, keeping her face still. When he was finished, she looked him up and down. 'You know, I think it's what you did to Sid that really repels me. She didn't stand a chance, did she? She was a child.'

Ed pressed his lips together and blew air out of his nose. 'She's always made her own decisions.'

'She thinks this is love.'

Ed couldn't prevent a smile from forming and Ali regretted giving him anything he could feed on. 'Love? Then she's stupid as well as ugly. She was just there.'

Ali didn't feel dizzy any more. 'You're one of those men now. Red eyes. Marked. Women will talk about you when you're not there, telling each other not to be alone with you. That's who you are.'

'It's a few fucks to alleviate the tedium and you think I'm Harvey Weinstein. Fuck off. Not one of those women had to be coaxed or cajoled, they hurl themselves at me.'

'But a few fucks isn't it. You don't need to pretend to love them to get sex. You're the guy with the microphone, you can take your pick. But you do pretend. You tell them… you tell us that we're the only one. You need control. All of the time. All of us. Just control.'

He leaned towards her again. 'Go back to your friends and shriek "me too" at each other all you want. I might be a cunt, but I'm not that cunt.'

She took a step back and he turned down the path, taking out his phone. She watched him go.

Ali stayed where she was until he was out of sight. Then she found the ground, sank to her knees and shook, her whole body felt like it was turning to air.

Thirty-Eight

Lost in the crowds on the Royal Mile, Ali pushed through the people to a passageway tucked between two shops and leaned against the wall, flattening her palms behind her against the cool of the stone.

She arrived back at the flat to find Summer out. With no one to debrief, she fell into bed and lay there feeling strange and empty.

She plugged her phone into her laptop and watched the download bar make its steady progress across the screen as the recording of Ed transferred. When it was a solid oblong of blue, she closed the lid and started a new message thread on her phone.

I talked to him. This is what he said.

She added a link and sent it to the group.

She scrolled back through her last messages with Sid. Long, chatty missives from Ali all met with short, polite replies. Sid never ignored her or left a message unanswered, even now, but she was keeping her away.

Ali looked at the picture of Ed's poster with the livid eyes and thought about how angry he was. How lonely Sid must feel, trapped with an angry bear.

Just letting you know we're here and we hope you're OK. And we miss you. A x

She pressed 'Send'.

The sun was sinking into the gardens opposite, dipping behind the trees. Tonight it would all be over. By morning, the clear-up would begin, teams of cleaners reclaiming the railings and lampposts, removing all evidence of the festival from walls and hoardings, leaving the grey and brown of the city exposed again.

Ali opened Twitter. The picture of Tom Weissman's dripping head had gone viral.

The hashtags were still gaining new entries. It was all women, rounding up months and years of pain in succinct posts.

'He's doing it to a new girl now and I knew she wouldn't listen to me. Punched the air when I saw his poster. Thank you. x'

'I woke up to him raping me. The police did nothing. Fuck him. Fuck all of them.'

When Summer came back the sky was turning grey and amber. She found Ali on the giant sofa, sleeping, the TV still on. Summer turned it off and Ali stirred.

'Hey. Did you hear?'

Ali sat up and rubbed the back of her neck. 'What?'

'Bethan's speech. She won. I've just been in her show. Promoters extending her tour. She's got a rocket strapped to her. She mentioned the Scolds. Well, she said she admired what they were doing, you know. She didn't out herself.'

Ali reached for her phone. 'That's amazing. She won? What time is it?'

Summer went to the window to roll a cigarette, then craned back over her shoulder to Ali. 'Tell me everything. What was he like?'

'Angry.'

'Did he try anything?' She held the roll-up by her mouth, waiting.

'He tried everything. Sad. Angry. Sorry. Not sorry. It was fucking mental, to be honest. You've got it all.'

Summer went for her phone.

'Don't listen to it now.'

She turned back to the window and lit her cigarette, exhaling under the sash, looking down at the street and the posters slapping the railings in the wind.

'Most shows finish tonight. Do you think Ed'll mention it? Will any of them? God, to be a fly on that wall.'

Ali thought for a moment and scrolled through her inbox, looking for something. She turned the screen around to show Summer.

She leaned over and read what she could see, looking confused. 'Bring a sexy friend? What's this got to do with flies on walls?'

'Two tickets to the wall,' said Ali, waggling her phone for effect.

Summer stubbed her fag out in a saucer and sat down next to her. 'Fuuuuuuck.'

Ali thought of the mad man on the mountain. With an audience, he'd have to keep it together. It's not like they'd be in any danger in a room full of people. They could sit in the dark, just shapes in the crowd.

Summer made a disapproving face. But Ali was already on a train of thought. 'How's he going to style this out? Are you telling me you don't want to see that?'

'Oh, I do want to see that. I'm just saying is it better to walk away? Leave him to it?'

Ali pretended to think about it. 'Nope.'

Thirty-Nine

Cider spilled from plastic pints as Summer carried them across the cobbled courtyard. This was the liveliest hub of the Fringe, an open-air space with bars and food trucks, rammed with festival goers between shows, surrounded on four sides by gig venues. The converted university rooms of the old building were draped in black every August and filled, hour after hour, with new audiences, drunker as the day went on, squeezed into small spaces to see comedians from the TV or new acts hoping for big things.

Summer found Ali leaning on a wall near the entrance. 'There's seats in the back.' She held out a cup.

Ali took the offered pint and sipped at the cold bubbles. She followed Summer back over the cobbles, past lines of people queuing for shows and into a quieter tented area with low tables and benches. It was busy but the next shows were going in and a few people hovered in small groups, waiting to take over tables as they emptied.

They sat at a table next to a stone wall, their skin tinted yellow by the canvas of the roof above.

Summer looked at her watch. 'Down these, then we'll head to the Dome. Why did you want to come here?'

'I just thought, I'm in Edinburgh, in August and I hadn't been to the courtyard. It's my festival too. I want it back.' They bumped their plastic cups together.

Ali took it in; the strings of fairy lights lining the roof, flyers scattered over tables, people in holiday mood, enjoying the lack of anything to do but see shows and get drunk. She finally felt like she was on holiday too.

She took a picture of herself and Summer, pints in the picture and sent it to Ava.

Summer leaned her chin on her hand. 'I wish Sid was here.'

Ali checked her messages, knowing there'd be nothing new there. 'I wonder what he told her about today. Not much, I'm guessing. Imagine still being in the bunker.'

They both contemplated it for a while, the idea of Ed being their whole world, how they'd both felt the strange comfort of Ed making all their decisions for them. Summer put her wrist against the cold cup. 'Bunker is right. No daylight, no friends. Just Fritzl.'

As she looked around at the other drinkers, Ali saw herself 20 years ago, in the same place, head down, poring over the schedule with Ava, wishing she had even some of the self-belief of the performers they were seeing. They'd seemed magic to her, without fear. Now she thought there was probably something wrong with a lot of them. All the talk about sad comedians, the tears of a clown, she didn't see it that way any more. They weren't sad, they were angry, any time they weren't holding the mic.

She wondered if she would enjoy stand-up comedy again one day without thinking about what the people on stage were doing to her. How they thrived on the control they had of a roomful of strangers.

Ali slid the flyers on the table around idly with her finger. 'Is this it for you? You still want to work in comedy?'

Summer laughed and put down her pint. 'Yeah. I still love it. Maybe it's time to fight for it.'

Ali didn't say anything about Summer's absence from the Scolds protest, not wanting to squash the good feeling between them.

'We're all part of it aren't we? Not just the women on stage. Other people have been trying to change it and I've just sat back and let them. You know, not speaking up if a headliner's going to bring in the crowds, no matter how dodgy he is. One less coward in the industry might mean there's a few less after this Fringe. Who knows.' Her smile was broad, the lipstick still perfect.

Ali looked at her with a mocking eyebrow. "Are you signing up to be…' She put both hands on the table, '…an angry woman?' Summer raised her middle finger, smiling. 'And what about you?'

Ali swallowed. 'I'm going to be unemployed.'

'They won't put you on a different show? That seems a bit harsh.'

'Not after they've read my email. I quit.'

Summer's goldfish impression confirmed Ali's suspicions. 'It's true, I've lost my mind, but I've got some savings. That'll buy me some time. Why stay if it makes me miserable? I've never said that out loud.' She puffed her cheeks out like she might vomit. 'I don't like my job. I was settling. I don't want to do it any more.'

Summer raised another toast. 'To not settling. Fucking hell. What will you do?'

'Good question.' Ali bobbed her head as though taking a run-up to something. 'I'll go freelance. Maybe podcasts. You can't go a metre without tripping over a podcast. I need to learn how to produce them. Can't be that different.'

A young man wearing a lanyard laid some flyers on their table and moved on. And there he was: Ed in a dinner jacket, eyes staring, the hard black lines either side of his mouth.

Summer turned to see what Ali was looking at and clocked Ed's face. 'This one looks shit. Let's see it.' She gulped her drink, burped discreetly and put on her sunglasses.

Ali put her shades on too and they linked arms, picking their way through the crush, bodies swaying with cider and sunshine.

Forty

As they emerged from the underpass, Ali saw a queue forming along the front of the union building and began to scan the queue. She pulled on Summer's arm until they were standing far enough away.

Summer was catching up. 'Aren't we going in?'

Ali directed her gaze towards the queue. 'Guess the show.'

The two of them looked for a while. Summer spoke first, eyes trained on the people waiting to go in. 'Tank Girl t-shirt. Tattoos.' She kept scanning. 'Penguin backpack. Goth girl on her own. This would be the line for Ed Catchpole's show.'

'One hundred per cent.'

When the queue began to move, they joined the back, taking off their shades, their laughter covering nerves like the ones you get before a rollercoaster.

As they came through the main door, the blonde woman in the Tank Girl t-shirt was confiding in a smaller woman next to her. They were both looking at Ed's poster. 'He's fit. But Jess saw him earlier in Tesco. She said his hair's gone Tory.'

Ali wanted to laugh out loud. She turned to Summer instead and mouthed: 'Tory hair.' They screwed up their eyes and gripped each other's hand as they filed up the stairs, stifling laughter, not wanting to draw attention to themselves.

The queue slowed and stopped as it reached the top of the stairs and Summer looked back. 'Do you still…' She breathed in, then out, keeping to a whisper. 'Sometimes, do you think about him and still get that flip? The physical thing, even as your brain is going "Noooooooo"?'

Ali thought about the cesspit she'd syphoned from his laptop and the way he'd sneered about Sid. 'No. Not any more.'

Summer looked chastened and Ali felt bad. 'But that's a recent thing. One day you won't either.'

'Yeah. Maybe Sid too?' The queue began to move again.

The room was a black box with raked seating taking up two-thirds of the space. Bodies filed in up the aisle and filled from the front, herded by ushers in yellow t-shirts. Black drapes hung around three sides of the stage and a mic stand stood just off-centre at the front. A white screen hung on the other side of the stage.

Ed's face smiled down from the screen, eyes blinking occasionally, a square section of his chin moving up and down like a ventriloquist's dummy.

'Hi, hello. You look nice. Come on in. Watch that cable.' Ali held her breath at the sound of his voice. It was a recording playing in time to the screen dummy. The girls ahead of them laughed shyly and looked up at the face like he could see them.

Ali knew he wouldn't be watching his audience come in. He'd be in his dressing room until the last moment, performing his ritual. A shot of whisky. He'd look at himself, mess his hair, imagine he was about to go on at a packed Apollo and head straight for the stage without acknowledging anyone.

An insistent guitar song was playing. David Bowie was singing about a man without a mouth. Ali didn't recognise the song.

She and Summer had hidden themselves in a corner, a couple of rows from the back. A few seats on their row were empty.

Ali nodded at the gap. 'Not sold out? Or people haven't shown up.'

As she turned to look behind her, wondering if Sid could see them from the control booth, the lights dimmed, the music faded and the audience chatter subsided. Ed's voice came over the PA. 'Ladies and gentlemen, please welcome… Ed Catchpole.'

As their eyes adjusted to the darkness, applause swelled and a figure strolled to centre stage, taking the mic out of its stand.

A couple of whoops of encouragement as bright light flooded his hair. It was cut shorter and now parted at the front like curtains. Ali wondered who'd cut his hair and if he was angry with them.

'It really is Tory,' whispered Summer. Ali snorted, unheard above the clapping.

Head cocked to one side and looking up at the audience, he waited. Before the applause was gone, he thrust straight into a rapid-fire sequence recounting how he came from humble beginnings – just him and his mum in a council house in Haywards Heath – to the C-list panel-show stalwart they saw before them.

Images from his childhood flashed up on the screen. Little Ed next to a pampas grass in red shorts, foot up on a football. Teenage Ed astride a silver Grifter in front of a green garage door, hair over his eyes.

Ali watched as he drew the room to him, switching from low status to high, defusing every boast with a bathetic rug-pull. So offensively charming. It was brilliant.

Ali wished she hadn't come. He was winning them over, the way he always did. She exchanged a look with Summer. He was going to ignore it all, the protest, the Scolds. In his world, none of it had happened. The other people in the room were either oblivious or didn't care what he did to women.

The hope drained from Ali and she sank in her seat. They both sat in the dark, looking ahead, waiting for the ride to be over.

Ali knew Summer would have gone along with whatever she'd suggested, that they were as sick as each other when it came to Ed. They'd wanted to be in a room with him again, another hit of drama to send a shiver down their spines. Now that she was here, Ali wanted to be anywhere else.

The spotlight on Ed went dark and now the screen was the only light in the room. The dummy's face reappeared.

She knew what came next. The dummy would speak, the real Ed would interrupt him, then a back and forth between them, carefully choreographed. The lights came back up on Ed to reveal him facing the puppet. 'Sorry, what are you doing?' The dummy's eyebrows were raised. 'Just a few notes.'

As the laughter rippled through the room, Ed went to black again and the dummy's mouth started to move in time to an audio track of Ed speaking. Somewhere at the back of the room, a door closed.

Ali nudged Summer. 'We could run for it now. This bit's a couple of minutes.'

They looked at each other in the half-light, searching for the answer, or at least the bravery to push past the people on their row and get down the stairs before the lights came back on. Summer swallowed as if about to make a pronouncement and then froze at the look on Ali's face.

The sound had changed. It was Ed's voice, but no longer in a studio, devoid of background noise. It sounded like he was outside. It sounded like it was raining. He was muffled, like he was speaking through gauze.

'My audience? I fucking hate them. They think we'd be mates, if we met. I fucking hate them. I fucking hate them.'

Ali recognised the monologue, Ed's hatred spewing from him, his face buckling with disgust. She couldn't take her eyes off the stage as she put her mouth to Summer's ear and whispered: 'This isn't the show.'

Summer tried to get some sign from her but Ali was transfixed by the dummy's jaw jerking up and down.

'They find me after the show. I fucking hate them. And they talk inanities at me. I fucking hate them. While their fat girlfriend tries to eye-fuck me. Their fat girlfriend. I fucking hate them. Their fat girlfriend. I fucking hate them. My audience? They disgust me.'

The dummy smiled inanely, jaw bouncing, eyes blinking.

'I'm bored,' it sneered down at the room. People shifted in their seats. No one was laughing. Ali couldn't see if Ed was still there in the dark. He must be.

'Fucking hell.' Ali wasn't looking at his giant face now. She was looking at them, the audience. The Tank Girl t-shirt was gawping at her friend. There was muttering, a nervous laugh.

The dummy continued, the angry phrases repeating, getting louder. Someone had added echo to the ends of his sentences.

'I'm bored. I fucking hate them. I'm bored.'

Ali craned again to see the small, high window at the back of the room, lit by a laptop, but she couldn't see anyone beyond the glow.

She found Summer's arm in the dark. 'He's talking to me. That's us, up the mountain.'

Summer looked at the stage too and the growing unrest in the room and it sank in. 'Fucking what?'

Ali tried to see into the darkness on Ed's side of the stage, but there was no movement, just a shape that could be him or a fold in the curtain. Then the sound of something falling over. A chair? The room hummed at the sound, punters starting to mutter to each other.

An usher in a yellow t-shirt came through the door at the front, looking at the control booth and back to the stage, which seemed to signal to the room that something was up. A couple of people took their phones out and started filming.

'Hanging around after gigs, offering it up on a fucking plate. On a fucking plate. On a fucking plate. All I do is say yes, occasionally, because I'm bored. I'm bored. I'm bored.'

Ali was thrilled and terrified, legs rigid. She could have run to the summit of Arthur's Seat and kept going, jumping from cloud to cloud and out to sea.

She wanted some sign that Ed knew this was happening. Where was he? The dummy kept going.

Another yellow t-shirt came back through the door at the front, blanching and fretting into a walkie-talkie. She muttered quickly, hovering at the side of the stage like a moth. A door slammed somewhere beyond the curtain, the usher jerking her head towards the stage, expecting to see the source of the bang.

'He's legging it.' Ali stood up to get a better look.

As the audience murmur began to grow, the usher clicked the button on her walkie-talkie. 'Can't you turn it off?'

'I have to face up to the cunt that I actually am. The cunt that I actually am. The cunt. The cunt. The cunt. I'm a mess. I'm bored. Their fat girlfriend. My audience? I fucking hate them. Stupid as well as ugly. Stupid. Ugly. Stupid. Ugly.'

The angry poem looped on.

Ali craned her neck again, trying to get a clear view of the small window into the control booth but her eyes struggled to adjust. The auditorium was slowly filling with little rectangles of light as more phones were held up to film the stage.

With her heart thumping, Ali began to make sense of the chaos. 'Sid.'

'Stupid. Ugly,' repeated the dummy.

Summer's mouth was open, looking around at the audience. Everyone was talking now, the commotion no longer self-conscious. Ali said it again, squeezing Summer's arm. 'He's talking about Sid.'

Somewhere behind them a knocking, then interference crackled, a panicked voice cutting through the static. 'It's locked. No. I can't open it.'

Two young women sitting at the front looked at each other, hands to their faces, enjoying the opportunity to be outraged. A couple at the end of a row got up and walked out, smirking, embarrassed. No one knew what to do but the spell was broken, like they were all coming around from a dream.

The screen finally cut to black and then the dummy came back, eyes livid red and a QR code slapped over its mouth.

The second yellow t-shirt came back to the side of stage and walked to the centre, looking up at the back of the room, finger to her ear. Still in darkness, some people were standing, trying to work out what to do. 'Ladies and gentlemen, we apologise for the technical problems with tonight's performance.' She gave up, unable to make herself heard above the cacophony. Two hundred confused people were swapping theories with one another about what had happened. Asking, where is Ed Catchpole? Was that part of the show? A man's voice boomed above the racket, demanding his money back.

Ali's phone screen lit up in her hand. 'It's from Sid.' She turned it to Summer.

RUN.

They pushed their way along the row, treading on coats and toes, whispering 'sorry' as they tried to contain their hysteria, hearts banging. Their feet thumped the metal steps up to the back of the room and out past the control booth door. The first yellow t-shirt stood outside, knuckles white around her radio. 'The master key,' she rasped into it. 'I don't know. There's no one in there.'

Ali and Summer bashed down the stairs to the exit, the din of confusion swelling behind them, and burst through the doors into the busy square. The rain strafed them as they held tight to each other's hands, running towards the floodlights and safety, breathless with laughter. They stopped under the awning of a burger van and Ali bent double, still helpless.

Summer was panting. 'What's so funny?'

Ali lifted her head, beaming. 'I don't know.'

Forty-One

Ali lay on her back, looking up at tree branches, slivers of blue sky visible through the green canopy. She couldn't remember the Edinburgh weather being this upbeat when she'd come here before. She usually got out before the end of the festival, leaving the last gasps of the party, fleeing the gloom and the endless Sunday rain.

Across the park, crews were dismantling the tents and pop-up bars, miles of coloured bulbs coiled onto large drums as the circus prepared to leave town.

Small groups had brought their hangovers out into the fresh air, kids queued for the slide next to a café while their parents stood with buggies, drinking coffee.

Summer stretched out a leg and kicked Ali's calf gently. 'Talk about making an entrance. Where is she?'

Ali sat up to see Sid striding across the grass towards them. 'I think she's earned it. Sid!'

Sid's smile was all new, the light glancing off the lenses of her sunglasses. The expression had conquered every muscle of her face.

Ali kicked Summer back and they both sat up to watch her.

Summer raised her coffee cup to the sky like it was Simba. 'Queen! Queen!'

Sid took off her shades and raised them in salute, looking shyly delighted.

Ali looked at her like she was a goddess on a plinth. 'Remind me never to piss you off.' Summer started clapping and whooping.

Sid looked healthy. She never looked healthy. 'Thank you. Thank you.'

Sid knelt on the grass and hugged them in turn. 'Even when I got there, I wasn't sure I was going to go through with it.'

Ali couldn't stop looking at her. She was wearing old Sid's clothes, but she was even sitting differently. 'What happened? To you. Start from the last time I saw you. No, start from last night.'

'Right.' She sat forward. 'Bethan texted me, asking if I'd heard anything about Ed. I didn't know what to say so I just didn't reply. After the Scolds finished their decorating, she got in touch to warn me about Ed's poster. Long story short, we met up and I told her everything. She was gutted she hadn't figured it out. She said she thought Ed was one of the good guys. She said she'd heard from another woman. I don't know if that was you or someone else.'

She looked at Ali and Ali shrugged. 'Maybe me saying something got them asking around?'

Sid continued. 'Then I listened to the recording. I knew all of it, but I'd never heard him say it. "She was just there." Like I was just a meat prop, something to wipe his dick on. And I realised I was angry, not heartbroken or sad. Fucking raging.'

Summer held her hand up and they high-fived. 'Yes!'

'I only had a couple of hours and I didn't know if I could use the recording or not. There was a lot of wind noise. I had to clean it up. But it did the trick.' The smile was back, pride and disbelief and something like triumph.

Ali and Summer looked at each other and back at the new Sid.

Sid carried on. 'I knew what I was doing. You don't interrupt them. You don't take their microphone away. I knew he'd never forgive me.'

They drank coffee and talked about the reaction in the room, the video all over the internet when they woke up.

Ali pinched Summer's tobacco tin. Sid took Summer's offered cup. 'You thought I'd gone back.'

'We just thought you needed, you know, time maybe.' Summer didn't sound convincing.

Sid stopped her. 'I did go back. I was pathetic. You kept messaging and I knew if I talked to you, either of you, I'd have to leave. Leave everything. And I just couldn't.'

Ali made to remonstrate. 'It's not pathetic. If anyone gets it, we do. He had you for ten years.'

Summer nodded emphatically.

Sid looked down, embarrassed. 'I was paralysed. After I told you about Deirdre, he disappeared for a week and I thought he knew. That he was punishing me. I thought about packing up, leaving London. I was fucking terrified. But when it came to it, I couldn't go.'

Ali shielded her eyes against the sun. 'He came back?'

Summer looked at Ali, reminding her to let Sid tell the story.

'Like nothing happened. Like always. We got on with the show, ran through cues, rehearsed. I rented a car. I didn't ask any questions and neither did he. But I couldn't get the little girl out of my head. Deirdre's daughter on her Instagram. I looked at her pictures every day, torturing myself.'

Summer and Ali exchanged another look.

'Then I messaged her friend, the one from Twitter. We ended up talking for about an hour. She's so young. I knew she was telling the truth, that he broke Deirdre down, destroyed her confidence. Because that's what he does. I told her about these women, these wise old hags that wouldn't give up on me, even when I shut them out. And how much it meant to me, knowing that they cared about me.'

Ali saw the tears in Summer's eyes and blinked away some from her own.

Sid took their hands. She was crying too. 'Sorry.' They squeezed back, forming a circle.

'I'm really fucking proud of you, Sid.' Ali squeezed Sid's hand and Sid squeezed it back.

'I fucking hope so. I had to leave my laptop.' Sid laughed, unable to believe it herself. 'I set the audio going and locked the control room door. Hoyed the key over the roof. I might look like a haunted whippet but fuck, I'm no runner. I thought I was going to die.'

Ali leaned forward laughing. 'And just texting "RUN". Who's the drama queen?'

Sid shook her head, laughing too. 'I saw it on *Dr Who*. I couldn't go back to the flat last night, so I used dad's Amex.' She took a card key from her pocket and waved it. 'Balmoral, baby. I ordered a martini in the bar, drank it on my own. I asked myself – what would Ali do?'

Ali couldn't picture this Sid apologising for existing. She was holding her head up like extra vertebrae had been added to her neck.

'Is that it now? Does he have anyone left?' asked Summer, draining her coffee.

Sid scratched her arm. 'There's always someone. He'll be glued to messenger, working on one from the discarded pile.'

Summer blew at her fringe. 'It's the work drying up that he won't be able to stand. The audiences going away. How many people have seen the video?'

Ali flicked at her phone screen and tapped a link. 'Seventy thousand on YouTube.'

A breeze was whipping up, threatening to bring new, less celebratory weather with it.

'So, what now?' Ali wanted this to last longer. The nearness of her friends felt good.

Sid sat forward. 'I've been having thoughts.'

'Oh?' Summer opened out a bag of crisps like a shiny picnic blanket.

'I want to study. I missed out on uni. I think I still want to go.'
Ali gawped. 'Study what?'

'Illustration. I'm considered "mature" now. If I can get an interview, some places might let me in. I fancy Glasgow.'

'Won't your dad cut you off?'

She smiled, shrugging. 'It's probably about time he did.'

Summer held her fringe back and let the air get to her forehead. 'Well, I'm going nowhere. I wanna watch it burn. It's time the women took over.'

'Well, good.' Sid looked happy, like she was free. She watched a crew dismantling a big top on the other side of the park. 'I only stopped drawing because Ed told me I was shit. He said if I tried to do it professionally, I'd embarrass myself.' She chewed her lip. 'Now I know it's because I was better than him. Courses start in October, next October now. Until then, I'll get a job.'

'We need a break,' Summer said, flexing the sides of her cup.

'A holiday!' Ali agreed, reaching for her phone. 'I could book something. Where do you want to go? We could do a cottage somewhere near a beach.'

'No, I think she means a break from this,' Sid said, pulling up a blade of grass and rolling it between her finger and thumb. 'We're still talking about him.'

Summer sat up. 'We should meet up in a year. Here. We'll come back and get wrecked and tell each other about our lives. Without him. Better make sure we've got something to talk about.' She looked at Ali, hopeful.

Ali felt like she was being sent on a lonely quest. She wanted them to go together but their courses were all plotted in different directions.

Sid tapped her foot against Ali's. 'We replaced him with this, sitting around a cauldron, making up curses. Swapping stories about the bad man and how he hurt us. I mean, I think it worked. But we can stop now.'

Ali closed her eyes and gave a slow nod. 'We can stop now.'

Summer said she never knew Sid was an artist and Sid showed her pictures of her art class sketches. Ali leaned back on her hands, stretching, taking in the park and watching her friends as they smoked and talked.

A lorry carrying stacks of metal barriers made slow progress along the park's perimeter. The colour of the clouds bruised ominously and the trees began to bend under the quickening wind.

Summer pinched the end of her cigarette. 'Right. Let's get a proper drink and no more shit men talk. We need to change the subject.'

A laugh erupted from Ali, pulling her into the present: sitting on the grass in a city she loved, nowhere to be. And with friends who asked nothing of her but to be herself.

She felt the clouds pass and the sun returning. They got to their feet.

'OK, what shall we talk about?'

Epilogue

Ed looked out at the room, hands in his pockets, satisfied it was a full house. The wooden plinth he was standing on raised him a few inches above his audience, but not far enough.

He was clean-shaven, hair combed back, making him less instantly recognisable as the comedian from the video, but this room knew. It was why they were here.

He ran his hand over his hair. 'Set upon by a gang of women. Literally, formed a mob and came for my nuts.' Ed mimed garden shears at the front row.

The beginnings of a chuckle in a couple of dry throats.

Ed's white shirt billowed around him, looking like a nightie, not something you would wear out of the house. His old stage shirts didn't fit any more.

He paused, wondering whether to continue with this bit, but he couldn't immediately recall any other material and this crowd weren't worth the effort.

A quick scan of the front row while he wiped the sweat from his top lip. 'Absolutely terrifying. It was like a witch hunt. But I was being hunted BY the witches.'

Most of the men looked like they spent their weekends with the curtains drawn, talking to each other online.

Ed wanted this done, then he could go back to his house and order a take-away. He told himself he'd only accepted the gig because it was so near to home. London was losing its shine anyway.

A woman sat next to her boyfriend at the end of the front row, looking thirstily at Ed, crossing her legs. He angled his body towards her and continued.

'Hands up, I've been a bit of a twat. Suffice to say, the booze wasn't helping. It feels good to be sober. It does.'

Some polite applause at this.

'But not when you're being chased by a pack of woke activists with PMT. Look at me. I'm not built for speed.'

The hum of approval was back. He looked at the ugly, pallid faces. Losers and farm boys, sitting on folding chairs. Two hundred of them in a village hall.

'You know me. I won't lie to you. I can't now.' More laughter. They were loosening up, knowing he was going to address the elephant in the room.

'No, you maybe saw the stuff in the papers. Turns out, so did a lot of TV commissioners. Oh no!' He put his hands to his face like Munch's *The Scream*, the mic missing the end of his exclamation.

'They had clearly been labouring under the misapprehension that I was a nice guy.' He shook his head slowly and elaborately, mouthing the word 'Nope'.

The laughs were rolling now.

Ed looked directly at the one with the girlfriend. 'I'm not your friend, pal.'

He ran a hand through his sideburn, turning back to the audience while the boyfriend shook his head, chuckling.

Ed gestured at the stage behind him, what there was of it. 'None of this is real.'

The room offered a hum of self-knowledge in response, as though silence would have meant they weren't clever enough.

'Is it a shock to you?' He looked at the woman on the front row now, allowing a little smirk to form. 'Are you shocked, madam?'

She shook her head shyly. The feeling grew that he was letting them in on the joke. They were starting to like it.

He stretched his hand out and cast it over the front row's heads.

'Aaaaall of this is fake. What's your name, sir?' He lowered the mic and then snatched it back again. 'Don't care. Literally not interested.'

There was more definite laughter now, the first dam breaking.

A small dose of something made its way through his veins. Not as good as the whisky he'd drink when this was over, but something.

'I am literally being paid to spend time with you. Make you feel good, does it?' He leaned forward, lowering his voice, pressing his lips against the mic. 'Not on the mouth.'

They really laughed now.

'There's one. But, trust me, when this runs down…' He paused here to take a kitchen timer out of his pocket and put it on a stool next to him. It was shaped like a red tomato.

'When the bell goes, that's your lot.'

The red plastic timer ticked and he put the mic next to it, amplifying the sound.

A few of them were really laughing, congratulating themselves. He pretended to look at his watch, biding his time as the ticking continued.

The woman on the front row was crinkling her eyes, leaning forward, touching her hair.

An hour later, Ed was sprawled on the floor of his lounge in his boxer shorts, leaning up against the sofa, chopping out a line of coke with his debit card on the glass coffee table.

A calendar notification chimed as he opened the web browser on his laptop: his new agent reminding him about his interview with Voice of the People, a new TV news channel hoping to get Ed on as a regular contributor.

He heaved himself up and picked up a plastic package from the coffee table, tearing a corner off with his teeth and unwrapping the new blue shirt inside. Once he was wearing it, he pulled the tag off the back of his neck and looked down at his bare legs.

He picked up a tumbler of whisky and took his laptop to the kitchen, checking on his webcam that the background behind him would be suitably bland, pine cupboards and a red kettle.

Don't forget the poppy.

As he took the red paper flower from the envelope on the counter and pinned it to his new shirt he felt a flutter of nerves, little pulses in his chest. He'd probably eaten that pizza too quickly.

The viewers wouldn't see anything below the waist, he thought, scratching himself and pulling his chair in to the kitchen table.

The line connected with the studio and a producer started talking him through the interview. He made affirmative noises and chopped out another line next to his keyboard where the camera couldn't see.

'OK, so we'll come to you in about a minute and you'll be speaking to Jessica. Happy?'

'Very.' Ed's expression remained blank.

Taking a rolled-up note from the table, he put his thumb over the camera and leaned down to the short white line in front of him.

As he lifted his head back up, his pulse became suddenly emphatic, his chest banging like someone inside was desperately trying to get out. A violent cramp spread from his armpit across his front, rising, locking his jaw. His thumb fell from the camera as he scraped his chair back.

For a beat he was suspended in mid-air, his vision clouding, and then a dull thud broke the silence as his head connected with the flagstone floor.

The channel jingle played from Ed's speakers and a woman with long blonde hair appeared in the corner of the laptop's screen. 'Welcome back. Joining us now is comedian Ed Catchpole. Ed, welcome.'

There was a pause, the woman's eyes betraying brief panic at the silence as it grew. 'Ed?' She listened to the gallery in her earpiece, a brief scan of the autocue and she moved smoothly on to the next item.

'Let's hope we can get Ed back, but for now, we seem to have lost him.'

Acknowledgements

About The Author

Image Credit © Rosalind Furlong

Julia Raeside is a journalist and broadcaster who has written for the *Guardian*, *Times*, *Observer* and *The Big Issue* among others. She makes regular contributions to BBC Radio, including review spots on Radio 4's *Front Row* and Lauren Laverne's *6 Music show*. She lives in London with her husband, kid and cat. *Don't Make Me Laugh* is her first novel.

X @JNRaeside
@juliaraesidewriter

Bedford
Square
Publishers

Bedford Square Publishers is an independent publisher of fiction and non-fiction, founded in 2022 in the historic streets of Bedford Square London and the sea mist shrouded green of Bedford Square Brighton.

Our goal is to discover irresistible stories and voices that illuminate our world.

We are passionate about connecting our authors to readers across the globe and our independence allows us to do this in original and nimble ways.

The team at Bedford Square Publishers has years of experience and we aim to use that knowledge and creative insight, alongside evolving technology, to reach the right readers for our books. From the ones who read a lot, to the ones who don't consider themselves readers, we aim to find those who will love our books and talk about them as much as we do.

We are hunting for vital new voices from all backgrounds – with books that take the reader to new places and transform perceptions of the world we live in.

Follow us on social media for the latest Bedford Square Publishers news.

🐦 @bedsqpublishers
f facebook.com/bedfordsq.publishers/
📷 @bedfordsq.publishers

https://bedfordsquarepublishers.co.uk/